GROOVY GIRL

2008 Amazon Breakthrough Novel Award Quarterfinalist
(Or was it semifinalist? And maybe 2007? "Hard to know"...)

ADVANCE PRAISE FOR gRooVY giRL

Wonderfully wicked words from a prized poet, a wondrous Wall Street tycoon, an articulate author, a totally tubular teacher-librarian, a canny copy-editor-turned-social-media-bigwig, an eagle-eyed expert of English, a copyist composer and cook, and a powerhouse Pilipina and her poised progeny, among others…

"*Groovy Girl* is uncannily timely and noisy; it is a cry for several types of justice. At times you want to cheer on this scrappy narrator—or scold her, then hug her."

"Just finished reading this vibrant, vociferous, and virulent novel. It is so many things and touched so many parts of my life."

"This literary masterwork will resonate with the young, dinosaur, sick, badass, gay, non-binary, misanthrope, immigrant, tyrant, oppressed, repressed, warrior, pious, slouch, kind human…and humankind."

"I snickered or gasped out loud at least once, I'm quite certain, after almost every other page of this highly spirited book."

"My reading glasses fogged up from my copious tears, both gladdened and glum."

"You will fall in love with this cool, funny, and smart girl, who tries to learn in real-time and assess in real-time, poking and prodding life in its side to get answers to questions that her much older sister has never asked, and never will."

"*Groovy Girl* was so character-driven that I find myself missing the Josés…"

"How is this author writing about my family to a tee? And I am white!"

"There are times when I had to pause, then take a slow breath…"

"It's you, it's me, and it's many more of us who haven't yet vocalized our experiences because we're still busy hustling."

"To me, this is a novel by a writer trying to grapple with the human condition, a classic struggle between honoring the family and spreading her wings."

"This is one of Ms. Casey Cui's gifts to the world. And I say 'one of' because hopefully it will be the first of many."

"It's told from first-person but doubles as third-person narration. There's so much to unpack… The author is a beautiful writer and brilliantly creative."

"Her work is an allegory of life."

a novel by i.b. casey cui

illustration by m. casey

This novel is a work of fiction.
Although its anatomy—and possibly major organs,
namely the heart—is that of a memoir, it is not (a memoir).
The quirks and chronicles of each character have been
embellished to suit the spirit of the book. Any references to
real people (living or dead), events, establishments, organizations,
or locales are intended only to give the book a sense of reality and
authenticity, and are fictitious (though dubiously). The judgments
expressed are those of the story's enigmatic protagonist and her
people, and therefore should not be confused with the author's.

first published in the united states of america by bookbaby
printed on acid-free paper
groovygirlnovel.com
insta: @groovygirlnovel

the ISBN of this edition of **gRooVY giRL** is located on the back cover.

cover design by *www.greatmemories.ca*
digital illustrations (cover and author photos) by *adi garnida*
title page design and illustration by *adi garnida* and *m. casey*

a portion of **gRooVY giRL's** proceeds will benefit:

STRIDES FOR LIFE COLON CANCER FOUNDATION
LORI ANN FOUNDATION
LUMITALA
MONA FOUNDATION

For yar, ocram, and oim

Three antitheses
of backward. You are not quite
palindromic, like
with the true meaning of "dog."
But oh, my dear gods you are.

MIL GRACIAS Y MARAMING SALAMAT

MS,
Was she a "wonder,"
like his "gait and crooked smile"?
Ah, they will be missed.

JS,
Your wariness of
this young, raw voice impelled me.
May it sing for you.

MK,
Fifteen years later
"an allegory of life"
'tis still. But whose life?

+J,
Which do thou love most?
She who put the groovy in
girl? Go: "There you are."

Deb,
Hollywood agent
My inspirer-friend, lending
dreams their wings to soar.

RA,
Truth "burns," but does it?
You peered over progressives:
blinded, then discerned

MoSully,
"Vociferous" girl!
Inspiration is to give
is to embrace, us.

CN,
The Cha-Icha link
Not "divine intervention"–
'twas woman action!

Kuya,
the "Flip" version of
the Joneses? No. baligtad
'to, my paragon.

en la memoria de…

She-She so feisty
"You designed a life you loved"
because you always
were still you: a butterfly
with winsome wings that took flight.

For you were the one
who knew the real niñita.
¿Siempre y para
siempre? Nope, no way, no how.
Mountains moved, god of knowledge.

King Chad, you preferred
action figures, not awards.
More than Black Panther,
streets ahead of trophies, you
did not get to finish life.

Go, girls! "Not the last."
Mea Domina, meaning
"my lady." To us,
it's honorable woman.
Like Shyamala, sin fin.

Sans the privilege
of knowing the warm, brazen
beauty you were, my
spirit's tamed. Watch over your
girls: greatly groovy like you.

#sheilabrucelaswhatshisnamechadwickbosemanshyamalaharrisamyhubbardnelson

"I don't know whether this world has a meaning that transcends it. But I know that I cannot know that meaning and that it is impossible for me just now to know it."

—Albert Camus

groovy girl

prologue: purple punishments and prayers

WHEN PAPA'S BROTHERS, MY *TITOS*, COME OVER TO THE HOUSE, they kick back in the dining room and make *kuwento*, which means telling stories.

Remember the house in Santa Mesa, back in Manila, they say.

Remember the clay tiles, the sacks of papayas in the kitchen?

Remember the tall vase of *sampaguitas?*

The national flower of the Philippines, which Mama says is lovelier and nicer-smelling than the jasmine growing outside our house in Arcadia, California.

I sit in the door frame between the kitchen and the dining room, hoping Mama won't glance up from loading the dishwasher and bark at me to help her or at least stop being unladylike and get off the dirty floor please. If you're ladylike, it means you're acting like Makena my *áte*, my big sister, who got out of having to wash dishes because she has pains in her belly. She lies on her bed, twisting the ends of her long, dark hair around her fingers, sighing and looking up at the ceiling like a princess who's in love or maybe just bored.

"Remember," the *titos* keep saying.

I wonder why they say *remember* over and over. Who forgets the house they grew up in? I'll always remember this house, with high ceilings that make you feel dizzy when you look up at them but also protected at the same time, and I really don't see how anything could smell prettier than jasmine on a warm night.

I look over at the *titos*, and they're staring back at me.

Maybe when they remember things out loud, they want to make sure I will remember them too.

I turn and watch Mama shake Sun Light powder into the dishwasher's little compartment. Her pink nails are bright against the yellow box. I'm kind of annoyed because I feel like everybody's trying to give me a lesson and it's Friday night, my favorite time of the week because it's the farthest from Monday, when it's so hard to get up early for school.

Tito Dante and Tito Carding and Tito Sal and Tito Vito are at the table with Papa, who is the oldest brother of the family. The only one missing is Tito Gus, the baby, the one they call *bakla*, which means he's gay.

"Remember Gus and the shoes," Tito Sal says.

"Gus and the shoes and the barrel," Tito Carding adds.

They cluck their tongues, making tsk-tsk-tsk sounds and muttering *sayang*, such a waste and what a shame, then they laugh big and snorty except for Papa, who frowns like he's remembering a business deal that didn't go the way he wanted it to.

Tito Dante calls to me, "You know, Isabel, your Tito Gus, when he was four years old, he waltzed into the living room wearing your Tita Choleng's red stilettos."

Tito Dante begins the story: "'Am I *bee-yoo-tee-pool?'* little Gus asked, looking up at everyone. All your *titas* giggled, even your Lola Carmen, who laughed so hard that teardrops were squirting out of her nostrils."

I could picture Lola Carmen, my grandmother, laughing like that because she was always so *masayang kasama*, which means you're fun to hang around with. *Masayang kasama* even with her brown and gray hairs pulled back tight and her rosary wound around her wrinkly hands.

I picture Tito Gus that night, his smiling and teetering, the clacking of skinny high heels on the tile. I see Papa, just a college student, walking into the living room to see what's going on, a copy of his favorite book, called *Society and Sanity*, in his hands. He drops the book when he sees little Gus, who is taking a bow like a cabaret dancer.

"Am I *bee-yoo-tee-pool?*"

Papa hears his own father, Lolo Martín, entering the house. Papa grabs a blue coverlet from the couch to hide his baby brother's feet, but he's too late. Lolo Martín walks in and looks around the room at his family, and his eyes flick down at the stilettos, like he would do if he spied a rat or a lizard standing still in the middle of the floor, trying not to be noticed. His teeth press together tight like pliers.

Lolo Martín has had enough of Gus and his *bakla* ways, how he cries like a girl, hands covering his face. How he steals the veils his sisters wear to mass and drapes them over his head while skipping along by the front gate for all the neighbors to see.

"Mierda, talaga kang puta!" he yells.

The house shakes, and Lola Carmen and Papa's sisters clutch at each other and reach out for Gus to take their hands. But Gus just stands there in his wobbly high heels.

Dante chews on the sleeve of his *kamiseta*, Sal hides behind Carding, Carding behind Papa. Vito is standing off to the side under the portrait of The Last Supper.

"*Qué desgracia,* you weak little queer. You are not my son," Lolo Martín hisses. He storms into the kitchen, leaving everyone frozen except for Gus, who is still bouncing in the heels.

Lolo Martín returns with a small wooden barrel over his shoulder, the barrel where Lola Carmen stores *isdang tuyo*, dried fish.

He walks outside to the driveway and empties the barrel. Maingay, the mutt next door, trots over to the pile of fish. He snorts like a hog because his nose is working hard, inhaling sharp, salty fumes. He lifts his leg and pees all over the *tuyo.*

Lolo Martín doesn't care. He taps his foot while the straps on both his *tsinelas* are starting to come loose.

"You and your brothers, *now*," Lolo Martín growls at Papa.

The boys rush over and stare. What plan does their father have with a barrel?

Lolo Martín instructs his older sons to put their little brother inside, secure the lid over the barrel, and roll little Gus around.

Papa blinks and swipes his wavy black hair away from his forehead.

"For how long?" he asks in a shaky voice.

"Until he has decided to be a man and not *bakla*," Lolo Martín answers. He slaps the top of the barrel like a drum, and he stamps his *tsinelas* into the house and drags Gus by his right ear outside to the driveway. Even with all the shrieking and flailing, Lolo Martín shoves his youngest son inside the barrel.

Papa decides to speak up.

"Rolling Gus around won't make him a man," he tells his father.

"I will be the creator of punishments in this house," Lolo Martín barks.

"The *creator*," Papa repeats to himself, low enough so that his father doesn't hear.

Lolo Martín tells his sons to keep rolling until Gus has made his decision. Papa's brothers chew on shirt sleeves and collars and try to hide, but there is nowhere to go.

Dante whispers to Sal, *"Ano ang bakla?"*

Sal rolls his eyes. "*Bakla* is Gus, you *ulol*. Being *bakla* is when you're a boy and you wanna be a girl."

Papa is the first to roll the barrel. He remembers the crunching sounds of dried-up leaves, pebbles being flattened into the ground. At each hollow, Gus wails. When the crying starts to hurt Papa's ears, Papa yells into the barrel.

"Ano ang problema mo? ¿Qué es tu problema?"

When Gus doesn't answer, Papa lifts the top of the barrel.

Gus' face twists into a scowl made especially for Papa.

"I hate you," he cries.

Papa gently pushes his brother's head deeper into the barrel and replaces the lid. He keeps rolling until the next brother's turn is up. He watches the sky change from lavender to purple, while shadows of banana leaves and coconut palms sway in the wind.

There's no room for ugliness on a night like this, he remembers thinking, looking up at the purple sky.

In the end, Gus is crusty, in a daze and reeking of fish, his body covered in small wounds from the pointy pieces of wood inside the barrel. But he makes no promises to be different.

At suppertime, Lolo Martín calls out to Papa and his brothers to hurry inside and eat. His regal posture has turned into a slouch, a look of defeat. He orders his sons to go straight to bed immediately or else. No one says one word or dares to let Lolo Martín hear them so much as breathe.

Lola Carmen runs the hot water for Gus' bath while the others get ready for bed. Papa is in charge of bathing Gus, whose tears seem to fall like raindrops into the basin. Papa scrubs off the bits of *tuyo* dangling from Gus' neck, then massages his legs and arms with white flower oil. When he's done, he changes Gus into a clean *kamiseta* and tucks him into bed.

Papa sits at his desk and flips through the index of *Society and Sanity*.

Man. What he is, why the question matters, man damaged.

Papa pulls the light switch and sits next to Gus' bed. He strokes Gus' smooth, round cheeks.

Gus opens his eyes and yawns. "Are we friends now, my *kuya?*"

Papa whispers, "You are not damaged."

Gus lies still, and Papa smells the earthy wood of the barrel, the remains of fish salt on Gus' skin.

"Come, say a prayer with me," Papa says.

Gus climbs out of bed and kneels beside Papa.

They make the sign of the cross together.

Now I lay me down to sleep
I pray the Lord my soul to keep

If I should die before I wake
I pray the Lord my soul to take

Gus taps Papa on the shoulder and asks what the prayer means.

"It means the Lord will take care of you, whether you're on earth or in heaven."

"But *Kuya*, will he take my soul even if I'm a weak little queer?"

After Papa tells the end of the story, the *titos* lean back in their chairs and sigh, just like they do after they've finished a heavy meal. Papa stares down at the table, shaking his head like he's trying to shake away the memory. I catch Tito Carding wiping his eyes, which meet mine and look away in a hurry.

He's making sure I don't remember his tears.

That night, I dream about being in the barrel, the creaking and the darkness and the stink of fish, but most of all the spinning.

Everything is spinning, spinning as the world spins. When I wake up, it's hard to breathe. Makena is standing over me.

"What were you dreaming of?" she asks, her cool finger on my forehead.

"I was in a barrel. I was rolling around inside. I couldn't stop spinning."

"Those *titos*," she says. "Too much *kuwento*."

"I was scared, Makena."

"Really?" She looks at me with crinkly eyebrows.

"Yes, I was spinning and everything was blurry and there was nothing I could do about it."

"But Isa, before you woke up, you were laughing," she says. "You were laughing in your sleep."

1. rocky road

"All hellz broke loose," which is what my big brother, my *kuya* Xavy says when the house gets loud and crazy. Mama's screaming "*Jesusmarijosep*, Xavy, you need to learn responsibility," because he fed our beagle Frida the leftover pork *adobo* from dinner last night, and now her breath smells like vinegar and soy sauce and she can't control her poo, which is in all kinds of mushy piles all over the kitchen floor and dining room.

And of course Xavy doesn't want to help Mama clean it up because he and Papa are the men of the house, so it's not their job to pick up after the dog.

Papa's in the driveway yelling and pointing his finger at Arturo, who is one of his subs. "Sub" is short for subcontractor and "super" is short for superintendent, and I know these things because Papa is in charge of all kinds of custom-built homes for rich people in Pasadena and La Cañada and other cities close by.

Arturo's workers stole a truckload of lumber from Papa's job site in La Cañada, so Papa's calling Arturo a *coño*, which means something horrible and nasty in Spanish according to Mama. She says when Papa curses *en español*, you sure don't want to be anywhere near him, but I don't mind because it's kind of neat seeing Papa be the boss and act all tough to other people.

Arturo once told me, "Your old man Antonio, he is like Mafioso, don't mess with him man or you be runnin' scared for your whole lifetime."

One time when Papa took me to his other job site in Pasadena, I saw him screaming like a baseball umpire into another man's face. This man also worked for Papa, and Xavy says he used to be the president of the Hell's Angels in all of San Fernando Valley. Ed Hardesty was his name, and he had the longest and most bushiest beard, and he always wore a shirt with the sleeves cut off that said "USA Rules and Screw the Rest."

Mama says the sight of Ed Hardesty's unkempt face with his nose and lip rings to match makes the baby hairs on the back of her neck stand up.

Xavy likes reminding me in his low and serious voice, "Dude. Dis gangsta once called Papa a coldblooded monster behind his back."

While the hell is breaking loose, I try to play with Sarita my favorite Groovy Girl with the poofy black hair, even though Makena thinks I'm too old to be playing with dolls because I'm already eight. Frida always tries to be sneaky and walk away slowly with Sarita tucked inside her mouth, but when I tell her she's a bad girl, her ears turn flat, so that's when she decides to just lie beside me while I play.

When I was in first grade, Papa and Mama bought me Sarita and Kayla and Kami. They even bought me the Groovy Girl Beautiful Bed, which comes in pink and purple and orange and feels so cushy soft like all my stuffed animals.

Makena's supposed to be home soon from her doctor's appointment, and I can't wait because she promised to take me to 31 Flavors. "We've had a goddamn scorching hot LA fall," says Papa, so every day's been the most perfect day for ice cream.

31 Flavors is really called Baskin-Robbins, but 31 Flavors sounds much cooler. The other kids at school make fun of me when I say 31 Flavors, but Mr. Baluga our neighbor next door doesn't. He just laughs his ha-ha's that sound deep like a gorilla's and tells everyone I'm the most cunning child he knows.

Papa and Mr. Baluga used to spend a lot of time together because Papa is the sole administrator of his estate, even though he isn't related to Mr. Baluga. I would hear them either in our garage, which is Papa's "second office" according to Mama, or in Mr. Baluga's backyard, where there's a big umbrella attached to a table so that they could be under the shade when the weather was hot.

Sometimes Papa would ask Mr. Baluga when he was going to tell his family about his money and properties, and sometimes they would talk about both their times in the military. But Papa's been getting busier these days working at his job sites, so he started sending me over to Mr. Baluga's house to help rake leaves or flatten boxes for recycling.

Mama doesn't like it when I hang around Mr. Baluga because she thinks he's an old crab and that he has no business hanging around youngsters. Papa always tells her, "It's okay, Mama, Isabel needs to get used to being around different characters, it'll do wonders for her confidence." Mama keeps arguing that I don't need to be any more confident than I already am, but Papa just ignores her and goes to his second office to smoke.

We're called the José family, and we're the only Filipinos besides Mr. Baluga and his wife who live on Carisbrook Drive in Arcadia, which is near the San Gabriel Mountains and surrounded by all kinds of grass that's trimmed super neat. It even has tall purple flowers called agapanthuses, named after the storm cloud according to Mama by a guy from Arcadia who bred this flower back in 1943, almost 60 whole years ago. There are also a bunch of oak trees with spirally leaves, and that's why many people want to move here, because who wouldn't want to live in a foothill landscape with lush greenery, which is what Makena likes to say.

Arcadia is full of white people we call *puti*, so some of our Flip friends from our old neighborhood in Eagle Rock say we're whitewashed, especially when we say "Flip" because that's an anti-Filipino sentiment, according to Makena, but Xavy says it stands for "Fine-Lookin' Island Peeps."

Not everyone here is *puti*. There are a lot of Chinese and Korean and Japanese and Indian and other Asian kids and also different kinds of Latino and Hispanic families and many cultures at my school, called Holly Reid Elementary.

Makena always tells me to never mind the color of everyone else's skin and just try to make some good friends, and when I told Mr. Baluga this while I was getting the *LA Times* and *Wall Street Journal* in our driveway for Papa one morning, he laughed his gorilla ha-ha's and patted me on the head and said,

"That sister of yours is so learned for a 19-year-old, and what a dear she is for giving you such wise words. But I've got a news flash for you, Kid. Our world isn't as open-minded as you think it is."

Maybe the world is so full of open minds and closed minds that it needs some halfway-open minds and halfway-closed minds to even things out. That's what I tell Sarita and Kami and Kayla as I'm changing them into different Groovy Girl outfits, and I wonder to myself which kinds of minds are better to have.

Makena and Xavy were supposed to be the only kids in this family, so when Mama found out she was pregnant with me almost 10 years after she had Xavy, boy did that turn this house upside-down because Mama had already given away all of Makena's and Xavy's clothes and all those bulky baby things, like the car seat and the stroller and the high chair.

Papa made Mama get rid of everything because he can't stand clutter. "There will be no pack rats living under my roof," Papa roars around the house whenever we ask him to put away our knickknacks in the storage closet or the garage. So the only thing Mama saved was Makena and Xavy's dark brown crib that faded to orange, and this is still at Lola Zeny's house.

Lola Zeny is Mama's mama, but we don't see her anymore because she and Mama's sisters accused Papa of stealing their inheritance, which is why Papa keeps reminding us, "You're never going to see that goddamn crib again."

Makena tells me that this is one of the biggest shames in life, being at daggers with your own flesh and blood. I don't like all the fighting either, but there really shouldn't be any shames in life at all.

I hear a car engine in the driveway. The sound of Makena's key in the lock makes my tongue feel heavy, and now all I can think about is rocky road with lots of marshmallows.

When Makena walks through the front door, her eyes are small and swollen. This is what happens to me if I cry right before I go to sleep. When I wake up in the morning, I look sort of Chinese like my great-grandmother Maymei from Xiamen, and

I try to fix it by putting Blue Ice over my eyelids, but that never works fast enough.

Makena sits on the curvy green couch in the living room that always makes Papa mutter under his breath, "It's too green and too goddamn curvy," but I don't think he really wants this to stay under his breath.

I walk over to Makena, making sure my steps are quiet and careful because puffy eyes always mean rotten bad news in this house. I want to ask about 31 Flavors, but Makena pulls me close to her and presses her lips against my head.

"*Hija,*" Papa says in a low voice from down the hallway. "What did the doctor say?"

"Shhh," Makena whispers into my ear, and the sound she makes is long and tired.

"Kena Beach," Papa calls out. He's standing in the door frame, trying to mask his frown by saying one of Makena's nicknames. Makena was named after Makena Beach in Maui, where Papa took Mama for their honeymoon back in the '80s.

Mama walks in, and she's holding a cantaloupe to her belly. I hear a cracking sound from the stairs, and we all look up and see Xavy biting into his bubble gum, making mini explosions with it inside his mouth, which I think is cool but really is low class, according to Papa.

"Colon cancer."

This is all Makena has to say.

Mama drops the cantaloupe, and it clunks onto the floor and rolls towards Frida, who sniffs at it. A soft sound comes from Mama's lips that quiver like a fiddle string, like a hum, like a siren you can hear from far away. She starts making the sign of the cross over and over as if it'll change the way things are.

All of a sudden, Papa slams his hand down on the dining room table, which makes Frida jump and lower her head like she did something wrong.

"That's a goddamn old man's disease," he says loud but not shouting. "How can this be?"

But Papa calms down on the double and wraps his thick and dark arms around Makena's small shoulders, pulling her away from me. Xavy stays on the stairs all hunched over and chews his gum harder. He yanks his bandana off his head, wringing it like it's wet or something, and he doesn't say one single word.

Colon Cancer.

If you ask me, I don't think Makena is that sick right now. She just looks like she needs a nap. I've seen her with a cold and the flu and even laryngitis one time, and that sure wasn't pretty because it made her voice sound raw and croaky, kind of like the koalas I saw at the San Diego Zoo last year.

Makena and Mama are always coming down with something, especially around Christmas when the weather isn't as warm, and sometimes even during the summer, which of course is no fun at all because blowing your nose and coughing up the gooey stuff inside your chest and throat when it's hot outside just isn't right.

Papa and Xavy always call Makena and Mama "sickly," and I wonder if that's what Papa's thinking right now. Mama always says, "Your father believes he's Superman," but maybe he really is and he can't tell us, like Clark Kent having to keep it secret from everyone until Lois Lane got nosy and found out.

Colon cancer.

I watch Makena with her sleepy face leaning against Papa, all limp and floppy, and I realize I don't feel sorry or scared.

I feel mad.

Why does she have to be so weak, I think to myself, even though I know it's wrong and terrible to be angry at someone who's sick. Mama doesn't like it when I call some of my girl classmates "weaklings," but it makes me super crazy hot on the inside when Callie Barone or Talula Lee pretend they can't go across the monkey bars because they don't want water blisters all over their soft little hands. A lot of my classmates have small bodies, and even Makena isn't much heavier than me, and she's almost 12 years older.

Everyone says I'm big-boned, but I've worked on it by drinking lots of Alta Dena milk and eating Spam and scrambled eggs and Ligo sardines with fried rice, which is what Papa likes to have in the morning before he goes to his job sites. Makena is petite but muscular too, just like Frida. They both have legs as lean as a racehorse's, Mama always says. Mine are like tree stumps, with kind of a big chunky butt to go with them.

Papa walks behind Makena up the stairs, his hand on her shoulder all cautious, like the cancer could make her fall. Xavy and I follow Mama to the kitchen.

Mama starts to grind coffee beans, which of course makes Frida bark and pace in circles because she hates screaky noises.

Xavy bites into a persimmon, not caring it's bitter.

Colon cancer.

My body is squirmy, and I think it's running a fever. "Can someone open a window please," I shout, even though the A/C is on, and that's when I start firing away with the questions.

"Is Makena hurting?"

No answer.

"How did this happen?"

Still nothing, but I'll bet they can hear me.

"How are the doctors going to fix her?"

I ask all of this out loud to anyone who will answer me, and when I realize my questions are the kinds you blurt out when you're worried, I feel wrong and terrible for being angry.

Mama shushes me, resting her hand on my back and noticing Frida's hair all over the Oski Bear on the front of my T-shirt. She starts picking hairs from only the Oski part and sometimes from the "California Berkeley" letters because beagle hairs are like neon glow necklaces on dark colors.

"Relax and sit down, please, sweetheart," she says, and all of a sudden I'm folding my arms across my chest like I'm making *tampo*, which means you're acting like a baby because you didn't get your way, but that's not really how I'm feeling.

Mama explains the part where Makena had stomach pains one day in her psychology class and could barely walk, so one of her classmates whose name is Junior, a quiet and sweet Samoan guy who lives in Arcadia too and we all know has a major crush on Makena, carried her all the way to the campus hospital. Then

Makena was sent to the emergency room at a bigger hospital because the doctor had a sinking feeling about her pains.

Makena also showed other symptoms before she was hurting, like making poo in the toilet that was black and thin like straws, but she couldn't bring herself to tell anyone because she was embarrassed.

Later when she found out that dark-colored poo meant she was losing blood, she decided to call Dr. Witt, whose wife is a nurse and one of Mama's good friends, and that's when he told Mama to have Makena fly back home from school.

I still can't relax because now I'm wondering why Makena didn't go to the doctor sooner.

I feel mad again but I don't want to be, so I start picking hairs from the ears and nose on Oski, and then I notice all the other beagle hairs blending into the glossy gold color of the rest of this Cal T-shirt that Makena brought back from school before she knew she had a disease.

colon cancer.

I need to brush Frida. I wonder if one of those huge rolls of packaging tape will work better than Mama's old lint brush. I keep plucking the hairs off one by one, trying hard not to frown.

"Take a nap, Isabel, we've had a long day," Mama says in her soft mother voice. Her fingers feel like a dewy washcloth against my cheeks. In my bed, I lie down in my T-shirt covered in beagle hairs, and I realize I'll never get them all off.

When I wake up, I notice the house is still. I pull out my chair from under my desk and open up the 2002-2003 calendar book that Makena gave me for my eighth birthday in June.

Today is September 27, 2002, and everyone is in different corners of the house. One of the black balloons from Xavy's party that we threw for his seventeenth birthday a few weeks ago is still hanging out in different spots around the ceiling of the family room.

Papa's smoking in his second office and throwing darts at Xavy's Britney Spears poster.

Mama's cleaning up in the kitchen. You can tell she's trying not to bang the pots and pans while she puts them away in the cabinets.

Makena's on her computer looking at emails, and you never heard such lickety-split typing. I poke my head quietly through her door and see her entering "colon cancer organizations" and "stage III colon cancer" on Yahoo Search, and now I'm wondering how many stages of cancer there are.

Xavy is in the backyard talking ghetto on the phone with his friends who Papa calls gangsters.

When it's time for bed, I watch Makena in the bathroom as she plucks and shapes her eyebrows into an arch in front of the medicine cabinet. She turns to me and says tweezing eyebrows shouldn't matter so much to her now, like a line from a sad and silly love song.

Why shouldn't it matter, I think to myself, and I decide I don't like her sad-song voice, like she doesn't want to try and who cares what my eyebrows look like anymore.

Then she tells me she's going to be fine and that she's taking some time off from school. She promises she'll keep hitting me tennis balls from the little red shopping cart that we forgot to take back to Luigi's Deli on Baldwin Avenue, right in our backyard where Papa built a tennis court all to ourselves, but how will she be able to do this if she has cancer?

Makena is teaching me how to play tennis. Her college teammates call her "Makenzer Wowzers" because when she hits a ball, it sounds like thunder and makes you want to say "Wowzers" and not just wow. Their eyes grow frog-eye wide and they whistle through their teeth, "Go, Makenzer Wowzers."

When I hit a ball, it just goes twang.

I ask Makena how someone like her could get sick with this kind of disease, and isn't cancer only for old people like Mr. Baluga? He has this long hair growing out of a fat mole on his right cheek, and he tells me he can't pull the hair out or else he'll catch skin cancer.

Makena says that's hogwash because both she and Mama have moles, smack on the right side of the upper corner of each of their mouths, in the same exact spot, and they always pluck the hair that grows from it. One of these days, I'll have to tell Mr. Baluga, but he might snap at me like his parrot Mokong used to do whenever I had Goldfish crackers for him.

Makena tells me that there are young people like her who have cancer too, and I ask her if I can catch it. That's when she reaches for my hands like they're Frida when she was a tiny puppy and wraps them around both of hers. She holds my hand during those horror movies Xavy likes to watch and thunderstorms that make me sleep with my head under the covers and Frida howl the whole night.

Makena held my hand during the earthquake that made me pee in my new Snoopy flannel pajamas when I was in kindergarten, and the best thing about all of this is she never tells Papa that I wasn't tough and brave.

She starts to explain to me that something called a polyp grows in your colon, which is your large intestine. Food is digested inside your stomach, then it moves from your small intestine to your colon. Polyps are growths that look like warts at first, but if they grow bigger like the size of cherries, they can become tumors. And if the tumor spreads all over your body before a doctor removes it, you need medicine to keep it from growing and spreading some more.

What I want to know is how the polyp started getting big in the first place, but I don't think it's the right time to fire away with my questions, so instead I imagine Mr. Baluga's mole with the long hair. I also think about Mama's and Makena's moles. Warts are like moles, so I'll bet moles are evil too, little speckles of black skin that can turn into something so ugly and multiply all over your body to make you weak. Makena says that colon cancer isn't contagious, so at least we still can live in the same house and be a family together with her.

I listen carefully and I try to remember everything, but it sure is a lot of information to hold inside my brain. The whole time Makena's explaining, I squeeze her cold and shaky hands, trying to push the warm blood back into them.

I notice her face looks pretty under her orange lampshade. I want to cheer her up, so I tell her that the light shining on her face makes her look like a beautiful angel. When she starts to cry, I don't know what to do, if I should cry with her or just sit there trying to hide being surprised by her tears, stuff that rolls out of my *áte*'s eyes usually only when Papa is acting like Mafioso, the coldblooded monster.

"Who wants to be an angel," she whispers, and it sounds like the beginning of a sad song.

2. *pasyal:* pig out and pee on perfection

Now that Makena is sick, I imagine everything that will change, like *pasyal*, which is one of my favorite things to do. *Pasyal* means to just go out somewhere. Sometimes we rent bikes at Playa del Rey and ride all the way to Redondo Beach and back, which I don't have any problem doing because I learned how to ride a bike earlier than all of my friends.

I can go far and long and up and down windy and bumpy paths. I can ride even farther than Mama, but she doesn't bike anymore because of her achy lower back, so she just waits for us while she pigs out on steamed crab with Tita Gwen, who is my favorite *tita*, Papa's youngest sister. She's getting married right after New Year's Day.

When we finally get to Redondo Beach, we eat crab and shrimp cocktail and fish and chips, which I found out are really French fries, and then we bike back to Playa del Rey and drive to Redondo to pick up Mama and Tita Gwen. And that's a whole 18 miles total, which Papa says is a lot for 8-year-old legs, even strong and stocky ones like mine.

Or sometimes *pasyal* means going to South Coast Plaza, which is a humungous mall that's close to Newport Beach. It has all the stores you can think of, like Gap Kids and Sanrio and even Gucci and Tiffany & Co. and Ferragamo and all those expensive brands that Papa likes.

Makena's favorite is Tiffany & Co. She says a lot of their stuff is elegant and simple, and she even saved the money she made from teaching tennis one summer and bought one of those bangles that Tiffany & Co. calls a love knot. It's perfect for Makena because it's the smallest bracelet ever, so only people with the tiniest wrists can wear it. There's no way Papa or Xavy or I can wear anything like it because we're husky and meaty like all the rest of the Josés.

Mama's side of the family is small, and that's how Makena got her wrists that look like twigs. Mama has twig wrists too, but jewelry isn't at the top of her list of favorite things. She'd rather shop for shoes. Sometimes we like to call her Imelda Marcos because she owns all kinds of shoes, 233 pairs to be exact, but she hates being compared to "the dragon lady who married that good-for-nothing dictator." Mama always says Ferdinand Marcos is the reason why the Philippines never progressed and why the country is in the shape it's been in for all these years, with a polluted environment and drugs and crime and way too many poor people without food and homes and jobs.

Xavy just waits for us while we shop. He picks up a car magazine somewhere and hangs out with other men who are waiting for their wives, or he watches the kids on the merry-go-round at Crystal Court, which is a different section of South Coast Plaza that has one of our favorite restaurants, called Ruby's. They have the tastiest chili because the meat isn't the ground beef you find in other kinds of chili. It's shredded, so it looks real and not processed according to Makena, who doesn't really eat meat.

I eat lots of meat, which means I'm a carnivore, but both Papa and Mama call me an omnivore because all I think and talk about is food, any kind of food.

Sometimes when Papa and Mama and Makena and Xavy and I make *pasyal*, we just keep driving and never get out of the car. One time we drove around Bel-Air and Hollywood Hills and admired all the grand houses with iron gates and flashy cars, like Aston Martins and Rolls-Royces parked in the long driveways.

We have a nice house here in Arcadia, but you can't compare the homes in our neighborhood to the ones on the west side of LA, mansions where the movie stars live. One of these days, I hope we run into someone like Freddie Prinze, Jr. or Phoebe from *Friends*, which is one of Xavy and Makena's favorite TV shows.

When I tell my classmates about *pasyal,* they tease me because all it means is to get out of the house and go have some fun, which everyone in the world has to do anyway. But I know they turn envious sometimes because their parents stay cooped up at home. Their mamas knit and cook and get arthritis, and their papas are always working until they get gray hair or no hair at all.

Papa works all week long and he still has some hair left, but he always saves time for *pasyal*. Frida gets to go with us sometimes, and one time she squatted for a longer time than usual to pee, right on someone's perfect green front lawn in Beverly Hills, and boy did we hear it from the owner of that house.

I don't care if *pasyal* means to just go out. There are so many things to see when we make *pasyal*, comparing fancy iron gates to the chain-link fences in neighborhoods where Mama says money is harder to make, watching Papa curse the lowriders all tricked-out, cruising like they don't have anywhere important to go and riding over speed bumps in a slow zigzag super gentle so that their bottoms don't get scratched. Then noticing Xavy chuckle under his breath because he drives over speed bumps the same exact way with his Volkswagen Bug.

Making oohs and wows at all the new shopping plazas with Starbucks and Ross and Bed Bath & Beyond, wondering how long it will take for all the short and skinny trees planted on those little cement islands in the parking lots to become tall and leafy and thick, which Papa says might take 10 to 20 years. And that's when Ross will turn shabby from old ladies hunting down bargains, messing up the clothes racks and shelves, keeping Mama from shopping there and complaining, "No way am I sorting through all that disarray."

Scrunching our faces at the cloud of smog sitting on top of Downtown LA which you can see from the 10 freeway, listening to Makena complain about how unhealthy it is to live here, how her chest hurts after tennis practice and what if it's the air that grew a tumor inside her colon and sent her on all kinds of emergency trips to the bathroom.

The cleaner air in Northern California is one of many reasons why she went to Cal instead of UCLA, which was her second choice for college even though their tennis team is better. Cal is the original University of California, Makena says, which is why some people call it Cal instead of UC Berkeley.

I like making *pasyal* because it means we can go out and be a normal family together, laughing and cursing and making our own comments about what we see and how we feel about it.

Pasyal makes our lives interesting, and Papa says you need an interesting life to matter in this world.

3. the pussycat and the pendulum

Sometimes when we aren't making *pasyal*, the hell starts to break loose in the house or on the tennis court in our backyard.

Right before Makena left for the school year last month in August, Papa called her a "choker" and a "pussycat" when she lost a practice set to Xavy.

Papa taught Makena and Xavy how to play tennis when they were younger, even younger than I am right now. Both of them have all kinds of talent and athletic ability according to Bill Van Gelder their coach, but "Makena has the mind to make it to the pros," he likes to brag. Mental toughness, which is what Papa calls it, is what it takes. He always says, "All Xavy does is screw around on the court like a goddamn bozo doing his circus act."

Xavy's never serious when he plays, but it sure is fun to watch him hit a shot from under his leg or do the fire hydrant when he's volleying, which means you step forward with the wrong foot and lift your other leg so that you look like a boy dog peeing.

Makena isn't supposed to lose to Xavy, even though Xavy's a boy. Papa says that Xavy has a stronger serve, and sometimes he even has harder put-away shots which are called winners, but Makena will wear you down with her steady groundstrokes with lots of pace, and boy does she aim for those corners and lines, making you work like a horse for every point.

Papa makes me watch Wimbledon and the US Open and all the major pro championships with him on cable, which is how I learned all the tennis jargon there is to know. Mama calls me Papa's "sidekick," and "Why are there so many of you," she always asks. She likes teasing Papa about his sidekicks because Papa can't do anything by himself, even if he's the one doing everything and his sidekick is just sitting there looking bored.

I don't think there's anything wrong with wanting someone to hang out with you, because at school, we learn that the need for belonging and community is a natural thing to feel, even for animals.

Makena and Xavy's practice set was long and tiring for them because it was 87 degrees outside, which made them take more water breaks. It was tiring even for me and Papa, whose right hip started to hurt during one of Makena and Xavy's rallies from the baseline that was all dragged out, making me wish I could press the fast-forward button on a remote.

I can still hear the skids from their tennis shoes on the court, also the heavy breathing from Xavy because his big body is filled with Sour Cream 'n' Onion Lay's and Mexi-Cokes, according to Mama. I remember Makena's piercing squeals when she reached far for a shot, her thin arms like elastic, and then she would return the ball to Xavy even harder than he hit it to her in the first place.

The set became a tiebreaker, which Papa says what happens when you're tied at 6-6. Xavy was up 8-7 in the tiebreaker, and he needed only one more point to win. There was another long rally, and even though I was rooting for Makena, I remember I kept wishing Xavy would just rush the net and end the point, which is what Papa sometimes yells at him to do because he says Xavy's volleys are full of power and precision. But Xavy's scared of Makena's passing shots, so he decided to hang out at the baseline and try to keep up with her groundstrokes.

My head turned right to left, left to right, watching the tennis ball get pounded across the net by my *áte* and *kuya*, their faces like hot peppers, all sweaty and competitive and who cares if I'm related to you.

All of a sudden, when one of Makena's shots barely touched the baseline, Xavy called the ball out. I looked at Makena who glared at Xavy and turned to Papa with a face that couldn't believe what happened, but Papa didn't do anything, he just stood there, making tsk-tsk-tsk sounds under his breath and shaking his head. I think he wanted Makena and Xavy to figure things out for themselves instead of him making the call because whenever Papa plays umpire, the person who got the short end of the stick never wants anything to do with him for the rest of the day.

"You have got to be kidding!" Makena screamed to Xavy across the net, but Xavy's racquet was already resting on the mark that the ball made near the baseline. He even pulled out the towel he keeps tucked inside his shorts because he sweats so much and then laid it next to the mark, the edge of the towel underlining it, like it was deciding who won and who lost.

Papa and I walked over to Xavy's side to get a better view, but it was hard to tell if the ball was in or out because there were so many other marks surrounding the one that Xavy was pointing his racquet to.

I asked Xavy if he was sure he was pointing to the right spot, but Papa made a "psst" sound, the kind that tells you to shut up because you talked at the wrong time. That's when Xavy gave me this look like I betrayed him and shouted, "You dipstick, just zip it."

I looked at Makena, who forced a smile at me to let me know she was grateful for being on her side, and when I looked back at Xavy, he was walking to the net towards Makena like he won, the set has ended and yeah right if you think that ball was in.

Makena walked over to the net too and held out her hand to shake Xavy's, which is what you're supposed to do after the match is over because Papa says it's proper etiquette. But when Xavy stuck his hand out, Papa stormed over and karate-chopped right into their handshake.

"You're just going to give up?" he asked Makena with a stare so sharp that it could split you into many pieces.

"It's not worth it, Papa," Makena answered. Her head was bowed, and her eyes were trying not to meet Papa's razor glare.

"That's how pussycats handle things," said Papa. "Your brother beat you at *your* game. Choker *ka talaga.* I don't know how you made it this far with that attitude."

Makena stood quiet and closed her eyes, and I wondered about all the things swirling in her head, if she hated Papa for what he said and if she believed any of it. She was holding the grip of her tennis racquet with just two fingers, like her racquet was a dirty towel, the kind Papa uses to wipe the bumpers of his Porsche and Suburban, all black and grimy mixed together with bumper cleaner.

All of a sudden, Makena's two fingers turned into a hand grip so tight that raised her racquet head high like she was going to hit something, which made Xavy flinch and Papa's feet scramble and my shoulders hunch close to my ears.

But then she stopped her racquet in the middle of the air and lowered the head of it slowly to the ground, letting it hang and sway next to her left foot, kind of like the pendulum of our grandfather clock.

Papa started to laugh, but the sounds coming from his mouth weren't the funny kinds of ha-ha's. They came out in slow motion, like he was calculating how many and what kinds of ha-ha's to let loose, careful and calm so that he could keep himself from punishing Makena for making us think she was going to whack us.

"That's what I thought," he said. He threw me a look that said "Let's go now," and he turned around and walked off the court, back towards the house. Xavy followed us and made skid sounds with his tennis shoes on purpose because he knows it annoys Makena.

Makena's head never moved the whole time she listened to Papa call her names and swung her racquet high like a sword. It just hung low, probably like the way she was feeling. I wish she fought back and told Xavy he was a bad cheater, but maybe she really thought her ball was out and didn't want to turn into a liar too. Or maybe she thought she'd be wasting her words on Xavy because Papa wasn't going to play umpire anyway.

There are names you can call other people when you're just playing around, like when Papa calls Xavy "TOL" which stands for "tub of lard" or when we give Mama the name "Gumby" because she has big gums and little teeth, but there are the kinds of names that never make it to the list of okay.

We all know Papa's gasket has exploded when he calls Makena a pussycat and a choker, but if any of us ever were to call him a coldblooded monster like Ed Hardesty did but instead straight to his face, he might just beat you to a pulp, which is what Xavy likes to say, and make you wish you never opened your enormous fat mouth.

4. stories: stay.

Mr. Baluga always says that in life, rotten luck is simply a rotten fact, like Papa getting sued because he takes a lot of risks in his real estate development business and Mama not talking to her own mama and sisters for a whole two years now.

Or Xavy not being able to score high enough on his practice SAT's so that he can get into UC Santa Barbara, where he says all the chicks who rock will be going to school.

Or Frida having knee surgery on both her hind legs, not just one, and even getting an abscessed canine, which means one of her fierce teeth in the front needed to be pulled out because it got infected.

The only problems I have are those fourth grade bullies at school, who keep making fun of my tree-stump legs and my big butt to match. One of these days, I sure would love to give them knuckle sandwiches, but Mama keeps telling me that violence is the wrong path to take.

Then there's Makena, who a lot of people are envious of because she's not only brainy but also nice-looking and such a natural at any sport she tries. She was always number one in her class ever since she was in kindergarten, and she skipped first grade and seventh grade because all of her subjects were too easy for her.

When she was five, she performed in a piano recital in front of President Reagan, and she was accepted to many famous universities like Cal and Harvard and Princeton and Yale, and all these schools offered her full rides, which Mama says are scholarships that pay for everything you need, like books and living expenses during your whole time there as a student.

Makena was a National Merit Scholar and made straight A's and participated in all kinds of activities, and she even got full rides from NCAA D1 tennis programs, which is almost unheard of, according to Papa.

Xavy says you'd think people like our sister have only one layer to them and just hit the books and play their one sport, but Makena also volunteers at the Pasadena SPCA. She wants to be an animal behaviorist and dog trainer because she'd rather work with animals' minds and not have to take care of sick bodies all the time, but Papa's making her become a veterinarian because it's the better route and it'll make you six figures, which means you make at least $100,000 a year.

They call her "Golden Girl" because she seems so perfect. Makena was on the football homecoming court in high school, but she lost to a cheerleader who was the most popular girl, even though she wasn't as pretty as Makena. But then Makena ended up winning prom queen anyway, so everything turned out even.

I watch my *áte* the golden girl, who doesn't have time for Frida anymore and still has some tricks and commands to teach her, who doesn't really have too many close friends except for Tracy Miller and Ally Ching and Antoinette Manalang, but they seem to annoy her so she's always brushing them off.

Her two best friends used to be Meena Madras and Shari Townsend, but Meena went back to Chennai which is in India, and Shari moved to Virginia a few years ago to attend this college prep school so that she would have a higher chance of getting into the Ivy League, which Papa says is where all the rich and snooty and conservative parents send their kids to college especially if they have legacy, which means they went to school there too and their kids automatically become accepted even if they didn't have straight A's.

Makena's never home, so she doesn't usually eat dinner with us. When she's around, she's either practicing piano or locked inside her bedroom listening to those Italian language CDs because she wants to travel to Italy next summer to take cooking classes after she graduates from Cal.

The other day when I was in the backyard playing fetch with Frida, I overheard Mr. Baluga talking to Mrs. Baluga, who we call Lola Evie. They were working in their vegetable garden, and Lola Evie kept making her hmmph sounds like my Tita Choleng, Papa's *áte* they call the scandalmonger, does when she thinks she's right.

I kept hearing mumbling and some arguing, and then I heard Lola Evie blurt out, "That older José girl, she wants to be everything and do everything, and I'll bet that's what made her sick."

Mr. Baluga snapped back with a bunch of Tagalog curse words and went on to say that not too many people can play a Beethoven concerto in front of the President of the United States and hundreds of people and make almost every single one of them sway and hum and weep in their seats.

I was shocked to hear Mr. Baluga stand up for Makena because they hardly ever talk. He says Makena used to just wave to him when she got home from tennis practice and would head straight inside the house to practice piano or study.

Mama doesn't talk to Mr. Baluga much either because she thinks he's crabby, but she always says that they don't have too many words to exchange with one another. That's where Makena inherited some of her aloof ways, according to Papa. To me, Makena just focuses and works hard, so I don't think that makes her aloof.

I'm gregarious, which is one of the SAT words that Xavy needs to memorize. I'm just like Papa and Xavy. I enjoy being around a lot of people and making *kuwento,* telling stories. I also love hearing *kuwento*. Through the stories we tell and hear, Papa says, we pass on wisdom and get different kinds in return.

I like *kuwento* because it reminds me of one of my favorite kinds of puzzles, called connect the dots. Each dot has a letter or a number, and you have to draw lines from one dot to another in whatever direction the puzzle tells you to. When everything is connected, the dots form a picture of an animal or a house or just something whole.

After I'm done making *kuwento*, I imagine dots inside my body looking for the next ones, not knowing what stories are coming next, which is neat because things sure would be boring if we knew all the stories we were going to share during our whole lifetime.

Mr. Baluga used to hang out with Papa and Xavy in our backyard patio sometimes, and they'd always high-five each other and make *kuwento* about grown-up things and shoo me away. Papa says, "Sometimes it's a welcome change to just laugh and enjoy your time with people and not have to worry about work, politics, appearances, and other goddamn crap like that."

If you ask me, sometimes I wish Makena would stop being everything and doing everything. If she could stop trying to be a golden girl and hang out and make *kuwento* and laugh with us more, maybe she'll stop being sick.

I could get her to drink Alta Dena instead of that icky soy milk she likes and make her start wanting to eat Spam, which she says is sodium nitrite mixed with processed pig, and even those sardines that probably have sodium nitrite too, the ones Papa and Xavy and I gorge right from the can.

I want her to sit still for one minute, like the way she trained Frida to down-stay, which means to go in a down position and stay put until your master says you can get up. You train dogs to down-stay so that everyone can relax when dogs get all riled up, and you attach leashes to their collars when they're walking to keep them from running away or getting hurt or lost and never ever coming back.

Down, Makena, I should tell her.

Stay.

5. poker and *pansit*

Frida and I are in our backyard, one of my favorite places to be because of all the colorful flowers that Mama likes to plant. Sometimes Frida likes to run loose on our tennis court, but it's still a goddamn scorching hot LA fall, even though I'm really not supposed to say goddamn.

Last week when I walked Frida around the playground at school, one of the pads on her front left paw started to crack and peel because the black asphalt burnt like hot charcoals, which I know only because I picked one up from the ground at a barbecue when I was six and squealed like a bat, so now we make sure the gate to our tennis court is always shut.

Frida's sniffing the petals on the orange marigolds that Mama planted last fall. Marigolds don't smell too great, kind of like the odor from the straw hat Lola Evie wears outside that got soaked after the rain, but Mama insists they repel all kinds of garden pests. Mama also says most people think marigolds look finest in the summer, but she read in her *House & Garden* magazine that the large-flowered ones bloom more profusely during autumn, which means they blossom like crazy.

I like marigolds because of all their wavy petals, together making a bunch of strong balls of bright yellow and orange and thick like a quilt of pom-poms laid out over our yard.

Mr. Baluga is making his whistling call over the fence, which means he wants me to go over to his house so that he can teach me how to play *pusoy dos*. It's called "super poker" in English, so you need to know how to play poker to catch on fast. Now that I've learned how to make a royal flush and straight flush and full house and all the different kinds of hands there are in poker, I can play *pusoy dos* with him.

When the front door swings open, a greasy fried noodle sort of smell seems to greet me, even before Mr. Baluga can say "*Kumusta,* Kid" which means "How's it going, Kid" and then pat me on my back. Lola Evie usually has too many noodles left from the *pansit* she makes for Mr. Baluga, so she deep-fries them like Lola Carmen used to do. This is what they call Hong Kong–style chow mein.

My nose also notices the minty coolness of white flower oil, which is a Chinese kind of Ben Gay but even better. I know so because Papa always moans good when Mama rubs it all over his back.

Lola Evie walks over and says she'll pray to the Lord to heal Makena. I stare at the way her hands reach out to me, all delicate and careful like they were just soaked in dishwashing liquid made of pity. Mr. Baluga doesn't like any kind of hullabaloo in his life, so all he says is "Hurry up, the cards are getting cold," which is what he barks at me when I'm moving too slow.

He sets up the poker table, which is really a *mahjong* table, then he pours Japanese rice crackers called *arare* into a little bowl next to my poker chips. He tells Lola Evie to buy *arare* at 99 Ranch the Asian supermarket for me because he knows I love the taste of seaweed.

In *pusoy dos*, you don't really need chips, but Mr. Baluga likes listening to them clicking against each other, the sweet sounds of gambling, he says. He also serves me a glass of kiwi strawberry juice with extra ice, and that's my favorite too.

He even finds the fanciest pillows in his house for me and stacks them onto my chair because I'm short. Sometimes he lets me sit on one red pillow with thick creases that he calls corduroy and one blue velvety pillow because they're both firm, but not too hard that my butt turns sore when I sit on them.

"I feel like the queen of a kingdom when I'm with you," I tell Mr. Baluga. He flashes his gold teeth at me and laughs his gorilla ha-ha's. Then he pets me on the head like I'm Frida or something.

Xavy keeps reminding me to ask Mr. Baluga about his part in World War II, but every time I try, he grunts and says he just wants to enjoy his card game and "Christ, Kid can we not talk about anything important today?!" Papa says Mr. Baluga was a guerrilla leader during the Japanese occupation in the Philippines, so I can see why the subject of war makes him cranky.

I'm glad *pusoy dos* is an easy card game to learn because if it were hard, Mr. Baluga would get huffy and hissy at me for being dumb or slow. Sometimes he even tells Lola Evie that someone hung a vacancy sign right inside her head, and all she does is sigh and walk away. Makena tells me when Mr. Baluga is mean to his wife, he's acting like the typical macho male, bossy and demanding and derogatory, and now I'm wondering what Lola Evie and Mama and all kinds of older women do to make men act this way.

Lola Evie is sort of pudgy like a hedgehog, with black and gray hair that's thin and straight like the bristles of a broom. She makes the tastiest *dinengdeng*, made of tilapia fish with eggplant and long beans and shrimp paste, and she enjoys growing all kinds of vegetables in her garden, like tomatillos and chayote and *upo* the winter melon. I know she enjoys *Survivor* and *CSI* and *Law & Order*, but she tells me she watches them only when Mr. Baluga is already asleep. She still uses a VCR and records them along with this soap opera called *One Life to Live*.

Makena says Mr. Baluga treats Lola Evie like dirt, which is one of the reasons why Makena shies away from Mr. Baluga. "He's too militant and chauvinistic and jeez, it wouldn't kill him to crack a smile once in a while," she keeps complaining about him. And she asks why he insists on all of us saying "Mister" when we can easily call him "Lolo Bennie," like we do with all of our Filipino old-man friends and relatives.

Sometimes I wonder if Makena's talking about someone else, because Mr. Baluga is different around me. When we're together, he wears honest smiles and likes patting me on my shoulder.

Xavy likes Mr. Baluga. He says, "Meester B's a hipster wit hiz cool-ass crew cut an' black trousers an' gray cardi, oh an' dat hellza clean white tee under it, an' dude he even wears dem off-white Converse high-tops to finish off hiz hipster-badass get-up."

A lot of our neighbors call Mr. Baluga a funny old man, and they're right, he really is funny and super crazy old. He cuts his nose hairs with the biggest pair of scissors you've ever seen, and sometimes he gets ingrown toenails, so Lola Evie has to squeeze drops of that red liquid called Merthiolate all over his toes. And of course that's when he has to walk around the whole neighborhood in his rubber *tsinelas* with his ugly red toes.

Mr. Baluga is the smartest person I know next to Papa and Makena. And Xavy says he's more down with the times than you think a geezer like him would be. He knows Makena's going to a university that's tops, but he has no worries about what she'll do with a biology and psychology degree if she doesn't become a doctor or a psychiatrist.

When Xavy and I tell him that Makena wants to be an animal behaviorist and dog trainer, he doesn't shake his head and make tsk-tsk-tsk sounds and mutter *sayang*, which is what all of Papa and Mama's Filipino friends do when they think Makena's throwing her brains and talent out the window.

Mr. Baluga was right. The world isn't as open-minded as you believe it is, and now I'm thinking closed minds aren't such great kinds to have, so those should be thrown out the window instead.

6. asap, *áte*

Mama picked me up half an hour before school got out so that I could go with her and Makena to see Dr. Vieri. He's the person who's supposed to take away Makena's tumor. Papa says he overheard that he's a world-renowned colorectal surgeon, but Mama thinks he's exaggerating.

My third grade teacher Ms. Langevin asked Kendra the aide to watch the classroom while she walked me to the front of school. As Mama's car drove away, I stared at Ms. Langevin through my window, standing there with her right hand held up, her dainty fingers fluttering up and down at me.

"That's the way timid ladies wave goodbye," Papa always teases, but I think it's polite because why would you want to swing and flap your hands and arms at someone whose sister has a disease?

Mama's A/C, which she calls *ehr-cone* because that's how most Filipinos say it, isn't working because Papa keeps forgetting to have it fixed, and the leather seats are sticking to my shorts that won't stop riding up my sweaty wet legs. My window is lowered as far as it can go, and I wish it would go down all the way, but the back windows in some family cars don't do this because they're supposed to be safe for kids and pets.

Makena is pointing at a row of agapanthuses as we turn on to Duarte Road, and I know she's just trying to keep me from whining about the heat because Mama's usually the only one who notices pretty flowers. Most of the agapanthuses in Arcadia are purple, but these are almost blue. A shocking electric blue, Makena says.

The flowers are extra tall, and their heads aren't droopy like the ones on other agapanthuses I've seen. They're high and mighty and noble like a princess.

The car ride to Dr. Vieri's office is making my head spin because Mama drives with two feet, so when she brakes, she brakes hard. Papa always makes fun of Mama's driving, but he's gotten way more tickets than Mama has. When Mama finally turns into the parking lot, I let out a deep sigh, but it was a little too loud because Mama's giving me her "Please don't be a pain in my neck" look.

Makena holds my hand all the way from the parking lot to the elevator. This is where my head starts to whirl even more because maybe this is what it feels like to be inside a rocket, flaring upward and then feeling as if your insides dropped into different corners of it afterwards.

I burst out another loud sigh but this time a sick and gagging kind, and that's when Makena snaps at me and tells me to stop acting so immature. You can tell she's nervous because she keeps pacing and rubbing her hands together like she's trying to make a fire with them, just like she did before her high school valedictorian speech.

Papa says that Dr. Vieri and Dr. Witt both went to medical school at Johns Hopkins, which always confuses me because why is there more than one John for Hopkins, and they even play golf together every Saturday. Dr. Witt's wife the nurse has become close friends with Papa too, so Mama and Papa and both doctors all got together one day to decide whether or not I should be a part of everything that's going on with Makena, even though I'm only eight. According to Mama, the two doctors had their reservations, but Papa kept insisting, "My Isabel is mature for her age, so don't give me that BS, of course she can handle it."

When Dr. Vieri walks into the room we're waiting in, I make Mama giggle when I whisper into her ear that he looks too short to be a surgeon. Dr. Vieri smiles at us with his high and chunky nose that Mama says is Italian and wishes she had because her nose is kind of flat.

Dr. Vieri tells us to wait while he checks Makena in the other room. When they get back, Makena's eyes are small and puffy, just like they were a few days ago when she announced she had colon cancer.

She tells me and Mama that Dr. Vieri needs to remove her tumor ASAP. I tap Mama on the shoulder, and she whispers, "*As soon as possible*, sweetheart," even though I already knew what it meant.

"ASAP because the tumor might grow bigger and burst?" I ask but not out loud, and I think Dr. Vieri feels my confusion because that's when he jumps into his explanation.

He points to a picture of a colon on a wall that's with pictures of other body parts, and he tells us where Makena's tumor is. Dr. Witt found it there during Makena's colonoscopy, the little doctor says to me and Mama. When I ask him what kind of doctor Dr. Witt is, Makena rolls her eyes and almost butts in, but Dr. Vieri puts his hand on my shoulder and tells me that Dr. Witt is Makena's gastroenterologist, which is a doctor you're supposed to see if you're having intestinal problems.

It's like listening to Ms. Langevin explain long multiplication, but it's much more complicated because of all the difficult words like "gastroenterologist" and "colonoscopy," and Dr. Vieri doesn't even have a chalkboard to draw and write on. When I raise my hand to ask what a colonoscopy is, Mama pulls my arm down and smiles and tells me to go ahead and ask my questions. That's when the little doctor decides to talk more slowly and explain everything one by one.

"A colonoscopy is a very simple procedure, Isabel," Dr. Vieri begins. "A tiny camera with a light is attached to the end of a tube, and that's what's inserted into your colon through your bottom. It sounds painful, but it's not, because another doctor gives you medicine that takes away any discomfort. The camera snaps pictures of your colon and looks for polyps, tumors, or anything out of the ordinary."

Now that Dr. Vieri's words don't seem so mysterious anymore, I'm starting to understand what's happening inside Makena's body.

I try not to think she's a weakling, but I keep imagining Papa grabbing his throat and yelling "Choker" and "Pussycat" to her from the stands, not caring that other parents are whispering to each other. Every time Makena hears Papa's rude names for her, she slaps the side of her leg like one of those jockeys at the races whips his horse, the only time she starts acting like a tiger.

So I'll bet Makena got sick because she's usually weak like a kitten and not fierce like a tiger.

I pay attention as closely as I can and I even stretch my neck towards the little doctor to make sure I'm hearing every detail, but it's hard to keep up sometimes. I finally get to ask Dr. Vieri why he has to remove Makena's tumor ASAP, and he explains that the tumor is blocking the passage of food through Makena's colon, which is why she's been having pains. He says he can feel a protrusion, which is a big lump near the right side of Makena's belly button, but I don't really believe him because how are you supposed to feel a bump that's way under your skin?

"It's all in the mind," Papa always says. I can hear his voice roaring in my head, and that's when I stop thinking of the bad lumps.

All of a sudden, the words break free from my mouth. "Just be fierce like a tiger, Makena."

I look straight at my *áte*'s face. It wears a mask made of surprise and anger, but the mask starts to turn solid and hard like marble, the kind that says boy you're in big trouble, little girl.

Makena growls for me and smiles. But I notice her growl isn't fierce and her smile curves up only halfway, and this is the moment I realize that it's time for her to be a tiger all the time, not just when she's losing.

7. ambivalently alive

Papa and Makena have a love and hate relationship, which is what Mama calls ambivalent. There are times when they're the most supreme buddies, like when they sit together on the couch and cheer for Miss USA or Miss Philippines or Miss Spain to win Miss Universe, even though it's annoying to hear Makena complain that the swimsuit competition is demeaning to women, because to me they all look like goddesses in their bathing suits and long flowy dresses during the evening gown part of the show.

Then there are times when Papa and Makena are archenemies, like in our backyard on the tennis court when Papa doesn't think Makena's topspin serve kicks high enough. Makena always snaps back, "Of course it does, look at that ball jump almost right over your head," and then they go back and forth until their faces turn sour.

Makena is the number one women's singles tennis player at Cal, but you'd never know it by the way Papa grabs his throat when he watches her play, all dramatic like he's choking and dying because Makena couldn't pass her opponent at the net or committed an unforced error, which is what happens when you miss an easy shot.

He screams at Makena when she slows down after 8,000 jumps of skipping rope outside in our driveway, right in front of the house for everyone to see so that they know how hard his eldest is working at being the greatest. Makena has to jump at least 10,000 jumps once a day to make her legs and feet move like the wind on the tennis court.

Sometimes Makena's calves start to cramp after all that jumping, like her muscles are turning into bags of gravel that are too heavy to live inside her skin. But Papa allows Makena only 20 seconds to stretch, and then she goes back to jumping like a tiger, not a pussycat, and "Don't forget to eat lots of bananas to avoid those goddamn charley horses in your calves," he always adds.

When Papa and Makena are friends, they enjoy doing Mama's errands together. They'll go find her some *bagoong* that fishy paste of anchovies or a 50-pound bag of jasmine rice from 99 Ranch, where there's all kinds of stuff you'll never find at Vons or Ralphs.

Sometimes I go with them and have to listen to their conversations about Gray Davis the governor doing a crappy job with California, and why Ruth Bader Ginsburg who is Makena's idol and is called RBG isn't just all about women's rights. And whether or not the Big Bang Theory is a Catholic creation, and how there's no way they'll ever forget where they were on 9/11, which is when Makena always says, "While we sat in front of the TV watching those people perish inside the Twin Towers, our tears weren't enough to speak the grief barreling through our hearts."

Then they'll start talking about sports, agreeing that both Venus and Serena would be able to kick Pete Sampras' butt or that the Lakers are the Yankees of basketball, and why Papa thinks the Warriors might get lucky someday if they can find a head coach who'll stay with the team for more than two years.

Or why Larry Itliong and Dolores Huerta didn't get a street named after them when Cesar Chavez got to have Army Street in San Francisco, and how does supermarket fiction sell more copies than literary fiction, and why the hell did Albert Camus have to die at such a young age?

I know that Papa and Makena are still friends even when it seems like they're arguing over who has a better opinion, because Papa always rubs the side of Makena's neck after the conversation is over, his gray eyes sparkling, so full of love and look at my brilliant daughter everyone. But he shakes his head when Makena says that RBG is the one who's brilliant because she convinces judges who are men to get rid of laws that treat women and men differently, and yeah right if you think the Warriors will ever win a championship again.

Makena is more than brilliant. She got a 1590 on her SAT which is almost a perfect score, and Papa says her IQ of 198 is off the charts. Makena doesn't like to show off all that knowledge and mind power, Papa says, but we all know she doesn't make life easy for people with regular brains. She expects more from you even if she knows you can't give it to her.

One time when Xavy couldn't remember the height of an isosceles triangle and kept saying it was the Pythagorean theorem, she told him to quit acting like an idiot, even though he was right about the name of the theorem but couldn't remember the exact formula. Ms. Langevin would have given us a bonus point for knowing part of the answer, but Makena wants it all, and no way are you getting any bonus points for half.

Papa and Makena act the same, which makes it harder for them to be friends sometimes. They're both analytical and moody and impatient, according to Mama.

Xavy says that the Josés come from a long line of attorneys and politicians in the Philippines, so "Don't evuh be talkin' smak wit dem dudes," all scholarly and huge fans of controversy. Papa's own papa and *tito* even topped their bar exams, which is the test you need to take to be a lawyer. Or *liar*, which is what Xavy likes to call them.

Papa and Makena are stubborn like the zippers on your jacket that are stuck but not really broken. And they sure don't like to be told. You can't tell them they're wrong because that just never happens, like when Papa insisted that "irregardless" wasn't a word and Makena said it was in the dictionary but hasn't been fully accepted into American speech yet.

They went back and forth about the meaning which means "despite everything," and if you put an "ir" in front of it, it's supposed to make the meaning a double negative. And Papa knows all about prefixes and suffixes because he studied Latin in college.

They kept arguing while I went looking for all the dictionaries in the house, and when I found one that had "irregardless" in it, Papa didn't look too happy with me. But he still didn't admit he was wrong and went on to say, "Most Americans can't speak king's English, which is why 'irregardless' made it to the goddamn dictionary."

Papa and Makena are the kinds of people you either love or hate, which matches their ambivalent relationship. The people who really love them would do anything for them like loyal dogs, but the people who can't stand them try to hurt them, like one of Papa's rivals in the construction business who burnt down the home that Papa was building near the Pasadena Racquet Club and accused Xavy's gangster friends of his crime.

Or one of Makena's high school classmates named Mavis King who spread a rumor that Papa paid off the principal, which had everyone believing for a while that this is why Makena got straight A's and was named valedictorian.

All this ambivalence feels like driving a bumper car at a carnival, making zigzags and sharp turns and even going backwards to try to ram into others and at the same time keep them from plowing into you.

You turn your head every which way to see who's coming at you, and you hate it and you love it all at once because when you get hit, it knocks the wind out of you and makes you give dirty looks to the person who caught you off guard, but when you're the one who does the hitting and the plowing, you want to pound your chest like an ape.

But the ape feelings don't last because you realize that the others got the wind knocked out of them too, and that's when you decide bumper cars aren't really that fun after all.

Makena says she doesn't really care about the people who hate her and Papa even though I know she does, and Papa keeps saying "Screw them all, they can take their hatred and envy with them to hell," which according to Xavy is exactly the kind of thinking that keeps the ambivalence alive.

8. crushing capricious

Ms. Langevin is giving us a new kind of writing project to work on, and it'll keep going until the end of the school year. She says she'll display whatever our class finishes by Back-to-School Night in October, which is coming up soon.

Our activity is called Automatic Writing. We're supposed to write at least one page about the people we love, and what's cool is we don't have to worry about grammar and punctuation for this project.

A truckload of boxes of paper was delivered to the front of the school the other day during first recess, so now we have lots of construction paper and regular white paper. If we want to make our words straight, there's even paper with the blue lines that are spread far apart, but that's the kind that the kindergarteners and first graders use to write their names on, so of course nobody's going near that stack.

Neil Decker, who always tries to copy my homework and cheat off me during quizzes, told Ms. Langevin he doesn't have enough people for his project, maybe only three or four. When Ms. Langevin asked if he has grandmothers and grandfathers and even dogs or cats, he slapped his forehead and said "Duh, man" and started to add his hamster named Hammy to his list.

Ms. Langevin says automatic writing is exactly what it says to do. You write quickly without thinking too much about what you know and feel as if the words are like a stream flowing from your heart and mind to your sheet of paper, and don't worry about making paragraphs at the correct spots and does the comma go before or after the quotation mark.

Ms. Langevin is a writer and not just a teacher, so a few students at our school have won writing awards, even in our whole district. Last year, a fourth grader named Yolanda

Gutierrez won first place in the "Why I Love America" contest with Ms. Langevin's help.

I'm going to start my project with Papa because Mama and Makena call him "capricious," which means his mood will change like the wind and you won't have a clue if he'll be sunny or stormy the next minute, like will he lecture us about our sour faces when Mama serves us leftovers for three days straight or will he sneak up from behind and wrap you up with his thick and hairy arms and tell you *"¡Eres increíble y lo haces tan feliz!"*

If you ask me, people like Papa make this world an interesting place to live because if things didn't change like the wind, they'd get stuck being flat and hidden under rocks and never be able to blow up like a giant bunch of colorful balloons and lose themselves while soaring in the sky. Maybe it's sort of like the way *pasyal* makes our lives interesting.

papa

you like listening to yourself say your full name which is "antonio nicolas de la viña yen josé" and don't forget that tilde which is the "en-yeh" sound en español *and yeah that accent mark on the "e" too and please don't pronounce it "ho-zay" like you're rhyming it with the month of may.*

you own a company called magni aedificii meaning "great building" in latin which is the language you learned in college. your friends and business partners say you're bright and savvy and cocky and macho as if they're calling you curse words and you're also the kind of guy you either adore or want to put a hit on.

you're six-foot-one and i'm only four-foot-one so you are a towering building that's menacing but also protects those who are inside of it. your skin is the color of olives when they're brown and not the blackest black when they're ripe and your hair is a dark and wiry nest that's starting to lose its twigs at the crown. your lips are like the chicken patties that mama pounds super thin for sandwiches along with your nose so high and pointy and all of these things make you look like a white man with dark skin. filipinos would say "puti *man" but don't worry that's not a curse word it just means you're a white man which is "all good" like xavy would say because being called* puti *or white by fine-lookin' island peeps should be a compliment.*

you are three-quarters spanish and one-quarter chinese and you always have to preach like you were made to be a priest to anyone who is listening and not rolling their eyes that filipinos have all kinds of genes and blood mixed together from the spaniards and the chinese and the malay race. you wear birkenstocks and khaki-colored shorts and shirts with floppy collars like it's your uniform and you never leave the house without a jacket even if it's a hundred degrees outside.

you buy the fanciest gold watches like this brand called audemars piguet whose name you keep reminding us of like it's important vocabulary and you insist these two fancy words come together to be classier and way more expensive than a rolex while mama complains that an audemars piguet costs all kinds of arms and legs and sometimes even more than a car.

back in santa mesa in manila all the titos *and* titas *used to call you "bookworm" even though you were still a bandit and lately i've noticed you with your eyeglasses hanging from your tall nose always reading books by your favorite author who is the french philosopher named albert camus and whose name you make sure has a silent "t" and "s" at the end. whenever you're feeling mushy or angry or you want to look back on your life and think hard about what you've done with it you start to quote "ahl-behr cah-moo" like for example "if something is going to happen to me i want to be there" because you like saying that life never waits for anyone.*

makena complains that albert camus isn't really french and he isn't even a true philosopher but she says it doesn't matter because his writing is direct and "astute" which is one of xavy's SAT words meaning your mind is sharp and filled with words that cut like you're a master swordsperson and words that make your characters teach you about being a human who should act human too. hmmm that sure sounds exactly like you papa the preacher the priest and that's why "papa got a love thang fur dat cah-moose dude" which you can't stand hearing xavy tease you about.

you smoke one whole pack of cigarettes a day even though you've been on the patch and mama even made you try that gum called nicorette which you complained tastes like cinnamon and then all of a sudden like a pepper bomb exploded inside your mouth. you keep telling us you'll live until you are ninety-six just like your lolo alejandro who drank and smoked and feasted weekly on crispy pata *which is pig's feet and not at all healthy for your heart.*

you say that your job for a whole lifetime is to give your family the most outstanding kind of living you can and to make sure we'll never grow gray hairs over money and that's when you become a skipping record and not a broken one like people say wrong and you harp on about coming to america with two dollars and thirty-six cents in your pocket when you were twenty years old.

you washed dishes that made your young hands look old in a hurry and you were even stopped on the street in new york city by a talent scout which everyone believes because tito dante says you look like a dark and older keanu reeves the guy who's in that matrix *movie and who makena thinks is hot but that's when xavy scrunches his face and says "ew dude datz gross so ya think papa's hot?!"*

xavy likes to call the papas of all our friends "apple pie america" the ones with the suits and the briefcases and the bodies so stiff and would no way ever fart inside a jar and open it up for their families to smell and gag and crack up about or show you how to flip people the bird when they're being bullies. there's also no way that apple pie america knows the meaning of kalokohan *which means the crazy and odd things you do just because to be goofy and sometimes a bit rascally.*

devi banda and bianca gonzalez my best friends at school are scared of you along with all my other friends so they come over to play only when they know you're at the construction sites because they don't like your booming voice which is the kind you hear in your nightmares that says you're messing up our house with your sticky little hands and don't you dare use our chair cushions as your personal hand towel.

they don't like the way you stare them down like you're the inspector of the way they breathe and move and wondering what kinds of parents brought them up hmmm maybe all sticky and breathing the wrong way too.

you are like the calluses on your hands that are hard and bumpy and rough and proof to everyone you don't have a life that's too easy to live and making sure it doesn't happen to your family too.

i want to be hard and bumpy and rough just like you papa and i want to have kalokohan *and i don't want apple pie america and i want to own a corporation and tell people what to do even if they think i'm like mafioso.*

i want to be capricious like you so that my life is interesting enough to matter in this world even though i just play with my groovy girl dolls and take frida on walks but someday i will matter and i will make differences that matter because my eyes never stop following people not just what they're doing but also how they're doing it and maybe that's what really matters in this world.

Ms. Langevin said she was "rendered speechless" but looked super crazy pleased with a wide-open mouth when she read my pages about Papa and told me that I just need to trim down his section a bit, but I know there's so much more I can write about him.

How do you fit someone you love into one page and still get to the important stuff? At first, I was sort of worried about being too honest and what if Papa finally goes to one of my back-to-school nights, but Ms. Langevin says she'll display only one person we love and wrote about and that we can decide whether or not we want our whole project to be "uncensored," which means you don't hold back on things that makes your insides roll or your face steam up like an iron.

Things like Papa wanting Makena to be a tiger and not a pussycat, like the time he smashed the silver watch he gave her for her sixteenth birthday.

I was only six years old, but that day is written like a Sharpie into my memory.

Mama and Xavy couldn't go to one of Makena's tennis tournaments in Palos Verdes, so Papa and Makena and I had to squeeze into Papa's Porsche convertible because his Suburban was in the shop, and Mama and Tita Gwen took Mama's Volvo to a quilt show.

Papa never lets Mama drive his Porsche, only if it's an emergency and it's the only car around to use. Mama kept having a cow because I wasn't supposed to ride in a two-seater and I still needed to use a car seat, but Papa promised her he'd drive like an *abuela,* hugging the steering wheel and making sure he wouldn't go more than five miles over the speed limit.

It was so windy that dust and dirt were blowing everywhere, and Makena hates playing in this kind of weather because it makes her topspin groundstrokes go every which way and hang too long in the air. Makena kept hitting the balls into the net or way outside the lines, and it looked like she was moving in slow motion, like she was trying to run through sand on the beach.

Of course Papa kept grabbing his throat and yelling "Pussycat," but that time, it didn't make Makena play any better.

When her match was finished, she was walking like she had nowhere to go, so Papa barked at her, "Move like you give a shit, *Princesa.*"

I remember walking way behind Papa all the way to the parking lot because this was one of those times you sure didn't want to be in his space. I can still see his car keys hanging from his pocket, rattling with each heavy step he took. The back of his blue T-shirt soaked with patches of sweat and the muscles in his calves pulsing as he got closer to the car are like ghosts that keep haunting my brain.

I almost stepped on my shoelace along the way and Makena was waiting for me to tie it, but I guess I was taking too long because she started to walk ahead of me.

When she opened the car door to let me in, Papa told her to go inside first, which didn't seem right because I'm shorter and smaller than Makena even though she's skinnier.

But I remember being okay with it because I was able to hold on tight to the door handle while Papa made fast turns, making the tires sound like they were shrieking and then giving Jesus Christ the middle initial H and yelling the mother-F-word at all the *abuela* drivers in his way.

All of a sudden, Papa stopped the car in front of Denny's and let out a long sigh, and it sure didn't sound like the overworked breaths he usually huffs.

"Let me see your watch," he said, all short and snippety.

Papa took Makena's wrist gently, like in TV shows where the doctor checks someone's pulse, and with his other hand, he reached for Makena's tennis racquet that was laid across both our laps.

All of a sudden, he raised the racquet as high as he could right there in the front seat and smashed it into the face of Makena's watch, like a hammer hitting a nail.

I squeezed Makena's arm and hid behind her and screamed her name, and I wanted to cry but Papa hates crybabies, so I held back my tears while Papa undid the strap of Makena's watch and opened his door and laid it on the street behind the front tire.

Then he set the gear in reverse and ran over it.

It went crunch, a sound like when Xavy would step on snails on our front porch after the rain but much louder.

Papa grabbed Makena's wrist again.

This time, he held it and rubbed it with both his hands. Teardrops raced down Makena's cheeks the whole time, even though she didn't make one peep or even one sniffle.

Papa started driving again, but he drove with only one hand. He held Makena's wrist with his other hand and rubbed it with his thumb except when he needed two hands to make a turn. He just looked straight ahead, his gray eyes darker than ever, staring at the road the whole way home while tears kept rolling down Makena's face and neck.

Now Makena is sick with colon cancer. I think of her running in slow motion, but where is she going? She can be a tiger or a pussycat, and so can I.

What will Papa think of that?

It plays over and over in my head, the tennis racquet crushing Makena's watch, but it's the tire that appears in my dreams. I don't know why it does because Makena and I never saw that tire, but I knew that's where her watch sat still and helpless during the last ticking of its lifetime.

I remember the look on Makena's face when it happened. It was like the shattered pieces that lay there on the street in front of Denny's, forced to be that way forever.

"You are not damaged," I imagine Papa saying to little Gus.

9. hippie hair hygiene

Papa and Mama and all the *titas* and *titos* call me "Hippie" and "Weirdo," and Xavy and some of the cousins call me "Geek Freak" because I don't care about my looks.

"Getting her to take a bath is such an ordeal," Mama complains to Tita Gwen, who just giggles when Mama gets worked up about my hippie ways.

Mama makes me wear a dress every Tuesday. That was our deal when I started second grade because all of a sudden when I turned seven, I didn't feel like wearing dresses anymore.

My best friend in second grade whose name is Kanoko Kim always had the neatest flared jeans from Gap Kids with small flower designs stitched near the bottom of the legs. She also wore long-sleeve T-shirts with words like "radical" and "epic" sewn on the front in sequins, and even those sporty and expensive shoes by the brand called Merrell that they sell at REI.

These three things together add up to the most comfortable outfit in the world ever.

I also hate long hair even though it looks *napakaganda* on Makena and Mama, which is a dramatic way of saying it looks beautiful. Mama used to tie my hair into a ponytail or pigtails, and when she left my hair down, she'd part it on the side and use a thick plastic clip to hold it up, but that never worked because the clip would be lost by the time I got home from school.

So I asked Lola Evie to cut my hair one day, and boy did Mama look like she was going to faint when she saw how short my bangs were along with the rest of my rice-bowl haircut that made me look like a boy.

Mama doesn't realize that bangs are so much easier, you just comb them down and you don't have to go find clips or bobby pins, which never stay in place anyway. A few weeks ago when Makena cut her long strands of hair into thick diagonal bangs that everyone calls side-swept, Mama and Papa thought she still was *napakaganda*, but I guess when you look like Makena, you can get away with any kind of hair.

When my hair starts to stick out in different places, I use my saliva to mat it down, and that's another reason why everyone calls me Hippie. Makena keeps reminding me it's bad hygiene and to just use her hair products, but I don't like putting gel or spray on my hair because it turns hard and crusty. Saliva works and it's my own anyway, so why should anyone else care?

Rice-bowl haircuts don't match dresses too nicely, so sometimes Mama forgets when Tuesday comes and doesn't say anything when I'm wearing pants. On Tuesday and Wednesday and Thursday nights, I lay my pants and T-shirts on top of my toy chest so that I don't have to think of which clothes to wear to school in the morning, and sometimes I'll even lay out the same exact outfit on Monday nights and pray hard that Mama forgets I'm supposed to be wearing a dress on Tuesday.

When I get stuck wearing dresses, I put on a pair of shorts over my panties because when I wear just panties, it makes me feel sexy, even though Xavy doesn't think I'm old enough to know what sexy is.

But I know what it means. It's when people stare at you because you're showing a lot of skin, and they give you the shivers, the kinds that make you want to cover yourself up in a hurry and not because you're cold.

I don't like people checking out my tree-stump legs, and that's the excuse I always give Mama when she remembers I have to wear a dress on Tuesday. Mama tells me to never mind what other people think and not to forget that those who make fun of me have personal issues of their own that they can't share with anyone, which is why they take out their insecurities on people like me.

The only thing I don't like is when other people stare and don't tell you what they're thinking because that's when you become irritated trying to read their minds instead of just knowing the truth. Even if "da truth bites," which is what Xavy likes to say.

I don't care what other people think, but no one ever believes me when I say this. If I really cared, I would listen to Mama and Papa and stop being a hippie and try to be more like my *áte*.

10. silly statue

It's only 71 degrees today. That's what the sign next to the red brick building called Washington Mutual Bank said when Mama was driving me home from school.

Makena's surgery is in two days, at 7:30 a.m. on October 2nd, and I hope the weather stays this way because Makena's armpits turn soaking wet when it's more than 80 degrees outside. They even stain her white T-shirts and blouses yellow, which means her sweat and deodorant combine to make a new type of chloride that's full of acid, according to what she read on the Internet. Makena gets so embarrassed by this that she carries the strongest antiperspirant called Secret Platinum in her purse all the time.

If Dr. Vieri notices her gross armpits while she's lying on the operating table, he might ask another doctor to perform her surgery, which would be a horrible thing because what if he isn't world-renowned?

Makena and I are walking Frida, and I keep thinking about all the long words that Dr. Vieri explained. It's making my head spin like a roller coaster ride again, so I try to think of something else in a hurry. I look down at Frida, and I giggle to myself because she walks like she's prancing to a silly song.

I turn to Makena to tell her that Frida wags her entire butt instead of her tail, but I guess it isn't the right thing to say because Makena's expression is droopy, which makes her look like Bianca's Chinese Shar Pei puppy. She keeps staring down at the sidewalk, sometimes walking right through piles of leaves and kicking pebbles without knowing it.

There's quiet for a super long moment. All I can hear are leaves rustling and pebbles rolling and scooting down the sidewalk.

"Are you okay, kiddo?" Makena asks sort of sudden and loud, like one time when Xavy started the engine in his Bug and a rap song screamed out of the speakers, making Papa curse about his loud gangster music.

"I'm fine," I tell her.

I glance up at the sky, hoping God isn't listening because I'm not feeling that fine.

Makena gives me that hard and stony look again, the same one Mama gives me when she's trying to make me go to bed.

"This is a lot to handle, isn't it?" she says. "Isa, do you understand everything that's going on?"

I want to ask her how a polyp gets there in the first place and how does it turn into cancer and what does a tumor look like and what color is it, but I really want to know only one thing.

"Are you going to die, Makena?"

My voice is squeaky because my words feel like they're tying my throat into a tight bow. I know I'm not supposed to ask questions like these, but the answer will be more important than polyps and colors of tumors.

I feel the jerk of Frida's leash. I grip it more tightly, even though I know Frida wants to keep going.

colon cancer colon cancer it's like it's screaming out of speakers inside my head and i can't find the knob that turns down the volume.

I don't know how I'd feel about someone so young taking a ride to heaven and not coming back, which is what Mr. Baluga says when we watch the news together about people who were killed in an airplane crash or didn't survive other kinds of freak accidents or were shot by someone who doesn't know right from wrong.

The only people I know who took that ride were sort of old, like Papa's parents Lolo Martín and Lola Carmen, and Lolo Carlo who was Mama's papa. Now I'm wondering if God separates the old people from the young ones in heaven and if

God will let the rest of our family live longer if he makes one of our family members take the ride earlier than they're supposed to.

Frida's starting to whine because Makena and I have been standing in one place for way too long. Her leash keeps pulling on my firm grip, and I can hear her paws slipping on the leaves, but I feel my eyes focusing like lasers on Makena's face, all scrunchy and thinking deep about my question.

I wonder if she'll tell me the truth because how do you tell another person that God is going to come knocking at your door and say it's time to go with him to heaven without sounding like you've been "telling one too many o' dem o'd wives' *kuwentos*," which Xavy likes to say.

"No, Isa, silly girl, I promise," Makena finally answers.

She straightens the collar of her shirt and steps on more leaves and kicks pebbles on purpose this time. When we start walking again, I notice Frida staring at us. Her tear stains are dark and crusty from being outside in the warm air that makes her eyes watery.

She's standing on a tall bed of shrubs and twigs. She's a beagle statue with tiny pieces of crisp brown leaves stuck to her mouth.

"You silly dog," I say to her.

I turn to Makena. She glances at Frida and then goes back to staring down at the ground.

But this time, she's giggling.

mama

your real name is maria angelina arevalo santos josé and you have two nicknames. the first one is what your filipino friends call you which is "jelleh" and the second one is what your puti *friends call you which is "ann." they say "jelly" like the jelly in jelly bean but you're really supposed to say it with an accent and make an "eh" sound at the end because that's how your mama lola zeny said it.* "ay naku aking *jelleh" which means "oh my jelleh" but more dramatic-sounding and according to lolo carlo this is what popped right out of her mouth when you popped right out of her belly.*

you have skin that's so milky and fair just like snow white's even though makena says this is the tritest analogy but who cares what trite means because snow white is beautiful. you wear hardly any makeup that's only a light shade of rose-colored lipstick and medium-brown eyebrow pencil to fill in your eyebrows which tita rina plucked out one by one when you were little and that you never forgave her for.

you are shy but you try to act cheerful and show your best manners to the people that papa brings over to the house so you bake all kinds of treats for them like cassava *cake which comes from the vegetable that looks like a sweet potato and also* ensaymada *which is the yummiest sweet bread ever. you make me go with you to church every sunday but you never ask papa or makena or xavy to go anymore because makena says you shouldn't impose religion on others even if they were born into it and that's when xavy says "yeah what she said" which gets papa to snort and you to make the sign of the cross and wanting to say bad words.*

i know you try hard not to swear too much especially in front of me but when you're at the end of your rope you say "ay buhay" *which means you're tired of life. that doesn't really count as a curse word even though it seems awful to be tired of life if you're still lucky to be living it so i guess the only bad word that tumbles out of your mouth once in a while is "shet."*

you say "shet" instead of "shit" because a lot of filipinos can't seem to get it straight. it's like when some asian people get their r's and l's mixed up so when they say "rice" you think they're saying "lice." papa knows how to say "shit" the right way because he speaks clear english with hardly any accent but you still have a bit of an accent because you've stayed at home a lot ever since you came to america from the philippines and when you don't go out you aren't able to spend time with as many people as papa who talks to them every day and tries to get them to invest their money in real estate and all kinds of ventures which you like to call "bullshetting people for a living."

makena hates it when you say "shet" and always tries to correct you which is rude if you ask me. she says how come you can say "bitter" like in the bitter melon you bake inside your ampalaya *casserole that we all grimace at and that's when you get irritated and tell makena to stop making fun of you and to please show some respect and then you blurt out that makena is arrogant like papa who always reminds us that he speaks king's english and why doesn't she go to the philippines to try to speak tagalog with her american accent and see how she feels when people start putting her down.*

i like the sound of "shet" better than "shit" because when mama says "shet" it doesn't sound low and rotten like everyone else who says it to make you feel like you were shot full of holes. one time when xavy called me a shitface after i ate all his candy last halloween it made me feel more angry than small and you fume like a bull that it got you to make xavy wash out his mouth with irish spring. usually i smile to myself all sneaky when xavy gets in trouble for his naughty ways even though i was scolded by you too for gobbling up his candy but that time i felt bad for him because irish spring must taste like shet.

mama i think your goal in life is to make everyone happy before yourself and that's what papa calls someone who doesn't have one single bad bone inside her body. so when you're telling me to stop being kuba *which means slouching and to watch fewer cartoons and "don't eat so many ice cream sandwiches that you will develop high cholesterol like your lola carmen and die when you're 66" i have to keep remembering all the good bones in your body that add up to you.*

11. sacrifices and sins

It's 5:45 a.m., October 2, 2002, and we're supposed to be at the hospital for Makena's surgery in 1 hour and 45 minutes. I made Xavy get up at 5:00 to go with me on Frida's walk because it was still dark outside, which wasn't a whole lot of fun because Xavy's a big whiner when he says you're disturbing his beauty slumber.

Something about the weather earlier this morning seemed wrong. Mama says it's always cooler in the mornings, but the air felt summery against my face. Makena calls it global warming, which means the sun is moving closer because of inconsiderate people polluting the earth and destroying our ozone layer, but to me, it was like God was making sure that Frida and I weren't cold, even though I think it's Mother Nature who's in charge of the weather. I even had to tie my jacket around my waist at the end of the walk, and when Xavy was forced to do the same with his sweatshirt, he turned even crabbier.

Yesterday was an all-over-the-place kind of day for us because of the preparation for Makena's surgery. Mama asked me to bring trays of food to Makena's bed and to make sure she had enough blankets and pillows, and Xavy said he would handle the entertainment, which meant distracting Makena from being grumpy about having to clear out her digestive system with liquids and this stuff called GoLytely.

Sometimes Xavy would deal out a game of *pusoy dos*, or he'd just start wiggling his ears and making his wacky elephant noises to remind Makena it was all right to laugh. Mama was busy in the kitchen preparing grape Jell-O and chicken broth, which are two of the foods that Makena was allowed to eat.

I remember hearing Frida's nails clicking on the floor from one room and back to another and the way she kept tilting her head and perking up her floppy ears, like she was asking me what was going on. Papa sat with Makena in the bathroom while she tried to drink a whole gallon of GoLytely so that Dr. Vieri the little doctor can see everything he needs to during her surgery.

Makena's not a good drinker, so Papa's job was to stay with her and give her lots of pats on the back and you-can-do-its. Dr. Vieri told us this GoLytely stuff makes your stools loose, which means you'll have to make poo piles that don't stick together and in a big nasty way, and to top that off, it forces some people to vomit too. When Makena's insides were finally empty, she told me she felt like a tornado had whirled right through her body.

After we were done helping Makena, I lay in my bed, pretending to play the piano on my belly while Frida kept digging at the blankets to bunch it up and make a cushy spot for herself. I couldn't figure out if I was feeling nervous or excited because it was hard to fall asleep.

Whenever we go to Disneyland, I can't sleep the night before because of all the talk of California Adventure and everyone planning their junk food breaks in between the rides, all these things buzzing in my ears to keep me from getting the rest I need so that I can walk around all day.

I shouldn't be excited about my *áte* going to the hospital to have a doctor cut her open, but the most excellent part will be Dr. Vieri finding the tumor and maybe chopping it into pieces so that it doesn't grow bigger like the Blob, which Xavy was watching on cable last night, and then sewing her back up so that she can come back home to live a happy life with us.

On our way to the hospital, I can't stop chewing on the hangnail on my pinky. In the waiting room, Papa keeps pushing my hand away from my mouth and patting his shirt pocket for cigarettes. Sometimes I follow Mama to the chapel and listen to her pray to God to save her daughter and recite all kinds of Hail Marys and Our Fathers. Xavy's just sitting there reading his car magazines and looking up at the clock once in a while.

When the nurse comes to get Makena, I bite on my hangnail some more. I watch this nurse, who's wearing a blue cloth that looks like a giant apron or maybe more like baggy pajamas, push Makena in a wheelchair through two double doors that have a tiny window on each one.

All of a sudden, I feel weak.

I cry "No, Makena" even though Papa told me to be strong, and then I run to Mama and wrap myself around her legs while Papa walks away and makes his tsk-tsk-tsk sounds. Xavy rushes over and picks me up and puts me on his lap and tells me to act like a big girl please but I don't feel like it, so I shove my elbow into his potbelly.

He yells, "Aw man, you little—" and then he stops and scans the room for someone who might scold him for the curse word he was about to say to me. I run back to Mama, who kisses my head and tells me to take some deep breaths. I glance sideways at Xavy while he shows me his fist and shakes his head like I'm a namby-pamby, which Mr. Baluga once told me is another way of saying you're a sissy.

The surgery is supposed to take up to two hours, but it seems like these two hours will be much longer than all the other hours that have ever existed. Mama wants me to stay with her in the chapel, but the picture of Jesus Christ in there looks spooky, even though I learned in catechism that he was the noblest man in history who sacrificed his life for us.

There's no way I'm staying with Xavy, so Mama takes me over to Papa. He's smoking outside in the area that he says is reserved for smokers but really isn't because I don't think you're allowed to light up anything near a hospital.

"Papa?"

"Yes, Love."

Papa rubs his cigarette in a patch of dirt that's surrounding some short and bushy plants. The cigarette is still long, but Papa knows he's not supposed to smoke around me too much because I'm still a kid.

"Is it a sin to be a weakling?"

Papa crinkles his dark eyebrows and tells me to come sit down on his lap. He finds a spot near a bunch of ferns, and I know they're ferns because we have some in our backyard. Xavy thinks they look like skeletons of plants that used to be, and one time he even pulled a giant leaf out of one of the ferns in our backyard and started fanning himself, which of course got Mama all worked up, reminding us how hard we make life for her sometimes.

"Love, it's not a sin. Remember, God doesn't judge you for who you are," he says, but he doesn't sound like he believes it himself.

I think of Makena's watch, and now I'm remembering how the glass broke clean when Papa struck it, how he looked more weary than angry. How weak he looked even while he raised the tennis racquet and wondering if he should have broken something else or even nothing at all.

Papa starts to get up and complain that I'm getting too heavy for his lap. This also means he doesn't feel like talking anymore, so I just follow him around all the ferns. I try not to step on the cracks on the cement even though Makena says it's a superstition, but who wants to take chances on Mama's back cracking?

There are weeds that look like parsley growing between some of the cement openings, and I make sure I don't walk behind Papa too closely because he gets annoyed when you're in his space and he's not in the mood for you to be there.

Papa keeps his hands inside his jacket pockets while he walks. Sometimes he mumbles stuff to himself and raises his chin to the sky like he's searching for something, and I wonder if he's asking God to save his daughter like Mama did in the chapel.

After almost three hours have gone by, Dr. Vieri appears in the waiting room and delivers the most epic news. He says Makena's tumor is all gone and it didn't spread to any of her major organs. I wonder if the little doctor chopped up the tumor, but I have to tap Mama on the shoulder about the major organs part. She explains that the tumor could have spread to Makena's liver or lungs or some other large organ and made her even sicker.

Xavy isn't giving me a hard time anymore. He high-fives me and picks me up and twirls me around, but my head is already spinning from being nervous or excited or maybe both, so all of a sudden, I throw up my breakfast of Pop Tarts and peanut butter toast and bananas all over his white skater shoes.

Usually Xavy curses me out just for stepping on his shoes, but all he does is look a little grossed out, and then he snorts and laughs and hugs me really tight, tighter than he's ever hugged me before.

Papa asks Dr. Vieri if we can visit Makena in the recovery room. Papa and Mama are telling me that I'm too young to go inside, but I think they're lying because Xavy probably told them I was acting like a baby. I start to feel better when Mama says she'll tell me everything when her turn is over. They all get to go in one by one, first Mama then Papa then Xavy.

When it was Xavy's turn, at first he poked his head inside because he got freaked out when he saw tubes going up Makena's nose. The nurse told him that Makena needed more oxygen because she just got out of surgery.

Mama says she smiled at Makena and touched the mole near her mouth. When Makena asked her if the cancer had spread, Mama told her it didn't and that she was going to be just like new.

Papa and Xavy tell me that Makena asked them the same exact thing when they visited her, so Makena's head must have been spinning too from all the medicine that let her sleep during her surgery.

I wish they let me in there to see my *áte*, but Papa says I just have to accept it. I keep imagining myself sneaking past the nurses behind the tall countertops and the row of wheelchairs that's not far from Makena's room.

It's getting late, and visiting hours are ending at 8:00. Dr. Vieri says we can come again in the morning if we want, but Makena might still be asleep. Mama insists on staying with Makena for at least the first night, and after a few pouty faces and some arguing with Papa, she gets her way. One of the nurses says she'll get a cot for Mama and promises Papa and Xavy and me that she'll take special care of Makena and Mama.

When Papa tucks me into bed, I ask him if Makena is really going to be fine now that the tumor is gone.

"Of course, Love," he says, but his voice doesn't sound firm and steady.

Now it's my turn to ask God to save my *áte.*

please god let my big sister keep the life she's supposed to be living with us because i don't think it'll wait for her so i promise i'll stop eating so many skittles and swedish fish that i take from the kitchen pantry right after dinner and i promise i won't ask for something else the next time i pray to you i swear really i swear.

12. damn him dubious

I'm wondering if all this stomach stuff I learned at Dr. Vieri's office has something to do with the summer before last when Makena came home after her second year at Cal. I knew something was different about her because she didn't call out my name and ask me to go with her to 31 Flavors when she walked into the house. She headed straight to her room and stayed there until it was time to eat dinner.

When I asked Xavy what was wrong with her, he said Papa told him that Makena didn't say one word the whole six and a half hours that he and Mama and Makena drove from Berkeley to Arcadia, even when they passed by Harris Ranch, which is where all those smelly cows hang out and then get turned into steaks. Usually they all play the license plate game or talk about our family's plans for the summer, but Makena just took naps or stared out her window the whole way home.

After one week back at the house, Makena still wasn't saying much. She answered all my questions, like did she get straight A's again this semester, but she'd just give me a soft-sounding yes and a nod and never even looked at me.

Mama and Papa kept talking hush-hush to each other, and you could tell that they wanted to ask Makena what was going on with her. Mama told me later why they didn't open their mouths, explaining that Makena needed time to get over her breakup with Eli Enki-Abrams.

Mama says "this stupid boyfriend" lasted nine months. Makena never talked about Eli at home because Papa always teased that Eli was a gangly *puti* boy, and he sure didn't like that Eli stood an inch taller than him, and boy he couldn't stand Eli's pompadour haircut, which I thought looked okay even though it sat a little high on his head.

But what Papa didn't like most of all was Eli's character. Papa could sense there was something dubious about him which means suspicious, but he could never tell Makena exactly what it was and that he had an off feeling about this hoodlum, which of course would make Makena red hot mad because Papa was already judging Eli before he got to know him.

I met Eli only once because he lives in this city called Fairfield in Connecticut, so I couldn't decide whether or not I thought he was a dubious character. But I know for sure that I liked Makena's boyfriend before Eli, whose name was Ryan Jeremy. He was my favorite one of all, even better than Kahlil Robb the linebacker from Iowa that played for Cal and who Papa said had eagle vision on the football field, or the mixed Taiwanese and *puti* boy named Stephen Joseph from Brentwood who wanted to be a firefighter and drove a black Corvette, and even the Flip boy from a city up north called Fremont who Mama says sang like a nightingale.

Papa had a love thang for Ryan like he did with Cah-moose, Xavy would always tease, and no one could compare to Ryan, so I can see why Makena wasn't a chatterbox when it came to Eli. Papa and Ryan joked around a lot together and even liked to high-five each other, and we all know Papa never high-fives any of Makena's boyfriends. He gives them what Mama calls a *malocchio* with his gray eyes from behind his newspaper and blows cigarette smoke in their direction when he gets the chance.

At night for three days straight, Makena cried in her bed. It made me wonder if Eli hurt her and if he did, I'd sure want to plan something mean and unholy for him. Whenever I went to Makena's bedroom to ask her what was wrong, she said nothing and pretended to sleep.

On the second day she cried, I remember checking my Snoopy and Woodstock clock, which said 1:24 a.m. Makena got up and went to the bathroom, and she stayed there for a long time. When I woke up and looked at my clock again, it said 2:32, so I started to feel high-strung, like Mama calls Makena when she worries too much. I wondered if Makena ate something spoiled earlier that morning, so I tiptoed to the bathroom and peeked inside.

The door wasn't closed all the way, and I could see Makena sitting on the floor with all kinds of bloody towels surrounding her. Her hands were clutching a spot below her belly while she moaned. Frida was there with her, her eyes filled with worry, stuck in a down-stay position and panting like she was in the desert.

Makena kept crying, "Damn him to hell, damn him to hell," and I was about to scream because I thought a bad man did this to her and all the blood was starting to scare me, but then Makena noticed me and hurried over and covered my mouth and told me she was okay and to please be quiet. But there was no way she could be fine because all kinds of towels soaked with blood were everywhere. It smelled like the emergency room when Xavy had to get stitches on his arm after he fell off the fence trying to pick persimmons, like a sickly gas filling the air, all thick and raw.

Makena told me, "Don't worry, I just got my period," but I didn't believe her because I don't think you're supposed to bleed that much when you get your period, otherwise they would make those Always feminine pads that she wears way wider and thicker.

I kept thinking that a criminal must have cut her up and he was hiding inside her walk-in closet and told her to shut up or else he would kill her, and when I told Makena this, she shushed me again and told me not to let my imagination run rampant and that she was bleeding more this time because she was sick and not to worry because she's feeling much better now.

She grabbed all the towels and saved only one, and then she wiped up the blood that spilled on the floor and sprayed Lysol everywhere and told me to go back to my bedroom.

When she came to me a few minutes later, I asked her why she saved that one towel, but all she did was keep staring at the blood on it. She sat next to me on my bed, and I noticed there was a shiny and gooey bump in the dark red blood. Every time Frida tried sniffing the towel, Makena would push her gently aside.

Frida and I were told to stay put, and then Makena said she needed to check something in the backyard and don't say one word please. She gave Frida the hand signal for "stay" and left my bedroom.

I couldn't help creeping down the stairs to the dining room and then peeking through the blinds, where I saw Makena rush over to our big oak tree and dig up a hole next to it and bury the towel with the shiny gooey blood bump in the ground.

She made the sign of the cross, and she walked slow and careful steps back to the house and to my bedroom. After she gave Frida a treat and me a hug, she said she'd sleep in my room and that we should all go to bed now.

But none of us slept that night, even Frida who kept licking Makena's face and then mine and getting shooed away because her licks felt like sandpaper buffing my cheeks.

All I thought about until it was time to wake up were the pains and the moans and the gooey blood bump on that one towel that Makena hid beneath the ground, the one thing I would promise to never ask her about during my whole lifetime.

13. caterpillar in a cocoon

Today is October 12, 2002, and Makena will be home from the hospital in five days.

The house hasn't been the same without her around.

Mama's quieter when she folds and separates the white and colored laundry. There's no humming of tunes in her high and sugary voice.

Xavy goes about his own business. He just makes sure his cars are spotless and keeps talking ghetto with his gangster friends on his phone when Papa isn't home.

Papa seems different now. He's usually in a grand mood when Makena is around, wanting to dance even if there isn't any music on, or make *pasyal* and buy us Krispy Kremes or 31 Flavors. Now he's always alone in his second office sweeping, or he just sits there on his beat-up wing chair smoking cigarettes and looking like his head is about to burst.

I still play with my Groovy Girls, or I read my *Anastasia Krupnik* books or hang out with Mr. Baluga, or I go to the backyard to run around with Frida or sometimes watch Mama cook. I love to watch her cut carrots and onions and tomatoes because her hands move like they're in a race, just like those Iron Chefs on the Food Network, but I don't think Mama could ever have her own show because she doesn't like talking to people.

"Isabel, can you get me the smaller chopping board for the garlic," Mama asks me while she scrubs potatoes in the sink. There are slivers of zucchini skin stuck to her apron.

I find the smallest chopping board way at the bottom of the cabinet under the heavier boards, and I place it next to the big wooden one with all of Mama's chopped vegetables. I make a happy face with the carrots and zucchini, and when Mama sees what I'm doing, her face twists into a sour scowl.

"*Ay naku*, Isa, stop playing," she says, and she pulls my hand away from the vegetables.

"Makena likes to make happy faces with her food, Mama," I try to explain, but her frown tells me she doesn't want to hear Makena's name.

"I don't care what your *áte* does. Let's not talk about her right now, please," Mama barks. I wonder if she really means what she's saying, because if I were a mama who was all crazy worried about her daughter being sick, chopping vegetables and even snapping once in a while would seem like things that were allowed.

Mama turns on the kitchen TV to Emeril, who is cutting vegetables like Mama is, but the difference is he looks like he's having fun while he's doing it, talking to the food and yelling "Bam" and "Let's kick it up a notch" and asking the audience if they're having a blast.

I decide to go find Xavy, who's on eBay shopping for car parts for his Bug. He has an old white Honda CRX that he fixed up too, and this used to be Makena's car in high school, but Papa put him in charge of it when Makena left for Berkeley.

Ever since Papa finally said we could have DSL to make the Internet go faster, Xavy's been taking up all the computer time. Whenever I tell him he's a computer hog even though I don't really use it, he calls me Geek Freak and to go play with Freedz.

"What if you buy something on eBay and the person doesn't send it to you," I ask Xavy, and I know he doesn't feel like talking to me because he's squinting his eyes at the screen, pretending not to hear me. But he answers my question anyway and says, "Den I'd git ma bruddas to kick da shit outta dem."

"But what if they live far away, like Australia or Zambia?"

"Aw come on, Isabel, just go hang with Frida," Xavy answers, tugging at the neck of his black Digital Underground shirt, and I know he's super annoyed because he's calling me and even Frida by our real names. Then he starts to scream "Freedz," loud enough for the neighborhood to hear.

Papa yells from downstairs at Xavy, "Lower your goddamn voice!" and he adds to his yelling that Frida's with him in the garage, which is where I should have tried to be in the first place.

Frida is sitting right in front of Papa and waiting for treats as usual. Papa has a jar full of Jump 'n' Sit Bits on top of his little round table next to his wing chair, and every time he reaches into the jar, all sorts of drippy drool hangs from Frida's mouth. Mama thinks it's the most disgusting thing ever, but I can't stop laughing whenever it happens because sometimes Frida's slobber comes really close to the ground without stretching apart and falling.

"How's my Love?" asks Papa, and I notice he already put out his cigarette.

"I'm kind of bored. Can we make *pasyal*?"

"We should just stay home. Mama's cooking us one of her delicious meals, *'di ba*?"

"Can we make *pasyal* tomorrow, then?"

That's when I remember something Papa always says to us when we're being whiny about trying new things.

"You always say that experiences are meant to be experienced and not just created," I say, and I feel like I'm sort of scolding him.

"Very nice, *hija*. But, I'm sorry, I have to go to the job sites in the morning. And Kena's coming home in a few days, so just sit tight."

"But she won't be able to make *pasyal* until she gets better."

"She'll be like new in no time," Papa tries to convince me. "Why don't you go help Mama with dinner?"

I walk heavy steps to my room on purpose, and I check each corner of it to get ideas for something to do. There's nothing interesting in my toy chest. I don't feel like playing with Groovy Girls or stuffed animals, and I don't want to watch TV or play video games. I look on my shelves for other books and think maybe I'm ready for my Spanish *Harry Potter* series, but it's more fun when Makena reads to me outside in our backyard.

go play with frida go help mama with dinner now can you just go away already so we can wait for makena to be like new in no time?

colon cancer why can't you just leave my brain alone colon cancer?!

Makena isn't loud and goofy like Xavy and Papa and the rest of the Josés, but she always makes things more fun, a different kind of *masayang kasama.*

Makena doesn't have to say much. She just sits there and giggles with us or holds up her hand for high-fives when someone makes a joke. She likes to give Xavy a hard time, firing away with her questions, like "What are you going to do with yourself after college" or "When do you plan on shedding some of that poundage," and boy does that get the whole family going, especially Papa, and of course that's when Xavy starts tickling Makena or bagging on her about her prissy ways.

Now I wonder if things are going to be the same when Makena gets home.

It's easy to remember how fun people are when they're away. When Papa used to go to the Philippines to take care of Lolo Carlo's and Mr. Baluga's properties and finally came back home, everything felt safe and right, even though we noticed how much hair he lost or how much darker he got, or how many more cigarettes he was smoking because Papa says that everyone in Asia smokes like a tank engine.

I love changing, but there are only a few kinds I'm okay with. I like switching my outfits twice a day even when my first set of clothes isn't dirty, just to pretend it's a brand-new day. When Xavy notices I'm wearing something different, he always tells me, "Well dat sho as hellz ain't hippie-like, ya dope Geek Freak Weirdo."

I enjoy moving my toy chest or nightstand and other furniture around in my room so that when I wake up in the morning, I feel like I'm in a hotel room far away from home.

I don't like leftovers, especially spaghetti with super dry sauce even though Mama says you shouldn't waste food, but how cool would it be if you didn't have to eat the same old thing every day?

When we moved from Eagle Rock to Arcadia, I thought it would be the most thrilling and awesome thing to happen to us ever, but there were so many things to pack, like books and CDs and clothes and kitchen gadgets and all kinds of delicate knickknacks. If you were caught filling up a box with too many heavy things or you didn't cover the knickknacks with bubble wrap or newspaper, you never heard Papa yell *puta* and *mierda* so loud in your life.

Having to say goodbye to my playmates Andi and Neranti and their extra huge swing set and epic treehouse with the secret tunnel that led to their bedroom almost made me want to cry, but Xavy was there when we all hugged and promised each other to keep in touch, so I didn't want him to notice and go running to Papa about my dumb wasted tears on those two rug rats who always messed up our house.

Moving made our family all nuts like one gigantic ball of nerves and you better be careful with that box or else, which is why I get picky about the changes in my life.

But when you're stuck in one spot for too long like a caterpillar in a cocoon, you want to jump up and down, like you're trying to keep from peeing in your pants. It's like having to get up in front of class and talk about what you did over the summer or waiting in all those long lines for a whole hour for It's a Small World and Pirates of the Caribbean.

When you mix all these feelings, you know they don't go together, like drinking Coke with your pancakes in the morning, so the only thing you can do is shake them out of you, like the way dogs shake their bodies from their heads to their butts when they're wet or after they've napped. And when you finally do, you feel like your world went from topsy-turvy to a picnic in the park.

When Makena gets home, we won't be forced into different corners of the house just doing our own thing and not caring if it's boring.

Xavy will make us laugh with his elephant sounds.

Mama will sing her sweet high notes.

Papa will do his goofy boogie dance while he passes out the Krispy Kremes.

We won't make *pasyal* as often, but we'll all be talking about how happy we are to have Makena back and how we'll help her become like new, like me and the rest of the world going through all kinds of changing.

14. the plowering plant

Makena keeps an ugly plant inside the bathroom we share, and it sits right on top of the toilet tank.

Her name is Ramona Quimby because Ramona is one of Makena's favorite childhood characters from those Ramona and Beezus and Henry books by Beverly Cleary. Makena doesn't know which plant Ramona Quimby is called because she doesn't think it matters, as long as she keeps it as green as it was from the time she first got it.

Mama told Makena she'd ask Mr. Baluga what kind of plant Ramona Quimby is because of his green thumb, which means you have a unique ability to make plants grow. Papa says Ramona Quimby might even be a weed, which is probably the reason why Makena doesn't want to know.

I know this plant is special because Makena's been taking care of it since she was seven years old, which means she's had it for almost 13 years so far. Sometimes Makena forgets to water Ramona Quimby for more than a week, but she's still alive. When she needs water, she lets Makena know by showing that some of her leaves are turning yellow.

There are people who talk to their plants and flowers, like Lola Evie does to the ones by her kitchen sink. Last winter, she gave Mama a pot of azaleas, complaining they would never bloom, even in the spring when they were supposed to.

When Lola Evie asked Mr. Baluga, "Bennie, pleece transplant dees plowers to a nice spot in da pront yard" in her clumsy accent like Lola Zeny's, Mr. Baluga copied her voice and told her that "dos plowers" wouldn't be able to handle the stress and to just "bid parewell to da stinking plant already."

Lola Evie knows that Mama has a green thumb too, and Mama sure proved her right when she decided to prune behind the parts where the petals are attached, which Xavy called giving it a bad haircut. Mama also repotted the whole thing, changing its soil and feeding it new fertilizer.

When the azaleas bloomed pink petals with white tips that spring, Lola Evie couldn't believe her eyes, and even though we all knew she wanted the plant back, she let Mama keep it for being its savior.

All Makena does with Ramona Quimby is make sure she's growing, and sometimes she fixes her vines so that they don't stick out of the pot, looking all slouchy and limp. Mama says talking to plants and spending time with them and making sure their soil is fresh and disease-free makes them live longer, but Makena doesn't believe that for one second.

Of course this gets Mama all riled up about Makena, and then she complains on and on to me about how you have to keep giving life like the Lord did and that she and Papa give us ours by not only making sure we're breathing but also by loving and being a family together.

That's when Papa butts into Mama's rambling and tells her, "Stop wasting your Catholic breath. Ramona Quimby might simply be a goddamn weed."

15. chemo can crumple

On Mama and Papa and Xavy's last day visiting Makena at the hospital, the air felt dry and breezy, which is what Ms. Langevin taught us is a kind of Santa Ana wind. Papa says the Santa Anas are in southwestern California and blow west through the canyons towards the coast. The only time they don't come is during the summer, which doesn't seem right because the winds are usually hot and dusty. "Playin' t-ball while dem Santa Anas blow iz wretched," Xavy always complains.

When the Santa Anas are extra dry, Xavy has to put Chapstick all over his lips, and he can't stand it because maybe that's what it feels like to wear lipstick, all waxy and unnatural.

He remembers rubbing Chapstick on his bottom lip right at the very moment Dr. Witt the gastroenterologist sat them down at the hospital, outside Makena's room while the nurse gave Makena a sponge bath.

"Dr. Witt's face," Xavy says, "wuz like a pint o' heavy, so I knew wut-evuhz he wuz 'bout to spit out sho wuzn't gunna be no newz to write home 'bout."

Dr. Witt placed his hand on Papa's shoulder, Xavy remembers, like he wasn't sure if he should have touched him.

Then Dr. Witt just busted out, "Makena's going to need a full year of chemotherapy."

It was the first time Xavy ever saw Papa cry. He could tell that Papa was trying to control his tears because he kept pretending to scratch his shoulder, hiding his face behind his big hairy arm. Then he crumpled himself up like a blanket in his chair and just sobbed.

What's strange is that Papa didn't cry when he found out Makena had colon cancer. He slammed his hand hard on the dining room table and said goddamn to this and that, and he comforted Makena like a papa is supposed to. But he didn't sob and crumple up.

I remember Makena telling me chemotherapy stops tumors from growing and spreading, and that's when I start to get confused again because Dr. Vieri said the tumor didn't go to any of her major organs. Xavy says the tumor spread to eight of Makena's lymph nodes but nowhere else.

"What are lymph nodes," I try to ask, but Xavy keeps explaining how chemotherapy is done and who Makena needs to see.

When Makena was finished with her sponge bath, Xavy says she lifted up her shirt and showed him something called an incision, where Dr. Vieri went inside her body to take out 20 inches of her colon along with her tumor that was the size of a big yellow peach.

I still wonder if he chopped it up into pieces, but Xavy goes on about sutures, which are staples that hold the incision together to make it heal right. Mama says the incision will become thick and red and will end up looking like the keloid that grew on her elbow after she fell off a tree when she was a little girl, which would actually be kind of neat because I love running my finger over Mama's red scar that looks like a comb, all smooth and cool to the touch.

Xavy tells me that Makena tried to make a joke about not wearing her two-piece anymore, and she even poked at his sides, which was a shock to everyone because Xavy usually does all the poking. We all know how much Makena enjoys the beach, so her joke didn't make anyone snicker. And Xavy wanted to keep her from laughing because every time Makena started to, she'd scrunch up her face and hug a pillow tight against her belly.

That's when Xavy scrunches up his face too. For a short moment, there are no more words, no poking sides or snorts or calling names. I just watch Xavy feel our *ate*'s pain.

When Papa came home from the hospital that day, I asked him about Makena. I thought he was going to shoo me away and tell me to go walk Frida, but he lifted me onto his lap and told me he was afraid the chemotherapy would take away not only Makena's bad cancer cells but also her spirit. I asked him what he meant and if it was like being *matapang*, which means you are aggressive and determined and sometimes can be feisty.

Papa told me to close my eyes and picture Makena on the tennis court, belting that tennis ball across the net and slapping the side of her thigh when she wins a point. Picture her radiant face when she's at the dinner table and yapping on about all the sick dogs and cats and other animals she helped at the shelter and how she can't wait to graduate from Cal and go to vet school.

"Isabel, Love. That's spirit, I tell you, that's spirit," Papa said, and then he asked me to please never lose mine.

16. a different drummer

Makena's friends from Cal call the house once in a while during summer break, and I've met only three of them, one at the dorms where Makena lived during her freshman year and the other two at the steak and oyster party that Mama and Papa threw in our backyard when it was only 62 degrees, one of the mildest days of summer last year, according to Papa.

Antoinette and Tracy and Ally are all sweet just like Mama but sure love to yap. Tracy and Ally live in LA too, and Tracy's house is in Claremont, which Xavy says takes more than an hour to get to sometimes because "dat 210 goin' east can be a beeatch."

They always offer to help Mama in the kitchen and Papa with his grilling, and Tracy and Ally even played stuffed animal beauty pageant with me in my bedroom while Makena was outside being social with our guests and everyone else was running around getting things ready for the party.

Xavy calls Antoinette "Alienation" because he says when she ties her shiny black hair back into a tight ponytail, she looks like an alien. Then he goes on about her forehead sticking out like a shelf over her eyes and her face looking smashed when she smiles. Antoinette drives a Saturn, which of course gets Xavy going off even more about her and Mama shaking her finger at him for being *pintasero*, which means all you do is look for flaws in people and call them out like you have no shame.

Antoinette treats everyone like royalty, especially Makena. She emails Makena just to say hi, and she even sends birthday and Christmas cards and sometimes care packages full of dried mango snacks and homemade *tapa* beef jerky all the way from Daly City, which Papa says is where most of the Filipinos flocked over to when they immigrated to America. One time, she even bought a singing telegram for Makena on Valentine's Day when Makena was already having problems with Eli.

But I see Antoinette's emails sit in Makena's inbox on our computer all in bold lettering, which means Makena hasn't read them, and I never see Makena sending cards to Antoinette or anyone else. Mama's always reminding Makena to be a better friend, but Makena barks back to Mama that being a good friend isn't all about correspondence and gifts.

Tracy and Ally are the same way, always keeping in touch with Makena. Whenever they drop by the house during the summer, they ask Makena to grab a bite to eat or go to the mall with them. One time when Makena was too busy practicing for a piano competition, Tracy and Ally took me instead.

Tracy looks like Barbie with her long legs and silky blonde hair, and Ally is Chinese, like a chubby kind of Lucy Liu, who I thought was the coolest angel in the *Charlie's Angels* movie. Tracy and Ally's favorite mall is Glendale Galleria, so we decided to shop there and eat at Bobby McGee's afterwards, where the people serving you dress as different characters. Ours was a pirate, and he kept saying "Ay matey" and making googly eyes at Ally, who I think he had a crush on. Every time the pirate winked, Tracy and Ally covered their mouths and tried hiding behind one another. I remember one time when someone winked at Makena when we were waiting in line for a drink during intermission at *Annie*, she rolled her eyes and said men can be so disgraceful.

Tracy and Ally are easy to be around. They like to hang out and giggle about things that seem dumb, but the things aren't really *that* dumb, like when Ally pretends she's Dory from *Finding Nemo* and keeps forgetting that she was already introduced to Nemo's dad.

I have fun with Makena too, but sometimes she makes you think about every little thing people do or say, like when this family in the booth next to us at Ruby's was talking about criminals deserving to die for killing innocent people, and boy her face sure went from light to pink to red in a hurry. All of a sudden, she couldn't mind her own business and told them that the death penalty is still considered by most civilized nations as a cruel and inhuman punishment.

When Tracy and Ally took me home, Makena was still practicing piano. She stood up from the bench and thanked her friends for taking me out and said they should get together sometime. I saw Tracy bump her elbow softly against Ally's so that Makena couldn't see, and that's when Tracy said, "All righty, Kenz, we'll email you," and both she and Ally turned to me to give me tight hugs and said "Ay matey" together and giggled. After they left, Makena asked me if I had a nice time, and of course I said yes.

That's when Mama flew into the room like a falcon and said, "Isabel, you can tell your *áte* all about it after you take Frida for a short walk."

While I was in my bedroom putting on my sweatshirt, I could hear Mama in her scolding voice, saying something about making time for other people, and then Makena snapping back as usual with her quote from *Walden*, which is a book by Henry David Thoreau that she read in high school. She quotes different parts of it all the time to Mama, especially when Mama's lecturing her about things like respect for elders and being an honest-to-goodness Catholic.

"If a woman doesn't keep pace with her companions, perhaps it's because she hears a different drummer. Let her step to the music she hears, however measured or far away," said Makena, trying to sound all intellectual even though she already is, and also changing the "man and he and him" parts to "woman and she and her."

Then Mama burst out, "I'm sick of hearing about different drummers. You need to stop alienating your friends."

For a second, I thought about Alienation Antoinette, even though I knew Mama was talking about a different sort of alienation. Papa taught me that some words have many meanings, and sometimes you can make a play on certain words, like the time when one of his business associates teased another about being a working stiff all his life and Papa butt in and said, "That's not the only type of stiff he can be."

When Papa realized I was in the room too, he shook his head and said "Aw, goddamn" and gave me one of those knuckle rubs on the head that's called a noogie.

I'm beginning to understand why Makena hears a different drummer, because Tracy and Ally and Alienation Antoinette are different drummers themselves. Maybe they all used to be the same drummers and also listen to the same music, but Makena all of a sudden started to hear something new and stopped hanging out with them so much.

Makena has always been her own kind of drummer, doing and being everything like Lola Evie said, and I think what's different about Tracy and Ally and Alienation Antoinette is they're trying too hard to keep pace.

But no one can keep pace with my *áte*.

17. rockin' and righteous

Papa and Mama asked Dr. Witt to get approval from Dr. Minor for me to go with Makena to her treatments, so today I get to be there for Makena's third chemotherapy, which I just call "chemo" now. It doesn't smell too great in the office, kind of like the medicine that Mama uses to wash the scrapes and cuts I get when I fall off my skateboard. Dr. Minor is Makena's oncologist which means cancer doctor, and this is where she's going to have chemo every week for a whole year.

While we sit and wait for the nurse to call Makena, we eat the yummy strawberry candies in the basket on the coffee table. We're surrounded by all kinds of old people in the waiting room. One wrinkly lady with black hair that looks like a wig, along with a shirt that says *Vaya con Dios,* keeps looking at Makena funny, and then she finally opens her mouth and asks Makena if she and I are there for our mom or dad or grandparent.

When Makena tells her that she's waiting to have her treatment, the wrinkly wig lady says, "Oh heavens, you're much too young to have to battle something like this."

Makena answers, "Yes, I absolutely am," and she just keeps chewing on her candy and listens for her name to be called.

A door swings open, and Makena's nurse named Dana appears. I like to call her Surfer Girl. Surfer Girl is an all-over-the-place kind of person, sort of like another one of Papa's *átes* named Tita Malou, who they call neurotic because she always repeats herself and asks questions she shouldn't be asking, like "Is your *áte* still a virgin," and then she ends up answering her own question anyway.

But Surfer Girl sure isn't neurotic, and I love hearing about her dog Sunny and her research on kidney cancer and all of her *kuwentos* about the beach and creative ideas for children's books.

Surfer Girl spots us and waves. She swings her head to the right, which whips her blonde bangs away from her eyes that are the color of hazel, which Mama told me is a mixture of green and gold and brown with little specks of blue, like the ones on the pretty glass vase she bought in Switzerland.

"Come on in, my sweethearts," she says, and then she asks me to go wait in the room with the chairs that look like La-Z-boys. When we first met Surfer Girl, she made dreamy eyes outside the window and wished she could bask in the sun all day long. I asked Surfer Girl what she would do in the sun, and she said she'd keep being a nurse because it's what God meant for her. But if she could be a nurse *and* bask in the sun, she'd be set for life.

Surfer Girl first weighs Makena and draws some blood from her arm before she brings her to the La-Z-boy room where I'm waiting. That's when she takes Makena's blood pressure and pulse and temperature. Sometimes I don't like watching the blood pressure part because that strappy band with the Velcro looks like it's squishing Makena's tiny arm.

Makena tells me to go get more strawberry candies while Dr. Minor checks her and asks her questions about how she's feeling. She tells me to wait for at least 10 minutes, and while I'm scooping up a handful of candies, the wrinkly wig lady asks, "How is your, um, babysitter doing?"

"She's my big sister," I answer in a flat but fierce voice.

She nods and clutches her brown leather bag with cracks all over it super tight, like I'm going to take off with it or something. Her bag is so huge like a gunnysack that you can't see her *Vaya con Dios* shirt anymore.

"How old are you, dear?" she asks.

"Eight."

"Which cancer does your sister have?" she goes on, and this time she pulls a Huggies wipe from her bag and pats her neck with it.

"The colon kind," I say. I usually don't give people short answers because I like making *kuwento*, but this lady seems kind of nosy, like a lot of my *titas* and girl cousins who always look for *tsismis*, which means gossip.

There's a difference between making *kuwento* and *tsismis.* They both can make you laugh or cry, but telling a story always leaves you feeling like you shared a part of yourself, like you connected some dots inside your body.

The door next to the lady in the booth swings open again, and a different nurse calls out the name Wilma Macias. Wrinkly Wilma with the wig and the leather bag cracks and baby wipes stands up and takes both my hands and says, "*Que Dios esté contigo y tu familia, pastelita.*"

But isn't God already with us, I think to myself, and I also wonder why she spoke Spanish all of a sudden.

When I go back to the La-Z-boy room, Surfer Girl is holding up what she calls a butterfly needle and tries to find a fat vein on top of Makena's hand, not a skinny weak one that won't let the medicine through to Makena's insides to make her better. Surfer Girl keeps telling Makena to squeeze her fist so that her veins start to bulge.

"Get the blood pumping, girl, let's see those veins pop out," Surfer Girl always says. I stare at the freckles all over Surfer Girl's arm as she slides the needle into the top part of Makena's hand, and this gives me the chills because it feels like the needle is poking right through my skin too.

Sometimes Makena and I watch soap operas or cartoons while the medicine is finding its way through her veins. Today we're watching Makena's favorite soap opera called *All My Children*, and Makena can't believe it when Anna finds out she has a long-lost brother. Dimitri doesn't trust this brother and neither does Edmund, but Anna reminds Dimitri and Edmund that they used to despise each other and look at them now.

I don't really care what's going on most of the time during the soap opera because it reminds me of all the nutty and dramatic things that Papa and Mama have to go through with their families. What I really like to do is watch the medicine pump through Makena's veins and pray hard it flushes away whatever wretched cancer is left inside her body.

Surfer Girl likes to say "dude" and "wicked" and "righteous" every time Makena tells her something interesting about herself, like playing on her college tennis team or hoping to be an animal behaviorist and dog trainer someday, even though Papa's making her study to become a veterinarian. Then Surfer Girl turns to me and asks what I want to be when I grow up.

"I think I'd like to be a doctor or a nurse instead of an animal behaviorist and dog trainer," I answer, "because I saw how hard it was to train my dog Frida when she was a puppy, and my mama thinks I have no patience just like my papa."

Surfer Girl claps and jumps and pinches my cheeks. "We'll work together someday," she says. "We'll have a rockin' office right there on the beach."

"Where we can say dude and wicked?" I ask, and I can feel my heart going ba-boom like a tuba.

"Righteous," she answers. Her grin is so wide that you can see her gums. "And bask in the golden, glad sun all day long."

18. goddem no good

One of Papa's younger brothers named Tito Carding whose real name is Ricardo used to be my second favorite *tito* after Tito Gus. Nobody has heard from Tito Gus, not even me and Makena even though he would always tell us we're his favorite nieces, which is really sad because he was the only one besides Xavy who could make you laugh when you felt blue.

Papa says Tito Gus is finding himself somewhere in Europe, but I don't understand how you're supposed to find yourself if you aren't lost. My new favorite is Tito Dante, who I've always liked anyway because he holds up his fist for fist bumps and wears lots of gold chains and colorful suits every time we see him. Tito Carding isn't allowed to be our favorite because "He's been a very bad seed lately," according to Mama.

Tito Carding married one of Mama's younger sisters named Tita Rina, so when I tell my friends that Papa's brother married Mama's sister, they think it's the most radical thing ever. What's even cooler is that our cousin Katie, who is Tito Carding and Tita Rina's oldest daughter, looks exactly like Xavy. They could even pass for twins. Their birthdays are only two months apart, so sometimes they get stuck in some of the same classes together, which Xavy complains about all the time because he says Katie is the most obnoxious butt-kisser there is.

But Tito Carding did a terrible thing a while back when he was in the Philippines, and a few years ago, everyone found out what he did, so that's why Papa's side of the family has been feuding, just like Mama's is.

Our relatives in the Philippines told us that Tito Carding is a "gigolo and a cheat and simply a downright no good piece of shet." He committed bigamy which means you go and marry someone else without telling the first person you picked, and he even has all kinds of kids with different mamas, so that means

Makena and Xavy and I have many more cousins in the Philippines.

Papa's side of the family started fighting because when Mama and Papa visited the Philippines a few years ago, one of Tito Carding's kids named Mikaela introduced herself to them. Papa even had her investigated, and when they found out she was telling the truth, boy did Papa and Mama have a huge cow.

"Mikaela's face was the same as Carding's, a carbon copy," Papa said, so Mama went and tattled to Tita Rina, who screamed to Papa and Mama that all they want to do is hurt her. Tita Rina somehow got it in her head that Papa and Mama hunted down Mikaela when it was really Mikaela who went to Papa and Mama. Papa's known for stirring up controversy, so of course he was the easiest person to blame.

The Tito Carding I knew didn't seem like a gigolo and a cheat. He'd hang out with the family and stay out of trouble, and he acted so wacky with Papa and was always *masayang kasama*, so fun to be around.

Wherever our family moved, Tito Carding and his family followed. Katie and her younger sister Marie were like sisters to us, so we were never apart. Katie and Makena even used to take baths together, but when they started growing boobies and hair on their private parts, they stopped. Now they don't talk because of everything that's happened.

When Tito Carding sneezed, he'd say "ah-ching" instead of "ah-choo," maybe because his nickname ends in "-ing." He used to fold up his eyelids, which would stay stuck there so that only the red veiny parts showed, and then he'd chase us all over the house and try to grab our legs when we ran up the stairs.

He also loved to sing. He taught Xavy "The Greatest Love of All" by Whitney Houston, which is one of the hardest songs to sing because Makena says it requires falsetto, which means you have to go way higher than your normal vocal range. And of course everyone would laugh and point at poor Xavy, Mama remembers, because his voice always cracked when he tried to reach the high notes.

Tito Carding taught Makena "Snowbird," an old song from the '70s, and everyone says she'd jiggle her hips exactly the way Tito Carding would. Then Tito Gus would join in, and boy did he have amazing rhythm, according to Makena. The *titos* and *titas* say that *baklas* are the smoothest dancers, and Tito Gus proved it. They called him "Disco King," and "He could outdo that John Travolta any day," according to Tito Sal, who isn't very graceful because he had polio when he was little, which means one of his legs is shorter than the other.

Tito Gus had nicknames for all of us. He called Xavy *Mamahuhu*, which means "laid-back and carefree" in Chinese, and he called Makena *Doña*, which of course she didn't like because *doña* in Spanish means you act like a princess.

He used to call me "Scrappy-Doo" who is Scooby-Doo's cousin, and I didn't like my nickname either because Scrappy is annoying and loud, if you ask me. But Tito Gus thought the name was perfect for me because Scrappy is *matapang*, feisty and tough and full of spirit.

Tito Gus was *masayang kasama* too, and if he were around, he'd be there for Makena and make her laugh with his jokes about his nose that looks like someone stuck a monster wad of Play-Doh in the middle of his face. He used to yell "I'm going to inhale you" every time he walked through our front door, and I'd laugh and cry so hard when he caught me and tickled me until my jaw turned really numb.

I miss my two *titos*, but if I ever shared this information with my family, they'd get all huffy and hissy and tell me to stop talking nonsense. Tito Gus and Tito Carding were my two favorite *titos*, but we aren't supposed to talk about them anymore because of "the unthinkable and selfish things they did," Makena tells me. Xavy says that most of the *titas* and *titos* took Tito Carding's side because they have bird brains or they owe him money, and only a few of the smarter ones didn't.

Then there's everyone being out of sorts because Tito Gus deserted the family, so this is another reason why Papa can't bring himself to talk to any of them anymore except for Tita Gwen, who has always been close to us.

Now the families on both sides aren't talking, which means they don't even know that Makena is sick. If everyone stayed friends again, they'd call and come over and dance and sing and be loud, which is what they're the best at. They'd also bring *pansit* noodles for long life or *hopia* that pastry with the sweet bean paste along with all kinds of other yummy Filipino treats.

Then abracadabra, we could all be one big nutty family again.

When Papa was still friends with Tito Carding and the rest of their family, he'd invite them to make *pasyal.* One time, Papa asked Tito Carding, Tita Choleng, and Tito Vito to go to Mission Viejo with us to look at these model homes in what they called a tract-home complex named Sorrento. Mama and Tita Rina had to take Katie and Marie to a birthday party that some of the other cousins were going to also, so the only cousin who could come with us was Janey, Tita Choleng's youngest daughter who was four years old at the time, the age where you don't do very well at birthday parties because you can't help spilling and breaking stuff.

Tito Carding lives in Eagle Rock and Tita Choleng in Montebello, and Tito Vito was visiting from the Philippines and staying with Tita Choleng, so Papa had to invite him too.

All of my friends always make fun of Tito Vito's rhyming name. Sometimes I try to get away with calling him just Vito, but then he flicks me behind my ears and tells me he's my elder, so I better say "Tito Vito" even though he thinks it sounds lame too.

It's easy to make fun of Tito Vito because he's only five-foot-one and acts a lot bigger than he really is. But you'd never know he has a third-degree black belt in Kajukenbo and a pacemaker to help keep his heartbeat steady.

Early that morning when we drove to the model homes, Papa told Tito Carding to follow us to Tita Choleng's house, where we were all supposed to meet. Of course Tita Choleng had all kinds of food there for us, like *bibingka* the sweet rice cake with real goat cheese and even leftover *sinigang,* which is what she cooked for her family the night before.

You could tell that they had *sinigang* because the house smelled sour. Tita Choleng says she likes to make her *sinigang* with lots of tamarind, not those green instant packets filled with MSG, which is a terribly worse form of salt according to Makena, and "That's what the lazy Flips use," says Mama, which always irritates Makena because she thinks Mama is stooping to being racist against her own kind, even though "own kind" sure doesn't sound right either.

Makena said she was supposed to go to the SPCA and help train some dogs and clean some kennels, but Papa insisted she spend time with the family. I knew Makena was making a fake excuse because she doesn't really like hanging out with some of the *titos* and *titas*.

Xavy loves that Tito Carding always tells corny Flip jokes, like use the word "tenacious" in a sentence, and that's when he asks you to please tie the laces on his "ten-ay-shoes." Then Xavy jokes that Tito Carding acts like he just got off the boat, but Makena always reminds me to ignore this remark because it belittles Asians, even though I don't think Flips came to America on a boat.

Tita Choleng talks so much and so loud that she makes people stare and whisper to each other, and Tito Vito speaks broken English and has the "most atrocious grammar ever" according to Makena, so imagine all of them put together, Xavy always says, they can easily star in a Flip sitcom.

When we got to Sorrento, Tita Choleng was full of hmmph kinds of comments, like "My husband needs to make more money" and "I need to live in a house like this." She kept going on and on about how her friend Brandi's kitchen was like the one in the model called Triana and how Brandi can't stop bragging about her subzero refrigerator which she calls Frigidaire and also her high-end granite and stainless-steel appliances. Xavy kept rolling his eyes at me while Tito Carding and Tito Vito imitated Tita Choleng's yapping right behind her.

Makena couldn't believe how elegantly these homes were decorated. She said the furniture looked like the stuff at Ethan Allen, really formal and fancy like the kind she hopes to have in her own house someday. Curvy legs for the dining room table and rugs with different shades of red and gold and all kinds of knickknacks that looked breakable and expensive, like this crystal cat that was sitting on top of the coffee table in one of the living rooms.

One of the bathrooms had the most curious-looking bathtub that just sat there by itself in the middle of the floor, and that's what Makena said was called a clawfoot. The bathroom smelled like the jasmine vines in our backyard but even more overpowering because of all the candles and potpourri everywhere. The towels looked like jelly rolls stacked on a serving tray, and the bathroom rug was the cushiest thing I had ever stepped on, like my feet were being snowed under by a cottony storm.

There was one model called Trevi with a view from the living room where all you could see were rolling green hills, and while we were looking out the window, Janey almost broke a shiny blue and white vase with naked people painted on them.

"What did I say about not touching anything?" Makena scolded Janey, and that's when Xavy told our cousin to never mind our uptight sister. He made a nanny-nanny-billy-goat face at Makena and started to pet the vase and kiss it, which of course turned Makena all pouty. She always has to ask Xavy to stop mocking her in front of other people, but of course that makes him do it even more.

All of a sudden, we heard cackles and snorts coming from upstairs, and there we saw Tito Carding and Tita Choleng rushing down the stairs like they were naughty little kids and Tito Vito right behind them. Tito Vito's jacket was all zipped up, and it looked like he was hiding something huge under it. Makena stopped him at the bottom of the stairs and asked him what he had there bulging from his jacket, but all Tito Vito did was wave his arms up in the air, trying to look innocent.

That's when Makena unzipped Tito Vito's jacket like she was cracking a whip and found a skinny white poodle statue, even taller than my stuffed giraffe at home. This poodle had the longest neck ever, with a hot pink satin bow tied around it. Makena started to pull the poodle away from Tito Vito, and before we knew it, my *tito* and *áte* were playing tug of war with an ugly white poodle that Tito Vito was going to steal from the model home called Trevi.

Instead of screaming at Tito Vito, Makena calmly said, "Put it back, please," but she sounded like she was talking to Janey.

Tito Vito noticed, so he didn't want to be calm.

"Shut your trap and live a little, you goddem little shet!" he yelled at Makena.

Now that's the best English I ever heard come out of Tito Vito's mouth, I remember thinking to myself. Then I noticed Xavy looking over at Tito Vito, and by the way his eyebrows curved up like upside-down u's, I could tell he was thinking the same exact thing.

Makena couldn't believe her ears too, and it sure looked like lava might ooze out of them when she answered back in his face, "I'm taller than you, so I'm not the little shit, and don't you tell me to shut up, you ignoramus—"

Before Makena could finish, Papa appeared and grabbed her shoulders and shouted in her face to respect her *tito*. He shook her so hard that she started to cry, and then she ran outside to the car and stayed there until Papa was done talking to one of his business associates who he bumped into at the model home called Como.

During the car ride home, no one said one word, but Papa finally decided to speak up when we got off the freeway to grab dinner at the drive-thru at Wendy's. He turned around and asked each of us what we wanted, and after Makena told him she wasn't hungry, he said, "I'll order you a goddamn classic double burger meal with biggie fries and a goddamn extra large Coke because you really do need to live a little."

19. scrabble and straights

When Makena isn't feeling too nauseated or tired from chemo, sometimes we sit in the backyard and read or watch Frida chase squirrels and roll around in the rosemary shrubs while Mama yells "Off, Frida" at her, and we laugh like loons because Frida just tilts her head at Mama and keeps doing it.

Makena's reading *The Wind in the Willows* to me, and it's the perfect book because the breeze sweeping through our oak tree makes me feel like I'm a part of the story.

Sometimes Makena and I play Scrabble, and we jump up and down together when I can use all my letters and score a whole 50 points, and that's 50 extra because you're supposed to add it to the points from the word you just made.

Or sometimes Makena turns up the volume to maximum high so I can feel the bass booming inside my chest, and we dance to a '70s song by Barry White called "You're the First, the Last, My Everything," one of Tito Gus' favorites.

Makena stands on the couch and grabs Mama's angel figurine and pretends it's a microphone. She sings, "The first, my last, my everything, and the answer to all my dreams," and then Papa joins in all of a sudden and does his funny boogie dance, the one where he bites down on his bottom lip and raises his chin up to the ceiling with his eyes shut, his hand on his belly, swaying back and forth, and he follows Makena's lyrics: "You're my sun, you're my moon, my guiding star, my kind of wonderful, that's what you are."

Then there's Xavy, who's copying every move that Papa makes, biting down on his bottom lip too, and that's when Mama decides to join in and picks up Frida and holds one of her paws like she's waltzing with her.

I sing and I dance with them, waving my hands and arms in the air so carefree, but I watch my family and wonder if people walking by our house peep through the window and think, "Wow, what a happy family they are," and of course they don't know my *áte* is sick and that life sometimes deals us straights instead of royal flushes, as Mr. Baluga likes to say.

20. sticky silence

"The ride you don't return from," that's what Mr. Baluga says, but I know it means you go to heaven. It's like Makena took the ride but came back kicking and screaming. Thinking about the ride rattles up my insides, making me wonder what you need to do to get a free ticket back.

Right before we found out that Lolo Martín was going to take the ride he wouldn't return from because he had a rare lung disease, the whole José family visited him at a nursing home, a place for old and sick people that's in Sherman Oaks, where some of the cousins live. Lolo Martín came to America right before I was born, so he didn't get to enjoy life here for too long, Mama tells me.

We threw Lolo Martín a small party in the courtyard, a shady area outside in between all the old people's rooms, and there were picnic tables and long pointy grass everywhere. Lola Carmen and Papa and the rest of the *titas* and *titos* pushed Lolo Martín all over the courtyard in his wheelchair, taking turns talking to him and telling him how much they loved him.

Lolo Martín looked tiny that day, all hunchback and shriveled up in his white hospital gown with purple dots that looked like stars from far away, and I remember thinking he shrank a lot since the last time we visited him. Papa said he used to have reddish-brown hair, but the Lolo Martín I knew always had gray hairs, even the ones on his arms and his legs. His skin started to look gray too, and when he smiled, his lips curled inward because he had no teeth.

Tita Choleng and Tita Malou and Tita Marijo kept crying like Lolo Martín already took the ride, while Tita Gwen stayed cool, even though the whites of her eyes were red and veiny. Lolo Martín sure couldn't stand all the tears, yelling at them to cut the drama and go make sure there were enough pork skewers and *inihaw na manok*, which is Filipino-style barbecue chicken that's both sweet and salty, for all his *nietos*.

Some of the boy cousins were playing with a Frisbee, and most of the older girl cousins were hanging out with all the *titas*, slapping their thighs hard every time someone came up with a great piece of *tsismis*, especially if it was something about one of the *titos*.

The funniest one I heard was about Tito Dante and all the hotel maids in Reno having a crush on him. Tita Carlie said one of them even looked like our cousin Mickey's pug dog, and when Makena reminded me not to be *pintasero* and to never speak that low about anyone, I thought, "What about the poor dog?!" because pugs make me smile, their jumbo eyes ready to pop out at you.

When it was Papa's turn to push, he took the longest time out of any of the *titos* and *titas*. He and Lolo Martín huddled together near the water fountain that had a horse statue in the middle of it, and they looked super serious, talking in their lower voices so that no one could hear. When one of the cousins walked by, Lolo Martín would yell "Scram, *niño*," and that's when the *titas* and girl cousins would start making *tsismis* again, whispering and pointing at the bad boy cousin who was told to stay away.

Xavy and Makena were in charge of the barbecue, and I knew Makena was watching the pork skewers and chicken only because she didn't want to gossip and whisper and point. Makena said when she talked to Lolo Martín, he told her how proud he was of all her accomplishments and to keep excelling. But she didn't like it when he told her it was a shame she couldn't carry on the José name.

Lolo Martín reminded Xavy to keep doing whatever Papa tells him to because Papa will steer him in the right direction. "Gangs, drugs, alcohol, and crime are for losers and if I ever hear you talk like a hoodlum again, you might just get a taste of my fist," he warned.

When my turn came, Lolo Martín said to try to take after my *áte* and always listen to Papa and Mama. "Do well in school, and don't you ever lose your ability to make people crack smiles, you hear." He told me everything in Spanish and English and Tagalog, and after he asked me to give him a kiss, he hugged my head with his left arm because he's left-handed like Makena. I think it was the first time ever that I saw Lolo Martín act a little mushy.

When it was Tito Gus' turn, there were hardly any lips moving, just Tito Gus pushing Lolo Martín's wheelchair. Once in a while, Lolo Martín scolded Tito Gus because he was pushing too fast. Makena and I sat and watched together, and her clothes smelled smoky, but they were a hickory smoky and not the cigarette kind like Papa's clothes always are, like Mama's wool sweaters that have stayed inside her closet for too long. Makena kept shaking her head and saying "Jeez, the irony," but I didn't understand what she meant.

Lolo Martín spotted me and Makena watching them, so he waved at me and said, "*Mi nietita*, come help your Tito Gus push my wheelchair."

Tito Gus rolled his eyes while he made room for me to stand next to him and help. We pushed for a long time, listening to the rowdy boy cousins playing in the background. Sometimes Lolo Martín asked us to slow down whenever we rolled over a deep crack on the cement.

All of a sudden, Lolo Martín turned his head around towards Tito Gus.

"Change your life," he said, and the words seemed to fall from his mouth like he was already losing his breath from his rare lung disease.

I could tell that Tito Gus was trying to hide his wide frog eyes, and right when I thought he was going to say something, he decided to hold his head low and just stand there. Lolo Martín's head was bowed too, and there was all this sticky silence, even worse than no talking because we weren't pushing the wheelchair anymore.

My insides started to twist from all the jitters, wondering who might break the silence, so I asked Lolo Martín if I could please be excused. When I did, he seemed surprised I was still there and said, "*Sí, ve ahora*, go to your mother."

I couldn't find Mama so I went straight to Makena, and she knew something was wrong because her eyebrows were crinkly. When she asked me what happened, I just told her that Lolo Martín and Tito Gus talked about serious stuff, but I didn't tell her what Lolo Martín told Tito Gus because I don't think I was supposed to hear it, and if it ever got back to Lolo Martín, I might just get a taste of his fist too.

How do you change your life? Do you start over and find a new name? Maybe that's why Tito Gus went away to the other side of the world to find himself. Maybe it was too much to ask and he couldn't do it.

Papa always tells me that God doesn't judge you for who you are, but Lolo Martín judged Tito Gus, a fun and funny kind of person who could make other people crack smiles too.

21. shining street smarts

Everyone says Makena is the genius and Xavy is the loafer and I'm in between.

Mr. Baluga says being in between is the place to be because no one wants to be a whiz kid or a goof-off. Mr. Baluga never had kids because he had to travel to Sacramento for his government job all the time, and by the time he and Lola Evie finally settled here in our neighborhood, they were too old to have kids. But if they had any, Mr. Baluga told me he would want them to be just like me.

He says Makena is too gifted for her own good and doesn't have street smarts, so what use do you have if you're all brains. Xavy has street smarts, but he's too lazy and he just wants everything to fall into his lap, everything like a job and some money here and there from Papa and Mama.

"But those in-betweeners like you, Kid, they are life's unsung heroes."

That's when I ask Mr. Baluga to slow down because how do you get street smarts, what are they, and what is unsung?

"Street smarts are what you need to survive life," says Mr. Baluga. He's observed Makena from the time we moved here, and she's the only one who hasn't tried climbing our oak tree right there in our backyard. He even caught Mama one time doing it, and I believe it because of the keloid on her elbow. Mama's a monkey when she wants to be. She can do 12 whole pull-ups on Xavy's exercise bar hanging across his bedroom door, which Papa insists he used to do 50 of in the Army.

Makena always asked Papa to help her with her bike when it had a flat or if the brakes weren't tight enough and never bothered to learn how to fix things, and when the Rodríguez family was building their house across the street from us in Eagle Rock, she didn't like the construction workers because they would nod at her with expressions that said she was too precious to associate with, she would tell me. But she didn't do anything about it, like maybe ask if they wanted some water or something, and just ran inside the house every day when she got home from school.

Mr. Baluga says I climb trees like a wildcat and taught myself how to fix my skateboard without asking for anyone's help. When the Sanders family renovated their house down the street, I asked the construction workers if they wanted Mama to make them *longanisa*, which is a sweet Filipino sausage made out of pork butt, along with fried eggs and *pan de sal*, the most thick and doughy and tasty dinner roll ever.

I sat with them during their breaks and asked them what it was like to build a real house, not one out of a deck of cards or some Magna-Tiles, and sometimes they even taught me how to dance the salsa and the rumba while they gobbled up their *longanisa* sandwiches.

"Don't get me wrong, Kid," Mr. Baluga says. "That sister of yours is a respectable girl and a tremendous success, but you're the unsung hero, the one who shines like a bright star but doesn't get any recognition or praise because you don't get straight A's or play the piano like those virtuosos at Juilliard or hit a tennis ball like Martina Navratilova. What you do is keep making people feel like there are some genuine people left in this ugly world."

Before I can ask Mr. Baluga why he thinks the world is ugly and why he's comparing Makena to Martina when he should be talking about Serena Williams, he's already putting away the *pusoy dos* cards and telling me to go on home before that scrumptious supper Mama cooked for us gets cold.

22. cuckoo curt captions

I think Makena's chemo is making her a little cuckoo. Mama warned me that Makena will be more emotional because of her treatments, so watch what you say around her and don't get stuck listening to her feeling sorry for herself.

Makena doesn't really ramble on in front of Papa or Mama or Xavy, only me. Sometimes she remembers the past, making *pasyal* and winning tennis tournaments, and sometimes she talks about the trees swaying outside, or is it the sky just moving or the earth revolving.

Does Mr. Baluga really hate her because she's a snob, and why can't she tell Papa she's going to be an animal behaviorist and that's that, and how does Mama put up with Papa's bigotry, and why does she keep adding bell peppers and raisins to the *torta* she makes for us when she knows that we all can't stand those two ingredients?

It's true, all you need are scrambled eggs and ground beef and onions and tomatoes and potatoes and all the right spices to create the perfect *torta*, and just when I'm imagining the most mouthwatering *torta* ever, with ketchup squirted into a happy face right on top, Makena jumps to her next *kuwento*, telling me why she would never date a celebrity if she had the chance.

But sometimes she sticks to just one subject, and boy she never leaves out one single detail, making you think hard about the life she's been living.

Makena is finally answering the question I've been wondering about since she told us she got colon cancer. She says there's nothing worse in the world than not having control, which is what it feels like to be on chemo. You have no idea what's going on inside you, if the treatment is reaching every lymph node or poisoning the bad, then wondering what was left behind.

I tell Makena if we could control what was going on inside our bodies, there would be no sickness in this world, no doctors and nurses and hospitals, and they would never have the chance to relieve pain and make lives long and comfortable. But from the look on her face, I can tell this isn't the answer she wants to hear. She decides to ignore me and says that the chemo is poisoning everything else in her life.

She lies awake at night and talks to God, but she doesn't question him anymore. She tells him how painful it is to sleep during the day. She fights the lethargy, which means being extra tired, another SAT word that Xavy needs to memorize.

She fights to keep her eyelids from shutting, not just from falling asleep but also from shutting out the world she wants so much to keep tackling. She should be practicing piano, fine-tuning her serve, preparing for vet school, and going for that summer internship.

I nod my head at Makena. I know what she's talking about, even though I'm not going through her pain and lethargy. I try to imagine what it would be like if I couldn't go outside and ride my skateboard, catching all kinds of fresh breaths when it's windy outside or walking to Luigi's Deli with Mr. Baluga and making *kuwento* or building tunnels for our sand castle mountains during recess. It would be like spending time in jail, except you didn't do anything unholy to get yourself locked up for a long time.

During the car ride home from Dr. Minor's office, she says, the queasiness starts to set in. Sometimes her stomach makes rumbly noises, like it's brewing up a disgusting stew, so Mama packs plenty of extra large Ziploc bags just in case Makena can't make it home in time to go to the bathroom.

One time when Makena was at chemo and I was stuck at home with Xavy, she left her journal on her desk. Papa and Mama always tell me to respect other people's privacy, but I noticed words like "appalling" and "sickening" in her journal.

All of a sudden, I couldn't stop reading, even though seeing those words made my throat close up, just like Makena says hers does right before she's about to vomit.

The bile, the chunks of digested matter rise up through my chest and throat and gush through my open mouth. Sometimes the rancidness is too much to bear, forcing me to heave again. Sometimes the acid from the bile burns the canker sores in my mouth. Sometimes I wish it would just burn them all off.

Why would she want to be in more pain from the burning, I wonder, and does she want to take that ride you never come back from so that she doesn't have to go through this monstrous kind of changing?

Papa says you need experiences like these to have character when you're older because if your life was always easy when you were young, people will be able to tell, and they'll never respect you.

Papa knows when someone has had an easy life. He checks out their hands, and he can tell if they ever did hard labor or played sports. If they don't have wrinkles on their face, they were never out in the sun working hard or just being out in the world, being out there so that things can happen to them.

I touch my head and feel the strands of hair that have grown back. Curt, coarse coils. I yank them out one by one, and they seem to grow angrier, thickening and multiplying with each extraction. Yet I struggle to find each and every one. I yearn for the smooth, the straight, and the undeviating.

Papa loves Mama's wavy hair, almost like Lola Carmen's, thick and sometimes tangly like it has a mind of its own. My hair isn't straight or curly. It's just one giant wave that flips the wrong way. Tito Gus used to tell me he'd teach me how to fix my hair with a curling iron, even though I'm scared of them because Xavy once tried to curl my flip the other way with one and burnt the top part of my ear. Tito Gus liked curly hair too and always said that it gives people more bounce and pep.

"Bouncy and peppy hair makes for a bouncier and peppier lifetime, my sweets," he used to say.

I lift up my shirt and stare at my seven-inch scar, a grim slash above my navel. I imagine the scalpel piercing through my flesh, gloved hands handling delicate instruments to remove the cancer invading my body. The cold parts of my body.

I can taste the poison. I marvel at its ability to both prolong and cripple life. I marvel at its ability to transform something into nothing.

There comes a point in suffering where no one can do anything for you. It's so lonesome, this pain.

I wonder how doctors keep their patients alive when they're operating, cutting into their bodies and making them lose all kinds of blood. Do they take the ride and wait while they're being sliced into and come back when it's time to wake up, when the doctor is finished taking out the cancer and putting their organs back where they were? And why does chemo have to pick the good stuff inside their bodies to mess with too?

I don't believe you can turn something into nothing. This isn't true, Makena, I want to cry out to her, but if I do, she'll know I looked inside her private little book. I could decide to be sneaky and hide her journal and even throw it away, but then Father Jack from catechism would make me say five Hail Marys and oh please forgive me God for I have sinned. Even if the trash collectors picked up her journal and burned it, it wouldn't become nothing. The ashes would float around and just go live with the air.

I'm still nodding at Makena. I watch her mouth, the way it moves, the soft flapping of her lips, and I block all the words coming out of it. She looks like a silent movie. There are captions on this movie, different sentences on the screen, but the words aren't telling me any kind of story.

23. grossly golden

Makena's asking me to pass around a bunch of colon cancer awareness cards at school and around the neighborhood. President Clinton who was our last president helped make the month of March "Colon Cancer Awareness Month," and this was a huge deal because Makena says no one used to have any clues about colon cancer but always seemed to know everything about breast cancer and lung cancer, which is what Tracy's grandfather took the ride for when he was 49 years old and he didn't even smoke.

Everyone remembers President Clinton because of Monica Lewinsky, but I like to remember him as the president right before George W. Bush whose father is President George Bush without the W but now puts H.W. in the middle, and also as the president who tried to help recognize people like my *áte* during the month of March.

Papa loves Clinton because he made the country's economic growth historic, and boy times were prosperous and people were spending all kinds of money, he says, so how could you not like a president like that, even though everyone says he did inappropriate things with an intern? When I asked Papa what President Clinton did, he says, "We all make mistakes. But Clinton didn't let himself become them."

Ms. Langevin tells me that I can pass out the cards, but she says it'll be more beneficial to have a speaker from a cancer organization talk about the illness first, so when I told Makena this, she was already nodding her head and walking over to her computer to look up a name.

Makena met a lady named Betty Glantz on a cancer patient forum, where people who have cancer can share their experiences with each other. Ms. Glantz has survived colon cancer for 15 years now and volunteers for the Colon Cancer

Coalition. Makena hopes she's willing to fly all the way from Pennsylvania to speak at my school about colon cancer.

Papa and Mama don't think it's wise to have someone talk to young children about colon cancer, but Principal Zalay and a bunch of other teachers believe it will be educational and might help kids who have sick *átes* or *abuelos* in their families too. Parents and members of the community will be invited, and now this whole thing is going to be a big affair all because Makena asked me to pass out a bunch of little cards that list the facts and symptoms of colon cancer and what you need to do if you have those symptoms, which all have something to do with the gross and dirty areas of your body.

Mama hates any kind of attention, and now she's getting super high-strung, thinking that the parents at PTA meetings will start feeling sad for her and oh you poor thing do you need help. Papa says all this exposure won't be healthy for me because what if the kids at school start hammering away at the questions. Xavy doesn't care either way, but he says, "Itz kickass dat mo foo's will know sum shit 'bout colon cancer now an' do sumtin da hellz 'bout it early if dey gits dem repugnant symptoms."

One of Makena's favorite celebrities is Katie Couric from *The Today Show*, and her husband died of colon cancer when he was only 42. Makena's secretly hoping Ms. Couric will visit our school so that she can meet her, even though Mama hears she didn't bother to go support the Colon Cancer March in Washington, D.C. that was 40 long miles because she had to interview Tom Cruise, which Mama thinks is such a crock of bullshet. Makena says Ms. Couric does a lot for colon cancer so cut her some slack, but how much are you supposed to cut for someone who can help spread the word better because she's famous and everyone will listen to her?

Papa was right, and now everyone at school is asking me about Makena. I didn't think I'd start feeling twisty on the inside about it, but when they start asking me if my sister's hair is falling out or is she going to survive or what's it like to have a family member with a disease, my throat starts to feel hacky dry. Ms. Langevin tells me to say that Makena is going to pull through this, and it's important to know about colon cancer because it's very treatable if you catch it early, just like Dr. Witt did when he gave Makena a colonoscopy.

colon cancer colon cancer there you are all over the place now please get out of my face.

I prayed to God again tonight, but I didn't really pray. All I did was ask him to make my *áte* a golden girl again.

24. warfare to witness

Today is October 29, 2002, and it's Makena's twentieth birthday.

"Birthdays should always be celebrated," Makena likes to say, but it seems that most of her birthdays end up not feeling like a party.

Xavy tells me that Papa used to take him and Mama and Makena to Manila Garden, this small Filipino restaurant next to Taddeo's Drycleaners and Pizza Boy, and it was owned by Papa's friend named Bong Ocampo, who used to help cater those grand parties that President Marcos and his wife the dragon lady threw all the time when they were in power, which is the way Filipinos describe people who run their country, Mr. Baluga tells me.

Tito Bong cooked every kind of Filipino food you could think of, from *kare-kare* that peanut-buttery dish with oxtail all the way to *pansit palabok*, which is my favorite *pansit* because of the fishy orange gravy and glassy noodles that look more like jelly sandals than regular spaghetti.

All kinds of hell used to break loose at Manila Garden, and Mama thinks it's because Tita Alfie, Tito Bong's first wife who knows voodoo, put a curse on him when he decided to leave their family and start a brand-new one here in America.

One time, a man with hair that Xavy says looked nappy walked into Manila Garden with his hand in his pocket, pretending he had a gun inside it and telling everyone, "Stick 'em up, if anyone moves they're dead meat," but Papa could tell right away that he didn't have a gun.

Papa waited until the man had his back towards him, and then he got up from his chair as fast as a whip and did one of his wrestling moves on him, the kind he learned in the Army. When Papa had Tito Bong empty the man's pockets, all he found were a bunch of rubber bands and a smashed pack of cigarettes.

Xavy remembers how scared he was that day, chewing rice until it got mushy in his mouth and his heart booming so hard and loud in his chest that he thought it would make the nappy-haired man turn loony and shoot them all.

Xavy says something more traumatic happened at Manila Garden, even worse than the man with the fake gun in his pocket, and that was the day Papa decided to show off Makena and the speech she was going to memorize in front of her whole school. It was her ninth birthday, two days before Halloween, and she and Xavy were planning to dress up as Sarah Connor and the Terminator.

Xavy remembers how excited Papa was when Makena decided to enter the speech contest. Papa used to win the same kinds of competitions too when he was younger, making Lolo Martín the proudest papa who'd also brag about his kid to his friends and business associates.

Papa didn't even realize that Makena had a knack for public speaking until he made both Makena and Xavy read the front page aloud to Papa one day while he was plucking his neck hairs. Maybe Papa thought Makena was such a natural at them because Xavy still isn't the fastest reader, even though he's going to college soon.

When Papa realized how clear and smooth Makena's voice sounded, he headed straight for his bookshelves and looked for his book called *Greatest American Speeches* and flipped through the pages until he got to "Give Me Liberty or Give Me Death." He told Makena and Xavy this was the same exact speech that won him first place in oratorical interpretation back in high school and that it earned him the admiration of the nuns especially, who thought Papa was just a hooligan living to stir up trouble.

When Papa found the page he was looking for, he pointed to the middle of it and instructed Makena to read.

"They tell us, sir, that we are weak; unable to cope with so formidable an adversary. But when shall we be stronger?"

Even Xavy had memorized all of "Give Me Liberty or Give Me Death" because Papa made Makena practice it over and over. He also remembered how hard Makena tried sounding tough and convincing, as if she were putting together a cavalry, just like Patrick Henry did when he made this speech many years ago.

Xavy says Makena read with as much feeling as a 9-year-old could "muster," which I thought might be one of his SAT words. But Papa still wasn't satisfied.

"Slower, *hija*," Papa would say, and he kept telling her to try not putting so much stress on the word "weak."

Papa and Makena practiced together for two weeks straight, and Papa would make Xavy and sometimes Mama when she wasn't busy cooking be the audience and clap and holler for Makena. Xavy would try to cross his eyes and flare his nostrils at Makena to make her laugh, but of course Papa backwards-slapped the side of his head every time he made Makena mess up.

When Papa thought Makena was ready, he decided to take her to Manila Garden and even pulled Tito Bong from the kitchen to watch. He made Makena stand right next to the cash register in front of a bunch of customers who didn't really care, wondering what all the fuss was about while their mouths were probably full of fried rice or that purple yam *ube* ice cream Xavy says is an oxymoron, his SAT word that he describes is like being ambivalent and opposite all at once.

But Papa got their attention fast with his deep voice that said, "Hey, listen to my eldest," and when all kinds of eyes were finally on Makena, Papa stooped down in front of Makena like a movie director, raising his thick eyebrows to let her know when to start.

Mama wasn't able to go to Manila Garden that day, and Xavy says he was even more nervous than Makena and thinks this was the first time ever that his hands felt clammy.

Xavy started to shrink in his chair when Makena made "weak" sound too loud and too harsh, and that's when he could tell that "Papa wuz 'bout to looz hiz shit."

"Weak. Not WEAK. Haven't I taught you anything? Christ."

Makena started to hiccup and she couldn't go on, which of course made Papa even more crazy mad.

"You're going to finish. Stop crying."

Papa circled Makena like a vulture and kept reciting parts of the speech in Makena's face.

"It is in vain, sir, to extenuate the matter. Gentlemen may cry, peace, peace—but there is no peace. The war is actually begun!"

Tito Bong started to feel sorry for Makena, so he tried to put his arm around her. But Papa pushed him away.

"What is it that gentlemen wish? What would they have?" Papa carried on, Xavy says, unstoppable like the Terminator.

"Is life so dear, or peace so sweet, as to be purchased at the price of chains and slavery? Forbid it, Almighty God! I know not what course others may take; but as for me, give me liberty or give me death!!"

That's when Papa slammed his hand down on the closest table to him and yelled, "What are you, a goddamn pussycat? I don't raise timid children!" Then he dragged Makena out of the restaurant by one of her long and skinny arms like a dog on a leash and screamed at her some more in the parking lot.

Papa didn't realize that he left Xavy inside, but Xavy had already bolted into the kitchen and hid under the sink while Tito Bong kept trying to comfort him, saying, "Don't worry, your father is just angry, he will get over himself soon."

But Xavy didn't believe him and wouldn't move from under the sink. He sang "Happy Birthday Makena" to himself over and over while chewing on his fingernails, hoping to God that Papa would leave him there with Tito Bong forever.

Tito Bong doesn't own Manila Garden anymore because he moved back to the Philippines to be with his first wife and first kids. Xavy still knows the entire speech by heart and of course Makena too, who ended up winning first place in not only her own school but also the whole district.

Xavy says she beat out a bunch of seventh graders and even made one of the man judges cry.

I watch Xavy's big body shaking while he finishes his *kuwento*, and he doesn't realize that his voice is doing the same thing.

I imagine Xavy coming out from under the sink, noticing everyone staring at him as he's walking out of the restaurant and still singing to himself, "Happy birthday dear Makena happy birthday to you."

The customers with fried rice or maybe *ube* still inside their mouths all have expressions that seem to tell him, "Dude, you just witnessed warfare," and their sorrow is like one of those shaggy mops, cleaning up the blood that Makena left behind, almost like the kind she lost when she damned Eli to hell.

25. mama and the marys

The world outside is bright and zippy, where teenagers in sporty cars like to cruise down our city's widest street called Huntington Drive and joggers wink at babies in strollers, even the not-so-great-looking ones, and they also smile at parents throwing a baseball or kicking a soccer ball with their kids on the cool green grass, right near the lawn bowling area at Arcadia Park.

But my family's world inside is like a dungeon that's dark and bleak, breeding long faces and heavy hearts and quarrels you start for no good reason.

Mama and Makena are fighting today because Mama gave Makena a statue of the Virgin Mary to pray to every day, but Makena insists on keeping it inside her closet. Mama wants Makena to put it on top of her desk or somewhere outside where people can see it, but Makena refuses to believe in displaying religious statues.

Mama turns huffy and hissy and tells Makena she's disrespectful and that she should be grateful to the Virgin Mary for saving her life. Makena asks how the Virgin Mary did just that, and Mama says she felt the Virgin Mary's presence in the hospital chapel during Makena's surgery.

I butt in and tell Mama that I heard her praying to God to save her daughter so where did the Virgin Mary come from, and that's when she all of a sudden cries, *"Ay buhay!"*

Mama shakes her finger at me and asks if I've learned anything at all in catechism and then walks away with stomping feet. She scares Frida in the hallway who's chewing on a peanut butter bone that Papa gave her to keep busy while our family tries to act like things are fine.

The statue is made of wood. I think it weighs as much as my piggy bank, and it also has a deep crack going down the middle of it. But don't ever say it's broken or ugly or else Mama will make you say a bunch of Hail Marys and Our Fathers and that other prayer you're supposed to recite when you've sinned.

When Mama isn't looking, Makena dusts the Virgin Mary statue and kisses it on the head every night before she goes to sleep. Then she puts it back inside the closet.

26. breathe breath and blossom

This morning when I walked Frida, I blew white fog from my mouth. The marigolds aren't blooming anymore because it's November. There's no more orange and sunny yellow, just all kinds of dull green. Our dogwood tree is sprouting white flowers, so at least there's one bright color left in our backyard.

But the pale green is everywhere. It blends in with everything else like it's nothing special, making you forget about what's around you that can blossom.

Papa and I are going with Makena to Arcadia Methodist hospital for her CT-scan. Mama has to stay at home to help Tita Gwen with her wedding favors. They're tying ivory bows around vanilla potpourri and ivory tulle, which is a scratchy kind of material you can see right through. The vanilla makes me sneeze even though I sometimes eat vanilla ice cream, so Makena's CT-scan sounds like a much better place to be this morning.

Papa says he'll take us to 31 Flavors afterwards, and that's when I dash to the car and buckle up my seat belt and dream about rocky road with lots of marshmallows all the way to the hospital.

When we get there, Makena has to check in at two different places. All kinds of people are crammed into the small waiting room, where some are old, some are young, and some are not looking very happy. One lady is reading *People* magazine, a little boy and his mama are sitting quietly on a kid-size couch that looks part furry and part fuzzy, and an old man who looks like he's Mr. Baluga's age keeps tapping his foot right next to the magazine stand, checking his watch every minute even though it's not helping.

Papa's not helping either because he keeps grumbling to himself and walking back and forth and looking over at the front desk to see what's taking so long. Makena asks Papa to sit down and relax please, but she can't stay in one place herself. She squirms in her chair like there are bugs crawling inside her pants, and that keeps even me from relaxing, and I'm usually the one who's hang-loose, according to all the *titos* and *titas*.

When Makena's turn finally comes, a man with a wiry beard sends us over to the radiology department, where a heavy lady with pointy glasses looking like her life is so boring sitting behind a counter gives Makena a large container of something that looks like milk. She says it's barium, which makes your body glow on the inside during CT-scans.

Then we all sit down in the waiting room and watch Makena drink.

Makena still isn't the greatest drinker, so we hang out in the waiting room for almost 45 minutes before she finishes the barium. Papa asks the bored counter lady if Makena has to drink all of it, and she answers in a snippety voice, "Yes she does or the radiologist won't be able to see everything she needs to."

I tell Makena to pretend it's her favorite drink, so she closes her eyes and says to the plastic container, "You're a tall glass of icy lemonade." She chants like those fortune tellers with their crystal balls and then gulps down every last drop.

Papa and I cheer and whistle and give Makena lots of high-fives, but Makena starts to gag and gets up to look for a rest room. Papa holds her back with his thick and hairy arm and keeps telling her to take deep breaths and says, "If you vomit, you won't glow, for crying out loud, and they'll make you drink even more."

Makena changes into a hospital gown after her tall icky drink. The nurse tells her to wear two, one backwards and one the right way so that she doesn't get cold and her butt doesn't show. Papa tells me to hold Makena's purse while he goes to the gift shop to get something, and I'll bet it's a pack of cigarettes and that he'll come back fuming mad because the shop doesn't sell them. When the nurse calls Makena, I watch Makena climb onto a table with a tunnel at the end of it.

The door shuts, and all of a sudden, I'm sitting in the hallway all alone with my *áte*'s purse in my lap. I feel like pressing my ear against the door, but I don't want anyone to catch me and kick me out of the hospital, so I close my eyes tight and listen.

I hear a voice say "Breathe in, hold your breath," and then a few seconds later, the voice says, "Breathe," and I wonder if Makena has the jitters. I keep looking down the hallway for Papa.

When Papa appears, I tell him about the voice and the tunnel. He says the tunnel is where Makena's insides are scanned to make sure there's no cancer. Every time the doctor takes a picture, Makena has to hold her breath. He says even breath can get in the way when the doctor's trying to make sense of the pictures.

What would happen if Makena didn't hold her breath long enough or if she breathed in at the wrong times? Then the doctor who is called a radiologist wouldn't be able to catch what she's supposed to because Makena's breath was blocking it in the picture. Even though breath is invisible when you're blowing it out of your mouth, maybe it shows up in X-rays, kind of like ghosts, which people don't usually see in real life but sometimes end up in pictures.

Makena has gone through a lot lately, which Mama says is called the wringer. She had a surgery called a right hemicolectomy which means they took out the right-hand side of her colon and even her appendix because Dr. Vieri cackled and said she didn't need it, which I thought seemed a bit looney, and she even had to live in a hospital for almost two weeks.

When Makena came home, she had to use this plastic thing that looks like a mini vacuum to help her breathe and get all the phlegmy stuff out of her insides. When she'd cough or sneeze or laugh, even squeezing a pillow against her belly wouldn't take away the pain.

Makena doesn't laugh as much as she used to, so she didn't need the pillow too many times when her incision was healing, but Xavy kept forgetting and got all kinds of scolding from Mama each time he tried to make everyone laugh, pulling his boxer shorts up to his chest and dancing disco or leaving a booger on our arms and asking us to watch it for him.

I guess I wouldn't want to laugh as much if I were Makena, having to go to chemo every single week and not being able to make *pasyal* because she might fall asleep or throw up in the car anyway.

Mama always tells me that laughter is the best medicine, because when you laugh, it's like you're jogging inside of yourself, exercising and making healthy hormones that are supposed to let out the bad ones turning you into a jumbling pile of nerves. If you don't have as many bad hormones, your insides are supposed to work better, like a machine oiled well, which means that Xavy really should keep trying to make us laugh, at least once a week so that when Makena gets chemo, it all cancels out and everything is even again.

After all the breathe-ins and breathe-outs and hold-your-breaths, Makena finally comes out of the room with a smile that makes my insides settle down. The radiologist says she didn't see anything out of the ordinary, but she'll have someone send Dr. Minor and Dr. Witt the official results in a few days.

"Let's go home," Papa tells us, and I give him a look that reminds him of 31 Flavors. He picks me up and squeezes me tight and says, "Oh yes, Love, we need to fill you up with some ice cream."

All Makena and I talk about in the car is what flavor we want. She's craving rum raisin, and of course I'm thinking about my rocky road with lots of marshmallows. Papa laughs and shakes his head and says we haven't had ice cream 'til we've experienced mango madness, which was Lola Carmen's favorite.

He even buys a few quarts of mango madness for Mama and Tita Gwen, and back at home, we all sit around the dining table, enjoying our dessert and admiring Tita Gwen's wedding favors, the vanilla potpourri that made me sneeze this morning, but now they're in lacy boxes shaped like hearts.

When no one is looking, I let Frida lick my cone, but she decides to be sneaky and bite it so that it crunches super loud for everyone to hear. Usually Makena or Mama or Papa scold me for giving Frida people kinds of food, but all they do is laugh, even

Makena, who starts to talk about all of her breathe-ins and breathe-outs.

Papa keeps nodding, telling everyone he wasn't that nervous even though I know he was busy looking for cigarettes, and Tita Gwen and Mama listen with wide frog eyes, looking up at the ceiling and thanking God and eating their ice cream.

I thank God too for making Makena okay, but I also thank him for all the laughing and ask him if he can just keep things the way they are, right at this very moment, even though I did sneak more Swedish Fish from the kitchen pantry before bed last night.

Then I lick my ice cream too.

27. understanding ugly

Mr. Baluga is requesting that I don't include him in my Automatic Writing project because we all know how he feels about any kind of hullabaloo, which I sure found out the hard way after the time I fell off my skateboard and started to cry.

He doesn't ask people for many favors, but he wants me to watch over Lola Evie after he goes away. I know what he means by "go away," which is another way of saying it'll be his turn to take that ride, because of course Lola Evie can take care of herself when he heads to the barber shop or to Luigi's Deli.

I ask him what it feels like to know he doesn't have as many years left on earth as somebody younger like me, and he says it's different for old-timers. He's been around the block and boulevard a few more times than a lot of other people. He hasn't traveled the world, but he reads all about it in newspapers and books. He can also study a person's face and tell you if the person is decent or no good, just like that.

He says that Papa can do the same thing, which is one of the reasons why he likes him. "We always used to hang out and shoot the bull," Mr. Baluga says. Papa says Lola Evie despises him, and this is true because I overheard Lola Evie telling her other next-door neighbor Mrs. Hathaway that Papa makes her feel like a second-class citizen. Mr. Baluga says both he and Papa can't tolerate ignorance and mediocrity and that's why they get along, but we all know Papa can put up with more than everyone thinks.

Mr. Baluga showed me his will one day, and that's where it says, "Antonio Nicolas de la Viña Yen José is the sole administrator of the estate of Benigno Jerónimo Sebastián Baluga." Papa's been taking care of Mr. Baluga's properties in the Philippines for years now, and he's made Mr. Baluga and his family a pretty penny here and there, which means a heap of money. But Papa gets thanks from only Mr. Baluga and no one else, especially not from Lola Evie or her five evil nieces.

It's all very complicated, the kind that can put you in a tizzy, and I know about it only because I'm always at Mr. Baluga's house playing *pusoy dos* or helping him with chores.

Sometimes Papa doesn't want me to hear about all this estate stuff and the feud that will break out after Mr. Baluga goes away because of what happened with Mama's family, but Mr. Baluga says I need to remember that he and Papa were close. Xavy knows too and says he'll be a witness if the case ever goes to court.

I don't know what kind of case there could be, and I ask why does everyone have to bother with lawyers and judges, so that's when Papa reminds me that Mr. Baluga chose his neighbor instead of his own family to handle his money, so how do I think that would make them feel?

"Oh, I guess that would be the same thing if you asked Mr. Baluga instead of Makena or Xavy to handle your money," I say.

"Right on, Love," Papa answers, and he gives me a noogie. "You've got a smart head on your shoulders."

Papa never wanted to be a part of this mess. But Mr. Baluga insisted and didn't speak one word to Papa for two whole weeks when Papa refused. Then Papa gave in because he says he loves Mr. Baluga like a father. He always warns Mr. Baluga that he needs to sit down with his family and let them in on what's going on, but Mr. Baluga keeps saying, "It will happen when it happens."

My family's full of the kind of deep worry that's heavy and dragging and makes creases on foreheads. Isn't it enough that Makena is sick and we all have to take care of her? Mr. Baluga always talks about life dealing us straights instead of royal flushes, but now I'm beginning to think that sometimes life doesn't even give us straights. Some people get only pairs or no pairs at all and all kinds of lame cards that don't go together, and I think some of those people are us.

Papa comes home to a sick Makena and sometimes stays up late to do paperwork that he didn't finish during the day, then there's Mama who's mad at Papa for getting involved with Mr. Baluga's estate because the same exact thing happened to her family when Lolo Carlo died, and now Lola Zeny and Mama's sisters can't stand Papa and don't ever talk to Mama or any of us anymore. They hate Papa so much that they accused him of having a mistress, and someone from their family hired a mafia police officer to get rid of him. They even had their lawyer put something called a lien on a huge property that's close to where Lolo Carlo and his family grew up, which Papa says could have made all of them rich.

I'm not supposed to know about these wicked things, but Xavy blabbed everything to me one day when he woke me up and was drunk in his bedroom at 1:42 a.m. Xavy says not to worry about the mafia police or anyone else because Papa has all kinds of bodyguards when he visits the Philippines, so no one would dare mess with our old man.

That's four birthday presents and four Christmas presents we won't be getting every year, but Xavy says to forget about them because they give us cheap gifts anyway. Makena scolds us and says we shouldn't be sad about the presents but about the people who don't want us in their lives anymore.

Sometimes we see Lola Zeny or Mama's sisters at Costco or the movie theater, and Xavy reminds me to act like I don't know them, but it's hard because Lola Zeny's face always looks like a basset hound's, with her long and droopy cheeks.

Makena used to be close to Mama's sisters and even went to visit one of them in Panama when she was little. They don't know that Makena is sick, which is why no one has come over to visit, but they're not allowed in our house anyway. They don't even meet secretly because deep down in Makena's blood boils all kinds of fury for what they did to Papa.

But she wants to let go of this anger soon, she says, because it never does you any good and just makes people ugly, and now I'm starting to understand why we live in an ugly world.

28. forever feminist

There are times I live in an ugly world, like earlier tonight when Papa and Mama and Xavy and I were about to drive home from Arcadia AMF Bowling Square.

Makena was too tired to come, so Xavy decided to act like even more of a pest than usual, telling me how stinky my hair was and how come I don't like taking baths. When we got closer to Papa's Suburban, he gave me a wet willy, which is when you lick your finger and stick it in someone's ear, and he kept poking my sides when I wasn't ready to be poked.

I wasn't in the mood to play with Xavy, so I cried to Papa and Mama to tell him to stop it. Mama threw me her shush-be-quiet face and said, "You're going to have a bath tonight," words I hate hearing the most because I can't stand taking them so close to bedtime. When I do, Mama has to blow-dry my hair right before I brush my teeth and it takes a crazy long time to dry, all those layers and layers that want to stay stubborn wet.

"No, Mama, can't I take my bath in the morning," I whined, and I started to pull on the back of her shirt.

All of a sudden, Papa barked, "I don't wanna hear your voice again, you goddamn hippie," and of course that's when Xavy started to call me Weirdo and Geek Freak.

I even heard Mama mumble under her breath, "How did I end up with such opposite daughters," which made my ears turn red hot and my fists clench tight.

When I got into the backseat, I decided to slam my door as loud as I could, and I sure did close it hard because I heard something crack.

Papa yelled the F word and charged over to my side of the car and grabbed my arm and pulled me out of my seat. He checked the door, and some of the seat belt was hanging out. When he noticed the part that got scratched or maybe even bent,

I tried to run away, but he grabbed as many hairs as he could on my head and pulled me back to him, like a fisherman reeling in his catch.

Then he shoved my shoulder against the door and shouted, *"Akala mo kung sino ka"* which means "Who do you think you are," and then he squeezed my arm like he was trying to pop it and kicked both my shins, like he couldn't find anything else better to hurt.

Mama screamed, "Antonio, stop it!" but she wouldn't come near us. Xavy sat frozen in his seat the whole time, and I sure hoped he was feeling guilty. When I got back into the car, he was wearing sorry eyes, all watery and you didn't deserve that, but he didn't bother to get up to remind Papa that he was the one who started it and just shrank deeper into the corner of his seat.

Every time Mama started to sniffle, Papa would tell her to knock it off, and then he'd step harder on the gas pedal. I sat there massaging my arm and shoulder that were hurting so bad, and I kept feeling for the bruises on my shins that would probably be purple in the morning when I woke up. Even my head was throbbing in the spot where Papa pulled all those hairs.

"She's becoming a prima donna like her sister," Papa told Mama. But Mama never answered Papa. She sat there cowering in her seat too, kind of how she looks when she crouches on the kitchen floor, like a housemaid that scrubs and scours.

Papa harped on, "Living in Berkeley is turning Kena into a goddamn feminist, and Isabel will end up becoming one too. These women think they have voices? I'll tell them a thing or two about their voices in this society. They will never be heard, my friend."

That's when I could tell that Papa wasn't talking to Mama or anyone else anymore because whenever he calls someone "my friend," he's usually talking only to his business partners or Mr. Baluga.

I sat there pressing down on my shoulder as gently as I could, along with my arm and my head and my leg too, and whenever I had the chance, I gave Xavy the dirtiest looks, the kinds you don't turn your head for. Instead, you move the colored part of your eyes way into the corners so that you look like a scoundrel, but I remember it started to make me sort of dizzy and carsick, so I stopped.

I imagined Makena resting at home and still making Papa go crazy mad. I sure would have to warn her soon about hiding her pictures of RBG and Dolores Huerta, because fourth grade is learning about them, so I know that they're feminists too.

Makena once told me that Dolores Huerta got two broken ribs and a spleen that ruptured from a baton swung by a policeman during a protest about President George W. Bush without the H. She said that George W. was being insensitive to the struggles of the working people, and boy do I remember how fuming mad she was when she shared this *kuwento.*

But I hated being compared to Makena, and I didn't care if everyone thought she was a golden girl, all perfect and gorgeous and so much going for her until she caught a disease that only old men are supposed to get.

Papa finally stopped talking, and he kept driving like he owned that super fast car that Xavy says he fantasizes about called a Ferrari Enzo, zipping through all kinds of yellow lights and even some red ones. I was angry at Xavy and Mama for staying in their seats like they were pussycats stuck in a gutter, but all I did was worry about the bruises that would cover my arms and shins the next morning, even though they wouldn't be broken like poor Dolores Huerta's ribs.

I couldn't talk back to Papa because no one does. He's the man of the house, like Mafioso and don't ever mess with him man, or you'll be running scared your whole lifetime.

But I don't want to run scared my whole lifetime.

I don't want to stay far away from him, even when he smashes your racquet like a hammer on the face of your favorite watch.

I don't want to hide under a sink and chew fingernails and wish he forgot about me forever.

I'm a hippie and a geek freak, and I want to keep being one of your sidekicks, Papa. I'm sorry I was born a girl.

29. souls, spirits, and sleeping

Makena asks me to say a prayer with her every night before we go to sleep. It's called "Now I Lay Me Down," the same prayer that Papa and Tito Gus recited together on the day Tito Gus got rolled around in a barrel.

We kneel side by side at the foot of her bed, me on the left closer to the window and Makena on my right. Makena's prayer hands are a fistful of embracing fingers. Mine are kissing fingers, just like the way Sister Velma taught us in catechism.

Now I lay me down to sleep
I pray the Lord my soul to keep
If I should die before I wake
I pray the Lord my soul to take

I've never really asked questions about the words to this prayer. I just say them with Makena and go straight to bed. But I thought about them tonight for the first time, and if you ask me, they really suck. Mama hates it when I say "sucks" instead of "That stinks" or "That's messed up." Xavy likes to say "Ooh dat bites" and sometimes Makena blurts out "That reeks," but I'd rather say it all just sucks.

"Makena, why do we have to say this prayer when it talks about dying and taking?" I ask. I try not to tap her too hard on her shoulder.

"Because we need to make sure our spirits don't die when God says it's time for us to go to heaven."

Makena stands up right away and stretches her long arms out to the ceiling after she answers my question, so I know she doesn't want to talk about the prayer anymore. She follows me to my bedroom to make sure I get into bed. After she blows me a kiss from my door, I pull the covers up to my chin and shut my eyes.

I remember Papa's words about Makena's spirit, but the part I don't get is why there's all this dying and taking right before you go to bed, where you have the whole night to dream about it, and will I open my eyes or take a ride to heaven when I wake up in the morning? If someone could take out the dying part and change the taking part to giving, I would sleep way better.

I think about Makena's spirit and everyone else's spirits. Do spirits go to heaven before bodies? Aren't spirits already gone before they reach heaven?

it means the lord will take care of you whether you're on earth or in heaven but will he take my soul even if i'm a weak little queer?

Mama keeps telling me that the spirits of Lolo Martín and Lola Carmen and Lolo Carlo live in all of us. Tito Gus' does too even though he's still alive, and Papa knows this only because Jerome, who is one of Tito Gus' ex-boyfriends, is Papa's friend and still keeps in touch with Tito Gus through emails, so sometimes he calls Papa to tell him what Tito Gus wrote. Papa cackles when Jerome says, "*Ay* Gus, he makes me so *huhu*" or "That *puta*, he is still gayer than gay."

Tito Gus better stay alive and always be gayer than gay. Xavy says, "Tito Gus, oh mang, he done pumped da 'fun' into dysfunctional," and boy do I miss his Play-Doh nose and playful pinches on my thighs, even though they would burn. I just always pray for him, and I hope he never gets lost again.

lola carmen

lola carmen when you were sick you gave me a small golden ring with my initials which are I.J. and i was just four years old so now the ring fits only on my pinky and oh i still remember your thick and wavy and shiny hair always looking like it was doing ballet whenever it was windy outside and when it wasn't tied up into a bun that you called your poofy chignon. you once told me that papa grew out his hair when he was a rebel at de la salle college and his hair looked exactly like yours but of course it wasn't as shiny.

you liked wearing a green checkered duster that sort of looks like a muumuu which are those dresses that ladies in hawaii wear to be comfortable and to hide the fat folds on their tummies. you also had the most cushiony pink tsinelas *that you always let me try on and then you'd giggle because you would say that my feet looked like chocolate-covered cotton candy.*

there were soft and wiggly bumps on your eyelids and around your eyes which you explained to me were cholesterol deposits from eating too much litson *roast pig along with bowls of mango madness for dessert which is why mama's always telling me to cut down on those ice cream sandwiches.*

you went to heaven four years ago when you were only 66 which is old but not super old so you weren't here long enough to be a family with us because of something called coronary artery disease which means your arteries were too narrow and blocked with stuff called plaque but not the teeth kind and this was keeping the blood from pumping to your heart so you had to take the ride to heaven but i think you died because your heart was beautiful and big.

you always made us feel like there was no such thing as a bad mood and boy were you the majesty of giving especially when you would plant sweet kisses on my nose every time i got you a glass of lychee juice.

you even bought me a little book called of all my favorite things i like you best *which you read to me over and over before bedtime whenever you would babysit us and this always made my eyelids grow heavy and then you would remind me to never tell makena or xavy or any of the cousins about this book because they might turn envious.*

mama says the most generous giving you ever did was the way you got papa and all the titos *and* titas *to forgive each other when they were fighting. you would say to your family "apologizing doesn't always mean you admit you did wrong" because you wanted everyone to be friends all the time and you couldn't stand all the bickering and making enemies which made your big beautiful heart weepy like an empty house that was just like the one you were left with when all your children left for america.*

your heart wept when tita choleng tattled to everyone about tito carding using rogaine and that's why his hair got crazy thick and way too noticeable. your heart wept more when tito vito cheated on tita marion who had giant man hands but was always so kind to everyone and your heart wept again when tita marijo stole tita malou's cartier watch and blamed one of the cousins.

your heart went on weeping when papa wouldn't bail tito gus out of jail for his second DUI *which is what happens if the police catch you driving when you're drunk or when you do drugs that aren't legal and that's when tito gus was left there to get beat up by a gang right inside the holding cell even though he knows kajukenbo and boy lola carmen it sure took you a long time to forgive papa for that one. you made everyone say sorry even if they didn't mean it and you would ask everyone to think hard about what they did which would remind them that hell is filled with torment and not such a swell place to end up after you're done wreaking havoc here on earth.*

"asking for forgiveness makes you a bigger person" you would tell all of your grandchildren and then you'd make us pile on top of you like we were your baby farm animals and peck your cheeks like chickens and even arms and ears and on top of your poofy chignon too. if you knew about the feuds and all the pointing fingers i wonder if you'd feel waves of shame in your big beautiful heart and i wonder if you would forgive even if you didn't think you were wrong.

there's a quote about hearts by albert camus even though it's really by saint francis de sales and it's inside a frame hanging above makena's RBG *and dolores huerta pictures and claude monet painting of water lilies. "blessed are the hearts that can bend they shall never be broken" is what it says so now i wonder if hearts like yours are breakable in heaven and if shame just keeps riding the waves.*

30. hi hi hi

It's getting closer to 2003, so hurray, it's going to be a brand-new year. We didn't celebrate Thanksgiving because Makena had chemo on Thursday that week. I'm not sure why, and Mama doesn't think it was because Makena's white-blood count was low, which is what happened three weeks ago.

All I know is we had El Pollo Loco for Thanksgiving dinner, and that was fine with me because I enjoy making mini burritos full of Spanish rice and *pico de gallo* with the meat on my drumsticks.

Makena didn't wake up until 11:00 that night, so Mama sat with Makena as she nibbled at her dinner, just the two of them in the kitchen.

I was still awake because it was a Saturday night. I watched Mama open her mouth each time Makena took a bite of her Pollo Loco, like Lola Zeny says she used to do when she'd feed us when we were babies, willing the food into our mouths so that we'd end up well-nourished like her.

Sometimes I picture Lola Zeny here in our house, helping Mama take care of Makena. Would she know what to do and how to act, and would she know how to make Jell-O? And how would she understand and pronounce all those long words like gastroenterology and chemotherapy when she calls Burger King "Barjoor Keeng"?

Makena and I sit in the waiting room of Dr. Minor's office for her eighth session of chemo. I'm not sure why Makena calls them "sessions" because it doesn't feel anything like a class that's in session.

Dr. Minor usually comes into the room after Surfer Girl takes Makena's pulse and blood pressure and temperature, and he greets us with three hi's. Makena knows I always wait for Dr. Minor's hi's, and she keeps telling me that one of these days, he might say hi only once so don't be disappointed.

"Hi hi hi," says Dr. Minor all of a sudden as he whooshes through the door with his long white coat and brown and gray hair, poofy and round like a tumbleweed. Then he flips through his folder full of notes and tells Makena what her white-blood count is. He asks Makena what her side effects were this week, and they're usually the same ones, nausea and fatigue and vomiting and canker sores and diarrhea. There are days when she's lucky, when her nausea doesn't turn into vomit inside the toilet and the sores inside her mouth decide not to grow and multiply, but her fatigue and nausea and diarrhea never leave her alone.

Sometimes Makena asks Dr. Minor about her colon cancer and what her chances are for a full recovery. One time she asked about 5FU, the name of the chemo pumping into her veins, like how effective is it and how long has it been around.

Ms. Langevin always encourages us to ask questions, but I think Makena's can be like fresh fruit or the sweet butter tart bars that Mama makes for special occasions. They're healthy and fresh for you because you should know what's going on inside your body but bad like sugar because sometimes you know way too much, and that's when your brain feels like it's coiling up into a Slinky.

Dr. Minor tells her about the different stages of colon cancer. The highest is four, which means the cancer has spread to a major organ. I remember Makena is at stage three, and the doctors found four lymph nodes with cancer in them, so there's a good or even great chance that they didn't spread to the other ones in her body.

This is when I finally find out that lymph nodes are what help get rid of bacteria and other strange things that aren't supposed to be in your system, but the doctors don't know for sure that the cancer spread to the others because you have thousands of them inside your body, all the way from your head to your toes, and that's the reason why Makena needs chemo for a whole year.

I think I'm becoming an expert at all this cancer and chemo stuff. Sometimes Tita Gwen asks me questions when she doesn't feel like asking the grown-ups, and when I explain to her everything I've learned, like lymph nodes and CT-scans and white-blood counts, she touches my face like it's breakable or something and tilts her head at me, and then she asks if I'm doing okay inside.

I feel that I'm giving her my confused face even though I know what she's talking about, but I can't help it because Tita Gwen usually doesn't fire away with deep kinds of questions. She just asks me if I'm hungry and how school is and if I have a lot of friends, while she draws and colors pictures with me or pretends to be Sarita, who is still my favorite Groovy Girl and who she always dresses in Juicy Jammies or the Ritzy Raincoat because their brighter and shinier colors match Sarita's chocolatey brown skin, which is just a bit darker than mine.

After Makena is finished with her questions, Dr. Minor makes her lie down, which means it's time for me to eat more strawberry candies. This is the part I'm not supposed to see because Dr. Minor has to check Makena's breathing and press down on different parts of her body, even her private areas to make sure there are no lumps.

After I grab a handful of candies but not too many because the old people in the waiting room are watching me, I go back to the La-Z-boy room, where Dr. Minor and Makena are talking about dogs and graduate school and stuff about our family and his own family. Dr. Minor is way cool and I like his three hi's, and I'm glad he's taking care of Makena's cancer.

When I ask Dr. Minor why he doesn't give Makena the chemo himself, he laughs and says it's because Dana is his boss. Doctors make more money than nurses so shouldn't they be in charge, I wonder, but that's when I remember Papa saying nurses get paid crap for what they do and get no respect, even though they're the ones stuck doing the caregiving. He also says, "But doctors deserve to make all that dough, because after all that goddamn schooling, they have loans up the ying-yang and have to wait too long to become rich."

Makena keeps telling me not to listen to Papa and reminds me that doctors and nurses save lots of lives every day, but of course there are some who just do it for the money and even get themselves tangled up in all sorts of malpractice suits, which means people sue them because they didn't do their job the right way and made innocent patients lose their lives. But Makena tells me not to worry because Dr. Minor and Surfer Girl and everyone else here are dedicated to what they do and care for their patients like their own kin.

Papa once saved someone's life in the Army while he was going through some grenade drills. He remembers the guy he dragged away from the exploding grenade sobbed like a baby and kept telling him he was his brother for life and that he would repay Papa one of these days.

Cathy, our family friend who's a nurse practitioner, which I think is sort of in between a nurse and a doctor, once saved one of her patient's lives by giving her a test to see if your baby is growing in the wrong part of your body, and it turned out the patient's doctor didn't even think of that. And of course this woman really did have a baby called ectopic growing in the wrong part, and that would have cost two lives instead of one, according to Cathy.

Even Xavy got to save a life when we were swimming at the pool and recreation center at Arcadia Park two summers ago. A boy I know who was going into first grade too fell into the eight-feet part, and he didn't come back up for a long time while everyone just stared in shock and all of a sudden seemed to be paralyzed, so Xavy dove in and pulled him from the bottom of the pool.

All kinds of parents were clapping, and one man even woohooed for Xavy when the boy started to cough up water and finally was able to sit up straight. Of course Xavy likes bringing up this *kuwento* about the pool, the only time in his life he ever felt important, he says, like he mattered to someone other than our family.

In Ms. Langevin's class, we're learning different ways of saving lives every day, like donating food and used clothing to the homeless or visiting lonely and sick people in nursing homes or giving blood, but that's something you do only when you're a grown-up who weighs at least 110 pounds, which could mean that Xavy can donate twice as much blood as other people can.

You really don't have to be a doctor or a nurse to save a life, but I want to be just like Dr. Minor and Surfer Girl. I would like to wear a stethoscope and be able to listen to heartbeats and breathing and know when something isn't right inside a person's body. I would also like to ask my patients how they are and learn stuff about their families and what they usually do for fun.

I want to take care of a life that is ending and a life that hasn't started to become one yet, even if I don't become a doctor or a nurse. One day, maybe I'll say "Hi hi hi" when I walk through the door to my patients so that they will crack smiles and their bodies will start to recognize and like this feeling, and then they'll want to hang out in the world a little longer.

31. the stormy scarecrow

I keep remembering the day when Makena and Papa and I got home from Makena's tennis match after Papa smashed Makena's watch, like when you rewind a movie to a part where you couldn't understand what the actors were saying or sometimes because you couldn't believe what happened and you want to make sure it really did.

When I rewind this day in my head, I realize that sometimes *tsismis* can be much better than *kuwento*. People usually forget about gossip, but stories stick to you like a bear's claws on honey.

Makena was about to go upstairs to her room, but Papa made her face our front door and stand there without making one move and told her she couldn't talk until he said she could.

He took her by her shoulders and positioned her under the hanging ceiling lamp, like he was planning for it to fall right on top of her head. Makena stood still as a painting for almost two hours, and I know this because when Papa was in his second office or somewhere he couldn't see me, I would sneak out to the hallway to see if Makena was still there and to check the cuckoo clock above the piano.

Makena's arms looked like tree branches glued to the sides of her body, and her hands seemed to just dangle right next to her thighs. You could tell a tennis ball was in her right pocket because it bulged out next to her wrist like it was getting in the way of how she was standing, like a soldier in training.

The blades of her shoulders looked bonier than usual, poking out the back of her T-shirt like wings. Her eyes were closed, and I wondered if she could see spots, just like when I squeeze my eyes shut and all of a sudden you see brown with all kinds of purple specks floating in the background, which I guess is what the inside of your eyelids look like.

I also wondered if she was imagining the bamboo stick and the leather belt that Papa was going to use on her if she moved or talked. Papa told her to be prepared to get either one, and I knew he wasn't kidding because one time when Xavy told Papa to go screw himself even though it was sort of under his breath, Papa whipped out his belt, and Xavy's leg sure did turn hot pink, which looked weird because his skin is the color of a light brown olive.

Papa hasn't used the stick or the belt on me or Makena yet, only Xavy, who doesn't think it's fair just because he's a boy and brags that he can take the pain better than Makena and I can, but boy is he wrong. Makena has gone through way more hurting with her surgery and now with her chemo, and the cousins keep saying that Scrappy-Doo is such a perfect nickname for me because he's all tough nails and always screams "Puppy Power," like nothing could ever make him weak.

Xavy always tells me it doesn't sting that much when Papa hits him, it's temporary and the bruises heal and disappear and you forget about them, but we know Xavy's all talk because Makena says he used to cry like a toddler inside his bedroom after his beatings from Papa.

When I tiptoed to the hallway for the third time to check on Makena, I remember she had moved. She didn't budge from under the ceiling lamp, but she turned her head to the right to look into the mirror hanging on the wall near the coat rack. I made soft steps down the stairs so that I could see the whole mirror, and when I looked closely, I thought I saw Papa's face.

Those cheeks that were starting to sag, like the ones on all the other Josés with high cheekbones.

The three crinkles near the corners of each of his gray tiger eyes.

Makena once told me all about Papa calling her a tiger for the first time. It was after she tried out for her high school varsity tennis team when she was only a freshman. Papa ran into our house calling for Mama and bragged about Makena beating the number one singles player on the team whose name was Mike Sewell, and when Mama asked why the number one girl had a boy's name, Papa took Makena by her shoulders and twirled her around and said she beat the number one singles player on the boys' varsity team.

"The *boys'* team," he kept repeating, then he turned to Makena and said she was his tiger and gave her a big kiss on her forehead.

Makena told me she smiled herself to sleep that night, whispering "I'm Papa's tiger" to the little pink bear lying beside her pillow.

Makena kept staring into the mirror, and I wondered if she saw Papa there too. I remembered her face looking old and tired but only 17 years old. It looked like the kind you see on scarecrows, all worn out and rumpled, just like the dried prunes that Lolo Carlo used to snack on while he read the newspaper.

Makena wrote about this experience in one of her sociology classes at Cal, and her paper was a whole 22 pages long. Her professor thought it was "riveting" and gave her an A+, not just a regular A. I guess she forgot about the part where she wrote about Papa smashing her watch because after she showed her paper to him, all proud of her A+, boy do I remember Papa's face turning sour when he got to the part about him.

"*This* makes me *sick* to my stomach," he said, and he started flicking the page, almost making a hole right through it. You could tell that Makena wanted to grab the paper from him, but she just stood there and frowned. Then Papa told Makena he thought it was funny, the parts of her life she remembered.

That's when Makena grabbed my hand and pulled me up the stairs with her, and while I was tripping over my feet from having to skip so many steps at one time, she mumbled under her breath, "Yeah, especially the part where you smash and run over my spirit, you fucking asshole."

Papa's been called horrible filthy curse words many times by drivers on the road or sometimes even his subs when they think he isn't close by, but to hear this come from Makena my *áte* made the world feel like a foreign place, sort of like the bizarro world that Xavy says Jerry Seinfeld talked about on his TV show one time when he made *kuwento* about Superman.

The bizarro world is a place where everything's opposite and not quite right, like alarm clocks telling you when to go to sleep and where ugly is beautiful, but it seemed like Makena was being more than opposite, like there was someone else living inside her and squirming to get out.

After Makena stood still before our front door for almost two hours, Papa walked over to her, but he didn't have the stick or the belt. He told her to go to her room and stay there until dinner.

I was happy because Makena wouldn't get a smacking or a whipping, but when I look closely at her face now, like those doctors called dermatologists do when they check your moles and zits, I keep seeing the same scarecrow. It doesn't look too much like a dried prune, but I feel that it stayed outside for too long, holding tight through too many storms.

32. *vergon* in a volvo

Makena had chemo four days ago, so it's a splendid day, like Mr. Baluga says when he gets three numbers on the Lotto and thinks he's closer to winning it.

It's December 3, 2002.

Christmas is in a few weeks.

We haven't had any rain for a while, which means a dry backyard for Frida to run around in and that her paws don't need to be wiped before coming into the house, even her toenails all coated with dirt. Which also means Papa won't have a cow about the mess she made on our family room couch, even though Mama tucks small blankets into the cushions so that Frida has a comfortable spot to rest and make smelly all she wants.

It sure is a splendid day.

Friday nights are fun because this is the time of week that's farthest from when Makena is sleepy and nauseated and throwing up and crabby, which goes on for almost four or sometimes five whole days. So at least Makena's in an okay kind of sort of cheerful mood for two or three whole days of the week, which is better than no days at all.

Fridays are the perfect time for making *kuwento* because everyone is relaxed. Sometimes Papa has to check in at his job sites on Saturdays, but he doesn't have to be there as early as Arturo and his other subs, so he gets to sleep in and ask Mama to brew him coffee and heat up some *ensaymada* the sweet pastry bread while he reads the newspaper in bed.

That's when Xavy gets Frida all riled up and asks her, "Where's Papa, where's Papa," and she hurries over to Mama and Papa's bedroom and jumps on the bed like it's a trampoline, and then right onto Papa and licks him all over his face. Papa keeps saying he can't stand Frida's slobber but lets her kiss him anyway.

Xavy and Makena and I follow and start laughing when we see Frida attacking Papa. We all lie on different parts of the bed and talk about picking up pastrami sandwiches from The Hat or Spike's Teriyaki Burgers for lunch or if Makena is feeling strong enough for a long car ride to Third Street Promenade, which is an outdoor mall in Santa Monica with a wide walkway for people to take their dogs and shop and eat and enjoy the beach weather.

Sometimes on Friday nights, we talk about which movies we want to rent, but tonight Xavy wants to make *kuwento* about the time Tito Gus got hellza pissed off, which I'm not allowed to say because the word "piss" sounds vulgar, according to Mama.

Makena presses her lips together into a scowl, which means the story has gossip and drama too, and now I feel myself getting shaky excited, even though I probably shouldn't be.

The *kuwento* starts with Tito Gus turning super huffy and hissy at Makena for writing "Gusdagard Vergon" on the envelope of the graduation announcement she gave him. *Vergon* is vulgar too, but Papa keeps saying that there's an actor named Randy Vergon in the Philippines.

This happened after Lolo Martín took the ride. Makena was graduating from Arcadia High School, and Xavy was turning 14 the same week, so both of them had all kinds of invitations to write and send to our family and friends. Tito Gus was coming over for dinner on the day that Makena and Xavy were finished with their invitations.

Makena says that while she sorted through her shoebox of announcements for Tito Gus' envelope, she heard the doorbell ring. She remembers feeling her heart flutter because she couldn't wait to see the look on Tito Gus' face when he read the name on the envelope. She was betting that everyone would think it was hilarious.

We all loved the way Tito Gus greeted us every time he came over to the house. "Where are my favorite *pamangkins*, my enchanting nieces and handsome nephew?!" Tito Gus would cry out, flaring his nostrils and sniffing the air.

Xavy remembers checking out Tito Gus from the top of the stairs, snickering at his turquoise blue silk blouse and baggy black trousers and his hair gelled straight and sleek, lying like black satin against his head. After Tito Gus was done sniffing, he would yell, "I am going to inhale the three of you if you do not come here and give your Tito Gus a smoochy!"

Xavy answered, "Yeah, yeah, we're coming, *Tita*," in his high-pitched girl voice, waving a freshly printed invitation in the air. Makena remembers cringing and scolding Xavy for his mocking and his homophobic remark, which means you're treating gay people with no consideration like they're a piece of shet, and I'm not supposed to say this either but can't stop doing it because it's starting to become a joke in the house, even though it isn't nice that we're making fun of Mama when we do it.

Xavy says I was following him close behind and trying to make my way past him down the stairs, but he kept blocking me with his arms and tickling me every time I tried to squeeze through. I was only five years old, and I remember how annoying Xavy was, making me squeal to Makena every time he poked my sides.

Makena didn't bother scolding Xavy that time because she knew the second that I got to the bottom of the stairs and clung on to Tito Gus' legs, I'd be a happy camper. And I sure was, because Tito Gus would let me hang on for a long time. Not like the other *titos*, who always shoo me away and tell me not to mess up their pants, or they won't even let me hug their legs in the first place because it usually makes them lose their balance.

Tito Gus raised his right eyebrow at Xavy because of Xavy's *Tita* remark, but his face changed in a hurry when Xavy handed him the invitation.

"Gusberto Ramón de la Viña Yen José," Tito Gus read. "*Ay* Xavy, my sweets, it is even printed in calligraphy." He placed his hand over his chest and cooed over his name, written perfectly across the envelope of his invitation.

Makena tells us that a girl who had a crush on Xavy at the time handwrote every single one of his invitations in calligraphy for him, which Mama always gives him a hard time about because Xavy used to tell her to please use Dry Idea Extra Strength and that she should consider waxing her mustache.

Makena handed Tito Gus her announcement and remembers rubbing her hands together in delight, like she was presenting Tito Gus a trophy.

"Ano 'to?!" Tito Gus demanded, pointing at the name on the envelope. He asked "What is this" all snippety in Tagalog, which he spoke only when he was mad or annoyed or both.

Makena asked Tito Gus if he thought it was funny, even though she knew right away by the way he was staring at the envelope, all confused and crinkly eyebrowed, that it wasn't. She remembers praying hard that a smile would start forming on his face, like any hint of something pleasant please.

"Who is Gusdagard Vergon? Did my asshole brother put you up to this?"

Xavy says he had to think for a second about which asshole brother, which of course made all of us snort. Makena joined in on the cackles too, but when Xavy went on about Makena admitting it was her idea and that she was being homophobic too, trying to explain to Tito Gus that Papa calls him *Vergon* all the time, she stopped laughing.

"Do you have any inkling as to what *vergon* means," Tito Gus asked.

Right when Makena asked if "Somebody Vergon" was an actor in the Philippines, Papa came out of his office with the phone pressed between his ear and his shoulder. Xavy remembers Papa flipping through a file folder full of documents, looking all busy and innocent.

"Who do you think you are, teaching your children a word like *vergon?!"* Tito Gus accused Papa.

Makena says that all Papa did was make a low hmmph sound and walk back into his office. Xavy remembers the hmmph too, the worst kind, the kind that says who the hell cares, why don't you take a pill.

"I know you put her up to this, you fucking piece of shet," Tito Gus snarled like a cat at the doorway of Papa's office.

Papa tells us that he really didn't know what was happening at the time, and if he had, he might have tried to kick Tito Gus' ass, and boy things sure would have turned much uglier because Xavy says that Papa has only a second-degree black belt in Karate.

But Makena says that nothing was uglier than Tito Gus shaking his head at her and glaring, his nostrils flaring wider than usual. Then he turned away and walked out of our house, down the stairway and into his black Volvo. His car looked like a hearse, with its tinted windows and all. It might as well have been a funeral car, Makena says, the way his glare bore a hole right through her.

Before Makena went to bed that night, she asked Papa what *vergon* meant, even though I think she already knew the answer. He insisted that Randy Vergon was a movie star, but Mama covered her face with both her hands while Papa kept repeating Randy Vergon's name.

Before Makena climbed into bed that night, she glanced over at her desk and saw some scribbling on a Post-it note. She picked it up and noticed Xavy's handwriting.

Vergon *means pussy and not like in pussycat, you invidious piece o' shet. (Ya diggin' my SAT word, beeatch?) It's dat udder kind, know wut I'm sayin'? Da one dat Tito Gus wishes he had.*

33. flawlessly foxy

Mama brought out some old photo boxes and books this morning to dust and organize, so Makena and I decide to look through them. Makena's eyelids are close to shutting even though she just got up from a nap, but all of a sudden while we're flipping through her college albums, she sees a picture of her and Ryan Jeremy in front of Lefty's the Left Hand Store at Fisherman's Wharf.

Ryan and Makena together look like dark and white chocolate, roast beef on white. Or vanilla and chocolate swirl, the kind you can get at Souplantation or Fresh Choice in the dessert section.

Ryan's skin is dark and smooth, with hardly any hairs growing out of it at all, but Papa thinks Ryan shaved his entire body because he's a swimmer and he plays water polo for Cal. Makena says it isn't true, he was born like that, and so many of her friends who always have to shave their legs and wax their arms and faces resent it, which Makena says is like being envious but also feeling that things aren't fair.

Ryan's eyes are light brown just like Makena's, only they're more golden, sort of like honey. "Honey Eyes," Mama used to call him, and sometimes Makena would be envious or maybe even resented Ryan because she thought she had the most golden eyes of them all.

Makena says when she's 30 years old, she'll find someone like Ryan or even Ryan himself and marry him. When I ask her where Ryan is now, she says he turned out to be like all college guys, wanting to go out with different girls.

"Oh, that was like Papa when he was younger," I say, and then we laugh and shake our heads together and say, "Men are just like colds, easy to catch and impossible to cure," which is what Tito Gus used to tell us all the time.

Makena says that Ryan was a rare gem of a human being. Their relationship was sometimes more like a sister and brother type, but when I ask if Ryan was like Xavy, Makena laughs and says, "Are you kidding me, not even close!" She means that Ryan could kid around and talk about anything and never had to pretend, just like he was part of the family.

Makena says that Papa met Ryan when Papa was in San Francisco on a business trip. They all had dinner together at Thanh Long, Papa's favorite crab restaurant. Makena thought Papa would be rough on Ryan like he was with all the other guys she dated, but Papa liked Ryan the moment he shook his hand. He even poked fun at Ryan's voice, which sounds like Mama's cousin Tito George's, scratchy and sour like juice being squeezed from his lemon throat.

Ryan laughed with Papa when he made fun of him, cracking his crab shells and even licking the butter and garlic off his fingers right in front of Papa. Ryan never became *pikon*, which means you can't take a joke, and that's what Makena is well-known for, "especially when she be actin' all uptight like a *princesa*," Xavy says.

I ask Makena what it's like to have a boyfriend, and she says if you find the right one, you feel like you're floating around the clock. "The dreamy ones let you know you're special," she goes on, "but not through flowers or chocolate or material items like that."

Ryan always liked pointing out that even though Makena wanted to work with animals and that her stronger subjects were math and science, she was such a wordsmith and a fan of alliteration, which means the same letter or sound repeats at the beginning of words that are close by or connected.

Ryan would tell Makena she was a "foxy, flawless fireball," and her heart would turn all gooey when she heard that kind of stuff. Ryan also said that Makena's drive and persistence would take her sky-high, which we all already know because she's a golden girl.

Makena says she and Ryan used to go to cheap movies called matinees and camp out together to try getting into impacted bio classes, which means too many students wanted to take bio and there wasn't enough space. They'd eat second-rate Chinese food at China King on Sundays because there was a discount between 2:00 and 4:00, and they'd act like tourists and go to that song booth at Pier 39 where you can record a song like a professional singer, and the workers laughed and covered their ears when Ryan tried to stay on pitch and even in rhythm with "Smells Like Nirvana" by Weird Al, which Makena said was fascinatingly queer because Ryan plays the tenor saxophone and bass guitar and is also a DJ, one that can stack sounds and beatmatch like nobody's business.

They'd scarf down hot fudge sundaes at Ghirardelli Square and ride a cable car to downtown and find their way to Japan Town and go bowling at Kabuki. Then they'd rent scooters and ride up to Strawberry Canyon in Berkeley Hills, lay out a picnic blanket, read parts of Walden and Camus novels together, and watch the sunset.

"We did so many things, but it wasn't all the gallivanting that made it fun. It was Ryan's energy and ambition," Makena says. "He didn't want to be a doctor, which his parents were almost forcing him to be. I admired that."

When I asked why, Makena told me that most people do what their parents tell them to because it's practical and it'll make you well-off, which means rich. When Ryan announced to his parents that he wanted to be an animal behaviorist and dog trainer just like Makena, I pictured his father, who Makena says is a cardiologist which is a heart doctor, grabbing his chest all dramatic, like he was going to have a heart attack that he couldn't save himself from. Ryan knew that Makena was going to take the veterinarian route because of Papa, which was one of the things they used to fight about.

One time, Ryan told Makena she was a coward, but Makena always found a way to change the subject, like talking about kitchen gadgets and even different types of soil because he enjoys cooking Italian food and growing vegetables in a garden with his mother.

The last time Makena and Ryan saw each other, Ryan decided he didn't want to be tied down to just one girl, so

Makena's promises to be braver couldn't keep them together anymore.

Makena and Ryan always talked about starting a business. They wanted to open up a dog resort called Lazybones, where there would be wide-open grass areas and trails and training classes and day care and pampering, and even snack bars for both dogs and people.

Makena goes on and on about Ryan, remembering his nerdy but cute smile with his two sharp teeth called cuspids in the front, and also his hefty upper body and thick calves, just like mine but with all kinds of man muscle. She appreciated the way he dressed, always in long khaki shorts, a T-shirt, and a hoodie, so comfy and natural like his personality.

"And those golden eyes of his sparkled, just like his mind," Makena adds with a sigh.

Makena was a happier person with Ryan, Xavy used to tell me, and now I believe him because while I listen to my *áte* talk about all the things she and Ryan used to do, she doesn't sound like the Makena we know, always locked inside her bedroom listening to music that we think sounds old-ladylike, or practicing piano or at the club hitting hundreds of tennis balls against anybody who will rally with her.

She talks like her mouth is a paintbrush, creating a picture of dark chocolate and white chocolate combining into a swirl. The Makena I see in this picture looks like Frida when I unhook her leash, her hind legs out of control from running so hard and so fast.

"Where do I go now," Frida seems to ask, turning her head this way and that. She moves in circles and long lines after anything that will let her chase it, even after nothing because she lives for noisy and peppy running.

let's run to the sky together makena let's be chocolate and vanilla swirl and go up up up and away sky-high.

lolo martín

lolo martín you were six-foot-one just like papa and we always looked up to you never at you just like people do with papa. you never lost a case when you argued in court and mama says if you think papa speaks king's english then you spoke the one better than that with your tongue so silver and polished.

papa says when you danced at the debutante balls with lola carmen all eyes were on you especially during the tango where you'd make lola carmen look like a twirling goddess while showing off your fancy kicks and making the other women oohing and aahing and saying "who needs a rose between your teeth when you already have passion?" you were filled with so much passion that you wanted eleven children with lola carmen papa says and boy that sure is a lot of passion but that makes sense because all the titos *and* titas *say that your love for your family was like the devil.*

papa says that honoré de balzac one of your favorite writers said it best which was "whom it has in its clutches it surrounds in flames" and this characterizes the spaniards papa goes on because they have a lot of passion in their personalities and music and the way they live. lolo martín sometimes you would tell me and the rest of your nietos *"if you don't have passion you're just a piece of white bread among all the sourdoughs and marble ryes and* pan de leche *rolls" and we would all scrunch up our faces and turn to each other and ask "but what about* pan de sal*?"*

Lolo Martín was like Mafioso too, and he was even scarier than Papa when he turned red hot mad. Lola Carmen told us he'd throw things and ruin furniture, and I still remember his voice like a big kind of thunder. One time, all the cousins hid from him under the bed when he stomped around the house like a giant, asking who spilled coffee all over his *Newsweek* magazines.

Whenever we talk about Lolo Martín, everyone remembers the barrel story. Tito Sal says he learned the true meaning of *bakla* that day, and when Makena asked him what he meant, he said he knew he wouldn't let his sons become *bakla* because you could never have a life like everyone else, always on trial for who you are and never for something bad you did.

Usually when Makena asks one of the *titos* what he means when he says something confusing or wrong, she expects to feel irked which she says means annoyed, but that time, Makena just kept nodding her head.

Tito Gus was even younger than me when he acted like a girl wearing brown pantyhose, and boy Papa sure had a cow when he spotted him in high heels because he knew Lolo Martín would be home any minute to notice them. Tito Gus' feet are sort of chunky and wide, so I'll bet Tita Choleng wasn't too happy with him when she got her shoes back.

Papa felt sorry for Tito Gus, but he had to listen to Lolo Martín or else choose the belt or the bamboo pole. The worst thing Lolo Martín ever made Papa do was walk on his knees all over the neighborhood with three thick books stacked on the palms of both his hands. Papa remembers his knees all bloody and his arms and shoulders feeling like cement for a whole week.

Tito Dante always laughs about the part where Tito Gus is rolling around inside the barrel with the stinky fish, but Papa starts to make tsk-tsk-tsk sounds every time he realizes that Tito Gus could have suffocated in there. One of Papa's other brothers, who was born in between Tito Dante and Tito Gus, took the ride while Papa was carrying him to the hospital when he was only three because he had meningitis, so Papa sure didn't want to have two baby brothers die on his watch.

Then Tito Vito tells everyone how Papa shook like a girl, but Papa cuts into his teasing like a hacksaw and snaps, "I wasn't afraid, you fucking dwarf, I just felt bad for the poor bastard."

Xavy always says to me, "Dude, I'd be scared shitless if Papa made me roll your dumb ass around in a barrel all over town."

I love the part where Tito Gus shows off his thick legs and matching chubby feet on a pair of skinny high heels because one of the *titos* always gets up and copies the way Tito Gus pranced, wiggling his butt and posing like a cha-cha dancer.

Sometimes Papa tells us how rotten-smelling the fish was when he gave Tito Gus a bath, how Tito Gus would squeal like a mouse when Papa was drying his body because it was covered with wounds.

How none of his brothers bothered to help him, not even his sisters, who cried and sniffled inside their bedrooms all night long.

I hear the barrel story again and again, connecting different dots inside my body each time because sometimes it's either funny or sad or both, depending on who the storyteller is. All the *titos* make it sound like it was a riot, but when Lola Carmen used to share her *kuwentos* about it, the higher parts of her cheeks would crease as she went through every little detail, like the vase of *sampaguitas* and her animal figurines cracked into pieces that were scattered like the colored sprinkles of a cupcake all over the floor, her back growing sore from bending over with the dustpan to make sure her children didn't step on sharp glass and ceramic when they played inside the house.

It was like Lolo Martín got a chisel and carved the scene into her memory. Makena thinks it's sad that even his own wife feared his wrath, but Mama's the same way, so maybe that's the way women are supposed to be.

When Papa feels like telling the barrel story, sometimes he tries to make it sound like a comedy, but you can tell his laughs and snorts are a façade, which is another word that Xavy learned for the SAT. Sometimes I can't tell if what's under his façade is sad or mad or sorry because Papa almost turned out to be just like Lolo Martín, smart and scary and passionate and mean to you for being a weak little kind of anything.

34. smiling sweet swishing sounds

It's nine days until Christmas, and we just got back from Makena's twelfth time at chemo. Makena's dashing straight to her bedroom to scream into the mirror about how hideous she is, pounding on her bed and making its springs twang hard, her cries drowned out by pillows and sweatshirts and whatever else she can bury her face in.

I want to stop the pounding and crying, but Papa tells me to stay away and just let her be. I sit with Mama and Frida in front of the TV, and I stroke Frida's floppy ears that feel like the black velvet jacket Mama hardly wears.

My insides are twisting and turning, and I can't sit in one place without squirming like an eel, so I go to my room and find the toy phone that Mama and Papa gave me for my fifth birthday. I press all kinds of numbers, as many as I can think of, 1-323-722-5744 Andi and Neranti, 288-2638 Lola Zeny, 573-3749 Mr. Baluga. The phone is smiling sweet, almost like it's proud, and it has a red nose and the bluest eyes, the kind of blue that smiles when the mouth does, all soothing and reminding me of the swishing sounds of the ocean.

When Makena screams that she doesn't want to be alive anymore, I keep pressing numbers on my smiling phone and hope God or someone with a kind heart will call back and tell my *áte* that living is really a remarkable thing you can do.

35. disco dreams

It's easy to remind Makena that living is remarkable when Xavy and I ask her to play *pusoy dos* with us, because it's like making *pasyal* inside the house.

Makena and Xavy both knew how to play the game long before Mr. Baluga taught me. Makena used to play at the dorms at Cal, and Xavy's gangster friends sometimes come over after school and bet two dollars a game while they snack on Sour Cream 'n' Onion Lay's and Nacho Cheese Corn Nuts and gulp down grape sodas and Mexi-Cokes.

Mama always tells Xavy that he eats too much junk food and should go on a diet, but she can't stop him because Xavy hates to be told and believes he just has baby fat and it'll melt away when he's older, and that's when Papa gives us his hardy-har-har laugh and says, "I've never seen baby fat on a goddamn sumo wrestler before."

When I first asked Makena and Xavy if I could play *pusoy dos* with them, Xavy gave Makena this look that said, "Yeah right," but Makena told him I'm quite the card shark now, especially since Mr. Baluga took me under his wing.

Xavy deals the cards while Makena gets up from the table to grab a can of vanilla Ensure from the fridge. Makena let me have a sip of Ensure yesterday, and boy it's pretty tasty, sort of like that vanilla crème drink Mama orders at Starbucks, which is surprising because it's supposed to have all these vitamins and nutrients.

Makena has eight big canker sores and a bunch of little ones, so it's still hard for her to eat solid foods. Last week she had 15 sores, and one of them was the same size as a dime. Makena says it stings worse than blisters that pop open on her toes when her feet sweat too much inside her shoes. Dr. Minor gave her some mouthwash that's pink like Pepto Bismol, and this helped her get rid of four more sores in just a few days.

"You first, Eezuh," Xavy says, and he's still giving Makena that "yeah right" look as if I'm too young and lame to play with them. Makena's rolling her eyes because she knows Xavy's in the mood to talk ghetto. She always complains that "his gangster lingo sounds desperately poser," which means phony, but I don't think she has enough energy to fight with him right now.

Xavy looks like a monkey, scratching his head and shoving his tongue under his upper lip. That's what he always does when he's concentrating hard. He even looks like he's studying his cards, which doesn't seem right because Xavy hardly does his homework.

I fan out my cards with both my hands, which I'm getting much better at, and my heart goes ba-boom when I see the two of diamonds, but I make sure I don't look excited so that I can fool Xavy and Makena into thinking my cards stink. Makena says the two of diamonds controls the whole game if you know how to use it right, and Mr. Baluga always reminds me that it's important to have a crafty poker face, even in life.

He made me practice my poker face the other day, and the best one he taught me is the one where I look serious and shake my head in slow motion and say "darn" softly but loud enough so that the other players can hear.

I throw down a straight, two three four five six, and Xavy laughs and beats it with a full house, three sevens and two tens. Makena has to pass, so now it's my turn to see if I can beat it. I have three eights, but I don't have a pair to make it a full house.

"Isa, would you mind getting me another can of Ensure," Makena asks while she hurries to the bathroom. There's a crease running across her face from one of the pillows on the couch where she took a nap. She looks super run-down, like time is beating up on her little body. I'm sure she feels this way because she couldn't sleep until 4:00 this morning. She naps long during the day, but Surfer Girl tells me that Makena needs consistent sleep at night. Some patients have insomnia, Dr. Minor says, which means you don't have the ability to get enough sleep.

When Makena gets back from the bathroom, her face looks like it's covered with a thin sheet of Elmer's glue, all splotchy and pale. I ask her if she had a bad time on the toilet, and Xavy says, "Ya diggin' on catchin' sum z's? How 'bout jus' a disco nap fur sum disco dreamin'?"

"I didn't go and I don't feel like sleeping," says Makena, and she sure looks and sounds irked. She throws down a pair of queens to beat Xavy's pair of jacks. When I show them my pair of aces, Xavy nods his head and twists his lips and says, "Datz wassup, Eesabel" in his thickest Tagalog accent. He tries to poke my sides, but my hands are too fast for him this time, ready to karate-chop and block.

"Do you guys ever have recurring dreams?" Makena all of a sudden asks me and Xavy, and I'm trying not to look at her pasty face. When I ask Makena what "recurring" means, she says it's when something happens over and over again.

Xavy tells us that he always dreams about being chased by someone. One time, he flew down a whole flight of stairs while he was running. "It'd be dis cool-ass kinda dream if dare wuzn't sum dude on ma tail," he adds.

Makena turns to me, and I say the only recurring dream I can think of is my school dream, but it's more like a nightmare. In this dream, I don't finish school because I haven't been going to class and doing my homework.

Makena gives me wide frog eyes when I tell her about my dream. She says she's had a similar dream for five days straight, and now it's consuming her. She used to get it only once or twice a year, ever since she was in middle school.

"Tell me more about this dream, Isa," Makena says. I notice she's pulling the sleeves of her sweatshirt over her hands, which are always cold and dewy. Even Xavy has wide frog eyes too, and that looks strange because it's hard to get Xavy's attention.

"All I remember is I don't go to school and I fall behind on my homework," I tell Makena. It always ends with Principal Zalay and Ms. Langevin telling me, "It's a shame, Isabel, that you can't go on to fourth grade."

I think of Makena having her recurring dream for five days straight, and boy do I feel sorry for her. Ms. Langevin and Principal Zalay are the bad guys in my dream, shaking their heads and making those tsk-tsk-tsk sounds that Papa and the *titos* and the other grown-ups do to rub it in when you're already feeling low about the thing you did wrong to get them to tsk-tsk-tsk in the first place, so every time I wake up in the morning and realize I'm in bed and none of this ever happened, I feel like I was an anchor that turned into a buoy and now drifts on top of the water instead of sinking.

Makena tells us about her dream. She misses her midterms, she doesn't keep up with the required reading, and when the final exam comes, she isn't ready, so she isn't allowed to graduate from college. Sometimes the subject is rhetoric which is an English logic type of class, and sometimes it's molecular biology or this one class called political economy of industrial societies, which I sure would have a nightmare about because even just hearing the name of it makes you feel dumb.

Makena says she started to look up dreams on the Internet recently, and she found one website that explained she has performance anxiety and isn't confident about her abilities. But Makena has the confidence of a lion, so that doesn't seem right. When she emailed one of those dream consultants and got an answer back, the person said there's something unfinished in her life, but Makena can't figure out what it is. She's done so many things and keeps them up and plans to complete the things that can be finished. Of course she'll never finish piano or tennis, she says, because she'll continue those activities for the rest of her life.

"What could be unfinished for you at the ripe old age of eight?" Makena turns to me and asks. Now I watch her blowing through the openings of her sleeves to warm up her hands.

"I think it's because I never finished being a Brownie so that I could go on to Girl Scouts," I say.

Then Xavy snorts and butts in, "Geek Freak, datz cuz dem bullies messed witcha pup tent on dat camping trip last summuh." When he starts to cluck like a chicken and flap his stupid arms, I punch his shoulder and yell at him to stop it.

Makena looks even more worn out and bothered now, but I don't think it's because Xavy and I are fighting. She taps her fingers on the table and stares at the walls, and then Xavy turns to Makena and says, "Dis game o' *pusoy dos* iz gonna be on yur list o' unfinished beeznezz if ya don't take yur turn, know wut I'm sayin'?"

Makena sits there like a zombie. Xavy stares at her and says, "Guurrl, don't be trippin' ovuh sum lame-ass dream," but Makena doesn't hear what he's saying because now she's too busy looking at her cards, and that's when she shows us her two of spades to beat Xavy's ace of clubs.

My heart bounces and I throw down my two of diamonds, it's my last card, and I almost fall out of my chair from all the excitement. Xavy's shaking his head and saying he can't believe he lost to me. He thought for sure that Makena had the two of diamonds and would save it until the end. Then he gives me a fist bump, and we start to go over everything that happened in the game, like when I beat his three-of-a-kind and when he stomped all over my pair of kings with his aces.

When we're finally putting away the cards, I notice Makena is falling asleep. She's curled up on the couch under the Cal blanket that Ryan gave her for her birthday when he was her boyfriend. She looks cushy and safe. Maybe she's thinking of Ryan, but I have a feeling that midterms and rhetoric or that one class with the long name will keep haunting her in her dreams.

36. *tabos* for toilets

Mama buys rolls and rolls of toilet paper at the supermarket every week. She picks Ultra Charmin because Makena says it's tops. Makena is always on the toilet, and when you have to go that much, it starts to sting down there, so you need the softest toilet paper in the world to make your butt feel cool and soothing.

When I ask Makena why all toilet papers can't be the same, Makena giggles and tells me to wait until I take economics in college, which is when I'll understand what capitalism is all about. That's when she gets my crinkly confused face because how did we go from toilet paper to capitalism, and Makena goes on laughing and says, "Don't worry, you just keep being you for now, Isa."

I tried some of Makena's Ultra Charmin this morning after I went poo, and boy did it feel satiny and gentle, just like that chenille blanket Mama bought from Target, the kind that's made only for babies. No wonder Mama keeps buying rolls and rolls of it for Makena. But it's the most expensive toilet paper out there, so Mama always tells me to watch out for coupons in the newspaper.

Lola Carmen and Lola Zeny used to wash their butts with something called a *tabo*, a big cup you fill with water, and that's what you're supposed to use after you go poo. Makena says only provincial or really old-school Filipinos use *tabos* these days, but I think a *tabo* would be the cleanest way, especially if the toilet paper can't get to all the dry poo that might be stuck deep at the edge of your butthole.

Xavy likes to wet a wad of toilet paper when he wipes, and he thinks that's the most superb way ever, but that works only if you can reach the sink to wet the wad of toilet paper in the first place. We always go back and forth about the best way to wipe, and of course that's when Papa laughs hard from his belly while Makena and Mama gross out and ask us to talk about something else please.

Other people turn super disgusted too when you talk about poo and pee and what happens in the bathroom, and that's fine because I learned there are things you shouldn't talk about in front of others, especially strangers, but that's what got Makena in trouble when she had black poo and those other symptoms and was too ashamed to tell anyone about it.

Now she's talking about Ultra Charmin the softest toilet paper, and she became a volunteer for the Colon Cancer Coalition, mailing T-shirts and pins and pamphlets and helping edit survivor stories to spread the word about colon cancer and all its symptoms that are embarrassing.

She tells me she wants to hold up a sign to the world that says not to let shame teach you a lesson.

37. the master of *mafran*

Makena talked back to Papa tonight at dinner because she didn't like the way Papa was treating Mama. Sometimes Papa acts like he's the master and Mama's his servant. He kept asking Mama to get things like *mafran* banana ketchup for the *embutido* meatloaf or some soy sauce and mayonnaise for his broccoli, and as Mama was taking her first bite of dinner, Papa announced he needed more ice in his Diet Coke.

That's when Makena blurted out, "Why can't you just get it yourself?!" which of course turned bodies stiff in their chairs, making silence and all kinds of exchanges of wide frog eyes while we waited for Papa to blow his top. Mama started to get up to fetch Papa's ice, but Makena pulled Mama's arm and her whole body back down to her chair. Mama's eyes seemed to stretch farther to each side of her face, and her mouth was halfway open, all shocked and how come I can't get one sound to come out, not even an ouch from my body thumping hard back into my chair.

Papa usually loses his temper fast, but he's been trying to hold back these days because Makena is sick. We all turned to Papa, who just sat there slicing his *embutido* like no one disrespected him, but I know he wanted to say something because there was a purple vein dancing on his forehead.

I turned to Xavy, who gave me this look that knew a war was going to break out. Then I looked at Makena, and her face was starting to turn hot pink.

boy it sure is haunting my brain again and i hope it doesn't visit my dreams too.

there's makena standing in the doorway forced into being frozen like a scarecrow on the day that papa smashed her watch and then all of a sudden she turns her head and checks out her reflection in the mirror and this time i hear lolo martín's husky voice demanding "change your life you weak little pussycat."

Papa decided to speak up, which wasn't one of the best things to do because he sounded like Napoleon Bonaparte, who we learned from Ms. Langevin was a French dictator that said offensive things about women. "The man is the head of the household and the woman serves him and never talks back to him," Papa seemed to announce, probably just like Napoleon preached to all the women he knew.

"Excuse me? What country and time period are you living in? Women aren't slaves to men," said Makena with her pink face. "You're such a misogynist."

"You do *not* speak that way to your father," Papa tried to say all super crazy calm, but he was clutching his steak knife so hard that veins appeared on his knuckles too.

"I can talk however I wish, especially when my father continues to treat my mother like hired help," Makena snapped back. "She works all day too. She cooks and cleans and does the laundry and dishes and takes care of me. You should try it sometime."

I wanted to butt in and add that Mama watches QVC the home shopping network most of the day, but I'm sure that would have made things worse.

I had never heard Makena talk this way to anyone in my whole life, except to some of the *titos* who always make her eyes roll, which is when I remembered what Surfer Girl told me when Makena first started chemo. She said sometimes the medicine will do all the talking. It makes people sensitive and jumpy and moody and all sorts of unpredictable things that our family sure won't like living with.

like being capricious but the bad kind that makes you walk like there aren't just eggshells everywhere but also the gooey yolk surrounding it which might be misogynists too.

Mama started to sink low in her chair, and I did in mine too because of Makena's and Papa's stinging tones, like when the nurse at Dr. Lisbin's office has to poke my finger for blood to put in their test tubes, poke and sting, making your insides clam up. Tonight Makena sure wasn't being a weakling, but this seemed like the wrong time to be a tiger because of Papa's purple veins.

Papa knew he couldn't grab Makena and swing her over his lap for a spanking, so instead he used filthy rotten words to make her feel small.

"You irreverent piece of crap. I don't care how fucking sick you are. No one acts like a *princesa* in my house. You've been a fucking prima donna from the day those doctors practically had to yank you out of your poor mother. You think you're so fucking intelligent with your 200 IQ and your Berkeley education. Keep trying to impress me, because you never will. Now go to your fucking room and cry to your fucking pictures of RBG and Dolores Huerta and all your women's rights heroines who think they're so fucking smart too."

Makena buried her face in Mama's good linen napkin and bolted to her room and slammed the door so hard that Frida jumped onto my lap from under the table and started licking me with her sandpaper tongue. She kept licking and licking and I couldn't make her stop, and Papa yelled more F words even louder so that Makena could hear him all the way from her bedroom.

All of a sudden, he noticed me and Frida and stormed over and lowered his face to Frida's.

"Stop fucking licking her, you goddamn stupid dog! And what the *fuck* is that stench?!"

Frida let out a long whimper and went scrambling under my chair. I didn't like the way her body was shaking, all jerking against my legs and please don't yell at me like that again, and that's when I noticed the huge dark brown diarrhea stain on my favorite Gap Kids pants that was covering the two purple hearts stitched at the bottom.

Right when Papa stood up and started to walk to the garage, my words tumbled out at him like a rockslide, even though they seemed like puny pebbles crawling out of my throat.

"Your F words made Frida go poo on my favorite pants, Papa," I said, and I felt my whole body turn weak as I said this.

All I could smell was the sewer mixed with rotten eggs, and I started to get annoyed by the clinking of the tags on Frida's collar, which sounded like the beginning of "Jingle Bells," but I went on.

"See, look what you did. She's scared of you now, Papa."

I forgot that Xavy was still at the table, and his face dropped in a hurry, like he didn't want anything to do with me, I don't know her, oh my God she's not my sister.

But Papa's face sure didn't drop. I think there was a knot of pain between his eyes, passing right through his head, maybe like a tumor.

What if he decided to grab me from my chair and push me to the ground?

push me to the ground papa i'm slamming the door hard and i'm breaking another seat belt.

I didn't know why I wanted Papa to beat me up again, like a pussycat that was so easy to hurt. But I felt like a mean tiger at that very moment.

come on papa what are you going to do about it this time kick my shins like a weakling?

Maybe this was the Twilight Zone, like that freaky TV show Xavy watches reruns of, where spooky things happen for no reason. I couldn't figure out why I decided to say something to Papa, but before I could start thinking of more feisty things to say to him, he was standing before me with his left hand in a fist, which seemed strange because he's right-handed.

"*Mabuti nga*," he said, which means good thing, good for you. "You should all be scared of me."

Then he left us there and stayed in his second office smoking cigarettes and throwing darts at Britney.

I took a long and steady breath while Xavy gawked at me, like I knocked some stuffing out of his Gang Starr shirt that makes him look like an Akebono sumo doll. My steps were quiet down the hallway to check on Makena, and I made sure Papa wasn't back inside the house yet. Her door was closed.

I could hear choking kinds of sobs that were being muffled by the pillow that she probably was burying her face into. Sometimes she cried, "I'll always be afraid of him," gasping like there wasn't enough air to go around.

Makena's scared of him too.

We're all afraid of Papa's stinging tones, making everyone feel miniature in their chairs. He shouts F words and awful nasty names and turns ambivalent about women, but I know the father hiding under his darkness.

Even though the things he says dig through your skin all the way to your insides and can hold your heart prisoner, he isn't someone to be afraid of. He's just Papa.

38. peaceful and pleasing

Observing my family sleep is something sneaky that I enjoy doing, but it's a good kind of sneaky.

One of my favorite things to do is to watch Frida fall asleep on my lap. She shrinks into a little puppy ball, and she makes me feel like a mama, even though I'm not really sure what that's supposed to be like. First Frida sighs, then she gets up to try to find a new place to rest her head, and when she finally plops into her perfect spot, happy and tingly feelings overpower my whole body, and I wish they would never go away.

The only time the house is still is when we're all asleep. Whenever it's one of those nights that I feel wide awake even though it's late, I watch Makena. She looks tender like a lamb when she's sleeping. She likes to nestle into a ball just like Frida, and most of the time she looks like she's dreaming of something wondrous, like rum raisin ice cream or Ryan's goofy cuspids or winning all kinds of tennis tournaments.

Xavy is creepy like a gargoyle when he sleeps because his mouth always hangs wide open, snoring like a grunting pig. And this isn't a regular snore like Mama's or Papa's. This kind makes his whole bed shake and creak, and it's so noisy that sometimes it'll wake me up, forcing me to go to his room to tap but more like poke him on the shoulder and tell him I can't fall asleep and that he should shove a sock down his throat, like what people on TV and the movies say they're going to do when someone's snoring or talking way too much.

But sometimes I don't really mind Xavy's snores because I'd rather hear loud hog sounds than "You turd" and "You dipstick" and all those hurtful words he shouts when he's angry.

Mama and Papa like to hold each other when they're sleeping, but I'm not sure they know they're doing it. Mama rests her head between Papa's shoulder and cheek, and Papa puts his arms around her like a big furry bear protecting her.

One of these days, I want to take a picture of everyone sleeping. Then I'll hang each photo on the fridge with my Snoopy magnets so that my family can see how peaceful and pleasing they look, even Xavy with his snorting pig sounds, when they aren't awake.

39. the falling fat-ass

"There's goddamn rain in the forecast for the next three days," Papa complained this morning while he was driving me to school.

Rain can be like a puzzle sometimes because there are so many different kinds, and you never know what's coming. Drizzling means there are only a few drops of rain here and there, and the drops are so weak that they feel like they're coming out of a spray bottle that's on the mist setting, not the high one. Showers are hard rain, the kind that feels menacing against the windshield of the car because you're moving so fast, but you know it's bad when your car is waiting at a stoplight and it's still coming down like it's blitzing.

Then there's also hail, which are small balls of ice, but that hardly happens here in Arcadia. Sprinkling is steady but light rain, not doing much damage but still making a difference, right in the middle. Kind of like me, the in-betweener, as Mr. Baluga always says.

Right now, it's sprinkling outside. Xavy and I decided to stay indoors so that he could teach me how to play Tony Hawk's Pro Skater on our PlayStation 2. I can't figure out all the different buttons and triggers and I want to give up and go play with my Groovy Girls, but when I watch him press the buttons like a pro video game player, it makes me want to have fancy trigger fingers just like him.

Makena is on the couch under a white comforter that Papa draped over her when he got home from his job sites, and I know that Frida is asleep right behind where Makena's legs are curved because sometimes I see a white mound near Makena's butt, which means Frida's adjusting her position.

When Xavy and I start to yell at the TV when our skaters fall, Makena tells us to shut up and have some consideration.

That's when Xavy lets her have it and roars, "Stop sleepin', an' git yur skinny ass off da couch already, ya beeatch!"

All of a sudden, Makena sits up from her lying-down position and snaps, "Have you forgotten I'm on chemo, you fucking self-absorbed brick-faced fat-ass?!"

The puffy white comforter wraps around her whole body like a marshmallow, but of course I'm not supposed to laugh at this silly sight, especially after her attack of hurtful words on Xavy, even though I had to hold in my snort when I heard "brick-faced fat-ass."

Xavy and I look at each other with the widest frog eyes and whisper "yikes" to each other, sitting there frozen quiet while our skaters keep skating and falling because our trigger fingers are frozen too, both of us waiting for Makena to lie back down and take her nap.

I remember the time that Makena called Papa the F word along with the A word, but she did it behind his back, like everyone else does.

I feel like saying something to Makena and right to her face. "Everyone thinks you're self-absorbed too," I could say, but how do you come up with something that won't make her feel small when we all know it's the medicine talking?

Xavy and I hold our tongues because it's probably the right thing to do.

"Why don't you say something back," I whisper to Xavy. I bump his elbow with mine, and he bumps it back harder.

"Why don't *you?* You're the pro at mouthing off now. You're lucky Papa didn't pop you right there the other night."

"If he did, would you have saved me?" I ask my *kuya.* My hands clench into tight fists while I remember when Papa sort of beat me up outside his car and Xavy just sat paralyzed in his seat.

But Xavy doesn't answer me. Instead, he swings his arm around me, pulling me close to him. We just sit there and watch the Tony Hawk skaters keep skating and falling, skating and falling.

40. later, *lumpia*

We used to have our big family parties at Tita Carlie and Tito Dante's house in San Fernando Valley which is the other valley, where it gets so hot that it doesn't matter whether it's 100 degrees or 110 degrees because it still feels like you're roasting in a goddamn oven, which is what Papa always says when we get closer to Canoga Park and he's cranking up the A/C.

The last time we were there was on Jeannie's birthday. Jeannie is Tita Carlie and Tito Dante's oldest daughter, who turned 13 that day. Katie and Erik and some other cousins call her "Friends of the Library" because she's quiet and boring, "An' don't fuh-git homely betty," which Xavy likes to add. But he says to watch out because sometimes those are "da chicks who be suh-prizin' ya, doze ugly ducklinz dat bloomz layta in life." I asked Xavy what he meant by that, and he said to check in with him when I turn 12, maybe 11 since I'll already be in middle school and taking sex education.

I remember watching my cousin Ricky practicing scales on their new baby grand piano, and boy were they making my insides sore. I don't play any instruments, but Makena thinks I have a keen ear for music, so I know when something doesn't sound right.

I wish Makena was there to show him how to hit the right notes, but she was upstairs in Jay and Ricky's bedroom, talking on the phone. She doesn't really like hanging out with the cousins and usually goes outside to read a book or takes a walk in the park across the street.

I also can't forget the smell of fried meat and oil coming from the kitchen while Ricky kept playing bad scales, so I decided to watch the *titas* cook. Tita Choleng was making sour faces in front of a pan filled with crackling oil and *lumpia*, which is like a Chinese egg roll and one of my favorite snacks. It's the Shanghai kind, which means it has meat inside a thin flour wrapper that's deep-fried. Mama likes the kind called fresh *lumpia,* with shrimps and different vegetables, but then there's also a vegetable and shrimp kind that you deep-fry like the Shanghai ones, and that's Papa's favorite.

There are always platters and bowls and Rubbermaid containers filled with food at these parties, all spread out on the table for everyone to choose from, which Mama says brings people together, even when they're fighting.

That's how Filipinos are, she says, it's all about the food. In the Philippines, I'm pretty sure you eat six times a day because you also get to have *meryenda*, which is what they call a snack in between breakfast and lunch, and also in between lunch and dinner and sometimes even after dinner.

Tita Carlie noticed I was there in the kitchen, so she asked me to mince some garlic for the vegetable *lumpia* dipping sauce. I still have no idea how to mince, and I'm all thumbs when it comes to cooking according to everyone, but I decided to try anyway.

When Mama saw that I was holding the knife all awkward and moving in slow motion, she grabbed the knife out of my hand and said she'd do it herself. Tita Gwen gave Mama a *malocchio* which sure looked like an oxymoron, and then she laid her kind and warm hand on my shoulder to let me know it was okay that I didn't have kitchen smarts.

Xavy says Mama's given both me and Makena major cooking complexes, but we don't mind because we'd really rather be doing something else, like walking Frida or even doing the laundry, which I enjoy because Downy is one of my favorite smells and makes all my clothes baby fresh.

Since I was getting in everyone's way in the kitchen, I went downstairs to the family room, where some of the *titas* and *titos* and girl cousins were dancing The Hustle. Xavy loves this dance and says it defined the '70s. He always talks about the '70s like they were the grandest of times even though he wasn't born yet, but Tito Gus taught him all the dances like The Hustle and The Bump and The Bus Stop, and he watches reruns of those radical cool shows like *Dance Fever* and *Starsky and Hutch.*

A bunch of other *titas* and *titos* were outside on the patio playing *mahjong*. Something about the sound of tiles clicking and clacking against each other when they're being shuffled after a game is done calms my insides. But whenever I ask one of the *titas* or *titos* to help them click and clack, they shoo me away.

I wondered if Makena was done talking on the phone, so I walked over towards the stairs. Erik, Benji, and Carter were playing with their Pokémon figures and trading cards. There must have been a hundred of these cards all over the place, so I couldn't get through the stairs without stepping on some of them.

They kept yelling "Hey man" and "Why don't you go play with the girl cousins," but I ignored them and stepped on their dumb cards anyway. Benji tried to grab my leg, but I was too fast for him. When I finally made it to the top of the stairs, I kicked some of Benji's cards right into his face and stuck my tongue out at all of them, even though Mama always says it'll stay that way permanently if I keep it up.

I opened the door to Jay and Ricky's bedroom, and there was Makena on Jay's bed, still talking on her cell phone. That's when Minnie and Darla, who are a few years older than Makena, walked in behind me and said, "Shet, she ees steel on da pone." They started to shake their heads and whisper stuff about Makena to each other, so of course Makena noticed and told whoever she was talking to that she had to run.

"What's your problem?" Makena asked, acting all huffy and hissy with our cousins.

"*You* ahr da *probe*-lem," said Darla with her accent that was even thicker. She and Minnie still have accents because they came from the Philippines just last year to live in America. Papa says he sponsored their whole family so that they could get their visas and have better opportunities.

"What did I do wrong now?" asked Makena. She kept rolling her eyes, which even I thought was rude, but it was hard to be mad at her because some of the girl cousins are crazy mean to Makena, always talking behind her back about how they just want to barf at her snooty and prissy ways.

Darla was about to say something back, but her words were all tangled up by tears and hard breathing, so she started walking away. That's when Minnie all of a sudden burst out in the best English she could come up with, even though most of the grammar was wrong.

"You never did hung out with us, Makena," she began. "You thought you're abob eberyone, hah?"

Then all kinds of Tagalog poured out, like "You don't know what it's like to come to a new country and feel so lost and you don't know the meaning of family."

I could tell that Makena wanted to say something, but all she did was shake her head, her eyes looking away but not rolling anymore. When she flipped her cell phone open and started to press numbers, Minnie yelled, "*Wala kang respeto at wala kang puso. Bruha ka talaga*, Makena," which means Makena has no respect and no heart and she really is a witch.

Minnie grabbed Darla's hand and even mine too, and she pulled us down the stairs to the dining room, where some of the cousins and *titos* and *titas* were singing "Happy Birthday" all rowdy and hitting all the wrong notes to Jeannie, who stood there next to her birthday cake with Barney on it, which I knew wasn't her idea because of her pink cheeks and neck and also because Barney is for babies.

After the cake-cutting, we went downstairs to the family room to watch Xavy, who was dancing The Hustle side by side with Tito Gus while Tito Carding and Tito Vito whistled and blew kisses at them, teasing Xavy that he might be *bakla* too, and then being stared down by my *kuya*.

Mama was busy in the kitchen frying more *lumpia* with Papa's sisters, even though she says she doesn't really get along with them but really does, and Papa was smoking outside in the front yard with some of the other *titos,* who always borrow money from him and never pay him back.

That day, I remember I was having fun like I usually do with the *titos* and *titas* and cousins, watching everyone be loud and crack corny Flip jokes and make fun of each other and just enjoy our time together.

But that was the first time it felt like we were all supposed to be there only because we were family. Like actors and actresses on those TV shows that last for many seasons, such as *ER* and *Friends* and *Everybody Loves Raymond*, memorizing our lines and getting paid for playing our parts.

When we got home after the party, I looked for Xavy's retro Magic 8 Ball, which Tita Gwen gave him for his sixteenth birthday. Xavy and his gangster friends always use one of its 20 answers in their emails to each other. Xavy likes to type, "Don't count on it, foo'," and Earl always answers, "Outlook not so good, guurrl," and that gets Xavy cracking up all rowdy at his computer and Mama and Papa shaking their heads.

When I finally found the Magic 8 Ball inside Frida's bed in the family room, I decided to ask it a question.

"Do you think Papa and Mama and Makena and Xavy and I will be on another TV show someday?"

We would play the same roles, but someone might have to look for the remote, because what if our family is on a different channel now, along with all those shows they call reality TV?

Our episodes would be the kinds that never stopped. The cameras would keep rolling, and there would be no cuts and take-twos and changing your mind because you would never be allowed to start over.

I remember when I shook the Magic 8 Ball for the answer, it said, "Ask again later."

41. grow, grass!

This morning the sky is heather gray, the same exact color of one of my favorite shirts from Gap Kids, and I'm playing with my Let's Go Camping Barbie, Stacy, and Kellie set.

All of a sudden like a train whooshing by, Makena screams from the shower. Papa and Mama and Xavy and I rush to the bathroom, where we find Makena sitting on the floor, wrapped up in a giant yellow towel.

She has a huge wad of hair sticking out of her fist, and she's holding on to it crazy tight. She won't stop staring, so I start to stare, not at the wad of hair in her fist but at the spot where her hair used to be, and my mouth must have hung open for too long because Mama put her hand over it and said to mind my manners and stop gawking at your *áte.*

If Tito Carding were here, he'd tell Makena to keep washing it because hair is like grass, you need water to keep it growing fast. That's one of the reasons why I don't like to take baths. If I took baths like Mama and Makena take their showers every morning, I'd have long girly hair like them.

If I started to lose my hair, I'd wear hats or wigs until my hair grew back. Papa might need to start wearing hats soon because he's already 52 years old, even though his hair is thick like steel wool. Frida's hair is all over the house, in little balls of fur under the couch and sitting right beside the legs of all the tables and chairs, but I never see any bald spots on her body, so dogs must grow their hair back faster than grass.

"It's just hair," I want to tell Makena, but when I look at her face, it shows all kinds of sadness and frustration and what am I going to do. I try not to look at her, but she's still squeezing that wad of hair in her fist like she wants to make it go poof into the skinny air.

Papa's trying to get Makena to stand up, but she won't, so he starts to grumble something in Tagalog and walks away.

Xavy's already gone.

Mama's tidying up in the bathroom.

I don't know what to do. Should I pray to God that Makena's hair starts growing like grass real soon, or should I go chew on a bone like Frida and just mind my manners?

42. the lotto lowdown

Xavy is in major trouble today and in way hotter water than I've ever been in, maybe even scalding, even hotter than the time I threw my Snoopy beanbag at Makena's face like a baseball pitcher would because she stuck him in the dryer and all of a sudden, he wasn't soft and fluffy anymore.

Makena and I were already sitting in the Volvo, waiting for Xavy to take us to Makena's chemo. Mama had to go out with Tita Gwen to shop for wedding shoes, so Xavy was in charge of driving Makena to chemo in Mama's car today. No one's allowed to drive Papa's Suburban except for Xavy, and Xavy treats his Bug like a trophy, according to Makena. He even uses those soft yellow cloths when he waxes it, and then he admires it and it just sits there doing nothing in the garage except take up space. Makena would have taken the CRX, but Xavy lent it to one of his gangster friends for the week, which of course Papa had some ugly words with Xavy about.

I ran to the backyard to see if Xavy was playing with Frida and then back inside to check all the rooms. When I hurried to the garage to tell Makena that Xavy was nowhere to be found, I knew at this moment that Xavy was in the biggest mess anyone could get himself into.

Makena swung open the door so hard that it looked like it might snap off. She stepped out of the car and slammed the door as hard as she could, which made me jump. She went around to the driver's side and looked through her purse, and then she pulled out some keys and plopped herself in and started the car.

"Makena, wait for me!" I screamed, but she was already backing out of the garage on the double and even left a few tire marks on the driveway, and I knew for sure that Papa wouldn't be very happy about that, but of course he would forgive her because he'd be too busy turning dramatic about what Xavy did to her.

Xavy's in even deeper and hotter water now because I'm home alone, even though I'm already eight years old and I can take care of myself. Mr. Baluga hardly leaves his house, so I took Frida with me next door. When I told Mr. Baluga what happened, he shook his head and said, "Atta boy, Xavy, way to make some more waves in the José household." Frida seemed to understand what he said because right when Mr. Baluga was shaking his head, she made her whole body waggle, like she was trying to shake off the shame that Xavy was bringing to our family.

Mr. Baluga and I didn't really feel like playing cards, so we decided to take a walk to Luigi's Deli and buy Lotto tickets. The streets were just cleaned, and you could tell because there were no leaves in sight, only bits and pieces of different shades of brown in the gutters.

The agapanthuses on the sidewalk were blooming wild and purple. Sometimes Frida tries to jump high and eat the agapanthus petals, and that always makes Mr. Baluga laugh his gorilla ha-ha's. He couldn't help being in a lively mood, telling me he was going to win the Lotto one of these days.

I asked him what he'd do with all that money, and he said he'd go to Spain and Italy and Iceland and Russia and Mauritius and Egypt and Singapore and a bunch of other countries he's always wanted to visit. Then he'd give the rest of his money to different places trying to find cures for lung cancer and colon cancer and other diseases. I asked him why there aren't any cures for all these cancers yet, and Mr. Baluga said God forgot to add that to his list of things to do when he was busy creating us.

If I won the Lotto, I'd ask Surfer Girl and Dr. Minor to tell their medical friends that I'd pay all kinds of money to find a cure for colon cancer and the other cancers and diseases wreaking havoc in the world, even though I think there are already brilliant scientists trying to do this, and boy I'll bet they don't do it for the money.

So instead, I think I'd pay someone to drive Makena to chemo every week.

I'd also buy Xavy a car that he could take out of the garage and drive without being too worried about it getting scratched.

I'd find Papa one of those reclining massage chairs to replace his grungy wing chair inside his second office so that he can feel super relaxed and won't need to smoke.

I'd hire a driver for Mama so that I don't get carsick every time she brakes hard with her left foot.

I'd get Frida her own Sarita doll so that she doesn't have to sneak out of my bedroom with mine and try to gnaw on her poofy hair or chew off her purple and pink skirt.

Then I'd call all the *titas* and *titos*, even Lola Zeny and Mama's sisters, and tell them I won the Lotto.

"Here's your money," I'd say in my hissy-huffiest voice, and then I'd throw it at their faces, even though that would be kind of lowdown and unholy. "But only if you promise to be a family to each other again."

43. hmmphs and hipsters

Makena and I are at Santa Anita Fashion Park because Makena needs bigger panties. She used to be a size extra small, but now she has to wear medium ones. All of her extra smalls are too tight and full of holes and even poo stains, but don't tell anyone I said that.

We walk over to Nordstrom, which is only 0.7 miles away from our house, according to Xavy, who likes clocking how far one place is to another. Nordstrom is one of Makena's favorite stores because their customer service is tops, she says. Salespeople in the shoe section bring your receipt right to where you're sitting, and you can even sign it right there on the shoe stool. There's also a concierge, which is where you can leave your bags if they get too heavy while you're shopping.

There are gold wreaths and thick garlands and star-shaped lights draped over railings and countertops where the perfume is and even on the mannequins, and it's all putting me into a party kind of mood, even though Makena and I are here only to buy big panties and then head straight home.

The saleslady in the panties department with the smooth French accent keeps showing Makena all kinds of different styles called thongs and high-cuts. All Makena wants are regular panties, which I found out are called hipsters. I was about to laugh out loud because Xavy called Mr. Baluga a hipster, but I decided Makena might get irked with me for being immature.

Makena tells me to find gray medium hipsters while she looks for black and white ones. Black and white and sometimes gray are her favorite colors of panties. Mine are purple and pink and green, and Makena says she knows my taste will change when I'm 20 years old like she is, but I don't think that's true because Makena's taste is sort of old-ladylike for her age, because how could anyone like the furniture at Ethan Allen, all tassels and scrolls and dark like they belong in a museum.

I find white medium ones after looking through piles of extra large and extra small ones, and Makena says four is enough, along with the three black mediums she found, so we take all the hipster panties to the French lady, who's finishing up with another customer at the cash register.

When Makena pulls out her credit card, the French lady asks to see her driver's license too. Usually salespeople don't check out driver's licenses for too long, and some don't even bother asking for them at all. But this lady isn't afraid to ask, and she sure is staring at Makena's picture for a little too long. She crinkles her blonde eyebrows that almost look invisible and insists that the picture doesn't look anything like Makena.

"The girl in this photo is slender and younger and much more attractive and chic," the saleslady says with a hmmph in her French accent that now seems to be squeezing through her nostrils.

Papa told me once that French people are very straightforward and sometimes impolite, and boy was this lady the most direct of them all, even more than the one at Luigi's Deli who always tells Mama that she should dye her hair.

I expect Makena to start telling her off, like "How dare you tell me I'm no longer slender and beautiful," but she just sighs and looks like she doesn't want to try.

But I want to try. No one tells my *áte* she isn't attractive, especially in a mean and disrespectful way, so I say to the French lady, "My sister gained 40 pounds because of chemotherapy. That's why she doesn't look like her driver's license anymore."

Makena rolls her eyes and throws me her "Why did you have to open your big mouth" look.

The French lady lets out a few nervous-sounding laughs and says, "Chemotherapy, oh that simply cannot be true."

But when Makena and I just stand there and give *malocchios* to the French lady, she decides to look closely at Makena and notices under her floppy blue hat that she doesn't have much hair.

"Oh dear, *pardone moi*, accept my apologies," the French lady bursts out, and she keeps her head bowed the whole time while she slides Makena's hipster panties into a gray Nordstrom shopping bag all super delicate and waits for the receipt to print for Makena to sign. All you can hear is the soft buzzing of the receipt coming out of the cash register.

Makena's grown from a size 0 to a size 8 in just six months. I wonder if she'll ever reach a size 16, which we all found out is what our cousin Glenda wears because a bunch of the cousins peeked inside the panties drawer in her bedroom. Whenever Xavy says Glenda has elephantiasis, Makena shakes her head and says, "Quit being insulting and narrow-minded. And so shallow."

Makena's eyelashes haven't grown back, and her eyebrow hairs are falling out one by one, so there's no need for plucking now. Her eyes are shrinking not only because of her stubbly eyelashes but also because they're buried deep in her face that looks like a *siaopao*, which are those round white and doughy pork buns that Papa sometimes picks up from 99 Ranch on his way home from his job sites.

I'm not supposed to tell Makena any of these things because her self-esteem is fading away as each day passes, Mama says. Makena wishes she can exercise to lose some weight, but she never has enough energy and always feels like throwing up. Fatigue and nausea are her worst enemies.

Makena has always been petite and beautiful with long and satiny hair, and now she has a *siaopao* face with a *siaopao* body to match. She isn't narrow-minded or shallow, and she always tells me that looks aren't important, but I'll bet they matter to her when nobody can believe what she once was.

44. brave beagle

Ms. Langevin says to me almost every day after school, "Do you know you're the bravest 8-year-old I've ever met," and I always grin wide for her, showing off all my teeth, even my fillings and the one tooth that Dr. Young is going to fix soon because it's supposed to be rectangular and not pointy like a cuspid.

But a couple of weeks ago when she asked me, right before the holiday break began, I couldn't hold back my tears, the ones making the spot on my nose between my eyes feel like it's going to pop.

I told Ms. Langevin that sometimes I don't feel like being a brave 8-year-old. Sometimes I want to be a beagle like Frida and just play in the backyard and admire all of Mama's plants, like her rosemary shrubs and white jasmine vines and enjoy being around all the animals that visit, like the squirrels and the birds and even knowing that coyotes and skunks and mountain lions have been spotted on our street.

Then I want to be able to go back inside my house to rest and eat and play some more and never understand the meaning of colon cancer and white-blood counts and chemotherapy and X-rays and colonoscopies and CT-scans.

After Ms. Langevin listened to my answer that was all over the place, she let me bury my head in her cushy lap. She stroked my head and my face, and when I asked her to please not tell my papa that I cried, she kept going. She pushed my bangs away from my forehead because they're getting long, scraggly strands hanging over my eyes and all soaking wet at the tips from my teardrops.

She moved her lips close to my ear and said she wouldn't tell a soul. I tilted my head up at her, my most marvelous teacher who became my friend too, and I breathed in the fruity apple scent from the soft black yarns of her thick sweater, feeling the back of her smooth and long fingers against my cheeks.

I thanked her for hiding my tears.

45. big bouncing booby butt

Mama and Papa were invited to Mama's friend Edith's twentieth wedding anniversary party at the Huntington Ritz Carlton, and they're going only because Makena convinced them to have some fun for once. Mama says that Makena will finally be able to get some shuteye tonight because she didn't sleep at all yesterday, which means Makena won't be able to look after me while they're gone.

Papa tells me he doesn't want to impose on Mr. Baluga and Lola Evie, so that leaves Xavy to watch over me, even though I keep telling Papa and Mama that I don't need babysitting anymore because I'm already in third grade.

Xavy's having what he calls a double quarter pounder which means heart attack because tonight he's supposed to hang out with Genevieve, who all his gangster friends call "Hot Thang."

Papa doesn't want Xavy dating sluts, which of course Mama had her own double quarter pounder about because Papa said "slut" in front of me, but nothing will stop Xavy because he learned from Papa who is the king of bullshet, according to Mama. That means Xavy's planning to tell Papa and Mama he'll be at Jason's playing video games, and of course he'll bring me along so that Jason's sister Nahla, who's two years older than I am, supposedly will watch me.

I don't really care for Nahla because one time when Xavy brought me with him to their house, I asked if I could have another ice cream sandwich, and she scowled and said my stubby legs would stay the way they are if I didn't watch it with the sweets.

Xavy wants to impress Genevieve with his Bug, which means that I finally get to ride in it. We're going miniature golfing at Golfland in El Monte, which I was surprised and excited to hear because Xavy knows that no one can beat me, not even Makena. I get a hole-in-one at least once every time we play, and Xavy always says that I have beginner's luck, but everyone knows I'm not a neophyte anymore, which was one of Xavy's coolest-sounding SAT words.

Xavy's revving up his Bug in the driveway, yelling that Genevieve is waiting in front of her house so hurry your ass up already.

"I'm going to tell Papa you said *ass* to me," I say to Xavy. I notice Mama's geraniums by the front door, and I choose a rosy red one that doesn't look too delicate to put inside the tiny vase in Xavy's Bug. All Bugs have bud vases on the dashboard, but Xavy always forgets to add flowers to it.

Xavy cracks a smile when I place the flower carefully inside the vase, and then I jump into the backseat, where I notice my booster is ready to go.

Before I can give Xavy a look of shock and wow you remembered, he says, "No one reminded me, Geek Freak. There's your dumb car seat, even though everyone knows you're too big for one."

I show him my fist, and he just laughs without turning around and says, "I can feel your look," which he always reminds me is one of his favorite lines from *Pulp Fiction*, a movie that Mama says is brash and savage and inappropriate and that I'm not allowed to watch until I'm way older.

When we get closer to Genevieve's house, I can see her big boobies from pretty far away. She's leaning against a mailbox with her tight blouse showing off a super low neck, and she's wearing tall black boots and a mini skirt made out of jeans. Her black leather purse that matches her boots is tiny, something that would be Frida's size if she carried a bag.

"*Ciao*, *bellos*," she says, and I can't help rolling my eyes because Makena taught me that in Italian, you don't make a word plural by adding an "s" to the end of it.

She kisses Xavy smack on his mouth. "*Gross*," I blurt out, and Xavy's glare is razor-sharp while I show him my fist again.

At Golfland, I pick course number two because it's the most zigzaggy and interesting one, and that's where the windmill is, one of my favorite holes to play on. Xavy asks me to keep score, and I roll my eyes again because I know he just wants more time for kissing and hugging.

Genevieve can't even hold her golf club the right way, and Xavy isn't concentrating on his own strokes because he keeps checking out Genevieve's boobies and butt. When his turn comes up on the fourth hole, he doesn't notice that my ball is waiting to pop out from the tube that's sticking out of the castle, so he hits his ball sooner than he should have, and then it comes flying through the tube right behind mine and knocks my ball way into the corner, far away from the hole, while his lands right beside it.

"Hey, you hit mine, you can't do that," I shout at Xavy, and I don't know why I feel my face and neck getting hot because we're just playing mini golf and I know there are times when I lose, which is fine because the one thing I always look forward to is going out to grab a Tommy's burger afterwards, where Makena and Xavy and Papa and Mama and I sit in a booth together and share fries and sip our sodas and talk about who hit the most epic shots of the day.

But now I'm here with Xavy and Hot Thang, and they're ignoring me because their hands are all over each other. Genevieve keeps giggling like she's all helpless, not strong enough to wriggle herself out of Xavy's hold.

So I keep walking, but I go past all the other holes and cut across a bridge, and I even almost step on someone's ball while I run inside the video arcade and right back out because I see a bunch of gangster-looking boys with low baggy pants that look like Xavy's friends.

That's when I decide to find the windmill and sit right behind it on a spot that faces the chain-link fence so that no one can see me, even when they're hitting their ball up the ramp and through the opening.

I sit and wait to see if Xavy will come find me. I think about Makena at home sleeping, why she couldn't stay up and look after me, why Papa and Mama couldn't ask Mr. Baluga and Lola Evie because they love having me at their house, why Xavy was all smiling and thoughtful in the car and all of a sudden acted like I was invisible and didn't care if I was beating him at mini golf, why it wouldn't be the same going to Tommy's afterwards, stuck inside a booth with Xavy and Genevieve, who doesn't even eat burgers because she's a vegetarian.

All of a sudden, I hear my name on the loudspeaker.

"*Isabel José,* if you are here at Golfland, please report to the front desk."

There's all this hullabaloo, people talking hush-hush like there's an emergency and all kinds of swift footsteps everywhere.

"Dude, Geek Freak's at the windmill," I hear someone who sounds like Earl, and I see him and Jason and Sean and Emilio, Xavy's best gangster friends, stick their cell phones into their back pockets when they spot me and start pointing, and boy do they look fuming mad.

But when Sean high-fives Earl, and Jason and Emilio pump their fists into the air, I know they aren't that angry.

I'm not fuming anymore either because Xavy called his homies to help find me, his little sister, and they all showed up on the double even though they were probably busy with their own hot thangs too.

Genevieve comes running up to me, her boobies bouncing up and down and her tiny purse swinging around and hitting her butt that's even bigger than mine.

"Xavy, she's okaaay!" she screams all dramatic, and Xavy appears and scoops me up and says without making pauses, which means he can't breathe from all his anger, "You scared the fuck out of me why would you go and do that what if some sicko decided to kidnap your sorry ass?!"

He starts crying, and I don't think he knows he is until Genevieve unzips her tiny purse and pulls out a miniature Kleenex and wipes his face. Then she turns to me and pats my cheeks gently, and that's when I realize that Genevieve isn't a slut and I'm just like my *kuya* at that very moment, even though everyone says we couldn't be more different.

46. of moose munch and men

I never sleep with my hair wet because Tito Dante once told me it would make me turn blind when I woke up in the morning. I don't blow-dry my hair the right way, I always miss a layer or two, and Mama doesn't like drying it before bedtime, so that's why I try to remember to take my baths in the morning, but only if I'm dirty enough to be cleaned. Makena says God frowns upon superstition, but that's confusing because Filipinos and Latinos and other Catholic families I know are both superstitious and religious.

Sometimes Papa is superstitious, especially with numbers. One of his best friends, whose name is Harry David Lim and likes to joke that he sells Chinese chocolate and Moose Munch gift baskets, taught Papa all the numbers in Chinese that are good and bad. He tries to avoid pointy numbers like four and seven which are bad luck, so he likes to bet on round numbers like eight and nine when he's playing roulette in Las Vegas or picking his Lotto numbers. That's why whoever owns 99 Ranch put those nines in there and why one of our favorite Chinese restaurants in Monterey Park is called 888 Ocean Seafood.

Mama believes in the Filipino superstition that if you drop a fork, a man will visit you, and if you do the same thing to a spoon, a woman will come. One time when Mama dropped a fork while she was loading the dishwasher, the UPS man knocked on the door with another package from QVC. Another time when she knocked over her huge spoon with holes that lets fat and oil drip through it, Lola Evie stopped by to borrow some *kalamansi*, which is like a cross between a lime and an orange but smaller, the same size as cherry tomatoes.

Tita Gwen believes that if your sister or brother gets married the same year you do, you'll be struck with bad luck forever. The man who's going to be her husband soon, whose name is Tito Rory, has a sister getting married next year in April, but Tita Gwen doesn't want to wait until the year after next to get married. That's why she's rushing and making us and Tito Rory's family and friends all crazy cuckoo by helping her tie bows on programs and hunt down wedding bubbles for kids to blow outside the church, and find a cheap DJ who will actually play the music you want to dance to at your wedding.

Xavy laughs when the *titos* and *titas* make *kuwento* about their superstitions, like always wearing polka dots on New Year's Eve because round things bring good fortune, or if you take a picture with three people in it, you'll get bad luck. But he always waxes his Bug the same exact way, nine circles in one spot, and he even counts to himself to make sure he doesn't lose track.

One time when Papa and Xavy and I were hanging out in the garage, I asked Xavy if something horrible would happen to his Bug if he didn't wax it exactly the same way every time. Of course he answered, "No way, you turd," and he shooed me away and said I've heard "one too many o' dem o'd wives' *kuwentos*." Then Papa snorted and said Xavy's birthday is September 9 which is 9/9, and that's why he's superstitious like the rest of us.

Papa says you're allowed to believe in superstitions once in a while because they add spice to our lives, even if they're ones we shouldn't be mixing in with the rest.

When I ask him why people mix spices that aren't supposed to go together, he answers, "Love, it's because life without risk is like a companionless dog. Or an empty house. And as your Lolo Martín used to say, 'Like a man without resolve.'"

47. hurray, huzzah, ha ha!

Xavy thinks he's the only one with a sense of humor in this house. He likes to kid around and tickle us and make silly kooky animal sounds, but it used to be funnier when Makena wasn't sick. Now it's irky annoying, which I guess is what it's like to be feel ambivalent.

Papa no longer tries to pin Xavy to the ground and pinch the inside of his thighs and make him whistle, which is what Tito Gus used to do to us all the time to make us laugh and cry all at once.

Mama screams at Xavy when he pokes her sides while she's washing the dishes, and Xavy still gives me wet willies. When I chase him around the dining room table to try to get him back, Papa yells that Makena is trying to get some sleep and we're being too goddamn rowdy. Makena doesn't seem to mind all of Xavy's pranks even when she's feeling tired or nauseated, but you can tell it's hard for her to laugh.

Makena's trying to record a new greeting on the retro answering machine that Xavy got her on eBay, and she can't seem to get it right. She sounds so floppy and blue, and when she tries to perk up, it seems fake.

Hi. This is Makena José. Please leave me a message, and I'll get back to you as soon as I can. Thanks.

She plays the greeting back and says, "I sound so dull. I should just let the standard greeting answer it. But God, that automated voice sounds like she's got a stick up her ass." Then Makena covers her mouth and apologizes to me, but she knows I've heard way worse than "ass" from Papa and Xavy.

After Makena tries recording her greeting four times, Xavy pokes his head into Makena's bedroom and announces that he will record the greatest greeting in the history of the world for Makena and she will be extremely pleased with it and might even want to pay him for it, trying to sound all bizarro ghetto. Makena gives him a hmmph and crosses her arms and says, "Oh yeah, then prove it."

That's when Xavy decides to do his Snagglepuss impression. He imitates all the cartoon characters like a pro, especially Scooby-Doo when he says "Ghosts" or "Shaggy" or "Scooby Snacks" in his scratchy and high-pitched voice, but for some reason he does Snagglepuss the best, and you just can't stop the cackles when you hear it.

He swings his arms everywhere all dramatic and girly and talks through his nose, just like the way Tita Malou used to right before she was about to go shopping with all the *titas.*

Heavens to Mergatroid!
'Tis I, Snagglepuss.
Press 1 for Yogi and Boo-Boo, or 2 for Makena José.
If you pressed 2, hurray! Huzzah! Good show, even!
So start talking...when you hear me exit, stage left!

The machine goes beep after Xavy is done, and all of a sudden, Makena and I let out the loudest laughs and buzzy snorts you ever heard. Before the beep, Makena had to cover her mouth while I buried my face in her pillow because we didn't want our laughing to be recorded, and boy was it torture.

Even Xavy almost snorted when he got to the "Hurray! Huzzah! Good show, even" part, but he stayed cool and finished the greeting without any mistakes. Makena's giggles are hard and choppy, and tears are starting to squirt out of her nose, and now Frida's getting all riled up, barking loud and doing circles on Makena's bed, which makes our bellies and jaws ache even more.

I hear Papa's and Mama's scrambly footsteps down the hallway, and they both ask all of us what's so funny. Makena's still giggling, which you can tell makes Mama feel good inside by the sweet smile lighting up her face. When Xavy presses the play button on Makena's answering machine, Papa asks, "Who the hell is that?"

Mama laughs and says, "It's your son doing that *loko* Snagglepuss impression of his." Papa smiles and asks us to play it again, and now we're all over the floor and on Makena's bed clutching our bellies and giving Xavy high-fives.

When the laughter tones down, Papa keeps telling Xavy that he should go into show business and he'll be his manager. Mama strokes Frida's ears, and Makena is leaning against the headboard of her bed with her eyes ready to shut. When she starts to cover her mouth, I can tell it's not from the laughing.

All of a sudden, she runs to the hallway bathroom, and we can hear her gagging over the toilet.

Papa and Xavy and Mama and I look at each other like the party's over. Everyone walks out of Makena's bedroom one by one, and there are no more laughs, no more words.

Mama goes to the bathroom to check on Makena and clean the toilet.

Papa walks downstairs to his second office to smoke.

Xavy turns on the TV to a rerun of *The Sopranos.*

I decide to go back to Makena's bedroom, and I listen to the Snagglepuss greeting over and over.

hmmm is snagglepuss bakla *and wait what why am i even asking this because just look at how he made everyone filled with gladness so golden for that one tiny moment when nobody cared if he was being a boy or a girl or maybe just a funny animal.*

I still keep laughing, but I make sure my ha-ha's aren't too loud.

48. mothertrucking murderers

Xavy says I could join the *pusoy dos* pro circuit if there was one, and I think Mr. Baluga knows it. Lola Evie keeps telling him I'm improving, saying "Give her a pat on the back, you grouchy old man," but he still believes that I have beginner's luck. Like sometimes I'll get three twos and even the two of diamonds, but the best cards to have are the ones you can put together to make full houses or high pairs or a bunch of high cards so that you can get rid of them faster.

I'm all out of kiwi strawberry juice, but Lola Evie disappeared to her bedroom, and I don't want to ask Mr. Baluga because he looks like he's concentrating hard. You're really not allowed to take that long when it's your turn, but Mr. Baluga doesn't care, he'll take all the time he needs to beat me, he always says.

"*Putangina*, my cards are so crappy," Mr. Baluga snaps. He isn't afraid to say bad words in front of me because he knows our family's always mouthing off, saying shit and shet and ass and goddamn and even the F word. Mama and Makena try to tell Papa and Xavy to take it easy on the cursing, but Papa's boiling hot temper and Xavy's gangster ways make them keep forgetting to when I'm around.

Putangina is a Tagalog curse word, and the full saying is *putanginamo*, which means your mama is a slut. Now that's even worse than shet or goddamn or even the F word if you ask me, but I hear it so much that it's starting to bounce right off my ears.

"Here, take *that,* Kid," Mr. Baluga says, picking at the long hair hanging from his mole.

He lays down a full house, but his three-of-a-kind is made up of just fives, which I can beat. So I throw down three tens and a pair of threes.

"'*Tangina*, Kid, you're so lucky."

I smile to myself and think of Lola Evie, who probably would have slapped Mr. Baluga on the head with a fly swatter and told him to apologize and say I'm becoming quite the hustler. That's what she always does. She usually hits Mr. Baluga with whatever she has in her hand. One time it was one of those feather dusters, and another time it was a dirty sponge. I hope if it's ever a frying pan, she remembers what she's holding.

"Why are some people luckier than others?" I ask Mr. Baluga, but he doesn't say anything because he's still trying to find a way to beat me. While I wait for his answer, I admire the pink and purple and white hydrangeas that Lola Evie arranged in the vase that Mama gave her for her birthday last year, which are big and round like marigolds but way prettier and have way more tiny and delicate-looking petals.

Then I look across the room to the hallway, where I notice for the first time that same picture of Jesus I saw in the hospital chapel. This one is wrapped inside a gold frame that has chips at the edges. I wonder if it's a sign, if Jesus is checking up on me and did I sin without knowing it.

"Kid, the things that fly out of your mouth. They aren't the questions of a typical third grader. You should take up philosophy when you get to college."

"Plato and Aristotle were philosophers," I tell him. "But I know who they are only because Makena learned about both of them in high school and would preach their philosophies to Mama and Papa."

"Christ, Kid, it's possible you're really sharper than that sister of yours. For all I know, you're schooled in all of that *cogito ergo sum* garbage."

I'm surprised that Mr. Baluga knows a philosophy quote which I think he said in Latin, but he can be capricious like Papa too. I want to tell Mr. Baluga I know just their names and not what their philosophies were all about, but now he's saying I might be smarter than Makena, which I think is super crazy awesome because hardly anyone has bigger brains than my *áte.*

"All right, Kid, you wanna know why some people are luckier than others?"

I answer, "Okay…" but I don't feel too sure because when I look more closely at Mr. Baluga's face, I notice it's starting to turn squishy and red.

"It's because the world is a crapshoot. God doesn't believe in luck. He has a different plan for each and every one of us. If we're hit by a bus, he's got a reason for it. If we win the Lotto, he's got two more reasons. If we get kidnapped or murdered or become famous or rich or both, he's got a mothertrucking boatload of reasons."

I've never heard Mr. Baluga say "mothertrucking," and I know he wanted to say the uncensored version, but I'm glad he didn't. I'm listening to every word he's saying because even though his tone seems to cut like a blade, it also massages my insides, which makes me feel ambivalent again.

"You just have to hope you're one of the luckier ones. But even if you're lucky one minute, you might not be the next. So, Kid, just keep living. That's my only advice to you. And stop asking all your questions. The answer will always be to keep living."

frida

frida you are my beagle who is light brown and black and white which means you're a tricolor with such a kind face that has dark brown eyes the color of hot chocolate when there's too much powder in the mug. you're also full of energy and just like makena you had surgery but yours was called a TPLO *which stands for tibial plateau leveling osteotomy and this means the vet cut your bone and rotated it to make it level instead of sloped so that it wouldn't tear any more of your knee ligaments.*

you throw up easily especially when i sneak people kinds of food to you like strawberries and the soy sauce and lemon beef steak dish without the onions that mama makes when she's lazy and boy do you have a problem with your anal sac so we were all surprised that papa didn't make us get rid of you when he discovered your foul habits. mama and makena think your anal problem is offensive-smelling like fish that wasn't supposed to be thrown away in the garbage and even worse than papa's and xavy's farts which filipinos call utots.

all dogs have an anal sac with two glands that store a fluid which usually comes out with their poo piles whenever they're marking scents or whenever they have to defend themselves like skunks do when they spray. xavy says he wishes he had an anal sac so that he could squirt the junk all over the people he gets pissed off at or on the ones who annoy him.

i enjoy watching you play because that's when your tail wags so hard and fast that your whole body seems like it's making a cool and funny dance move. i also love to stare at you when you take naps because you look innocent which mama always says about babies but no one seems to remember that dogs stay innocent their whole lives because babies grow up to know the meaning of money and why it makes families fight and what holding a grudge is and what wars and killing and being mean and nasty to people on purpose are.

my favorite kuwento *about you is the one about el portal drycleaners which is where mama picks up or drops off the dressy clothes that papa wears only when he's meeting with his business associates. even though el portal is a spanish name the people who own the store are asian-looking with one lady named penelope whose arms are covered with light brown age spots just like lola zeny's.*

penelope likes checking out papa's clothes and touching them like they're all silky rich and then she squeezes her lips together and makes hmmph kinds of sounds but never says anything to mama. the other worker is a young woman named chloe who is probably her daughter and right when we walk out of their store mama always says "i've never seen such gorgeous creamy white skin that's even smoother than makena's but don't ever tell your áte *i said that."*

i think i saw chloe smile once but it looked like someone painted it on her face which mama says is the kind of smile that just wants our business. penelope is the same way and just shows her teeth and nods but that's not what a smile is all about if you ask me. mama says el portal is the cheapest and most high-quality drycleaners so she's willing to put up with their fake ways.

one day when mama and i took you to the vet we stopped by el portal on the way home. when it isn't too hot you usually stay in the car with the window open if we have to go do a quick errand but you kept whining like you had to go pee or poo and that's when mama remembered there was a tree with a patch of dirt right in front of el portal so she told me to take you to that spot while she picked up papa's fancy pants.

when i brought you over to the tree that's when chloe ran out of the store right over to us and asked "is this your dog" and i was surprised to hear her say something to me and wow i also couldn't believe the wide grin on her face. i never noticed she had the whitest and most sparkly teeth ever the kinds you see only in commercials for crest whitestrips.

frida you are such an attention hog and you always think the whole world has treats for you so of course you kept wagging your tail and your butt and whenever chloe bent down to pet you. i couldn't believe it but you jumped onto chloe's lap and started to lick her face and this could not be a good thing because a scuffy tongue and smooth creamy skin are an oxymoron but chloe let you kiss her anyway.

all of a sudden penelope came charging out of the store with a shocked-looking mama right behind her. penelope couldn't stop pointing and giggling and then she ran back inside and reached behind the counter and when she came back there in the palm of her hand were two huge doggy biscuits shaped like cats for you, which of course you snatched right up and that's when you started licking penelope all over her creamy smooth face too.

on the day i cried in ms. langevin's lap about makena i told her i just want to be a beagle because sometimes i really do want to be like you frida.

someone who for sure will stay innocent her whole life and someone who can make you show the better person behind your sparkly crest whitestrips teeth and best of all someone who thinks the world is a treat.

p.s. sorry ms. langevin this section needs to be trimmed down too but i don't think you'll be rendered speechless this time because if you spell "dog" backwards you will have many words for what i'm talking about.

49. bristly bangs

It's 11:21, way past my bedtime, but it's hard to sleep because Christmas Eve is tomorrow. I hear Makena's bedroom door creak, so I get up and tiptoe to the hallway. Her door is open just a crack, and when I peek through it, I see Papa standing over Makena's bed.

Makena is lying flat on her back even though she's been sleeping for an hour now, which means she's had a dragging long day. She starts out on her back, but when she gets more comfortable, she turns to her side, sort of like Frida does, but Frida likes to dig through the sheets and blankets and pillows first and pace in circles before plopping on the spot she was digging.

Papa touches Makena's forehead, then his fingers slide over the three moles on her left cheek, which is when he whispers, "The Three Kings" even though most people call these stars in our sky "Orion's Belt."

Makena looks like a baby in a crib, surrounded by fleecy pillows that let her head sink deep into them and maybe escape to her dreams. I wonder if Makena will wake up because Papa's hands usually feel bristly after he's been at his job sites all day.

Papa whispers, "Was I too hard on you, *hija*?"

He brushes Makena's bangs to the side, but they fall right back to where they were, in the most perfect diagonal lines.

Now I also wonder if Makena can hear Papa but doesn't want to say anything because Papa won't like the answer she gives him. Lolo Peping, who is Papa's *tito*, once told Papa he's too hard on Makena, but that never stopped Papa from acting like Mafioso on the tennis court with her, screaming when her backhands were dinky and not powerful like his.

Makena tells me that Papa's tougher on her because firstborn children are expected to set the right example for their younger siblings. She'd rather have Papa be strict with her than let her get away with being lazy and unmotivated, but I don't think Makena was ever that way in the first place.

is this a rule that kids who are born first have to be examples because xavy says that in china they used to kill firstborns if they were girls and there were so many of them that the government had to control the population that was growing too fast but i think it's because everyone thought that boys were better than girls and if you ask me that's what it means to be a misogynist.

The other day when Tita Gwen came over to get help from Mama with last-minute wedding details, Mama asked Tita Gwen what Papa was like when he was younger.

"We weren't close until I was in high school, but Sal says he was a spitfire," Tita Gwen answered. "And he would get angry at you for calling him one because the term usually refers to a girl or a woman. That brother of mine, he's always been so full of machismo. It was our father's fault. He was harder on Antonio than the rest of us, even Choleng and Malou. But Antonio was the love of *Don* Martín's life. We all know he was our mother's favorite too, but to be the apple of our father's eye was the most coveted prize in the José household."

That was the longest I had ever heard Tita Gwen talk, even when she told me and Makena all about Tito Rory's disgusting habits, like cutting his toenails over the toilet seat which means he puts his dirty feet on the part you sit on, or leaving his boogers on their headboard and not bothering to wipe off the crusty leftovers.

I always wondered what it would be like if I could see right through my eyelids. If Makena could see through hers right now and look at Papa's face, so gentle and smooth like a dove, with no crinkles around his eyes and forehead like when he's breaking the hell loose, I'll bet she'd pretend she was sleeping.

50. fraidy fairy foxtrot fun

Tita Gwen's wedding day is here, January 4, 2003.

There were thunderstorms yesterday, but this time I felt daring and strong and didn't sleep under the covers. I listened to the raindrops, heavy showers crashing onto the skylight above our stairway, like they were trying to break through our house and make a tidal wave or something.

Today the streets are still wet and some of the gutters look like they're overflowing, but Tita Gwen's lucky because the weather people on NBC4 promised that the skies would be blue.

Christmas was a little better than Thanksgiving because Mama found some time to decorate, hanging her berry garlands all over the house and displaying the delicate nativity scene with Baby Jesus that she bought in Florence two summers ago. Papa and Xavy didn't bring home a live tree this year because Makena's sensitive to all kinds of smells, but I think the real reason is that they didn't want to deal with the mess.

I don't know why these live trees seem to make hullabaloo for them. All you do is get the Dustbuster out, and you can even buy a tree bag or use an old king-size bedsheet for carrying the tree in and out of your house if you don't want to leave trails of pine needles all over your floor and carpet.

For my Christmas gift, Papa and Mama filled a big basket full of Pochaco notebooks, Snoopy stationery, My Melody stickers, a Cinnamoroll pencil case, and a stuffed animal of each of my favorite Sanrio characters for me. They also got me the Groovy Girls Supersize Awesome Chair, which is big enough for me to sit in.

Xavy got me a Snoopy lunchbox. He says it's retro so you can't find it anywhere, and "How hellzacoo' will ya look at schoo' now, Geek Freak." It's plastic yellow and shaped like a doghouse, and he outbid everyone on eBay to buy it for me. Devi and Bianca and the rest of the gang will be envious for sure.

Makena didn't buy anyone gifts this year. She said she had zero energy to shop on the Internet, which she doesn't really like anyway because you can't hold the thing you're buying in your hands until you open the package that's sent to you.

Mama told me not to say anything, but it was Makena's idea to get me the Snoopy lunchbox.

I'm counting on my fingers and toes all the *titos* and *titas* on both sides of the family and also Lola Zeny, the only grandparent who hasn't taken the ride yet.

Lola Zeny is number 11 on my big toe when I go back to my left foot, so that's 11 presents I didn't get. But the only thing I should be sad about is the people who don't want us in their lives anymore.

I couldn't sleep last night because I can't wait to be a flower girl, even though everyone says I'm sort of old to be one. But I'm excited mostly because I'm finally going to see all the cousins and *titos* and *titas*, who we haven't seen in at least two years, some I think in three whole years. Maybe they'll have presents and maybe everyone will finally make up, but Makena keeps telling me not to get my hopes up.

I heard that Tito Carding might be there, and when Papa first found out about this, he told Tita Gwen he wasn't attending any wedding where that goddamn bigamist was welcome too. Tita Gwen has the most level head in the family, so she didn't have a double quarter pounder like the other *titas* and *titos* would have.

She was able to convince Papa to go and told him that his table would be at opposite ends of the room from Tito Carding's if he showed up, and she even had the courage to tell Papa this was her day and certainly not his and to just be happy for his youngest sister. Then they hugged, which of course made Papa all soft and crumply.

Tita Gwen is more beautiful than ever, just like sunshine with her bright red lipstick and orange-like-autumn eye shadow. Her dark brown hair is slicked back into a tight bun, like Lola

Carmen used to wear hers, and her veil reminds me of the one I wore for my first communion but way fancier, called a lace mantilla that's Spanish-style and made of French lace and drapes all the way to the floor.

Her bridesmaids are in Makena's bathroom getting ready, some with bobby pins sticking out of their mouths and curling irons in their hands, and others with only their bras and panties on or already dressed and fanning their faces so that their makeup doesn't get smudged.

Everyone's wearing ivory, which Mama wasn't too happy about because she says only the bride should wear ivory or white, but Tita Gwen insisted because ivory is one of her favorite colors, so pure and understated. She almost had all the men wear tuxedos the color of cream, but Xavy convinced her that everyone would look like those dudes from *Miami Vice*, a TV show from the '80s that Tita Gwen always makes fun of.

Makena is one of the bridesmaids, but she was close to not being one because her dress wouldn't fit. She was measured right after her surgery when she was still skinny, and last night when she tried on her top, she couldn't fasten the bottom three hooks. When her skirt didn't zip up, she peeled everything off and crumpled it together into a ball and threw it on her bed and told Tita Gwen to find another fat niece to squeeze into this hideous two-piece dress that looks like ivory curtains.

But Tita Gwen didn't get huffy and hissy with Makena because she's the coolheaded one, and she knew that Kate Andrews our neighbor the seamstress could fix the dress like a wizard because that's what she does for a living.

I don't really care for my dress too much because it looks like something a princess should wear, all frilly and long and flowing. But it'll cover my tree-stump legs, which means that none of the cousins and *titas* and *titos* will make fun of me. The florist made me a wreath with rice flowers and creamy roses to wear on my head, and even a kissing ball with the same colors, which I get to hold while I walk down the aisle.

Mama rubbed a tiny bit of gloss on my lips so that they don't look dry in the wedding pictures. It's watermelon one of my favorite flavors, and she said I could use more later if I want to, but I told her only when no one's looking so that the family doesn't think I'm turning too ladylike.

Papa's smoking in his second office, and he's yelling through the door at anyone who will listen to him that he's been in his uncomfortable tuxedo for two hours now and the limo will be here any minute. He's smoking because I know he's nervous about seeing his brothers and sisters again, even though he won't admit it.

I check out Makena in the ivory curtains that Kate Andrews magically made bigger, and it reminds me of the French lady at Nordstrom saying that Makena didn't look like her driver's license, all beautiful and chic and slender. The curtains are still tight, and her skin matches the color of an eggplant that's about to go rotten. Surfer Girl told us that the chemo would affect her pigmentation which just means color, especially her hands because that's where she pokes her veins every week.

Makena can't wear mascara because her eyelashes are still stubbly, and she refuses to wear fake eyelashes. Mama even had to help her fill in the bare spots where some of her eyebrow hairs used to be, all with eyebrow pencil whose color was called cocoa. The florist made Makena a bouquet kind of hat that looks like my wreath, but it covers most of her head since she's lost a lot of hair.

When it's time for all of us to hop into the limousine, Tita Gwen is admiring everyone, throwing compliments here and there and being the lovable *tita* she always is. She tells me I look like Cinderella, which makes my neck turn super crazy hot because no one's ever told me that I look pretty.

Then she turns to Makena and says, "Oh Kena, you look like an angel." Makena smiles at Tita Gwen and tells her, "Thank you, but you're the angel today," and Tita Gwen laughs and says, "Yes, I guess it takes an angel to try to get this *loko* family back together again."

Makena laughs too, and while everyone else giggles and snorts, Makena squeezes my hand tight, trying to keep her own from shaking.

When I look at her, she's all laughs on the outside, but on the inside, I know she doesn't ever want to become an angel.

The wedding ceremony was like a fairy tale, with all kinds of white roses and giant and grand-looking ivory tulle draping the pews like capes. The mass went so fast that Papa didn't even have time to think about the *titos* and *titas*, who were sitting on the groom's side because they all arrived late and there was hardly any room left on the bride's side.

The music was soothing and melodic because Makena helped Tita Gwen pick most of it, like "Air on the G String" for when Tita Gwen and Tito Rory presented the Virgin Mary with the bouquet, a song that makes you sway and hum and even close your eyes because you want to concentrate on each and every syrupy sweet note. Xavy tried to ruin it by poking fun at "G string," which is a thin strip kind of panty that the older girl cousins like to wear, but I kept my eyes shut and let the music play into my brain to make memories.

The reception is the part of the day that Xavy's looking forward to because he wants to observe Papa and all the *titos* and *titas*, especially Tito Carding, who we didn't see at the ceremony. Mama told me to be kind to everyone, including the cousins who never did anything wrong, but don't be too friendly and don't you dare tell anyone that Makena has cancer.

"How can you keep hiding it when Makena looks sick?" I ask Mama, but she isn't paying attention to me because some guy is asking her if he should put the guest book and engagement pictures of Tita Gwen and Tito Rory outside in the courtyard or inside near the gift table.

That's when Tita Lourdes walks up to me, and her smile looks fake and creased like her ruffly dress. She says in a high voice that sounds like she's talking to a puppy, "Oh, you've grown so much *at napakaganda mo* in your long gown, and you can't even see your chunky legs." Then she looks down at my ankles to check if there's anything more to make fun of.

Tita Lourdes is the wife of Tito Pao, who is Papa's second cousin. Even though she said I look so beautiful, Papa says she lives for making *tsismis*, so now I'm feeling ambivalent. I'll bet the next thing she does is *tsismis* to another one of the *titas* that I'm wearing a gown to cover my tree-stump legs.

Tito Vito taps me on the shoulder and says he wants to dance the salsa with me later. He's wearing a velvety jacket with shiny purple pants and white shoes with purple laces, and I know he thinks he looks handsome by the way he's walking. I love the salsa, but Papa might get mad at me for dancing with him because Tito Vito took Tito Carding's side in the family feud.

Tita Malou walks up to me and asks me what's wrong with Makena and why is she wearing a hat. Her gown is bright and glittery, and I almost laugh when I remember Xavy telling me during the ceremony that she looks like the whale we saw at Sea World but in a repugnant blue dress. I tell her nothing is wrong, and she keeps asking why Makena's hair is short and why her skin got dark and how come she's so fat now. But I keep my mouth shut like Mama said, and I walk away quietly when Tita Marijo taps her on the shoulder to share more *tsismis*.

I see Katie and Marie sitting at their table, and I almost don't recognize them because Katie's makeup reminds me of Marilyn Manson the ghoulish rock singer, and Marie's boobies grew into the size of melons. When their eyes meet mine, they turn away fast. We used to do cartwheels together and spray each other with the hose in Lola Zeny and Lolo Carlo's backyard, and we'd have camping parties where we would tie our bed sheets to the bedpost and the door to make a tent. Now we can't even look at each other.

All of a sudden, a bunch of the boy cousins run past me, and I feel my dress whoosh all the way above my head. Benji snorts while he holds the skirt part up high, pointing and yelling, "Hey, check out dem thunder thighs," and now everyone can see my legs and even my pink Hello Kitty panties because Mama wouldn't let me wear shorts underneath.

I try to yank my dress out of Benji's hands as fast as I can and scream at him to stop it. I look around left and right, and then to the left again and all over the room for Papa or Xavy to save me.

Xavy makes like a giant boulder rolling from across the room, ready to squash whoever dares mess with me. He pulls Benji over to the side and grabs him by the collar of his shirt and threatens to tell his old man about his gangster ways. He shoves

Benji's pale fraidy-cat face into mine, forcing him to say he's sorry and there's no way in hellz he'll do it again, wrapping Benji's collar around his neck even tighter.

When Benji finally squeaks out his apology, Xavy tells me to ignore everyone and just have fun. But now I think it's too late.

Xavy's still waiting for some grown-up drama to happen, but it looks like the only thing going on is everyone avoiding each other or giving each other dirty looks. Papa has the meanest *malocchio* of them all, and none of them would dare look back at him, even Tita Choleng, who isn't afraid of too many people.

Xavy bumps his elbow against mine and tells me to check out Tito Pedro and Tito Jo-Jo, Papa's cousins, who both had strokes a few months ago, according to Papa. They're walking towards each other to shake hands and can't even lift up their right arms. Tito Jo-Jo tries to say something to Tito Pedro, but both of them are still slurring their words. When they finally figure out that they can shake with their left hands, everyone starts laughing and pointing as if having a stroke is no big deal.

Tito Dante yells from across the room, "It's hard to kill off the sons of bitches of this world!" and of course Tito Pedro and Tito Jo-Jo hear him and start yelling *putanginamo* and laughing evil, slapping each other's thighs with their left hands.

Xavy says he can't get enough of all the José *kalokohan.* He shakes his head and laughs and claps, enjoying the show, and then he tells me he misses the fun times when everyone was still friends.

I miss these times too.

I miss them even if our family is the kind that makes *tsismis* and pokes fun at having heart problems and strokes and all the bad grammar that flies out of our *titos'* mouths, and even at your tree-stump legs, having your dress pulled up for everyone to see, even though you want nothing more than to give Benji and all the boy cousins knuckle sandwiches.

All of them asking why your *áte* is fat and ugly now, stealing jewelry from each other and showing off your velvety jacket and shiny pants when you shouldn't be proud of that kind of outfit.

I miss the karaoke and silly cackles and all the presents at Christmas with Tito Carding dressed as Santa Claus, being with people who are easy to be around, just like Makena's friends Ally and Tracy.

All of a sudden, "The Way You Look Tonight" starts playing, and I think of Lolo Carlo and how he used to enjoy dancing the foxtrot to this song, so I go find Papa to see if he wants to dance with me.

I hear someone from across the room yell to me, "Isa, this is our song!"

It's Carter, who is the kindest cousin in the family if you ask me, but sometimes he's too nice and doesn't fight back when everyone calls him the "Flip Michelin Man" because his body is big and bumpy. He walks with me to the dance floor, where I try to imagine Lolo Carlo wiggling his shoulders and smiling wide like the Cheshire Cat.

I don't even care when all the cousins and *titos* and *titas* are doing their pointing and laughing again because this is Tita Gwen's day, don't make *tampo*, just be a good sport. Carter's an excellent leader, so he knows when to do the brush step, which is the move you make when too many people crowd you on the dance floor. When there's more room, we do the promenade and the swing step, and he surprises me by twirling me during the swing step, which Lolo Carlo never tried before.

Papa and Mama are dancing too. My eyes follow Papa's as they move closer to us, and boy are they twinkling proud. Papa seems relaxed, probably because Tito Carding never came, and Mama sure looks shocked because I don't think she ever saw me do the foxtrot, only the salsa and other Latin dances with those construction workers who used to work down the street from us.

I hear Makena shouting, "Woohoo, Isa," and when I turn towards the table she's sitting at, she looks like she wants to rest her head right there on her dinner plate, and I don't blame her because she had chemo on Thursday instead of Tuesday this week.

She's not that pretty today, but she really does look like an angel, so delicate like a package that says fragile please handle with care, all soft and crumply like Papa was when Tita Gwen scolded him this morning.

I want to go over there and tell her to stop worrying about being an angel and to just have fun, even if you think it's too late.

Then I hear Mr. Baluga's words tickling my ear: "The answer will always be to keep living."

But isn't there more to life than just living?

51. indelibly incredible imbecile

When Makena thinks I'm sleeping, she and Xavy sometimes stay up and talk until super crazy late into the night. Makena and Xavy are pals, peas and carrots like Forrest Gump said in the movie, even though Mama says, "Those two siblings of yours always seem to be at war." They make *kuwento* in Xavy's room and close the door and try to be all hush-hush, but I can still hear them.

"I was forced to punch a panhandler in the face because he attacked me and tried to rob me," Makena says in her low and serious voice. "This is how I always begin my story."

I already didn't like the sound of this, but of course I couldn't stop listening, so I crept like an alligator over to Xavy's bedroom door.

"It was almost 7:00, and Eli was supposed to be at my apartment at 6:00. I must have called his home and cell numbers at least 20 times each. Where in God's name is he, I kept asking myself. He's never late. He can't stand flakiness. 'If you can't be on time for people, you sure as hell don't give a flying fuck about them,' he'd always preach to me.

"Tracy called at two minutes to seven. 'Kenz,' she started, and I could already hear the way her voice was hesitating. 'Hon, we just picked up Eli at the frat house. He's totally hammered. What do you want us to do?' Poor Tracy was practically pleading with me.

"So I asked her to bring him over to my apartment. I didn't care if Eli was drunk, even if we were supposed to go out and celebrate his acceptance to Yale Law. Ally and Adam were already waiting at The Gold Mirror, one of my favorite Italian restaurants in the city. Ally had mentioned their server was getting all uptight and wanted to move them to a smaller table if the rest of their party didn't arrive soon.

"Suddenly, I heard loud voices and stomping outside in the hallway. When I opened the front door, Tracy and Antoinette were standing near the elevator. Their bodies were stiff and staying as far away from Eli as they could. He was running up and down the hallway, yelling 'Get the fuck away from me' at the top of his lungs every time Sanjay and Johnny tried to grab him. Sanjay was finally able to pin Eli down when Eli tripped over his own feet. Then he and Johnny dragged Eli down the hallway and shoved him into my apartment.

"'Here's your loser of a boyfriend,' Sanjay said to me. I remember how sad I felt when I saw the disgusted look on his face. He was usually all toothy smiles, like nothing could ever make him bitter. Johnny just stood there with narrow eyes, eyes that followed Eli everywhere he stumbled in my living room.

"'I'm *nombre uno*,' Eli announced to me, and he saluted and pointed to himself as if he were a gift of God. I was mortified by his Spanish. 'It's *número uno*, you jackass. And number one you absolutely are *not*.'"

Xavy snorted so loud that I almost did too. Hearing Makena curse is like Papa telling one of his sidekicks that he should take grammar lessons from his eldest instead of shaking his head and blurting out, "*Tu inglés es miserable, tonto*."

"I turned to Sanjay and Johnny and apologized, and I remember them looking sorrier than I was feeling—but only after they couldn't help laughing about Eli being called a jackass. Then I had to tell them how horrible I felt and asked them to just go ahead to the restaurant with Tracy and Antoinette.

"My two girlfriends were now standing at the door and poking their heads inside whenever they got the chance. They were careful not to set one foot into my apartment. Antoinette's eyebrows were drawn together into a thick black line, and Tracy's arms were folded tightly against her chest. Her face looked like someone had slapped it around like pizza dough. I wondered what else Eli had done and said to them.

"After they all left, Eli grabbed my face and planted an obnoxious kiss on my mouth. Even though his breath reeked of booze and he was acting like such an asshole, his soft lips still made me weak at the knees.

"'What the fuck do you think you're doing?' I said to him. Eli hated the sound of the F word coming from my 'proper mouth,' which he always gave me grief about.

"Then he pushed me. He shoved my right shoulder, then my left one. I felt my entire body hitting the living room wall and crashing into a bunch of folding chairs I hadn't put away from the party I threw for him the night before, which I had really regretted at that moment. Shockingly, he pulled me up from the floor. I screamed at him to get his hands off me, but he bent down and laid his finger over my lips.

"'*Cálmate, mi niñita,*' he said to me. He rubbed my cheek softly with his callused fingers. I loathed him calling me his *niñita*, especially with his atrocious Spanish and his despicable smugness.

"He stood up abruptly and ran to the bathroom. A few minutes later, as he laid in my bed, he tried hard to keep from passing out. I don't know why, but I felt compelled to stroke his forehead. I smoothed his silky brown hair and walked my fingers down to his flushed neck. I placed the silver mixing bowl that I had grabbed from the kitchen beside his head in case he needed to vomit again. Why was I being so nice to this prick?

"'I love you, Christy,' he whispered, peering into my eyes with his bluish gray ones. His hands fondled my breasts and started to slide their way into my blouse and behind the cups of my bra. I wanted to vomit into that silver bowl."

I could hear Makena's voice getting squeaky like she was about to cry, and that's when I start to feel my body shiver, but I don't have those kinds of chills, like when you're cold or scared. They're the ones you get when you're not supposed to be listening because you're only a kid and it's wrong to hear words like "prick" and "fondle" and "breasts" and a *puti* boy named Eli Enki-Abrams speaking Spanish and touching my *áte* so rude and unholy.

"'What? Christy?!' I couldn't help shouting. Eli had never told me he loved me, even after nine indelible months together. Christy was his ex, the girl he shared a condo with when they were freshmen. I was beside myself."

I was wondering what "indelible" meant and if Makena meant "incredible," but I could tell that this part of her story was making her fuming mad by the way her voice went from squeaky soft to booming loud and clear, so I kept listening.

"Eli sprung up as if someone had woken him from a nightmare. His pink face turned white pretty darn quickly. That's when I decided to punch that stupid white face. Right in between his perfectly sculpted nose and those full-fleshed, rosy lips.

"A precise left hook, just like Papa had taught me. If I wanted to hurt the imbecile, all I would've had to do was use the ball of my palm and shove it upward into his nose. This maneuver, Papa explained to me, could kill someone instantly."

I couldn't help raising my fists and almost punching Xavy's door when Makena got to this part of her *kuwento*. I even busted out a "Yes" and "Hurt the imbecile" and not really under my breath, but I didn't care. I heard Xavy say, "Ma seestah da badass" and pictured his fists in the air too.

"At first, there wasn't any pain from the force of my punch, but out of nowhere, I felt a fist land between my left eye and cheekbone. It stung as if a hundred needles were piercing their way through my flesh. Papa had also taught me how to block a punch, but never in my life did I expect my own boyfriend to hit me back.

"I glared at Eli while he cupped his hand over his nose. When he saw his entire palm covered with blood, he yelled, 'Fucking hell. You cunt. You make me sick!'"

I could tell that it was hard for Makena to say these vulgar words, even though she was just repeating them. The nastiness made my body twist and curl up tight, like Mama's fusilli that she makes way too *al dente*.

Sins are sins because they make you do the wrong thing, Sister Velma tells us in catechism class. I always go to confession, but I'm not sure I'd be able to tell Father Jack about "cunt" and "F'ing hell" and a "flying F" and about a dreadful bad boyfriend hitting my *áte* and treating her like she was a piece of spoiled food, the kind you decided not to throw out because it would make the whole trash can stink.

"Seconds later, I heard the thundering slam of my front door. I felt for the spot near my eye and drew back my hand quickly when it burned again. I stared at that silver mixing bowl sitting beside my pillow and saw my reflection. I could barely make out my face, but from what I could see, the image was warped. It was imperfect."

is imperfect the same as damaged and why do boys keep making girls feel this way?

Makena went on to tell Xavy that Papa knew Eli would hurt her. "Papa never gave Eli the time of day, as charming as Eli was. Mama ate up that 'Aw shucks I'm so awkwardly adorable and boyish' act, but Papa stared it down and wanted to challenge it to a fistfight. Papa had said that all he needed to know was Eli was Jewish with divorced parents."

Makena complains all the time that Papa can bc "sadly xenophobic," which means he's hostile when it comes to other ethnic groups and just different people in general, which is confusing because one of Papa's best friends named Jacob Lebow is Jewish. And whenever Christmas comes around, Papa always cackles when he hears Adam Sandler's Hanukkah song that makes me snort too even though Xavy says, "I knowz ya dun't git most o' dem Jewish jokes an' references, foo'."

Ms. Langevin likes reminding us to see things in color and treat everyone equally. There are people who come from other parts of the world and believe in things we aren't familiar or comfortable with, but I think there are many who see in black and white their whole lifetime, kind of like what I learned about dogs in my book about beagles, but Makena found out that they aren't fully colorblind and see only combinations of blue and yellow.

why do i keep feeling ambivalent over and over and boy it's not comfortable at all because you can't decide which feeling is stronger than the others you're having and sometimes the feelings all take turns being the boss.

Makena tells Xavy that she would have to explain the red splotch between her right eye and cheek to everyone, even strangers who might want to know what happened to her. The smear on her face that would soon be black and blue, like the bruises of wives getting beat up by their husbands who believe that men are superior and have the right to be this way.

to be this way what does that mean is this who they really are?

When Makena tells this story, she changes the beginning and the end. Xavy knows how it really turns out, but Makena says she always finishes her *kuwento* like this:

"The panhandler started to tug at my purse, and I yanked back as hard as I could. When the strap broke, he came after me again. The moment his face met mine, he landed a punch right between my right eye and cheekbone. After I felt the sting, I laid a jab straight to his upper lip. He fell to the ground, calling me a cunt and a bitch. Then I sprinted down Durant Avenue.

"When I was far enough away from him, I emptied the contents of my purse and tucked them into my jacket pockets. I dumped the purse into the nearest garbage can, shoving it to the bottom. Deep down with the rest of the filth, ensuring its nonexistence."

52. sitting still sitting

It's March 20, 2003, and it's the first day of spring.

The only noise I can hear right now is the washing machine running, warm water gushing through creaky pipes, which is a wondrous kind of sound because now I can play with my Groovy Girls in peace.

Mama bought me Trini last week, and I think she's radical cool. Her hair is dark and short, just like mine. I'm hoping someday to get the Groovin' Scooter and of course more pink and purple and neon green clothes for Trini and Kayla and Sarita and Kami. Especially Kayla, who doesn't have many outfits because there aren't too many things that fit nicely on her, but she's still at the top of my list of favorite Groovy Girls.

When Xavy announced this morning from the top of the stairs that he'd walk Frida, I couldn't help saying, "No way, dude." Papa looked surprised too, and he even added that a goddamn bombshell just dropped right onto our stairway.

Xavy took the retractable leash, and I was hoping he knew how to use it because you can get the worst slashes from the long cord if you aren't careful, especially if Frida sees a cat or a squirrel and goes bonkers.

One time, she did circles around me when she saw a mouse running across the street and then under one of Lola Evie's rose bushes, and boy did the cord burn. I remember bright red lines streaking across where the creases of the back of my legs are, and I'll never forget all the antiseptic and Neosporin that Mama had to rub on my gashes that day.

Mama's making fried eggs and *longanisa*, which I think is way better than linguica or chorizo. Most Filipinos dip it in vinegar and garlic and eat it with fried rice instead of putting it inside a *pan de sal* sandwich. Mama made sure to start cooking after Makena left because she can't stand all kinds of odors, especially fried meat.

These days, the smell of chemo is starting to make Makena gag. She says it's like a medicine cabinet, with alcohol kinds of fumes that live inside your nose and your memory for a long time.

Papa took Makena to Dr. Minor's office, and when they get back, Papa might have some time to go with us to 31 Flavors before he heads to his job sites.

I hear the garage open, and the door that connects it to the house swings open right after.

I expect to see just Papa and Makena. But they come in with Xavy, and they're all walking in slow and heavy steps. I watch Frida's dark brown eyes following their moves, and her tail isn't doing the windshield wiper kind of wag she's so good at, especially after she's had a walk. It just points down to the floor and hangs close to her legs.

"Jell."

"Isabel."

Papa's voice recites our names quiet and deep. He tells us to go to the living room.

I sit on our small brown leather chair that's next to the green couch, which Xavy told me the other day is from Ethan Allen, and boy did that make me snort.

Frida jumps right onto my lap. This is what she does only when she feels like she needs protection.

Makena's at one end of the ugly Ethan Allen couch.

Xavy's on the other.

Mama's sitting on the piano bench, which doesn't look normal because I've never seen Mama near the piano.

"What's wrong, Antonio," Mama asks. She's eyeing Papa hard as if her glare will squeeze the answer out of him.

I hate all the staring and stiffness, so I try to get Makena's attention by curling my lip to the tip of my nose, which usually gets some giggles. Even though no one feels like laughing or smiling, it might get everyone to talk about something pleasant.

But Makena just stands up and ignores me. She clutches the back of her neck and rubs it, and she says her words clearly but with a strange-sounding and halting kind of tone, almost like she's reading to kids in preschool.

"Dr. Minor, gave me, the results, of my CT-scan. There's, a tumor, in my liver."

When Mama first found out that Makena had colon cancer, she made a soft humming noise, like a siren far off in the distance, like there was a chance that the siren might not stop at our house. Now Mama's wailing at the top of her lungs, and it's kind of hurting my ears.

I keep folding my lip up to my nose not because I want to make people laugh or even change the subject, but because it's fun.

there's a tumor in your liver and we don't have fun anymore.

Everyone's always splitting up to different rooms in the house and trying to find their own happy things to do but always looking like living life is super crazy hard.

there's a tumor in your liver so now what.

I know my *áte* is sick, but Papa reminds me to keep playing and being me, so that's what I've been doing. I play with my Groovy Girls and test out new neon pink outfits for Trini and Sarita and Kami, and I can't now because we're stuck in a family circle.

No one says anything for a long time. All you can hear are Mama's sharp cries.

there's a tumor in your liver and it all just sucks.

I decide to ask Makena if she needs another surgery, but she's already shaking her head no before I finish asking the question, which I don't like one bit.

"Isa, the tumor can't be operated on. It's tricky when it's in the liver."

"How about chemo," I ask, and I feel better when she doesn't shake her head this time.

"Dr. Minor's going to try Camptosar with my 5FU treatment every two weeks. It's much stronger, so it'll make me really weak."

"Not *weak*, and it'll work," Papa bursts out, raising his fist to the air. "Let's be aggressive here. They say Camptosar is the best that's around right now."

"Yes," says Makena.

I can't tell how she's feeling. Her expression is like a stone, like something that could never be soft again and never even was to begin with.

there's a tumor in your liver so what does that mean and how did it get there if you were on chemo?!

I wonder why it's tricky to operate there, but I don't fire away with any more questions because it doesn't look like anyone is in the mood to answer them right now.

Finally, I feel the sadness settling into my body. It's heavy and it's making me sink into the chair cushion like I'm being gulped up by a furniture whirlpool. I look around the room, and there's no hugging, not even any more tears from Mama.

We just sit still.

I think about Makena's first CT-scan and how we went to 31 Flavors afterwards, then looking up at the ceiling and thanking God or was it the Lord.

there's a tumor in your liver. a tumor a tumor a tumor.

This is all I hear in my head, and now there's nothing to thank anyone about.

I stroke Frida's ears, which are extra smooth today because Mama gave her a bath a few days ago. She doesn't get baths too often because her hair is short and sheds like crazy mad, and my beagle book says if you bathe beagles frequently, they might develop skin diseases, and we sure don't need another disease in this house. That's why you're supposed to just brush beagles and let the natural oils from their skin ooze out.

When everyone leaves the room, I find Frida's brush inside her chest full of dog supplies in the kitchen pantry, right next to the large Ziploc bag of Swedish Fish. I brush long and full strokes on her body. Frida likes being brushed because I can tell it feels like a massage to her, with her eyelids draping over just the top half of her eyes from being so relaxed. I keep going until her brush fills up with hair, but this time it makes her whine and pull away like I'm hurting her.

there's a goddamn tumor in your liver a goddamn tumor a goddamn tumor ha ha i'm saying goddamn like a skipping record goddamn so now is it time to make my crafty poker face?

I just keep picking Frida's hairs from the bristles. I brush again, and then I toss the hairs over to the side and start all over.

Xavy appears behind me and asks me what I'm doing, bending down and trying to take the brush all careful and calm from my hand that won't stop shaking.

I answer, "What does it look like I'm doing."

When I realize my words sound flat and crabby, Xavy doesn't show me his fist or say something all smarty pants.

He lets go of the brush and stands up. He rubs my shoulder a few times, almost like he's massaging it, and then he walks away slowly like he's Sasquatch the Bigfoot on tiptoes, but boy it sure isn't making me crack any sort of smile.

tito gus

oh tito gus you were a marvelous uncle and my memories of our times together are tucked away in a special corner of my brain. when makena and xavy and i were all younger we had such a ball peeping through the curtains of the living room window and watching you walk up the brick steps to the front door and i remember you always walked like you were balancing a vase on your head. your clothes were comfy and colorful you know the kinds that flowed like the sail on a sailboat and you would tell us that you wore these clothes to hide your taba *which means your fat and sometimes i'd find some of your* taba *and pinch it and you'd shout "i'm going to inhale you" and chase us all over the house.*

papa used to warn us about your nose because you could probably inhale all three of us but hmmm maybe not xavy. then papa would joke that your nose formed its own face and insist that only baklas *are cursed with pug noses and i'm not really sure why that's a curse. you would point to your stumpy nose and explain to me that filipinos have this thing about noses. you would always say that if you have a* mestizo *nose that's high and long like those* puti *movie stars then you are bee-yoo-tee-pool. when you said "beautiful" you'd close and open your eyes like they were wings flapping and your eyelashes looked like the wispy feathers of a peacock.*

i don't believe for one second that only baklas *are cursed with pug noses because mama has sort of a puggish nose and a lot of my classmates have stubby noses even mario caldwell who is half-*puti *and one of the most macho boys at school.*

makena says that gay people really live up to their name because most of them are happy and masayang kasama *and xavy likes to add that* "baklas *dey a'ight man dey tellz it like 'tiz an' dey have major* cajones *fur being who dey iz."*

papa says all the baklas *he has ever met are hard workers but sometimes they play harder and most of them he knows are flaky which is like saying you'll be at someone's party but then you forget to show up or decide to go somewhere else without telling the party host.*

papa believes that you my tito gus were born gay and it's in the genes which is why he thinks our cousin shannon is bakla. *he always says "that son of a bitch has a girl's name and likes to cook and sew and your tita marijo says he wants to be a goddamn nurse when he grows up."*

i think baklas *are like enigmas which was another one of xavy's SAT words that means you're hard to figure out so i think that enigmas like you make this world a more interesting place to live. all the things that people say about* baklas *even the bad stuff like playing too hard and being flakes makes me forget they're supposed to be just weak little queers but i think that if the way makena uses "queer" which is like when people say "you're odd" or "that's strange" is the true meaning of this word then boy would it be epic to be a strong little queer.*

53. boojie-boo baseball

I'm trying to find a safe place for my Snoopy beanbag inside my luggage because we're finally making *pasyal*. Not just regular *pasyal* but a small kind of vacation for the whole family. We're packing our bags and driving to San Francisco for four whole days. While we're there, we're going to watch Makena and Papa's favorite baseball team, the San Francisco Giants.

Papa refuses to let the news of Makena's tumor bring us down, so he made sure to plan our short vacation before Makena starts Campsotar, no I mean Camptosar.

It's going to be a splendid four days.

The Giants game we're attending is an exhibition called the Dog Days of Spring, which means Frida can be there too. There's also a Dog Days of Summer that's in August, so I hope we can all visit San Francisco again to be at the summer game.

Papa wasn't too happy about "this whole Dog Days bullshit" at first because we have to sit in the bleachers, the only place where dogs are allowed. Papa promises that next time he'll find us the finest seats in the park, right behind the plate so that we can see just how hard Barry Bonds hits.

Xavy thinks Barry is dope even though Papa thinks he cheated with steroids, which make your muscles huge and keep you from having all kinds of injuries, and that's when Makena jumps in and says, "Most players wouldn't be able to hit a baseball like that even if you pumped drugs into them. It's all about hand-eye coordination and bat speed."

Most people choose Barry as their favorite because he hits all kinds of home runs, but I like J.T. Snow because he moves like a white lion that doesn't need to try and still catches balls you aren't supposed to at first base. Papa says that J.T. isn't hitting so well this season, but he has stellar defense for a first baseman so he deserves the Gold Glove, which is what you win if you are the best at your position. Papa has taught me lots about both tennis and baseball, since those are two of his favorite sports.

Papa isn't a Dodger fan like everyone else in LA because he can't stand Tommy Lasorda, and when I ask Papa what Tommy Lasorda ever did to him, he answers, "That Lasorda would fight with umpires just to get more time on TV. He also has a short fuse and is cocky and outspoken," and this makes Xavy snort and cackle because Papa might as well be talking about himself.

Papa enjoys football too, but it turns confusing when all the referees throw so many of those yellow flags on the field. Papa always gets irked every time I ask him what happened after each flag.

At Pacific Bell Park which everyone calls Pac Bell, it smells fresh because I remember Makena saying that the air up north is healthier, and I can see why because there's crisp light blue everywhere I turn. We brought our own seat cushions because the bleachers are benches, not real seats like in the movie theater.

Baseball fans are everywhere, they're in front of me and walking right at me, and they're also behind me pushing on my backpack. Sometimes I look back at them and give them a *malocchio* when they shove me, but they don't even know what they did, so I feel bad about looking feisty in the first place.

There are many things to see, like the screen called a JumboTron that's full of announcements and a list of the home and visiting teams and their numbers called stats, which show you how the players are doing. And the 25-foot-tall baseball glove that Papa says is overkill and even the matching giant Coke bottle, where inside of it are slides for kids that Xavy says we'll check out during the seventh-inning stretch.

Then there's the overpriced food that Mama was complaining to me about, but it's so yummy and it tastes even better when you're finally sitting in your seat and letting everything around you soak into your body.

We all can't wait to walk on the field for the dog parade because Makena told us that "Pac Bell is one of the most well-built and aesthetically pleasing ballparks, so classic and scenic." Some of the dogs are in costumes, but Frida can't wear one because she hates wearing hats or any kinds of clothes we put on her and just chews them right off.

the baseball field is wide and green like a refreshment to my eyes oh i love it so much that i feel my insides grinning and boy i don't ever want to leave.

No one fought during the whole car ride which was 6 hours and 26 minutes, and Papa didn't even have any curse words for the stinky cows at Harris Ranch. Mama was crocheting red roses on the afghan she's making for Makena, and she usually stays quiet while she's busy with her hands, but she even took some time to turn around and talk to me and Makena and Xavy.

She asked us if Frida was hanging in there because sometimes she starts to pant and shake when the car's going fast, but this time she just stayed in an obedient down position in her car crate or used my lap to look through my window once in a while. Papa's Suburban is one of the biggest cars there is, and it's comfortable for our family because Makena and I get our own seats in the middle row and Xavy gets the whole backseat to himself.

No one mentioned tumors or Camptosar or sickness once, and the only time Makena had to go to the bathroom was when we stopped in Kettleman City to get gas. We had lunch at In-N-Out, which makes Xavy and Makena's favorite burger in the whole world.

I don't see what the fuss about In-N-Out is, but people say their meat and lettuce and tomatoes are the freshest and their fries are cooked in canola oil, so they're healthier compared with other fries, like the ones at McDonald's.

But no one can ever beat McDonald's fries, not too soggy and not too crispy, even though Makena read on the Internet that all sorts of chemicals are added to the vegetable oil and that the fries are pretty much a concoction of dextrose, salt, and beef fat.

There's nothing hard to think about today, so my brain feels like it can finally take a break. I wish I could record this day and be able to play it over during the times when everything feels topsy-turvy. Maybe someday an inventor will build a machine like a camera, something that can freeze incredible or maybe even indelible times like these, just like a picture.

But instead of a picture, you get a special little box that keeps the good moments safe, and when things start to turn every which way and can't find where they're supposed to be, you can slide the box into another machine and let it play until you breathe easy again.

When we walk by the Giants dugout during the dog parade, Makena's super shaky excited, hoping she gets a decent look at Barry. I see a boy who's older than me but younger than Xavy and he's holding out his hand, and all of a sudden he's petting Frida and saying "boojie-boo" to her, which is both funny and comforting because sometimes we talk baby to her just like that.

Xavy says, "Hey, that's Barry Bonds' son," and we all say cool and all right to each other.

When we get closer to left field, Frida's butthole is bulging, and I think *uh-oh* because I know she won't be able to hold it. When she starts to squat, everyone laughs and points, and one of the security people is shaking his head at me because dogs aren't allowed to walk on the grass.

Papa says, "Look where she's going, right there in left field," and Makena tells me I better pick up every single last bit of her mess because Barry isn't going to like it.

Then Xavy shouts, "Check out Freedz on the JumboTron!" and of course we're all embarrassed because our dog is making a tall poo pile in front of everyone who's watching the game today, and there are all kinds of people here because the Giants are playing the Cubs, even though they're going to stink this season, according to Papa.

Makena came to see Barry hit a homer into McCovey Cove, and Papa's betting Makena a Giants cap that he can't. Xavy is an Angels fan, but he sure loves all the food at this ballpark and says he's already spent more than $25 on just garlic fries, a large soda, Krispy Kremes, and a Polish sausage.

After the dog parade, we go back to our seats in the bleachers. Even Frida gets her own seat, and you can tell she's having a grand old time, checking out all the other dogs and waiting for someone to feed her garlic fries or drop one by accident. We're sitting in left field, so Barry might throw us a ball if we're lucky.

Xavy is getting ready to keep score in the Giants programs that the workers at the entrance handed to us. His sumo wrestler body is taking up a whole seat and a half, but Makena's takes up only half, so everything's turning out even.

Mama is pointing at the view of the Bay Bridge, and her wavy brown hair looks like swan feathers floating lightly in the breeze.

Papa is lecturing Mama about the bridge's history, even though she's heard it many times before. He doesn't have a cigarette sticking out of his mouth because you aren't allowed to smoke in the ballpark, but I don't think he needed one today anyway.

I'm looking for J.T. Snow. Near the bottom of the JumboTron, it says that some guy named Damon Minor is playing for J.T. today. I wonder if he's related to Dr. Minor and if he says "Hi hi hi" too.

Makena tells me, "Don't worry, we'll look for J.T. after the game," but I'm fine, because today is the most magnificent time our family has had in a long while.

I think we need way more days like these.

If we're lucky, this day will keep going, even when we get back to all the craziness and sadness that is our house in Arcadia.

54. wanna wretch

When I opened up my calendar book today, March 31, 2003, it said, "4:00 p.m.: Mama and Xavy and I are picking up Makena from her first round of Camsoptar. I mean CAMPTOSAR."

I can't stay with Makena during her chemo anymore because Camptosar takes an hour and a half to pump through her veins, and this is a lot longer than the 5FU that's been trying to heal the insides of her body. Mama told Xavy and me to stay put in the waiting room while she runs across the street to the bank, and then we're going to Ralphs to buy some whole chickens.

Mama wants to cook *arroz caldo* for Makena tonight. It's a thick kind of chicken rice soup with ginger and green onions and garlic, but Mama's planning on cutting back on all these ingredients so that the *arroz caldo* doesn't make Makena's nose crinkle and force her to gag.

It feels like the bizarro world at Dr. Minor's office now. The antisepticky fumes don't bother me like they used to, and patients in the waiting room don't stare anymore because they know who we are and we know who they are. But now that we're all friends, I feel bad because Surfer Girl tells me that a few of them might not be around much longer.

Surfer Girl isn't afraid to tell me about people taking the ride and not coming back because they were too sick to live, and I don't mind because everyone else tries to change the subject whenever I ask about dying. Ms. Langevin says it's a natural thing we all have to go through in life so don't be scared, but I can't imagine Makena being up there in heaven while Mama and Papa and Xavy and Frida and I are all the way down here on Earth. Most of the time I try not to think about it, and why should I anyway because Makena promised me that she wouldn't leave us.

Mrs. Mojtabai is looking straight at me, and I think she's wondering why I wasn't staring at her fuzzy thin hair, which usually looks like it might all of a sudden drift away. I smile back and say her name slowly after I greet her to show her I've been practicing pronouncing it.

Mrs. Mojtabai has pancreatic cancer, and she sees Dr. Minor right after Makena. She's always here early because Papa says the older you become, the earlier you get to places. I guess that's why Papa likes to arrive at the airport two hours before the plane leaves instead of the one hour that all those people at the ticket counters tell us when we try to get a boarding pass, but when we get to the airport, they tell us that the plane isn't there yet so just relax.

"How's your sister, dear?" asks Mrs. Mojtabai.

"She's having a different type of chemo now," I tell her.

"Do you know what it's called?"

"Camsoptar. I mean Campostar. No, that's not right either," I say, and that's when I start to feel confused and hot.

"*Camptosar*," Xavy answers for me, and he says it like I'm too dumb to be here.

Mrs. Mojtabai lets out a long sigh and straightens her eyeglasses, even though they weren't crooked. All of a sudden, I hear Surfer Girl trying to say Mrs. Moj-ta-bai's name.

"Mrs. M., let's go hop on the scale," says Surfer Girl, and I notice she isn't as loud and bouncy as she usually is.

"Surfer Girl," I call, but she doesn't hear me.

"*Dana*," I say instead, and she looks at me and tilts her blonde head. She walks over and gives me a tight hug and tells me that Makena is doing swell and how is Fridaboo and the rest of the José clan. She notices Xavy and squeezes his arm.

"*Shaaa*-vier, have you been beefing up for your gal pals?"

Xavy's face goes from brown to pink, and Surfer Girl says, "I have to go now, be good to each other you two sweet cakes."

Xavy shakes his head and asks himself, "How does she do it, man?"

"How does she do what?"

"How does she come in here every day and watch these people hit the skids and still be able to call people sweet cakes and have all that pep to make you wanna wretch?"

That's when Mr. Shoemaker and his wife turn to Xavy with scolding frog eyes, and they check me to make sure I'm okay or something. The front door to the office flies open and there's Mama, tearing through her purse and saying, "*Shet*, where are my keys?" Xavy jingles them in his hand and stands up and whips me out of my chair. My right shoulder makes a cracking sound.

While we walk to the parking lot, Xavy's still yanking my arm and I squeal at him to let go of me, but he pulls harder.

After we get inside the car, I tell him, "You're a ghetto poser, and I think you need to go wretch yourself."

Mama doesn't hear me because she's already complaining that there'll be a long line at Ralphs, which is a good thing because she might have insisted on a bath for me tonight for being vulgar, even though she said *shet* in front of all those strangers.

Xavy doesn't even turn his head from the front seat. He just copies what I said in his nanny-nanny-billy-goat voice, and then he adds, "You should try drinking your own bile, you dipstick."

the bile and the chunks of digested matter rise up through my chest and throat and gush through my open mouth and sometimes the rancidness is too much to bear which is forcing me to heave again.

this is what makena wrote in her journal that i wasn't supposed to read but it was so brainy and gross and dramatic that i couldn't stop and it's all because there's a stupid tumor in her liver.

I can't help sighing out loud and thinking that our small vacation ended way too soon.

Now it's just a sweet memory that you aren't supposed to try to fit into a special little box, which I guess is fine with me because Mama always tells me it isn't healthy to cling to the past.

I wonder if my *kuya* knows how bile tastes, and boy would I love to pour a whole jug of it down his throat right now. Will he ever be funny and kooky and not care about anything again? I want to blame Makena for everything that's happening to our family, but that would make me a dreadful person because you can't be mad at someone like her, so I'm probably already a bad kind of seed for wanting my own *kuya* to taste bile.

I look outside my window as we're driving away from Dr. Minor's office, a small building with white shutters and the greenest grass I've ever seen surrounding it, a place where Makena gets to see a nurse so sunny and glad whose job is to make everyone feel like the fizz of an icy glass of soda.

She makes me feel like I'm rising up to the top of the glass, where I can just spill over the rim and ooze everywhere, even when I'm feeling flat and stale.

55. the order of the oppressors

I got Mama to plant electric blue agapanthuses, five in a row right outside our tennis court.

I've been keeping an eye on them, and I can't wait to see them blossom even though that won't be until the end of summer, but that's fine because it's only five months away, and there are many other flowers in our backyard that bloom in the spring anyway.

I want to admire the electric blue that holds their flowery heads high.

Tall and mighty like an empress, someone with the power to make ugliness a crime in her empire.

It's the first day of group tennis classes at South Pasadena Racquet Centre, and I don't really feel like going, so I might make a fake excuse. But Mama doesn't want me to waste the discount we were able to get because of Makena's clout, which means she has influence because she's a college tennis player.

Mama also thinks I need to get away from the house once in a while. Xavy is one of the student teachers, so at least I'll have my *kuya* around to protect me if those bullies Joanne Miyahara and Laura Ledesma and Tawny Davis start to make fun of my tree-stump legs and my big butt again.

Joanne and Laura and Tawny are in GATE, which stands for "gifted and talented education." Makena was always in GATE, where she was one of few students to get a perfect score on the test to be accepted. The bullies are in Mrs. Cooper's fourth grade class, and I'm stuck seeing their sour faces every day because our classrooms are connected.

Ms. Langevin always has to ask Mrs. Cooper to tell her students to stop teasing us, but they keep saying we're nerdy and smelly and that all we'll be doing when we grow up is flipping burgers, which I don't think would be such a terrible thing to do if the restaurant gave you a free burger once in a while.

Xavy told me he'd tell those snobs off if they kept bullying me, and boy I sure would love to hear some of his foul words make them feel small, but Mark Leonard the head teacher would kick Xavy out and me next for being Xavy's sister. Then of course Makena would get embarrassed and all fuming mad at Xavy and me because Mark Leonard used to be her coach and she's supposed to have clout.

Luckily I'm not in the same group as the bullies, so I hope my group ends up on one side of the club, where there are two tennis courts. The other side has eight courts, which is where they usually put all the A group players.

Joanne and Laura and Tawny are in the B group, but they all think they should be in A. They want to be in A only because of Nick Longshore, who they all have a crush on because he has the bluest ocean-blue eyes. He's also the quickest and strongest dodgeball player in all of fourth grade, and I heard he's an LDS member, which means everyone who goes to his church is Mormon, the kind of people Xavy thinks are the most "hellza virtuous an' so dang nice dat ya wish ya wuz like dem but dude dat'll happen when hellz be freezin' ovuh."

Today my luck has run out because the C group and the B group are next to each other, the C group on the first court and the B group on the second court. Xavy teaches one of the A groups, and Mark Leonard decided to squeeze them into the two courts on the other side of the club.

"Isabel, I think your legs and butt are gonna stay plump fuh-evuh-evuh," says Joanne, the leader of the bullies, who everyone calls "Hapa" because she's half-Asian and half-*puti.* I feel my lips bending out of shape at the way she says "forever." I notice her bamboo pole legs, and both her butt and chest are flat like they got trapped under a steamroller, and boy do I want to say this out loud.

Lavelle Lynch, who is the B group teacher in charge of Joanne's group, yells across the net to Joanne that oppressors don't have a place here and she'll have to run five laps around the court if she keeps it up. The oppressors start talking all hush-hush to themselves, but they're loud enough so that I can hear them.

Tawny, who walks like a stork and always hates being called black because she says we're all supposed to say "African-American," starts the loud whispering.

"Hey Laura," she says, "I took that cancer symptom card home to my mom a few months ago, and she couldn't believe they were passing them out at school. It said stuff like stools and bloating and other things that are totally gross."

Then Laura, who Xavy says smells like Del Taco bean and cheese burritos and always has to add "Chill da hellz out, dat ain't racist cuz Mexicans don't eat dat shet," decides to join in with her yapping voice.

"Yeah, and it was all because of Isabel's sister. My brother thinks she isn't even sick. She just wanted to meet Katie Couric. And how could anything bad ever happen to Miss Perfection anyway? My cousin Amy was stuck in all her classes, and she said Isabel's sister made all the other students look stupid. Prom Queen and National Merit Scholar and all that. It's like she isn't human or something."

All of a sudden, Nate Hawkins, the worst player in the C group, is calling my name and shouting that it's my turn to hit forehands to Debbi Betta, our C group teacher.

I can't concentrate because of all the ugly things they're saying about Makena, and when Debbi tells me to keep my eye on the ball and bend my knees, I smack one of my forehands way over the fence to the next court where the bullies are, and of course they laugh and point and tell me how much I suck.

That's when both Lavelle and Debbi scream at the same time at all three oppressors, and Lavelle orders them to run 20 laps around the court. Now everyone else is laughing and pointing at them, even the C group, because that's the most laps ever that a teacher has asked anyone to run.

yeah you all go run those laps while we live in this ugly world where we call each other names even though "plump" isn't all that bad and also in this ugly world where we can't say black to some black people when we go and call white people white and is it only mexicans who don't like del taco? so how about my friend oscar who is salvadoran or joselita who is argentinian? they might like del taco too because there are more than tacos and wait i hear that people from norway love tacos and aren't they all white in that country so i'll bet joanne miyahara will stop making fun of my tree-stump legs and my big butt to match if i told her that i eat arare *japanese crackers.*

do we all make fun of different races without really knowing it and are we not kind and not gentle and not respectful which means we're all sadly xenophobic or maybe just racist because makena says this is what we become when we think our backgrounds and cultures and even our bloodlines are better than everyone else's which is kind of like misogynist boys who think they're in charge of girls.

I get stuck watching the oppressors run around and around with their sour faces, and I'm the only one who isn't laughing because I know all those laps will just make their legs sore and won't change who they are or who they will become.

56. oxymorons overpower opera

It's April 5, 2003, and hurray, spring break starts now.

The moon is usually big and bright, but tonight the sky is black, not the in-between dark blue that it looks like when I wake up in the middle of the night. I made Mama tuck my blankets tight into the mattress because after I saw parts of *Friday the 13th*, which Xavy was watching from his DVD player last night, I kept imagining someone under my bed grabbing my ankles.

The hallway floors are squeaking, and I wonder if Papa or Mama is awake. It's already 3:04 a.m., according to my Snoopy and Woodstock clock. Frida is curled up behind my legs. Usually Frida knows when there's danger, so I wasn't too worried when I kept hearing the floors creak.

One time, Frida started barking at 2:23 in the morning when she heard something outside. Her bark wasn't her regular one, boy was it super deep, and she even growled which she never does and she wouldn't stop barking, so that's when we knew something was up. Papa looked outside his bedroom window and saw someone running between our tall bushes, so he called 911 right away.

The police told him there were teenagers teepeeing our property, which means they were going to cover our house and yard in toilet paper. Most likely it was a prank, but Papa thinks a lot of people can be bought, which he says is asking to have something done that's dastardly and paying the person money for it. Then he started to mutter a bunch of unholy words about Lola Zeny and her *loko* family hiring more thugs.

I knew what Papa meant, but I didn't really want to hear anything more because whenever it has something to do with Lola Zeny, it's something God awful bad.

I get up and tiptoe down the hallway. I peek down the stairs, and there's someone sitting at the bottom step.

It's Papa.

I keep making light steps down until I can see his whole body. He turns around and looks up at me, and his face is shiny.

"Hello, Love," Papa says, and he holds out his hand to me and uses his other one to wipe his face. There's slow music playing, and when I listen closely, I can tell it's Frank Sinatra. He has that big-show kind of voice that reminds me of all the singers in *Les Miserables.*

The song is called "My Way," which is one of Papa's favorites. It seems like it's number one on the top 10 hits for many old men who have those potbellies and think they have melodic voices.

But they just can't sing the right notes and end up ruining the song, and this makes me and Xavy howl every time we have to sit and listen to Old Man Karaoke, which is what Xavy likes to call a lot of those parties we used to have with the *titos* and *titas* and cousins.

The *titos* would gather around one microphone with their arms around each other's shoulders like a football huddle, and they'd keep poking each other's sides and teasing, "You sound like Frank Sinatra, no *you* sound like Sinatra."

Papa picks me up and takes my right hand, and he starts to sing in a big-show but quieter kind of stage voice.

When the "Much more than this I did it my way" part comes, Papa likes to sing louder and hold out his hand to the ceiling like those opera singers do when they're hitting the high notes.

I lean closer to him because I love getting whiffs of his aftershave, which is called Pinaud. It smells like a mixture of soap along with laundry right when Mama takes it out of the dryer, but it's also sweet and manly, even though those two things aren't supposed to go together, just like an oxymoron.

Papa says it's from Paris, and that's when Mama laughs and tells me you can buy it at CVS for $2.99, so don't believe a word your bullshetting father says.

I rest my head on Papa's shoulder and yawn. I pretend I didn't see him cry, but I think he knows that I did.

Papa's voice overpowers the whole room, filling it up with feelings he lets go from his heart when no one is looking.

He must have been singing for a long time because I notice I'm in my bed with Frida behind my legs again. I check Snoopy and it's 4:09 a.m., and the fresh manly scent of Papa's aftershave floats into my room.

I wonder if my papa wants to keep on singing.

57. peachy pitch perfect

April 14, 2003: Makena just got back from her second round of Camptosar, and I'm watching her water Ramona Quimby.

Ramona Quimby hasn't been doing very well lately, but Makena keeps filling her copper watering pot and pouring like mad into the tiny white planter that she lives in. She even talks to Ramona Quimby now, promising her she's going to be just peachy and dandy, like all the old people in the chemo waiting room keep saying to her.

Some of Ramona Quimby's yellow leaves are behind the toilet, where I have to reach far and low so that Papa doesn't yell at me and Makena about the mess in our bathroom. There are other yellow leaves with green specks, or maybe they're green with yellow specks, and those are the enigmas. You can't tell if the green will just decide to disappear or if it'll tell the yellow to take a hike, hey I'm in charge now and don't you dare go and fall behind the toilet.

I've seen my *áte* every day lately, but today I notice her eyelashes are long and curly, not straight like they used to be. Her skin isn't dark anymore, not as light as Mama's and not as dark as Papa's, just in between. It's the softest skin you ever touched, especially on her cheeks and her arms, which feel like those satin sheets we saw at the model home called Trevi a long time ago when Tito Vito told Makena that she was a goddem little shet.

Makena is like Mama's camellias that are light pink with leafy petals, all delicate and feminine, and also like some of Mama's frilly purses that look too nice to carry. This makes me giggle a little because when Xavy was reading a ladies' magazine at Dr. Minor's office the last time we were there, he noticed an article about "feminine items originally made for men," and handbags were number six on the list.

Even though Makena's lost all her weight, and her long legs are like the branches of Mama's ficus tree that you can easily snap in half, I can't stop looking at her. I'll bet the *titos* and *titas* and cousins who kept whispering and pointing at Makena at Tita Gwen's wedding wouldn't recognize her today.

Sometimes I catch Makena singing '80s songs, like "Hold Me Now" by the Thompson Twins or "True" by Spandau Ballet. Makena's voice isn't high and sweet like Mama's, it's lower but not like a man's, so full of warm-sounding tones, and she can hit exactly the right notes without getting help from a piano or any other kind of instrument, which Papa says is having perfect pitch. She fills our house with music from her mouth and with her hands, something no one else in this house can do.

Makena hangs out with Mama in the kitchen now, chopping and dicing and even making carrots julienne, which means cutting into small strips. When Makena's hands start to move like molasses, Mama holds her tongue and just thanks God that her eldest is in better spirits.

Xavy says when Makena helped him with his US history homework, she actually laughed out loud and snorty when he said, trying to sound scholarly and all official-like, "The 'D' in D-Day stands for 'deadbeat.' Deadbeat Day, my friends, should be celebrated every damn day in honor of your deadbeat yet dapper brother, Sir Xavier Christopher Santos José."

Papa cups his hands around his mouth and pretends to holler, "Dees cancer shet deed Makena som gooood," and of course we laugh and high-five when Mama smacks him on the arm for making fun of her accent, which we all love because she's never *pikon*, what Makena always becomes whenever Xavy tells her that she should work for Ethan Allen after she graduates from Cal.

maybe you won't need camptosar anymore hurray i think i can finally pronounce it even though i'm not saying it out loud for someone to say if it's right or wrong but wait i think that's the problem because why do we have to keep making sure it's right to other people and not just to ourselves?

Now Makena's saying she wants to climb our oak tree with me tomorrow, which makes me want to believe that Ramona Quimby's leaves will be turning green again very soon.

58. pumpkin pie

It's April 28, 2003, and we're on the way home from Makena's third round of Camptosar, Papa and Mama and Xavy and Makena and me, and we're all glad to be together because sometimes only Mama and I pick up Makena from Dr. Minor's office. Or me and Xavy or just me and Papa.

I'm usually there for Makena when she's done because her appointments are at 3:30, when I'm already out of school. Xavy keeps saying he'll take Makena by himself and even wait for her so that everyone can relax at home, but Papa tells everyone to keep dreaming because that will happen only when *kalabaws* fly, which is funnier than imagining a pig because a buffalo's body is kind of stumpy.

After Makena's treatment, we picked up Spike's, one of our favorite fast-food places that has teriyaki beef and chicken bowls and teriyaki avocado burgers and even wet fries, which have gravy poured all over them.

We're driving back up San Gabriel Boulevard, and Makena and Xavy and I are playing our usual game, the one where you find as many gas stations and drycleaners as you can, and the person who's counted the highest number total by the time we drive into our garage wins.

All of a sudden, Makena announces that she has to go to the bathroom. Papa says, "We're almost home, just hold it, for crying out loud," but Makena can't. I look at my poor *áte*, and there are beads of sweat ready to roll down her forehead.

Makena looks around the car all super crazy panicky, and then she stands up as high as she can right there in the backseat with me and Xavy and starts to shove her pants down to her ankles and asks Mama for a bag or something, anything, now, and that's when I spot the Kleenex box that's stuck between my butt and Xavy's and decide to yank out all the tissues.

"Here, Makena, go here!" I scream.

"No way am I going in there!" she screams back.

Then Papa butts in, "You bet you're going in there, Miss José! Because there's no way you're going on my leather seats!"

That's when Mama starts to shake her finger at Papa and ask why is he so callous, and before we all know it, my *áte* is pooing inside the Kleenex box I shoved under her tiny butt and using almost every single piece of Kleenex that I hand to her to wipe.

Xavy sticks his head out of the car as far as he can and yells "*DUDE.*" I lift my shirt to cover my mouth and my nose and I try to hold my breath while Papa lowers his own window and shouts "Mother of God," and then I see Mama burying her face in her hands, but that's not really working for her because now she's coughing like a seal.

I look inside the Kleenex box even though I shouldn't have, and Makena's poo looks worse than Frida's, like a rotten pumpkin pie with mushy chunks of orange and brown, which is making me gag now because I had a few slices of pumpkin bread for breakfast this morning.

Papa pulls over to the side of the road in front of a tall yellow house with lots of agapanthuses and bushes and trees and tells Makena to throw the Kleenex box right there in the bushes that are lining the sidewalk next to the house.

Mama all of a sudden snaps, "Antonio, how would you like it if someone dumped a Kleenex box full of shet near your house," and I look at Makena and she starts laughing, but she's crying too because she just pooed a huge pile in the backseat of Papa's new BMW and how is she going to show her face to anyone when they find out that she couldn't hold it in the car.

Xavy starts to crack up too, and now he's asking us if we still want our teriyaki burgers, but I can't laugh with them because it smells like the zoo.

All of a sudden, I throw up in my lap and all over Papa's fancy leather seats.

My eyebrows feel like they've reached the top of my forehead as I sit still like a rock that Papa will want to throw out his window, but all Papa does is shake his head, and boy does he look like he has given up on his family. Mama bursts into silly giggles, and then the rest of us start to howl and snort together, even though I have a Kleenex box full of pumpkin pie poo next to my feet and don't forget my vomit that's also orange and brown and splattered all over Papa's new car.

59. freedom fighting

That was the last time we all laughed together, when Makena and I stunk up Papa's BMW and made so much nasty mess that Papa's car guy named Eugene York charged him almost double what he usually pays to have his cars detailed.

These days, I wait for Xavy to pull up his boxer shorts to his chest or make walrus sounds while his front teeth hang over his bottom lip, but I just keep waiting.

I wonder if I'm the only one who thinks Makena is looking better. She's glowing and rosy and more pleasant to be around, our new bizarro *áte.*

Our house needs more laughter. Everyone says it's the best medicine, but it looks like the cackles and snorts by themselves won't be able to make Makena's tumor shrink and disappear so that her insides don't need Camptosar and 5FU anymore.

Xavy has stopped being the way he is, the joker and the *mamahuhu*, and he's also starting to act like Mr. Baluga does around other people, wanting to snap your head right off.

After Xavy loses to me at *pusoy dos*, he throws the cards up in the air and makes me pick them up, and he always orders me to scoot over on the couch after I've already warmed up my spot. The worst thing is that he takes up all the room with his wide body and stocky legs all spread out on purpose.

When I try to ask Xavy if he's praying hard for Makena, his voice goes kaboom on my insides.

"I. Don't. Wanna. Talk. 'Bout. Dat. Shiiieeet!"

But I can tell that he wants to let out his feelings by the way his eyes start to wander all over the room, like he's not really there talking to me because his brain is thinking about serious things in another corner.

Mama says that most men and boys can't express what's on their minds because they just bottle it all up inside their bodies and hearts, thinking they aren't strong if their emotions are too exposed.

One of my favorite *kuwentos* ever told by Xavy, along with Makena helping him with the details, is about Papa being the center of attention at the Pomona Swap Meet, but mostly because Papa showed another side of himself.

Xavy recorded Papa on the Handycam Camcorder that he still carries around all the time to catch funny or cool or wow kinds of moments. When Sony came out with kickass technology video, he says, he begged Papa to get him a camcorder, but Papa bought it only after he gave Xavy a hard time about all the digital cameras he's wasted his goddamn money on all these years.

Xavy says he'll always remember the woman with the gray beret and the long floral sweater, who walked up to Papa and wrapped him up in a super tight hug that would last for not just a few seconds but for a whole lifetime.

It was a Saturday morning, Xavy says, and Papa had decided to make *pasyal* with him and browse the swap meet while he went on the hunt for more vintage parts for his Bug, which he was crazy excited about because the swap meet allows auto-parts vendors to sell their goods only every other month.

Makena adds that Papa had stopped at a table that displayed different art collectibles from all over Europe, and he noticed a beer stein. Papa said he liked this particular stein because of the patriotic scene that was hand-carved on it, and he gave the art-collectibles vendor two-hundred dollars for it even though the price tag said "$30."

The vendor couldn't believe what his eyes were seeing in his hands after Papa handed him two one-hundred-dollar bills, then he asked Papa why he paid so much for the stein.

Xavy all of a sudden showed up with a radio block-off plate and a banjo steering wheel that he says he scored just around the corner from where he spotted Papa. Other people who were shopping nearby began to notice Papa's deep and steady storytelling voice that easily commanded attention, even when it wasn't looking for it.

That's when Xavy says he decided to bust out his Camcorder.

"I remember seeing a beer stein like this one in Hamburg when I was 18 years old," Papa began. "I had just arrived in Germany from the Philippines with my best friend, Butch Ramirez. One of our first acquaintances, a gentleman named Ryker, happened to know Rudi Dutschke.

"Rudi led the German student movement in the late '60s. He and a bunch of other activists were angry about former Nazis who still held powerful positions in Germany. Not to mention the poor living conditions of university students.

"It was such a revolutionary time. People like Rudi wanted to make the world a better place, but my father was afraid for my life because he knew all too well that rebellions started by the subordinate class never ended well."

This is where I was getting kind of sort of bored with Papa's *kuwento* because of the words "revolutionary" and "rebellion," but of course he kept harping on.

"I refused to listen to my father. I wanted to help Rudi and the other students stand for something important. But I couldn't shake the feeling that this is when my father's health started to deteriorate—he was both sad and disappointed I left our country when I was so young."

That's when I notice all the people, even though the video is sort of fuzzy, who are surrounding Papa and making their way closer to him and forming a giant huddle so that they can hear him better, even a skater dude who has a scorpion-looking tattoo on his chest and is carrying his longboard, which looks weird because Pomona isn't near a beach.

"It felt romantic," Papa continued. "I was an idealistic teenager who had just fled the Philippines. An executive-level position at IBM was waiting for me after my graduation from college, but the Jabidah massacre left me feeling…disenchanted. Moro Army recruits were killed, and the government wanted to cover it up.

"There've been disputes about the accounts of the slaughter, but my father knew one of the fishermen who'd rescued the Muslim man. He ended up being the lone survivor of the Philippine Armed Forces' attack on his group. There were some who actually thought the massacre was a ploy by the Liberal Party to get in the way of President Marcos' re-election bid. I was so goddamn fed up with the country's corruption."

Now I see a bunch of older ladies near Papa with floppy hats start nodding their heads with eyes that are frog-eye wide. I could hear the wind whooshing in the background and wondered how their hats were staying put on their heads.

"My father warned me I was heading to a place with just as much political unrest. But I wanted to find out for myself and also start exploring the world.

"Butch and I hung out with Rudi and his girlfriend, Greta. She truly believed we could change things. She had us mingle with crowds and hand out pamphlets. Germany's post-war political system was authoritarian, so we opposed the Vietnam War and fought against oppressive systems."

I was starting to get bored again because he kept showing off more long words that didn't mean anything to me yet, but boy this massive huddle was listening as if Papa's words were gold.

"Soon enough, however, Rudi became an enemy of the state. I watched students get beaten up by the *Landespolizei*, the law enforcement on the streets. Butch wanted to go back to Hamburg because West Berlin was starting to become dangerous. He convinced me to leave with him, and we ended up back in Hamburg, then eventually in New York on a working visa.

"I read in the paper that Rudi had been shot in the head and that he survived, but around 10 years later, he died of brain damage from a seizure."

I think I covered my mouth right when everyone else in the video did, and they also let out a bunch of wows and oh my Gods and jeezes and turned to one another to show they were all feeling the same way.

I imagined that being shot anywhere on my body would be like a hundred bee stings and burning flames all mixed into one feeling.

"The oppressed never win, my friends," Papa said, soft but firm. "I helped fight for change, but I haven't seen much in my lifetime. Times change, people don't. I've frowned upon the powerless, the helpless, like my father did, but we both vowed to protect them to the end of the line."

Now the floppy hats on those old ladies were starting to come off, but they held them down tight to listen to the rest of Papa's story. The scorpion-tattoo guy with the longboard was sitting right next to them now.

"One of the best things that the French philosopher Albert Camus said was 'the only way to deal with an unfree world is to become so absolutely free that your very existence is an act of rebellion.'"

I couldn't hear any words or sounds from Papa's audience while he finished his *kuwento*. I counted 77 people surrounding him like he was Jesus and they were his disciples but way more of them, and I could see there were others trying to listen, stretching their necks out like cranes and talking hush-hush to each other and pointing at Papa like he was a celebrity.

I was hoping that Papa would describe what it was like in Germany and if he saw the Rhine River with all its castles like in Mama's coffee table books, because then I could tell Mr. Baluga all about it and he would add Germany to his list of places he would travel to if he won the Lotto.

After Papa finished his story, he started to help the vendor put away the collectibles and wrapped each one delicately like they were his own. The other shoppers who stayed to listen walked up to him one by one to pat him on the back or were shaking their heads in shock, saying, "You knew a famous activist" and "Dang, sir, you played a small part of the events of 1968" and that it was a turning point in history.

Xavy had been watching this one woman closely, which you could tell while the video was playing because he would zoom in on her round and rosy face sometimes while Papa was talking. She was standing off to the side, away from the crowd. Xavy says, "Dare wuz sumtin sorta hard-ass but comfy-cozy 'bout dis chick."

She waited until everyone else left and then made her way towards Papa and nodded, just like those ladies in the floppy hats, but her eyes were like gimlets, which is the SAT word that Xavy uses now when he tells me that my gimlet eyes don't match my big chunga fists when I'm pissed off at him.

Suddenly, this stranger held Papa, and together they started to cry. Papa let her hold him, and he didn't care about the tears sliding down his cheeks and that a bunch of other people who were walking by the art-collectibles table kept checking them out.

The woman's long floral sweater draped over Papa's shoulder like the shawl of an *abuela*, almost like it was protecting him.

This is what I want to see from my *kuya*. Right now, Xavy needs to be like the sun when it pops out from behind the sea, beating its rays down on anything and everything, like a freedom fighter showing who he is when everyone is looking.

60. spitting stella

Makena's favorite *tita* on Mama's side used to be Tita Stella, who was the most furious one on the day of Lolo Carlo's funeral when she and her sisters and Lola Zeny asked Papa about Lolo Carlo's properties in the Philippines. Makena couldn't believe that she was the meanest one of them all, but Mama was the star witness who saw with her very own eyes how greedy her own sisters and mama really are.

Makena liked Tita Stella because she's wise and adventurous and enjoys traveling the world. She joined the Foreign Service right after high school, so she got to live in all kinds of countries, like Bhutan and Panama and Mexico. Makena visited Tita Stella in Panama and remembers being bitten on the foot by a huge red ant while she spent her twelfth birthday there.

When Tita Stella lived in Mexico City, she bought me the tiniest and most colorful dolls made out of twisty wire and fabric scraps and yarn, called worry dolls, which you're supposed to put under your pillow after sharing all your problems with them. When you wake up in the morning, your worries are wiped away, which is why I like sleeping with Sarita, but keeping her under my pillow would be wicked if you ask me.

Makena said she was appalled by the poverty in Panama, which you can easily compare to the kind in the Philippines. It made her feel blue, but she also felt privileged to be able to see this part of the world and how other people who aren't as lucky as us live, and then try to help them in some little way that she could, like writing letters to kids or sending whatever money she made from teaching tennis.

Papa never really got along with Tita Stella because according to everyone, she's opinionated and kind of uptight. She didn't like it when Papa and Xavy made fun of her spitting, which is what she does when she's talking and getting excited. Papa says she acts like she's above all of us just because she got a master's degree in Southeast Asian studies, which Papa says is useless because you can never make a lot of money with that kind of education.

But Makena admired Tita Stella's passion, and she also loved that Tita Stella did her own thing and never cared about what anyone else thought. Tita Stella left home when she was 18, which of course Lolo Carlo wasn't too happy about, so that put a strain on their relationship all those years, according to Mama.

Lolo Carlo shared many things with Papa, and the one secret that Xavy found out one night when he wasn't supposed to be listening was that Lolo Carlo never forgave Tita Stella for leaving home at such a young age and then marrying a *puti* man.

Tita Stella's husband, who we call Uncle Jack because he doesn't feel comfortable with the name "Tito Jack," comes from a rich family in Long Island which is in New York, and he has a Ph.D in physics. But Papa doesn't mind him because he acts low-key and even holds his hand up all awkward for a high-five after he and Papa together make jokes about white people.

Lolo Carlo didn't go to Tita Stella and Uncle Jack's wedding, which Mama says made Tita Stella's tears ruin her makeup on her wedding day. Makena thought it was inexcusable of Lolo Carlo, but Papa explained to us that Lolo Carlo was from the old school and set in his ways, so don't knock his conservative beliefs and values because that's all he knew while he was growing up.

I also found out that Lolo Carlo was angry at Tita Stella for never having children, even though Uncle Jack didn't have the goods, according to Xavy. They could have adopted, but by the time Tita Stella and Uncle Jack were open to adoption, they were too old and concerned about caring for an infant in their early forties, which Mama thought was such a crock of bullshet because Lola Zeny can take care of all kinds of infants and toddlers, and she's already 71 years old.

The last time we saw Tita Stella was right after Lolo Carlo took the express ride to heaven because he had a brain aneurysm. Tita Doti told me that Lolo Carlo was dipping his peanut butter and sugar sandwich in his coffee when all of a sudden, he grabbed his head and yelled at Lola Zeny to call 911. Tita Doti said it was the most horrifying experience, watching her father fall to the ground and then trying CPR on him but already knowing it was too late.

I remember Tita Doti calling our house and Papa screaming at all of us, "Let's go, your *abuelo* is gone," which made all kinds of people appear at our house that week, including Tita Stella who had been on vacation at her house in The Hamptons and flew in the next day, and boy was she the most emotional one of them all, spitting and crying and carrying around a picture of Lolo Carlo and telling it she was so sorry for leaving the family and marrying a white man.

Tita Gwen came to the funeral, which everyone says was big of her because Papa's and Mama's families don't really get along. I watched Tita Gwen hug and kiss people she didn't know too well, and she cried together with Lola Zeny and held her hand for a long time and kept adjusting her veil and patting her tears dry with her bright white handkerchief during the wake, which is where everyone saw Lolo Carlo looking like someone painted bright and waxy makeup on his face, even though he was a man and already took the ride.

Papa's always comparing Tita Gwen and Tita Stella because they're my two smartest *titas*, but of course Papa brags about Tita Gwen because she's his baby sister and because he thinks Tita Stella is *mayabang*, which means you're a showoff, and that cracks all of us up because sometimes Papa is the biggest showoff there is.

Tita Gwen has an MBA from USC, and she got all kinds of offers to be an executive at different companies, so now she's a senior vice president at Bank of America. But you'd never know she makes six figures because she's so humble, says Mama, who wishes the rest of the Josés were just like her.

But ever since Tita Gwen came here from the Philippines, she hasn't really traveled outside of California, only Heber City in Utah, which is where some of the *titas* and *titos* live. And she doesn't do a whole lot of things except watch romantic comedies that are called chick flicks and also pig out on Filipino food and spend time with our family, and I think she hangs out with us even more than Makena does.

Then there's Tita Stella the world traveler, fluent in Spanish and Dzonghka the Bhutanese language and highly knowledgeable in politics and the arts, Makena likes to brag. Tita Stella runs marathons with Uncle Jack, so she's muscular and skinny like Makena was, but "She sho as hellz ain't a looka," according to Xavy.

"You can fit a whole goddamn soccer ball inside that trap of hers," Papa always teases, "and ping-pong balls would get lost inside her nostrils," but I don't think he's joking around. Tita Stella does have a wide mouth, which reminds me of the one on the bowhead whale skeleton I saw during the field trip to the Los Angeles Natural History Museum in second grade.

Xavy says when you're having a conversation with both *titas*, you might think that Tita Stella is the more interesting one, because she'll go off on Hillary Clinton being so accomplished and that she would be a more savvy president than her husband was, or harp on about animal rights and those beagles that these scientists tried to use for medical testing, while Tita Gwen will just give you a sweet smile and ask if you want something to eat.

Xavy and I don't care for Tita Stella much because sometimes she does act all big like she's better than everyone, especially when she's around Uncle Jack. She always has to introduce him as Dr. Jack Grant just because he has a Ph.D, which Xavy thinks is snotty and pretentious.

One time she had the biggest cow when Xavy started talking ghetto, saying "Wassup Stella" and asking her "Ya down, Stella G" when Mama and her other sisters were talking about having a Kris Kringle for Christmas.

"What do you mean am I down, and please address me as Tita Stella," she kept spitting. Then she scolded Xavy and asked him to speak proper English, which of course made Xavy talk ghetto even more.

I don't know what's better, being loyal to your family and staying close to home and working at a bank all day, or leaving home when you're still a teenager and seeing the world and being able to discuss the arts.

Everyone knows Makena would rather be like Tita Stella even though she adores Tita Gwen, and everyone knows Xavy could care less.

I wish everyone would just let Tita Stella be snotty and call her husband a doctor and also be okay with Tita Gwen staying kind and polite and not so well-rounded.

I want to be the in-betweener that Mr. Baluga always calls me. That way, nobody would ever talk about me behind my back and keep comparing me to another cousin or a family friend, or someone else my age who could compete with me.

can't i be a girl with a regular kind of life that people never need to talk about and won't ever dare mess with because all i want is for everyone to just be nicer to each other please okay?!

61. cold-cocking cancer

Mama says that the trumpet trees at the Arboretum look like pink sunshades. They're her favorite kind of tree because they start blooming at the end January when it's still winter, and now they're looking even prettier in the month of May. The Arboretum is a botanical garden that goes on for acres, one of the best places ever to have a picnic.

I keep checking Ramona Quimby's leaves, and they aren't green yet. I know Ramona Quimby is an indoor plant, but sometimes I hope that the season outside has something to do with leaves turning green indoors.

"I can't fucking eat and I just want to sleep," Makena says, and she gets up from her chair at the dining room table and pounds her footsteps like an elephant to her bedroom.

Makena said the F word in front of me again, but it doesn't matter anymore because Mama and Papa let Makena say anything these days. Xavy didn't even give me wide frog eyes, and Papa just kept taking huge bites out of the Burrito Supreme that he picked up at Taco Bell, and I was betting he'd smell like his lunch right after he was done even though he isn't Mexican. Mama's already in the kitchen shoving all the foil and paper wrappers down the trash can, and I can hear her murmuring something to herself, probably another prayer.

"Makena's gone downhill so fast," I heard Mama tell Papa in their bedroom last night. Makena's appetite is gone, and it's true that all she wants to do is sleep. The bags under her eyes that are puffy like water blisters don't help the rest of her face that's turning yellow. A light kind of yellow, but not as bright as the leaves on Ramona Quimby.

Makena told me the other day that she has jaundice, and don't be afraid to look at her if the whites of her eyes start to turn yellow too because that's what happens when this disease gets worse. But I'm not worried, because I remember on the Discovery Channel seeing babies who had jaundice when they were first born, and it usually disappears after one week, which is when they're allowed to go home from the hospital to their families.

Mama wants me to see the counselor at school who's supposed to help me deal with Makena's sickness, especially now because Makena's all yellow and thin and low on the energy, but Papa doesn't want me to talk to any goddamn therapist. When Papa holds my face and looks deep into my eyes with his own dark gray ones and tells me to be strong and come to him or Mama anytime I want to talk, I say, "Okay, Papa" just to make him stop.

I don't feel like talking. I just want to sit and watch *Shrek* again because I like Fiona, who Xavy says is a badass. I want to play with my Groovy Girls, and I'm still waiting for Papa to buy me the small Awesome Armchair so that there are more places for Trini and Kami and Sarita to sit.

Talking is hard even though everyone says it's healthy to use your words, which is something I learned a long time ago when I was in preschool, when Teacher Larissa told me to use my words after Danny Shapiro grabbed the bouncy ball from my hands and kicked my shin.

"Tell him how you feel, Isabel," she kept saying as she tried holding Danny by his shoulders as steady as she could because he was trying to get away.

So I said to him, "I'm feeling that you're a jerk-off who needs to be cold-cocked," which is what the *titos* told me to say if anyone bullied me. That's when Teacher Larissa's mouth formed into a giant O, and then she made me sit in the corner for five minutes to think about how I'd feel if someone said hurtful things to me, and then she stuck Danny in another corner to imagine what it would be like if someone kicked him.

After we were done sitting in our corners, Teacher Larissa lectured the whole class during circle time about inappropriate words and why they don't have a place anywhere, not at school or at home or even in the bathroom when you're all alone. She called Papa but he didn't scold me, because he says I told that goddamn rug rat exactly how I felt.

Talking is easy only if you know what to say and if you can be sure you won't get in trouble for saying it. If I could talk to Makena right now, the wrong words would come out.

I would say that she made this family sad, even though it wasn't her fault for becoming weak.

How could you look so pretty one day and all of a sudden turn into a sickly yellow thing?

How could you be only 20 years old and play tennis with that hard rocket body like all the boys describe it and all of a sudden get something called colon cancer?

Everyone tells me that young people get cancer too, but why did it have to be you, so beautiful and smart and always kind to me? What did you ever do to make God turn on you?

Mama says never question God, but boy do I have a million things to ask him. She keeps reminding me, "Don't ever ask why us, Isabel, God has his mysterious ways," but all his mysteries suck and make me want to call him a jerk-off too.

62. pushing for pamplona

Sometimes I'd go with Makena to her tennis lessons in one of the rougher parts of LA, which Papa says is where more crimes happen because of stuff he didn't feel like telling me about at that moment, and this is where her tennis coach Bill Van Gelder taught at these apartments called Cedarwood.

Papa always had a hard time finding parking on the street, so sometimes he'd drop me and Makena off right in front of the gate that opens only if a car is entering or leaving or if someone is walking in or out. One time, both the car gate and the people gate were broken, so Makena and I walked right in. I remember I kept looking around for someone to yell "Hey" and get us in trouble, even though we're Bill Van Gelder's friends.

It was always dark in the parking lot that we needed to pass through to get to the tennis courts, so I'd never let go of Makena's hand. But my eyes and ears would follow every movement and noise around us, and I could tell that Makena was on the lookout too. Her head would turn in all kinds of directions, this way and that, and she held her tennis racquet bag tight and close to her body.

is this what papa didn't feel like telling me about?

was makena afraid because of the dark or because she thought that a crime would happen here where someone like eli enki-abrams would jump out of the bushes and grab her bag and punch her in the face? but what makena didn't know was that my right hand which wasn't the hand holding her other one was always prepared with a strong and super crazy tight fist.

When we finally got to the tennis courts, I'd let out deep sighs and relax my fist because all of a sudden, there were bright white lights, and even the sound of Bill Van Gelder's rough voice yelling "Come on, you got lead in your feet or something?!" to the man he teaches before Makena was comfy and even cozy to my ears.

I overheard Bill Van Gelder telling Papa and Xavy that the man with lead feet is a hitman, and Papa made sure to tell Xavy right away not to say anything to Mama because she sure wouldn't want Makena and me going here anymore if she knew.

Bill Van Gelder lives near Montecito which is where Oprah lives, but he drives to LA twice a week to teach Makena and whoever else in the Cedarwood Apartments wants to learn tennis. His best friend was Bobby Riggs, who Papa says challenged Billie Jean King to a "battle of the sexes" tennis match a long time ago. Bobby Riggs wasn't the winner, like everyone thought he would be, and Bill Van Gelder always tells us, "I never stopped giving Bobby hell for losing to a girl."

Bobby Riggs took the ride many years ago, and I wonder how much longer Bill Van Gelder will last because he's been looking sort of pasty gray and slow-moving. Sometimes I think he might have lead in his feet too, but don't ever tell him that because he'll scream like a disaster in your face.

One time, Xavy and I were playing leapfrog and making all kinds of ribbit noises right outside Bill Van Gelder's tennis shop, and boy was he yelling the nastiest words at us, the kinds that Papa and Xavy save up for when they're really fuming. The dirty rotten words didn't just make you feel small but wish you were invisible.

Xavy learned tennis from Bill Van Gelder too, but he was more like a drill sergeant with Makena. After Xavy was done with his lesson, he'd watch Makena hit hundreds of forehands and backhands back to Bill Van Gelder. She'd run from one end of the court to the other like a puppet on a string and even rush the net when Bill Van Gelder decided to give her a drop shot or a short ball in no-man's land, which is where you aren't supposed to stand when you're rallying. If someone hits a ball deep to the baseline, you won't have enough time to take your racquet back and swing because you were standing where you weren't supposed to.

Bill Van Gelder even made Makena run in the rain, and sometimes the raindrops would fly straight at Makena's face that she says felt like pins, making her blink so much that she could barely see the ball. Bill Van Gelder made Makena run one lap for every ball she missed, and on those rainy days, she still had to finish her laps while we all sat in the tennis shop. Mama stopped going with us to Makena's tennis lessons because she thinks Bill Van Gelder is like all men, that's why we have wars and egos and violence.

The last time we watched Bill Van Gelder teach Makena, she had to get at least 12 serves in a row inside the box that you have to hit the serves into.

The first four balls had to be hard and inside the box that's on the side called "deuce," where Bill Van Gelder placed those orange cones on the spots where Makena was supposed to hit them.

I remember imagining that the cones were the orange baboon tarantulas I saw during a movie in my second grade science class that gave me nightmares for a whole week, so I wondered if that might get Makena to knock down all the cones.

Then Bill Van Gelder told her that she had to hit the next four balls fast and solid on the side called "advantage" and do the same thing with the orange cones again.

For the last four serves, she was supposed to hit second serves, which aren't as strong as first serves, but Bill Van Gelder made her give them different spins, like slice and topspin. Makena usually got the first eight serves in and hit all the cones, but then she'd barely miss the cone by a few inches when she tried a second serve, so Bill Van Gelder made her start over and told her, "You'll never run with the bulls in Pamplona with dinky serves like those."

Watching Makena hit her serves always made me feel like I was the one who ran all those laps in the rain. Seeing her arms and shoulders and legs start to move like a sloth's, just like the hitman with lead in his feet, and then listening to her breathe and cough hard and slap herself on the sides of her thighs every time she missed an easy shot sure made me glad that I suck at tennis.

"Come on, keep pushing yourself," Bill Van Gelder would yell at Makena when her forehands got weaker or her feet just couldn't go anymore.

Papa loves watching Makena's lessons, and sometimes he'd even punch the air when Makena passed Bill Van Gelder at the net. Then Bill Van Gelder would slip his racquet head under his armpit and start clapping for Makena's good shot and tell her, "You have almost everything it takes to make it to the pros. Just grow a few more inches," he'd tell Makena, his thick arm trying to swing around her but instead resting on her shoulder, as they were walking off the court after the lesson was over, which always looked funny because Bill Van Gelder is six-foot-three and Makena's only five-foot-four. Mama tells me that you stop growing after you're done with puberty, and I think Makena already went past this stage, even though Tracy with the long Barbie legs became three inches taller during their third year at Cal.

The last time I went to one of Makena's lessons, Bill Van Gelder wouldn't let Makena go home until all four of her second serves hit the orange cones. Even if she missed only one, he'd make her start over all the way from the eight hard and fast serves. I remember we were there for 3 hours and 28 minutes, because when I looked at the clock in the tennis shop, it was already 9:28, and we were supposed to leave at 8:00. I started to feel sleepy, so Papa told me to lie down on the couch in the shop, but I wanted to see Makena hit all her serves inside the box so that she could run with the bulls in Pamplona.

"You're throwing the ball behind you, the ball's dropping, you can't let it drop more than an inch, bend those knees," Bill Van Gelder kept nagging Makena, shaking his almost bald head with a few curly gray hairs sticking out and then scratching it all furious like he had fleas.

Sometimes Makena's eyes started to tear up, but Bill Van Gelder did nothing to make her feel better. He just kept telling her to concentrate and push herself. When Makena's body started to look stiff and wooden, Bill Van Gelder would tell her, "Loosen up, you're looking like a machine."

Even Papa stopped watching after a while. He'd walk past the shop to smoke, and every time he checked on Makena and saw she wasn't finished yet, he'd shake his head and mumble a bunch of Spanish and Tagalog words to himself.

Mama called Papa a few times to ask what was taking so long, and Papa finally told her, "Makena isn't pushing herself hard enough, goddamn it's getting late."

Mama always tells me to push myself in school, try my best and that's what counts, but all the pushing Makena did her whole life never seemed to be enough. Makena keeps pushing herself, but what if you have lead in your feet like the hitman or you have nothing left to push?

63. floaty fingers and sky into the sea

When I was in second grade, I went through Mama's things to find the bracelet that Lola Zeny gave me when I was just a baby. It's made of silver called sterling, and it says "Isabelle" in block kinds of letters. Mama couldn't believe her own mother misspelled my name, scolding Lola Zeny for never paying attention and are we French or something, so Mama told me she'd put the bracelet in safekeeping and get a jewelry maker to remove the "-le" at the end and add more chain links to it so that she could turn it into a necklace when I got older.

I always thought about that bracelet because I love the gold pinky ring that Lola Carmen gave me, so how cool would it be to wear another piece of jewelry, one each from two *abuelas* and not just one?

One day when Mama was at 99 Ranch, I decided to look for the bracelet. Xavy left for tennis practice and Makena was in Berkeley, and right when Papa picked me up after school, he got stuck on the phone with one of his subs, so I snuck into his and Mama's bedroom and started to hunt through her dresser drawers.

Of course the first place I checked was Mama's jewelry box, which had hardly anything in it, only her gold wedding ring and two old-ladylike necklaces, along with a gold and black leather watch with "Chanel" written on the face, a white necklace box that said "Mikimoto," and a pair of glittery diamond earrings that were actually shaped like diamonds, which I'm not sure why made me laugh out loud.

I didn't want to go through Mama's panties and bras drawer because those things are private, so I went inside her closet and found a brown metal box behind a bunch of shoeboxes and purses.

The smell of stale laundry and old perfume started to make me dizzy. I stared at the metal box and decided to take it with me to my bedroom. Inside of it were all kinds of letters from Papa to Mama when he was in the Army. When I lifted the envelopes to see if something was at the bottom, I saw a picture of Mama, three women, and two men, and one of the men had his arm around Mama.

I looked closely to see who it was, and it was someone I remember meeting when I was in kindergarten on my first day of school and who came over to our house one time to help paint signs. His eyes were sparkly blue and his hair was golden brown, and he wore a smile that made you think he'd take care of you, even though he didn't know you.

I remember the way Mama smiled that day, and also the way she brushed her hair away from her eyes, her hands all graceful and floaty. The man was Damian Stanley's papa, and he was the only papa in our kindergarten class who didn't have a wife, which means Damian probably didn't have a mama anymore.

Mama and Damian Stanley's papa and a bunch of other mamas joined the PTA together, and that's how Mama started going to meetings with other parents and helping organize the art auction and selling school merchandise, like T-shirts and sweatshirts, to raise money for my school. Papa would make fun of her because she never got involved when Makena and Xavy were younger and why now, so he'd always say that Mama had a boyfriend in the PTA.

"He's one of those chivalrous men who open the door for you when you get out of the car and stand up if you say you're going to the ladies' room," Papa would tease. Mama always waved him off, insisting there were mostly mothers in their group, but you could tell she was thinking about Damian Stanley's papa because her neck would turn pink.

Right before my kindergarten graduation, Papa took a trip to the Philippines for a whole month. Business was picking up in Southeast Asia, he told all of us, and construction was slow, so he had put together some deals in Hong Kong and Manila.

Mama told Papa that she was planning on having a PTA meeting at our house and asked if it was okay to move his Suburban and Porsche outside to the driveway, and of course everyone was all full of shock and no-ways when Papa said yes, as long as Mama covered the Porsche and made sure to put the cars back inside once the party was over. Mama needed the garage because she and the PTA mothers were going to paint signs for the graduation.

Damian Stanley's papa was the only man there that night, and boy did all the mothers adore him, laughing and pushing their hair away from their faces with their own floaty hands, touching him on the shoulder and arm whenever they had the chance. Xavy once taught me how to observe men and women at Darla's *debu,* which is what Filipinos call birthday galas for when their kids turn eighteen. He said to notice the way they flirt with each other, and he'd always make me laugh and snort when he'd copy their feminine hands and girly giggles.

Mama baked the most scrumptious desserts for the meeting that night, and I remember Xavy being surprised that she was making key lime pie and Kahlúa cheesecake instead of *bibingka* or *kutsinta*, which is a sticky orange pudding with coconut that I don't care too much for because the fresh coconut sprinkles smell like wood that got dunked in milk. She even made creampuffs from scratch, and Makena knows these aren't the easiest things to make because one time when she was stirring the filling inside a saucepan, she burnt it and had to start over.

Mama and Damian Stanley's papa spent a lot of time in the kitchen while she made the other mamas work on the posters inside the garage. Mama bossed around the other mamas, making sure the colors they were using were bright enough and to keep their hands off Antonio's belongings there in the garage or else.

I'll never forget the way that Mama pointed her floaty fingers and directed everyone, like one of those airplane runway workers who control traffic. It was the only time I ever saw Mama take charge of other people.

Mama and Damian Stanley's papa didn't know that I was sitting at the dining room table coloring my connect-the-dots pictures because Mama had closed the sliding door between the kitchen and the dining room. That's when I found out that my classmate Damian Stanley was "Damian Jr." and remembered that Mama's *puti* friends call her "Ann" instead of "Jelly."

"Damian," asked Mama, "may I ask why you never remarried?"

"Marriage is just a label. But I know this isn't something that a devout Catholic like Ms. Ann José wants to hear."

Mama burst out "Damian!" and you could tell she did more than touch his shoulder because Damian Sr. said "ouch."

"My focus is on Damian Jr. right now," Damian Sr. told Mama. "He's had a hard time since his mom passed."

"Oh gosh, I didn't know," said Mama in her soothing voice, the one she uses when I'm not feeling so good.

"Not many people do. Hey, can I help you with that? It looks heavy."

"You're such a kind man," said Mama, and I'll bet she was handing Damian Sr. one of her enormous casserole dishes that she makes her mac 'n' cheese inside of when she wants leftovers she knows I'll eat.

"My wife and I used to split all our duties, even the laundry. Don't take this the wrong way, I wasn't a pushover or anything. I just wanted to help. She was a stay-at-home mom like you, and I didn't realize how tough of a job it was. Sometimes even harder than my work at the firm."

"You're such a kind man," Mama said softly.

"You already said that," Damian Sr. answered even more softly.

Then it turned super quiet for a couple of minutes, so I stood up and tiptoed towards the kitchen, making sure I didn't touch the door because sliding doors like those usually wobble.

"Hey Geek Freak, spyin' on Mama, eh," Xavy all of a sudden shouted from upstairs. I remember giving Xavy my gimlet eyes and feeling like ants were crawling up my back, afraid of what was coming next.

The door slid open, and there stood Mama with her dainty hands on her hips.

"Your room. Now," she said, pointing at the stairs.

Damian Sr. looked at me, and all I could remember were his eyes so shimmering blue and his smile so kind that I didn't care I was being sent to my room.

I look closely at the picture again, and Mama's smile shows kindness too. I can't tell if her arm is around Damian Sr., but maybe it's hidden because she couldn't reach to the other side of his muscular body.

I wanted to keep the picture, but Mama would have noticed and made me say prayers like mad and go to church with her on a weekday to ask for God's grace, which I'll have to do anyway because I went through her stuff and invaded her privacy. So I put it back the way it was behind her shoeboxes and purses and never told anyone about Damian Sr.'s eyes like the sky melted into the sea and never asked Mama about my bracelet again.

64. singing sappiness

Today is May 10, 2003, and I'm pretty sure Makena's in love.

But she's in love with a voice and not the person who owns it. His name is Josh Groban, a singer who's around Makena's age. Before he became famous, Mama noticed him on one of the season finales of *Ally McBeal*, which used to be Mama and Makena's favorite show.

Josh Groban was on *Oprah* yesterday, and right when the first few notes of his song floated out of his mouth, Papa sat up straight in his chair and said, "Who the hell is that, Christ he sounds like an angel."

Papa couldn't believe all the beautiful sounds that were coming out of such a young geek. Josh Groban is kind of nerdy like that business tycoon they call Bill Gates and also this boy at school named Andrew Haas, who wears pants that reach only to the top of his ankles and always has a stack of snotty tissues piled high on his desk.

Makena can't stop listening to Josh Groban's CD. She keeps pressing the repeat button on the CD player in her bedroom, especially after a song called "You're Still You," which is the one that Josh Groban sang at his prom when he was a guest star on *Ally McBeal.* Makena closes her eyes, swaying like Stevie Wonder does when he plays the piano and sings. When she falls asleep after all the rocking back and forth, Papa drapes a blanket over her.

she sings her melody over his shadowy harmony, and then he watches her light up like a fire, maybe even a spitfire. he knows she will always feel her big beautiful heart going thud inside his own, and he will never forget who she is.

he lifts her up to a purple sky that they can scream their love to, on top of a platform super high that they share and can just be who they are together.

Josh Groban's voice is deep like Papa's, but there's something about it that makes you get the chills and remember the times you felt blue. Like at Lola Carmen's funeral, where Makena played this classical song called "Chopin," which Lola Carmen always asked Makena to play on the piano for her when she was still alive.

Every time Lola Carmen came over to our house, she would beg Makena to play it. Then she'd sway and hum and close her eyes and cry like a baby and ask, "One more time, oh please, *mija, isa pa*," so of course Makena kept hitting the same sorrowful notes over and over until Papa yelled at her to pick another song or Mama came over to tell us that dinner was getting cold.

Makena goes on about Josh Groban and says that he has the richest baritone voice, and everyone should watch out because he will develop it even more when he gets older and then he will truly shine. And of course Makena knows what she's talking about because she has perfect pitch.

Xavy likes hip-hop and disco, and funk and soul too, and everyone thinks I like bubblegum pop and R&B, but if I ever told anyone I like Billie Joe Armstrong, they would take away all the Green Day posters hidden under my bed and make them go poof in the fireplace. Makena thinks Billie Joe is freaky with his jaggedy teeth and his psycho bulging eyes, and he's much too vulgar and full of angst for an 8-year-old like me.

No one in our house likes rock, but to me, it's the only kind of music that doesn't sound phony because a rock band plays instruments, like guitars and drums, instead of using a bass track or synthesizers in the background to make them sound better, which I know because of Ryan, and boy would he scowl at me if he knew what I thought because DJs use all kinds of fancy equipment that aren't real instruments, but Ryan insists that DJs are real musicians, even though he already is one because he plays the saxophone and even bass guitar too.

And I'd sure rather hear words like "Tears down your face, leaving traces of my mistakes" in songs instead of stuff like remembering the girl or the boy who gave you your first kiss.

Billie Joe would never write sappiness like that, and he can scream all his notes and still sound like he's singing you a lullaby.

he cherishes all the things she is, and in her golden sparkly eyes, he doesn't do any sort of wrong. they have loved each other for so very long, but after they trade their wicked words, they both need to return to who they were.

Josh Groban's voice reminds me of happy times, like when Papa and Mama and Xavy and Makena and I sing in the car together. One time we all sang "On My Own," which is everyone's favorite song from *Les Miserables*. We were making *pasyal*, driving up Pacific Coast Highway and trying to be louder than the person next to us when we reached the high notes. I was laughing so hard until my sides ached, just like they do after I eat and drink and go play too soon afterwards.

Josh Groban's baritone voice lives in our house now, and I don't mind because one of my favorite things to do is listen to good music.

Papa says music makes him sane when he's stressing out at his job sites.

Xavy tells me that music helps him chill and vibe.

Mama's always humming different tunes in her high voice while she's cooking, so I know she likes music too.

When musical notes come together to make a perfect combination, I wonder how people make up a song, do they hear it in their heads before they write it down or do they test out all kinds of notes before the enchanting ones find each other and turn into a melody?

I like to listen to the words of a song too, which Makena told me are called lyrics. They make *kuwento,* even though the song's story usually is about needing and hurting and why did you leave me, but one thing for sure is that the lyrics always have something to do with love, whether it's good or bad, and you can even create your own song from the lyrics by changing some of the words and adding your heart's story.

she feels all his needing, and when the watch on her wrist that was smashed under the tire of hurting all of a sudden comes back to life and starts ticking, it changes every single thing, and the only truth that's left is that she is still herself. but is he still himself?

65. defective damage

Mama and Papa are concerned about Makena because they say that all her rambling is so uncensored these days. She just yaps on like an R-rated movie, not realizing there's a minor which is me in the room.

Mama keeps saying, "Makena should watch what she says around Isabel," but I like that Makena doesn't care anymore because that's the way she should have been living her life in the first place. Our family never holds back anyway, so I think Mama's the one who should stop caring about other people's opinions even if they're lame.

Makena's making *kuwento* about one day last week when she forced herself out of bed, and I'm not too sure if this story will end up R-rated or PG.

While she walked down the hallway, the wood floor felt cold against the bottom of her feet, she says, almost damp.

Papa was working at his job sites, and Xavy and I were still at school. Makena poked her head into Papa and Mama's bedroom, where Mama lay asleep with a *Harlequin* novel resting on her chest. She remembers Mama not looking very comfortable, her right arm hanging from the edge of the bed and her reading glasses crooked on her face.

Makena went to the bathroom and opened the medicine cabinet. She swallowed a nausea pill, gagged into the sink once, and looked into the mirror at her pink face and pink eyes to match. She heaved again while she held her tongue steady and took a few slow breaths so that her vomit wouldn't start gushing out.

She went downstairs to the living room, opened the window, and inhaled the fresh air. She felt selfish as she took this breath, like it wasn't hers to take, she says. She looked around the room for a comfortable place to sit and found Frida asleep in the tiny swivel seat that looks like a tall dog bed. We all know Frida's favorite place to nap, the only chair that wraps around her body so perfect. Makena kissed Frida on the head and decided to keep wandering around.

Makena remembers thinking about our house, the one that Papa asked his subs to start working on for us three years ago. She says she still can recall the day that he bought the lot.

"We're moving to Arcadia in eight months, *mi familia*." Papa gave everyone high-fives, even Mama, who usually hold ups her hand kind of fluttery for them.

"I'm building a home for us," Papa added to his announcement.

Makena also remembers how proud he sounded.

She ended up in Papa's office, the neatest and tidiest room in the house. She sank into the cushions of Papa's chocolate brown leather sofa. Not a trace of dog hair, not one whisker or stain of drool on it. Frida knows for sure that this room is off limits.

Makena also remembers the way everything was laid out in Papa's office. Art placed in just the right spots to keep it from fading because of the sun's rays gleaming through the special French windows that he himself had installed; Papa's brass stapler, paper clip holder, and tape dispenser set up in a straight line to the left of his leather desk pad; and every book and magazine organized in categories, from philosophy and theology to contemporary fiction and business.

remember the house in arcadia, remember everything in place, remember his pride.

Makena stood up and stared at Papa's bookshelves, which took up two tall walls of the room. *The Godfather* by Mario Puzo, *Graphic Guide to Frame Construction* by Rob Thallon, all kinds of issues of *BusinessWeek*, a research paper by Papa about Larry Itliong and the Delano Grape Strike, *The Stranger* by Albert Camus, *Society and Sanity* by F.J. Sheed.

Makena's eyes stopped at *Society and Sanity*, a book that Papa read for his sociology class in college. The red lettering on the cover was faded, and the binding was torn and taped back together. Makena slid the book from its spot and opened it to page 43. Two sentences were underlined in pencil, straight and perfect lines, like it was done with a ruler.

"The Christian believes that owing to a wrong choice made by the common ancestor of the human race, we have all inherited a damaged nature, and that it is one of the effects of the damage that it tends to further damage unless we take powerful action against it."

"Jeez," Makena said, and not under her breath. "What am I reading?"

"But even one who does not accept the story of that catastrophe at man's origin will not deny that man is a pretty defective being; that, though the degree of defect varies from man to man, none are without it..."

Then Makena flipped to the next page with more underlining. Page 53:

"Realism means, and must be seen to mean, taking all the facts into account—the essence of man, by which man is an object of reverence; the variety of man, by which man is himself; the defectiveness of man, by which man is an object of compassion."

Makena says it was like stumbling upon a Ouija board and a treasure map rolled into one. She remembers feeling her eyebrows stretching out and across her forehead from all her shock and wonder. Her heart thumped, and each beat was so forceful that she had to press both her hands against her chest.

A familiar but unusual feeling took over her body, she says, almost the same kind that makes the baby hairs on the back of her neck stand up when she's nervous. Then all of a sudden, she felt an embrace, like a quilt, the serenity of it warming her soul.

"The defectiveness of man."

We all know when Makena is done making her *kuwentos* because she always ends with a dramatic sentence, the kind that makes only your brain hurt and not really your head. When I try to think deep about her *kuwento*, I notice she didn't go over the part about man being an object of compassion.

Mr. Baluga always talks about compassion. He says people who are moved by compassion are the kinds who struggle to overcome suffering, which catches my attention because Makena rambled on about suffering and pain.

"Kid, your suffering can be anything from a sore leg to sorrow from someone making you feel like you don't matter," he once told me. "And for most of us who have compassion, we have it for those like ourselves."

xavy

hey xavy, my kuya! did you know that everyone thinks you look like a mini sumo wrestler because you're big-boned like me and papa? but you also have big skin, which makes you look like a menace too. and oh yeah, papa and mama and makena say you're also irresponsible and easygoing and even likable like a dog.

papa bought you a 1962 volkswagen bug, which you painted pine green and cream so that it looks vintage, and you're always on the lookout for parts for your cars. you can't get into what papa calls a top-tier university because of your first SAT score, which was mediocre according to makena, but papa thinks you'll get a tennis scholarship at one of the cal state schools and still get a solid education and even free tennis equipment, and he says you'll learn some discipline and end up being an upstanding citizen like the rest of us.

one of the most epic kuwentos *about you happened one summer when our family and all the* titos *and* titas *and cousins went to huntington beach to celebrate katie's birthday. our oldest cousin don-don was trying to build a sand castle that looked like the taj mahal and got all the other cousins to join in on the fun. makena and mama and a few of the* titas *were kicking back under one of those huge umbrellas when all of a sudden, a boy wearing long shorts that went to the middle of his calves tiptoed over with a sly kind of smile and stood right behind makena.*

we could all see that the boy was hiding one of those fart whoopee cushions behind his back, so that's when you, my crazy kuya, *decided to sneak up behind him and lift your right leg like a boy dog and let out the loudest and most bubbly and rotten* utot, *the kind that kept going like tomato sauce that splatters out of a saucepan without a lid when it boils for too long.*

of course everyone who wasn't under the giant umbrella started to fall down on the sand from laughing so hard at poor makena and mama and the titas, *who were all pinching their noses and fanning the air, but nothing was funnier than the look that this boy in the long silly shorts gave you, and boy was it a face that kept checking out your butt and wow what just happened and how gross was that, but you know what, i think funny and disgusting make the world a more interesting place to live.*

the only time you aren't funny is when papa acts like mafioso to you, and that's when he gives you the leather belt or the bamboo stick whenever you shoot off your mouth because you're already in high school and shouldn't get spankings anymore. you try not to cry when you get the belt or the stick and just bite down on your bottom lip while your face and ears and neck turn pink to match the spot on your butt that papa smacked. we all try to hide our tears from papa, because he isn't the kind of person who will catch them for you.

"don't ever show papa you're a wuss" is what you always tell me, but you kiss papa's butt like a pro butt-kisser, and you know exactly how and when to put him in the right mood, like you wrote it down on a cheat sheet that's hiding inside your brain. one time when papa was about to punish all three of us for fighting over the TV, which there are five of in the house, all of a sudden you remembered that one of papa's favorite shows called survivor *was on at a special time. that's when papa's voice jumped from deep bass to squeaky soprano, so all of us ended up in front of the same TV right there in the family room. makena had her arms folded tight across her chest, of course making* tampo, *and you kept snickering because you knew that you won, even though you didn't get to watch* 3rd rock from the sun.

i knew it was also because you're the one who got papa to forget that he was planning to make our bottoms pink and bruised, but i think you would have been the only one to get beat up.

you and papa can be buddies, just like makena and papa sometimes are, but you act like a friend who's also a servant, always the first to fetch papa's tall glass with lots of ice for his diet coke, or a bowl of pistachios along with an empty bowl for the shells. or papa's cell phone, which he always forgets in his second office, or his faded cal baseball cap that's somewhere in his porsche or a place where mama and makena and i don't have the patience to run around the house looking for.

i never say that you're scared of papa because you might just sit your big body full of sour cream 'n' onion lay's and mexi-cokes right on top of me, but man you are such a fraidy cat, and you couldn't get the right SAT score, and you take care of your cars before anyone else, but as long as you keep making me laugh and saving me when it matters, life will always be fine and dandy. you will matter in this world, siempre y para siempre, *which lola carmen loved to say, and to me that means "always and for always," not "always and forever," because whenever people use the word "forever," it has to do with something they don't want to happen or be.*

66. shriek, stare, stop

This morning the sky is a kind of gray that Mama calls dreary, and Dr. Witt and Dr. Minor are here at our house. Mama has become friends with Dr. Minor's wife too because of the PTA, so that's why Dr. Witt and Dr. Minor have taken extra special care of Makena since I started third grade, back when the weather was scorching hot.

I'm in the backyard with Frida, trying to teach her how to say her prayers so that we have one more family member rooting for Makena. I taught her how to put her paws up on my knees, but she won't keep her head down long enough to make it look like she's praying because she knows I have treats to reward her.

Mama's been squeezing her rosary tight and murmuring lots of prayers lately, which means things aren't going so well for Makena. Sometimes after Makena threw up in the toilet or slept the whole day until dinner, Mama would make the sign of the cross and say a short prayer. But now she's reciting this never-ending prayer called a novena, which is even longer than the Apostle's Creed.

I've been saying prayers more these days too, trying to learn other ones besides "Now I Lay Me Down," because Makena looks weary. Her belly is huge and round like someone pumped air into it, which makes me feel ambivalent because she weighs only 75 pounds now, and that's only 15 more than I am. Xavy says that her stomach is filling up with fluid, and this all has to do with the tumor that's blocking her bile ducts.

If you ask me, I don't care about all these new and fancy words anymore because they aren't making Makena better. I hate it when Papa or Xavy blurt out words like "bilirubin levels," more medical language they heard at Dr. Minor's office, because it all means there's something besides the tumor in Makena's liver that's wreaking havoc inside her body.

Makena's also been acting like she lost all her smarts. I always have to repeat everything I say to her, even just to tell her I'm taking Frida on a walk.

"What do you mean a *walk,*" she'll ask super snippety, and then she'll tell me I already took Frida out this morning. I answer that Frida gets at least three walks a day, and even four if it isn't too cold or dark outside after dinner, but we go back and forth, and Makena will keep saying I already went out.

Mama says to ignore Makena and don't let her get to you please. When Frida and I walk through the front door, Makena orders me to take Frida out for some exercise.

"But we just got back," I try to explain to Makena, and that's when Xavy or Mama finally shoo me away.

I'm a puny nobody around Makena. I never thought she could make me feel this way, but I have to remember that she isn't doing it on purpose because Mama and Surfer Girl and everyone else keep saying it's her illness, so we all need to be more patient.

I don't like being a person who doesn't matter. Xavy used to be the only one in this family who could make me feel this low and rotten.

It's like my whole body turned into a vase, but someone dropped it and made it shatter into pieces that you can't even pick up with your fingers because some of the tiny bits turned into dust.

Dr. Witt and Dr. Minor are sitting at the dining room table with Mama and Papa and Xavy and talking in mumbly voices, but I can still hear some of the things they're saying because the window in the dining room is open.

They're telling Mama and Papa and Xavy that they never had a colon cancer patient this young, and they keep wondering how someone like Makena got sick with this type of cancer. I hear Dr. Minor saying it was a random freak occurrence and Dr. Witt muttering something about family history, and he keeps asking Mama and Papa to try to remember if any of their relatives had polyps or other diseases related to colon cancer, like irritable bowel syndrome or colitis or Lynch syndrome. Mama asks them why it matters if there is family history because of course we will all have to get screened.

Then Papa jumps in, "What do you mean get screened?"

Dr. Witt answers, "You'll all need to schedule a colonoscopy except for Isabel, who won't need to be tested 'til she's in her teens."

Papa snaps, "No way am I getting a colonoscopy after what my daughter went through."

That's when the fights begin. Mama's saying *"Ay Diyos ko"* and "Shet I can't believe what I'm hearing," and now Xavy's insisting he doesn't need one either because he doesn't have any symptoms.

Mama all of a sudden shrieks, "How can you not want to get screened after finding out your daughter has only a couple of months to live?"

My heart goes thud and I push Frida off me and I run inside the house and my shoulders keep bumping into every corner of each wall I pass because my body can't keep up with my legs.

There's a tumor in your liver, and now the only way it'll disappear is if you disappear too.

When I get to the dining room, everyone just stares.

"What do you mean a couple of months?" My voice feels like it's shouting inside my throat and my chest but not coming out.

No one answers me. They all just give me sad or blank kinds of expressions, and then Papa gets up and tells Xavy to take me back outside and says, "Dr. Witt and Dr. Minor are leaving soon, Love, just stay put there with your brother."

Then he closes the window so that I can't hear anything, but *there's a tumor in your liver* and *a couple of months to live* are on maximum high volume inside my brain.

Xavy takes me and Frida to the wooden bench where Makena usually reads to me, and I sit there and look around our backyard. Our tennis court is covered with leaves and dirt, like a dump truck drove right through it by mistake.

I stare hard at the stones and pebbles and ferns near the steps that lead to our house because this is all I can do about anything right now, right at this very moment.

Xavy has his arm around me. He doesn't say anything. He never does when I want him to, but I don't care this time.

I keep thinking, "A couple of months to live, a couple of months to live," and today is May 18 so does that mean Makena will be gone on July 18, but how do those doctors know that for sure?

I don't know if I should cry because Papa wouldn't want that.

But shouldn't I be allowed to?!

Makena is breaking her promise to me. Maybe the doctors are wrong and she has a couple of *years* to live, which is way better than just months. Makena's taking a nap and I wonder if she already knows, but I don't understand why the doctors would tell Mama and Papa and Xavy first and not Makena.

I can't believe my *áte* lied. She lied to Ramona Quimby too. When I asked her if she was going to die, that was the hardest question I ever had to ask anyone in my whole life, even worse than the time I had to ask the bus driver Mr. Babbitt with the spooky purple bunny heart earring on his chin to drive me home because I fell asleep and missed my stop.

My body isn't supposed to be feeling this way. It's fuming hot and wanting to burn all the letters Makena wrote to me while she was away up north at Cal.

There's a goddamn tumor in your liver. Now you have a couple of months and not years here before you take the ride, so goodbye. Always and forever, goodbye.

I need to wear my crafty poker face now, the one that shows I'm tough and *matapang* and don't worry about me please.

Papa finally calls me and Xavy and says, "Mama's with Makena in her bedroom, come let's go now."

When we get there, Mama is sitting like the top half of her body is going to tip her over. She doesn't look sad or mad or anything else, just tired.

Makena is the queen of tired because her face looks like a sack full of potatoes. She's also even skinnier than that day I watched her water Ramona Quimby, which I can't believe because it was only a few months ago that she looked fat and ugly and had to wear medium-sized hipsters.

We're all sitting on Makena's bed, and Papa starts to talk. He says we're going to hang in there and we won't listen to the doctors because sometimes they're wrong.

But Makena starts shaking her head. Her eyes are shut, and her eyelashes are still curly but seem to lie flat against her face, like spiders I see resting near the corners of the walls of my bedroom, not sure of where to crawl to next.

She lets out a calm but begging kind of whisper, and now I'm not mad at her anymore for being weak.

"Papa, stop it. Just stop."

67. ching chong china

My calendar book says it's May 29, 2003.

I hate Dolby Peters.

I hate him even more than those fourth grade bullies. Dolby is the biggest bully in third grade and I think even all the grades. His gang always chases mine, and one time they made Devi fall on both of her knees right there on the black asphalt, and boy did his gang get it from Ms. Langevin and the teacher in charge of recess that day.

Dolby sits behind me, and he always kicks the back of my chair on purpose. I know Ms. Langevin doesn't care for him much, but she tries to be fair and gives Dolby lots of chances to be good, just like with the rest of us. One time, all he had to do was sit in the quiet corner after he scribbled all over Annabelle Hart's picture of Mahatma Ghandi and his robe, which was actually a dhoti and a shawl according to Mama.

One day when Ms. Langevin passed out the *Scholastic* magazines, I was about to hand the last one to Dolby, but Pyne Badwey turned around and asked if she could have it because hers was torn, so I gave it to her.

That's when Dolby grabbed the sleeve of my T-shirt and said, "That was mine," so I told him to relax and go find another one.

He raised his hand to ask Ms. Langevin, but she said there were no more, and of course he didn't want the torn one from Pyne, which means that I had to share my copy with him.

Ms. Langevin had Dolby pull up a chair next to me, and I couldn't stand being so close to him. All the girls in our class feel the same way because Dolby makes you uncomfortable like a rooster stuck in a lake. He likes to copy my voice, trying to make it all girly and high, but there's no way I sound like that.

"I'm not fat, I just have a big butt," he squeaks, or he tells me I smell like my dog. When he's feeling extra mean and rude, he'll sing "Ching Chong China" in his dumb fake accent to me and Thao Nguyen who's Vietnamese, thinking all Asians look Chinese or something, and that's when my hands start to squeeze into fists that want to cold-cock this sadly xenophobic boy with the stupid stereo name, even though I do have some Chinese relatives from Papa's side of the family who think "Ching Chong China" is the lamest song ever, which makes them start singing it together in an old-man kind of huddle while cracking up.

Dolby wears sneaky smiles, and his hair is greasy like someone rubbed Vaseline all over it. His white shirts always look like they're turning permanently light brown because all he does is play in the sand and ruin other kids' sand creations during recess.

After lunch earlier today, Devi and Bianca and Maya and some of our other gang went ahead of me to recess because I had go to the girls' rest room.

Devi had come up with this radical idea of making a sand mountain with a water slide, so I decided to just go pee and to hold in my poo pile. I washed my hands for 10 seconds instead of the 20 seconds Mama taught me to, and then I started to take super quick steps and remembered not to use my running feet so that I wouldn't get caught by a hall monitor.

One of my fast footsteps tripped over something that felt like a leg, and when my hands and knees hit the ground all at once, I heard Dolby's evil cackle, the deep ha-ha-ha kind that shows he's the leading bad guy.

I could already feel my palms and knees stinging, and I knew that Mama would have to put antiseptic and Neosporin and all kinds of bandages over my wounds later.

Come on, Dolby, what are you going to do about it? Kick my shins like a weakling?

All of a sudden, I decided not to pay attention to my pain.

I started to get up right there in front of Dolby, and when I was close to his private parts, I pounded them with the strongest fist I could make. I even made sure that my thumb wasn't stuck inside my grip because Papa says you can break or sprain it if you hit someone that way.

All kinds of howls and ows flew out of Dolby's mouth, and when his large oval eyes turned into circles, I think he wanted to cold-cock me too, so as he stood up in slow motion like an *abuela*, I kicked the back of his knees just like Papa taught me, and of course he fell right back down to the ground again.

That's when Dolby's gang started laughing and pointing and teasing him about getting beat up by a girl and how can we hang around someone like that from now on.

One boy named Robby Jordan even held my arm up to the sky, just like those referees in the boxing rings do for the fighter who wins, and when his gang started to clap and chant "Big Butt, Big Butt," I yanked my arm away from Robby and made all of them get lost before I told Principal Zalay.

It didn't feel right when I hit Dolby Peters.

I turned into the bully, the bad guy in control and the one who the gang wanted to follow.

It also didn't feel right when I heard all the ows and screaming come from someone like Dolby, all tough and mean and Vaseline hair.

Papa always tells me how invigorating it is when the bullies go down. He'll say, "Those goddamn assholes, they deserve what's coming to them."

I don't think Dolby Peters deserved to feel like a weakling in front of his gang, even though he's a bad kind of seed that makes girls feel like they can never be the boss.

But he might always be a misogynist, misogynist
A sadly xenophobic, brick-faced racist and misogynist

There are many times I wish I were a boy so that I could hang out in my second office and smoke and throw darts and be in charge of a family and scream at my workers who steal stuff.

But I like playing hopscotch and jumping rope. I like trading Hello Kitty and My Melody stickers and writing letters on my Pochaco stationery.

I like Snoopy and my Groovy Girls.

Lola Zeny

Lola Zeny, I'm not supposed to feel any love for you, but I think I always will. You're skinny and short, and your clothes smell like Spam, and boy do you like to gamble. You make Tita Rina drive you to the horse races at Santa Anita Park, which sits right across the way from Arcadia Methodist Hospital, and one time when Lolo Carlo told you to stop going because you were spinning out of control, you didn't listen, and that's how you ended up blowing your life savings, which Xavy tells me was supposed to be part of the inheritance for Mama and her sisters.

You used to go with us to Las Vegas, and you'd plop yourself right in front of only one slot machine the whole time we were there, even if it kept eating up all your money. Sometimes you'd win jackpots, like $1,000 or even $5,000, but you'd push all the coins right back into the same machine because you thought you'd collect even more. You still gave everyone balato, *which means a share of your winnings, even when you were thousands of dollars poorer. I always liked that part because I'd use my* balato *to play all the games at Circus Circus and MGM Grand and Excalibur with Makena and Xavy and the cousins.*

You always wear hand-me-down clothes and never like to buy anything new, and even the food you cook is recycled according to Papa, who says you can whip up an omelet out of any goddamn morsel of food. One time, Mama got sick from an omelet that you made out of chicken relyeno, *which was stuffed with pork sausage and raisins and sitting for a whole week on your kitchen table without any plastic wrap over it.*

Papa and Xavy go on and on about your faults, but you sure were masayang kasama, *always yelling "Come on, baby!" at the slot machine, even though I wasn't supposed to be watching, and that's when you'd tell me to marry into money and save everything I earn so that I could have a grand house of my own when I grow up.*

The only time I remember you weren't masayang kasama *was when the family would tell you to stop gambling, and that sure would make you angry like a typhoon.*

"Eet ees my only hoppi-ness," you used to tell me, and whenever Makena hears this, she shakes her head and tells me if gambling is your only happiness, then you certainly don't have your priorities straight.

This was all a long time ago. Now Lola Zeny looks like a dragon whenever we run into her and my *titas* at the mall or at Ralphs. When she sees us, her mouth screws up like a poisonous little flower, and it's all because she thinks that Papa cheated her and the rest of her family out of a heap of money.

Papa was in charge of Lolo Carlo's properties, along with Mr. Baluga's, in the Philippines. Papa even had to deal with Lolo Carlo's youngest brother, who was trying to steal all the land for himself. So Papa used his connections in the Philippines and worked with a lawyer to make sure the properties were split up evenly. And when he did, he made Lolo Carlo and the whole Santos family that heap of money they didn't really deserve.

It was Lolo Carlo's brother who hired the mafia police officer in the Philippines to make Papa disappear, but one of Papa's bodyguards found out, and Xavy says he sure gave it to that cop, telling him he'd make him dissolve into thin air too if he so much as laid a finger on Papa.

Lola Zeny and Mama's sisters never found out about these terrible things because all they cared about was their money, so they never asked Papa or Lolo Carlo any questions about the properties. None of them seemed to mind that Papa was doing all the work when they should have been the ones handling it all along, because Papa wasn't even related by blood to Lolo Carlo or Lola Zeny.

But Lolo Carlo didn't trust anyone else besides Papa. He thought Papa was one of the smartest men he ever met and even considered him to be the son he never had.

Sometimes I listen to Mama talking about this family feud with Tita Gwen in the kitchen, and her words sound like they're coming from a hissing snake. I heard that Lola Zeny and Mama's sisters all had sour ugly faces and wouldn't stop pointing their fingers at Papa, yelling and screaming when it was time to talk about the inheritance.

"They were going ballistic," Mama kept repeating, which I didn't have to know the meaning of because the word itself already sounds like it's flying into a mad rage.

Papa was so offended by them when they called him a crook that he finally showed them Lolo Carlo's will, which said, "Antonio Nicolas de la Viña Yen José is the sole administrator of the estate of Carlo Basa Santos" and that there would be "no interference from anyone, in particular from Zenaida Arevalo Santos, the wife of Carlo Basa Santos."

Xavy thinks what's crazy cuckoo is that Lolo Carlo wrote the will in his own handwriting, which is called holographic, and "Wutz messed up, dude, iz Lolo Carlz wuz da one who wanted Lola Zenz to butt da hellz out."

Xavy says Papa busted out the will all super arrogant and I'm the boss now, which of course made everyone hate him even more. But if someone called me a crook when all I ever did was try to help their family for so many years, I would have acted rotten and bossy too. And if I had an anal sac like Frida, I would have sprayed my stinky fish fluid all over them, but don't ever tell anyone I said that.

68. girl god

It's June 9, 2003, and I am now nine years old. Tomorrow is the last day of third grade, so Ms. Langevin let us out an hour earlier. She gave me an A+ for my Automatic Writing project, even though I haven't finished my section on Makena yet. An A+, not just a regular A, and the next highest grade in the class was a B+.

It also would have been Lolo Martín's eightieth birthday. Today is Monday, so we're going to celebrate this weekend. Mama says that Papa doesn't want too much hullabaloo anymore over birthdays, this year especially, but Mama promised she'd take me and Devi and Bianca and Maya to Golfland, and then to Spike's afterwards. I don't mind that I'm not having a real party this year. There would be so much to clean up again, and Mama has had a double workload for many months now.

Mama's taking me to church because yesterday we were so late to mass that she turned the car around and said, "*Ay naku*, we'll just go tomorrow." We're planning to light a candle for Lolo Martín and of course for Makena too and then pray to God.

I wish we could go to church only to light candles and have the communion bread, even though it feels like the thinnest paper wafer on your tongue, and not have to listen to old preachy priests and say prayers with all those thees and thous out loud with everyone else and listen to them sing the wrong notes, especially during the "Alleluia" song, which we seem to chant a lot during the whole mass.

When Mama and I walk into Holy Trinity Church, it seems dark and orange, so I wonder if someone twisted the wrong kinds of light bulbs into all the chandeliers and ceiling lights. An older lady who reminds me of the ones at Dr. Minor's office is kneeling at the altar, and on top of her head there's a black veil sitting like a doily, just like the one that Lola Zeny wore at Lola Carmen's funeral. The other two people I see look like a husband and a wife from behind, and when Mama and I walk past them, I notice they're holding hands.

I follow Mama into the first row on the left side. She tells me to pray for a while, and then we'll go light a candle for Makena and Lolo Martín.

Mama kneels and makes the sign of the cross, and she locks all her fingers together into one big fist and closes her eyes. Her lips are moving fast and her voice is low and mumbly, so I can't tell what she's saying.

I'm sure she's talking about Makena, and I wonder if she has other prayers.

"Mama?" I tap her on the shoulder real light.

"Yes, sweetheart," Mama answers. Her eyelids hang heavy like blinds over a window, and I notice her eyes are darker than they usually are, the color of rain clouds.

"What else are you asking God for?" I try to put my voice on low volume because I notice a priest walking near the altar. I can tell Mama's proud of me because she tries to smile.

The dimples near each corner of Mama's mouth no longer exist because it feels like there's a face towel of sadness in our house that's been wiping all her smiles away. Mama murmurs the last of her prayers and makes another sign of the cross before she slides back into her spot, and she checks her skirt to see if it got bunched up.

One time during Sunday mass when she made me wear a dress, I forgot to smooth and pull my skirt flat and tight before I sat down, so when I stood up, it was wrinkled and soaked in my sweat. When Mama noticed the creases all over my butt, she shook her head and told me I never listen.

"Isabel," Mama finally answers, "Prayer doesn't mean just asking God for things. When you pray, talk to *Diyos*, tell him how you are. He listens to you and gives you strength. He's our friend."

"Then how come everyone fears God," I ask. "Even Lola Zeny is afraid of him, and she used to tell me that God would punish me if I committed too many sins and didn't go to church and ask for his grace. And how do we know if God is a man or a woman?"

That's when Mama makes wide frog eyes, but then she gives me one of those looks that feel sorry for me.

"Sweetheart, that's how Lola Zeny and many other Catholics grew up."

"Makena told me that's how you grew up too. She says you think life is an entrance exam to get into heaven, and that's why you made her display the statue of the Virgin Mary in her bedroom."

Mama rolls her eyes and sighs *"Diyos ko"* and *"Ay buhay,"* but she stops and turns to me and says, "Isabel, I have a difficult time expressing myself. It always seems to come out the wrong way. I just want all of you to have religion in your lives. Your father, Makena, Xavy, they're all so smooth with the talking. I grew up in a house that never talked."

"Lola Zeny and Lolo Carlo didn't talk to you?"

Now I give Mama one of those looks that feel sorry because if talking weren't allowed, I know for sure that my head would never stop spinning from all the words trapped inside.

"They did, *hija*, but all they ever told me and your *titas* was do this, go get that, don't go there, don't you dare touch that. Do your homework and do your chores. Don't talk back to your elders. Don't ever take the Lord's name in vain. When you, Makena, Xavy, Papa, and I talk, we ask questions. We like to learn things about each other. Papa and I always make sure you're enjoying school and you have nice friends."

"Your talking is smooth right now," I tell Mama, and that's when she wraps both her arms around me.

"*Ikaw ang isang mabait na batang babae*," she says, which means, "You are such a kindhearted little girl."

This makes my insides feel gooey and warm, so I hold Mama for a little longer. I can smell some of Papa's Pinaud on her shoulder, and it starts to cool down my warm and gooey insides in a wondrous kind of way.

When I hear sniffles during our long hug, I ask Mama if she feels blue about Makena.

"I'm sad about other things too, Isabel." She opens her purse and pulls out a travel pack of Kleenex. For a second, I think about Makena's poo pile in the Kleenex box, but I erase those thoughts in a hurry before God catches me thinking about gross things in church.

"What else are you sad about, Mama?"

"I miss your Lola Zeny and Lolo Carlo. My sisters too."

Mama's making loud and croaky crying sounds now, and she's burying her face in the whole pack of tiny tissue and blowing her nose way too hard.

I check behind us to see if Mama is making a scene, and I notice that the couple holding hands is staring at us. The woman has a pearly white face and black hair like coal, and the man has a hefty body whose skin is bronzy dark.

I want to show Mama this couple because they look like Makena and Ryan in the future, even though Ryan isn't Catholic because he's Episcopalian, which means "Catholic Lite" according to Xavy.

Mama is still hiding behind the Kleenex, weeping for her lost family.

"Why is it so hard for everyone to be friends?"

I give Mama a long time to answer because she's still trying to catch her breath. I know this kind of feeling, when you're crying and you feel like you're choking and you try to squeeze the words out, but people can't understand them until you just take slow and deep breaths and imagine waves of soothing inside yourself and then let everything out.

"We'll always love each other, but sometimes there's too much grief between everyone to be together. Too many grudges, egos, and hurt feelings."

Mama blows into the tissue again. I move the strands of hair that are stuck to her cheek away from her face. Her breathing is steadier now, and her voice isn't rocky anymore, so it's much easier to understand her words.

"Is it all because of Papa?"

While I wait for Mama's answer, I think to myself about the family feud and how Lolo Carlo chose Papa over his family.

"No, *hija*, he's the one who helped your Lolo Carlo all those years. It was an 'agreement between two men,' your *lolo* had told me. Something that people like you and me are never supposed to understand."

When Mama and I light two of the white candles near the altar for Makena and Lolo Martín, we kneel and pray for a few more minutes. I look over my shoulder to check out the couple again, and the woman smiles at me.

Why do I feel like she knows me? And what are people like Mama and me never supposed to understand? People like Mama and me, and the pretty girl who's making me feel warm and gooey, and even Makena and Ms. Langevin and Lola Evie, and Surfer Girl and Lola Carmen and Lola Zeny?

I turn back around and close my eyes. Of course I pray for Makena, but I pray for Mama too.

And this time, I pray to *Ms.* God.

Ms. God, I'm sorry for saying that your mysterious ways make me want to call you a jerk-off, but that was when I thought you were a man-boy.

Ms. God, I think Papa was right. Mama really doesn't have one single bad bone in her body.

Ms. God, even though Mama grew up in a house that didn't talk and became a mama and a wife who does whatever her husband tells her to do at home, you sure gave her a lot of strength, the kind that isn't afraid to show tears in front of her kids, and also the kind that has to live a life without her own mama and sisters.

Ms. God, my mama deserves all kinds of royal flushes, and not just a bunch of cards that don't go together.

Oh, and Ms. God, I'd like to ask for one thing if that's okay with you. Can I please have some birthday hullaballoo next year?

Mama's ways are strong and quiet kinds. She keeps cooking and cleaning and caring for Makena and all of us, murmuring her novenas late into the night.

You don't love her or hate her. You just love her.

69. tater tot

Before the feud, things were different, but not meaning "separate" or "unlike," which is the definition that was on the vocabulary list that Ms. Langevin gave us last week.

One summer, Mama and Papa went on a trip to Madrid for two whole weeks to see where Lolo Martín grew up. I was only five years old, and that was the longest time we ever spent apart. Makena was away at Berkeley, and Xavy went to a summer tennis camp in Florida, so they made Frida and me hang out with Lolo Carlo and Lola Zeny and Tita Doti the whole time.

It got kind of boring over there after three weeks, since all they do is stay home and watch TV or go to 99 Ranch and Costco, but when Frida and I went back home, I really missed all three of them.

I think Frida missed them too because of all the extra treats and attention, especially from Lolo Carlo, who was a dog lover. When he was out in the backyard gardening, he and Frida would play fetch with a new toy that he picked up for her at Petco every two days. He bought new ones so often because Frida would end up breaking the squeaker and pulling out the stuffing from the toy once they were done playing.

The best times were at night when Tita Doti got home from work. She's Mama's favorite sister, and she's only 13 years older than Makena. She's a microbiologist, the kind who looks at different cells under a microscope all day and analyzes them. She isn't married yet, so she still lives at home with Lolo Carlo and Lola Zeny.

Sometimes we'd listen to Tita Doti's favorite songs, music from the '80s, like "Billie Jean" by Michael Jackson and "When Doves Cry" by Prince, and "I'll Be Over You" by Toto. Makena and Xavy love '80s music too, even though they were just babies during that time.

Papa always tell me that things were simpler back then. "There were no PDAs and laptops and Internet and all that BS, and people actually talked to each other in-person or on the phone instead of emailing," he says.

Tita Doti taught me how to dance '80s style, like moving my shoulders like a wave to The Snake and then tightening them up for The Running Man and The Robocop, along with all kinds of other neat moves that Makena's and Xavy's friends make fun of.

I think The Snake is coming back because the other morning, I saw Kelly Ripa from *Live With Regis and Kelly* do it, and she's super fun and hip. Xavy says she's dope, which Makena can't believe because Kelly Ripa is twice his age.

Tita Doti would boil those packages of corn made by Green Giant when we were ready to watch TV. She'd buy the kind with extra butter, so when you took one spoonful of the corn, sometimes all you could taste was the thick cream melting in your mouth.

Sometimes we'd watch *Who Wants to Be a Millionaire*, but at 9:00, we always had to check out a *Lawrence Welk* rerun. This was Lolo Carlo's favorite show, even though it was canceled a long time ago. I was supposed to be in bed by 8:30 every night, but Lolo Carlo let me stay up because he wanted me to dance with him at the end of his show.

Tita Doti made shoestring French fries or tater tots too if she didn't feel like having corn. Lola Zeny would fry Vienna sausages and Spam with rice, but the Spam was the low-sodium kind because she wasn't allowed to have too much salt. I can munch on tater tots all day long, especially with a Sloppy Joe, which is one of the yummiest lunches at school that we get only once a month.

Lola Zeny's favorite show was *Who Wants to Be a Millionaire.* Tita Doti told me that Lola Zeny would marry Regis Philbin if Lolo Carlo weren't around, which would always make Lolo Carlo cackle. But this didn't stop Lola Zeny from saying that Regis was so debonair and handsome in those expensive-looking suits of his.

Regis annoys me sometimes because he can't even read the questions correctly to the contestants, or he pronounces the names of celebrities wrong, like "Welsley" Snipes or David "Boowie." One time he said "heighth" instead of height, and Lolo Carlo started to pretend to punch the TV.

"Even my 5-year-old granddaughter can speak better than you, you *hayop*," he yelled. In Tagalog, when you call someone a *hayop*, it means you're lower than an animal, which I think is a rotten thing to say about Regis because animals are even more supreme than dope. Everyone knows that Regis can act dumb and lame, but I think he's a smiley old man who isn't afraid of making fun of himself.

Lola Zeny would answer all the easy questions in the beginning, but she needed her lifelines for the ones that stumped her. Lolo Carlo and Tita Doti always knew the answers to even the hard questions and never had to use their lifelines, but they both had to ask the audience one time when they didn't know Sean P. Diddy Combs' old name, which is Puff Daddy.

When it was time for *Lawrence Welk*, my eyelids would be so close to shutting for the night, but Lolo Carlo always nudged me for the last song, which I call "Good Night, Sleep Tight." When Lawrence Welk started grabbing people from the audience and dancing with them, Lolo Carlo would wiggle his shoulders and clap his hands and pull me up from the couch to do the foxtrot. I never remember the lyrics to this song because there are different parts in different languages, so when I trotted like a fox with my *abuelo*, I came up with my own words.

Buena noche *until we see each other again, bye bye*
Even though we're sad when we're apart
You know I will keep you inside my big and beautiful heart
Magandang gabi *until we see each other again,* adiós

At the end of the song, Lolo Carlo would blow up his right cheek into a mini balloon and make me give him a goodnight kiss. Sometimes I had to hold my breath because of his stinky Listerine mouth, and I'd kiss him as fast as I could and say *adiós*.

Then he'd ask, "How about *auf weidersehen* and *au revoir?"* and I'd just stand there all frozen quiet because I couldn't pronounce the words in different languages. That's when he'd snort and slap his knees and tell me, "*Ikaw, aking Tater Tot, mahal na mahal kita*," which means "You, my Tater Tot, I love you very, very much."

Tita Doti would take me to the bathroom to floss and brush our teeth together afterwards. She would remind me to scrub my tongue well so that I wouldn't have horrid breath like Lolo Carlo, and we'd cover our mouths full of foamy toothpaste and giggle. Sometimes I wonder if Tita Doti still brushes her tongue and makes Green Giant corn with extra butter for all the other cousins and kids who go to her house.

When it was time for bed, I'd ask Lola Zeny if I could sleep in the orange crib that used to be brown and that I was already too big for. She and Lolo Carlo sometimes babysat the neighbors' babies, which is why they never put the crib away. Being surrounded by the baby powder scent of my snuggly orange crib made me feel sheltered, even though Papa always preaches that he doesn't want any of his kids to have a sheltered life.

Lola Zeny loved to sing her favorite song called "Oh My Papa," but she'd change the words to "Oh my Isa" for me. Her voice would creak and shake, just like Katherine Hepburn's when she sang "Happy Birthday" to Henry Fonda in the movie *On Golden Pond*, which Mama and Papa watched on HBO the other night.

Oh my Eesa, to me you ahr so wahn-dehr-pool

That was my most favorite part of staying with Lolo Carlo and Lola Zeny and Tita Doti, dancing to the "Good Night" song with Lolo Carlo even though I was already sleepy, then lying in the orange crib that I wasn't supposed to be sleeping in anymore and knowing that Tita Doti was right next door to me, asleep in her own bed, and feeling that nothing could ever be different.

Oh my lolas *and* lolos, *I will keep you all inside my big and beautiful heart until I see you again…*

Then I'd breathe in the greasy tater tot and Spam smells of Lola Zeny's clothes, listening to her special song for me, whose words I know she changes for the neighbors' babies she sings to now.

70. gallbladders and geezers

Papa's been having some pains in his stomach, and when I ask him if it's a tumor, he barks, "No way am I the cause of all this," and then he tells me to go walk Frida.

Xavy joins me and Frida because it's getting dark outside, and when I ask him what Papa meant when he said that he wasn't the cause, all Xavy says is I know way too much for an 8-year-old, which annoys me because he should know that I just turned nine.

When we get back home from our walk, Papa is on the ground in crazy mad pain, and Mama is talking all out of breath to 911. Makena keeps asking Papa where it hurts, but I don't think that's helping at all. Papa's shouting that he has a goddamn hernia, and I tap Xavy's shoulder even though it's more like poking because my nerves are piling up, one on top of the other.

"What is a hernia, what is a hernia," I ask, and he gives me the same old answer about an 8-year-old knowing way too much, and when I scream at him that I'm nine now, he tells me to chill da hellz out.

Papa can't even stand up. The pain hurts him so much that he starts to grab and squeeze one of the legs of the coffee table really tight. I know so because his knuckles are turning lighter brown with blue veins that look like roads on a map.

Is there a tumor in his liver too, and how come all of a sudden it's so hard to breathe?!

I remember Ms. Langevin announcing in class one day that Sam Caudill would be moving away to Kansas to be with his grandparents because a vein popped in his father's neck and he died right there in front of Sam, and I know all these awful details because Jolie Johnson who we call the gossip princess found out from her papa, who is friends with Sam's papa.

My papa likes to dance the salsa with me, and sometimes he lets me sit on his lap when I'm in trouble with Mama or just feeling blue. He taught me how to pinch arms on the inside of elbows and poke eyeballs if someone tries to kidnap me, and he's the last person to say goodnight before I go to sleep. He tries to be quiet like a spy as he walks into my room, but I know he's there, calling me his Love and kissing me on the nose like Lola Carmen used to.

Then he tucks my blankets tighter into my mattress and closes my door only halfway, halfway because he wants me to be able to hear dubious sounds outside and be ready to fight just in case someone tries to mess with us.

I thought about Sam Caudill and how he lost his papa, just like that, in one tiny and quick moment of his lifetime.

Papa earns a lot of money so that we can live without too many worries, and he always makes us feel safe like a father should.

Xavy's cars are like his children, so he wouldn't have time to look after us if Papa took the ride.

Mama and Makena are women, so they might not make us feel protected like the way Papa does, but I know they would take charge of this family like Ms. God takes care of our world.

911 gets to our house on the double, and it makes Makena and Xavy wonder if Papa has connections with the paramedics in Arcadia. When we are all waiting in the emergency room lobby, Mama keeps reciting prayers and clutching her rosary, and her dark brown hair is in twisty tangles.

Makena's sitting on her hands because the A/C feels like it's set to only 60 degrees, and her shoes that have wooden soles and short heels, because they were the only ones she could find when we rushed out the door, won't stop tapping and clicking on the floor.

Makena still looks yellow, and people are probably wondering why that sickly girl is here and shouldn't she be at home resting, but she insisted on coming.

Xavy's slumped in his chair and his butt is hanging off the edge of it. If he slips and falls, at least we're already at a hospital.

I wonder if my *áte* and *kuya* are both scared and sad and full of worry, and what if they're thinking that it's Papa's time to take the ride? I wish they would say something, even if it's to tell me to stop staring at them please.

I'm scared and sad and full of worry, but I don't think Papa will take any kind of ride because he believes he's Superman.

All of sudden, Mr. Baluga walks in and catches everyone all shocked and wow, that grouchy geezer got out of the house, especially Makena because we all know she isn't comfortable around him.

Mr. Baluga walks over to Mama first, and they mutter softly to each other and nod and squeeze each other's hands, just like people do at a funeral. Mr. Baluga comes to me and says, "*Kumusta,* Kid," and he raises his bushy gray eyebrows and recites Makena's and Xavy's names like they're on a list, which is his greeting to them. He says he wants to make sure his good friend and neighbor is well and that we keep the crying and drama to a minimum because Antonio isn't a fan of hullabaloo either.

The doctor finally appears in the waiting room and tells Mama something, and she turns to us and says that Papa is hanging in there and we can go see him now.

But we all thought Makena was fine after her first CT-scan, and then we went out for ice cream, and now there's a tumor in her liver that's making her yellow, so why should we believe this doctor at all?

I tap Mama on the shoulder, and she whispers something about Papa's gallbladder but that he'll need only a laparoscopic procedure, which isn't major surgery like what Makena had. Mr. Baluga tells Mama he'll take me home and says, "Remind Antonio to behave."

I can't decide if I want to cry or scream. I don't know what's better because what is a gallbladder and does it grow tumors inside of it and why does Papa still need surgery even though it's just a mini one, but I remember there will be no hullabaloo, so I bite down on my bottom lip and breathe deep breaths to keep the tears from streaming down my face. Mr.

Baluga can tell I'm about to cry because I notice that his right eyebrow is higher than his left one, but he doesn't scold me for hullabaloo this time because it's just part hullabaloo and not a full one.

I feel better when we're outside, breathing in air so cool and fresh, and I tell Mr. Baluga that I didn't know he could drive. He lets out his gorilla ha-ha's and says he isn't really supposed to be driving because he can see well out of only one eye, but he promises he'll drive slow like a grandpa, even though he isn't one.

I buckle my seat belt and I don't care that there isn't a booster seat in the back, and then I hold on to the door handle tight as Mr. Baluga tries to back his car out of the small parking space he squeezed into. He drives a light blue Chevy Impala, the kind that carmakers don't build anymore. It's like a boat, the most gargantuan car I've ever seen.

When we get to his house, Lola Evie asks us right away if Papa is okay, and I can't help wondering if she really means it. Mr. Baluga tells her all about Papa's gallbladder and that it needs to be removed.

When Lola Evie starts to pour me a glass of orange juice, Mr. Baluga snaps, "No, *putangina,* no" and throws her a look that says the vacancy sign inside her head went up again and gets me kiwi strawberry juice instead.

I ask Mr. Baluga if Papa will make it through his mini surgery.

He answers, "Yes, Kid, it's a standard procedure."

Why can't everything be a standard procedure, I wonder, but I don't ask my question out loud because Mr. Baluga will complain that I'm too inquisitive for my own good and much too young to be losing hope.

71. quintessential and queer

I sit with Makena in her bedroom just to be with her and to make sure that someone is watching over her to see if she needs anything, like another pair of socks because her toes feel icy or the remote control which dropped in between her bed and her nightstand or is stuck under Frida, who likes to sleep really close to Makena these days because dogs are supposed to know when there's something wrong inside a person.

I can't find my calendar book, but I think it's June 13, 2003. It's Friday the 13th, which Xavy always makes a big deal about because he's superstitious and it's one of his favorite movies, but nothing bad has ever happened to any of us on this day of rotten luck.

Sometimes I listen to Makena going on and on about the Giants most likely not making it to the World Series because their bullpen sucks, or that she missed a whole season of Cal football, or why does Mama keeps saying those novenas which are just words you keep repeating, and do they really work?

She wonders if God is real, and I decide not to tell her that God is a "Ms." to me, even though I know she would be so glad and proud. Papa told me not to make one peep when Makena harps on because sometimes she might not even realize that someone's sitting in the room with her.

Mama warns me that if Makena starts to talk about dying, get up and walk away quietly and let her or Papa know, but I can't seem to make myself budge when Makena tells me she can't bear to look in the mirror anymore because she's swelling up like a balloon.

Her entire life, she says, people have told her she's beautiful.

It's true what she's saying because everyone keeps telling me how stunning my *áte* is and so exotic-looking with those light brown eyes and fair skin and long and shiny black hair, like the women in all those shampoo commercials. They all probably wonder what happened to me and Xavy, who are darker and stockier like some of the locals we saw in Hawaii the year before the last one, during Christmas break.

The quiet in Makena's bedroom isn't the peaceful kind. It's making me crazy wired-up, like when we're waiting in line at Costco and I'm wondering where all the shoppers are going to store all those rolls of paper towels and 48-packs of water bottles stacked inside their carts.

Makena finds the remote right under Frida, who sighs every time someone disturbs her nap because she has to go and make a new sleeping position for herself. It takes a while for Makena to turn off the TV because she doesn't remember we have cable and you have to switch the button to "TV" from "cable" before you turn it off.

All of a sudden, she says all she can think about is how she looks and who she is to everyone else in the world. She's a scholar and a concert pianist and a top-ranked NCAA tennis player, and boy is she *napakaganda*.

Xavy does the best impression of Papa when he's bragging to his friends about Makena. He pretends he's lighting up a cigarette and waves and points his finger, making sure everyone is listening to him. Then he'll throw in a lot of "goddamns" and "Christs" and "my friends" because when you talk about someone as dope as Makena, you better make a lot of drama.

Sometimes I catch Papa's friends rolling their eyes when Papa isn't looking because they're sick of hearing about Papa's amazing daughter and think, "Hey, my kids are just as special as yours."

Then I wonder if Makena gets embarrassed when Papa brags so much because sometimes I do, especially when he tells his friends that I set the world record for multiplication tables, even though I was the fastest only this one time in Mrs. Cooper's class when Principal Zalay couldn't find a substitute teacher for Ms. Langevin.

Or how Mama can outbake anyone at those culinary pastry schools or that his only son Xavy is the next Eddie Murphy or Dave Chappelle, even though he acts more like Jim Carrey, who can crack you up with his faces that look like they're made of Laffy Taffy.

Sometimes Papa likes to make the truth sound better, but I don't think he needs to because the truth can stay exactly the way it was in the first place and everything would be fine.

Makena must have read my mind because just as I was thinking about all those people who thought I set a world record, she started to brag about Papa.

"Papa attended De La Salle, one of the elite universities in the Philippines, and on a full academic scholarship."

Makena likes to use the word "elite," which irks Xavy and a lot of other people, but I guess that's what happens when you're an elite kind of person.

"Papa was in an entire class by himself. Valedictorian, Summa Cum Laude, out of college by the time he was 16. He excelled in basketball. He was invincible in tennis and let everyone know it by pumping his fists into the air after every winner he hit.

"Quintessential Papa: pumping his fists. Tita Gwen once took the most perfect picture of Papa, the moment I won my first USTA tournament. What's intriguing and queer is the picture is focused on me, walking to the net to shake hands with my opponent, right after match point. Papa is merely a speck in the background, but Tita Gwen managed to catch him immediately after he rose from his seat, running, his right fist clenched and pumping it toward the sky."

This is the most epic photo taken of Papa, even though you can barely see him. Every time I look at this picture, I feel like it's telling a story. Makena's face doesn't wear any expression, and her shoulders are kind of hunched, which looks weird because she always has great posture just like Tito Gus, like she's balancing something breakable on her head and trying not to make it fall.

Then you see Papa who looks the opposite, jumping all over the place like an orangutan, all big smiles and punching air, and you can't tell where he's going, if he's hurrying over to greet Makena to congratulate her, or to other people who were also watching to announce to them that Makena is his daughter, look at her, she just won a whole tournament.

But I don't think he's running anywhere because he's just running happy.

Xavy says he never heard anyone yell "Yeah" so loud and even felt it booming like bass and echoing inside his chest.

Mama says she never saw anyone hold his head so high.

He's high and mighty and noble and quintessential, even though sometimes quintessential means "usual and typical." I know the meaning of this word because I never put away all those dictionaries that didn't have "irregardless" in them. Quintessential wasn't even one of Xavy's SAT words, so I think I'll give myself a pat on the head or something. If you ask me, quintessential is what Papa is not, and boy I sure like the word "quintessential," because I think it sounds way cooler than being elite.

"I can visualize Papa pumping his fists after Tita Rose gave him his first $20 bill, when he was a wide-eyed 19-year-old ready to tackle America. He punched tickets at the movie theater, he washed dishes, he even held the title of janitor. Last year, he was recognized as one of the top real estate developers in Southern California. He makes a pretty penny, and he claims to have given his family everything."

It's true, Papa has given us everything we ever wanted. Like Xavy's vintage Bug, and Makena's hefty allowance even though she got full rides, along with Mama's once-a-month shopping sprees and all of my Gap Kids clothes and Sanrio trinkets.

But there was one time he told me he was going to buy me the entire Groovy Girls wardrobe if I got three A's on my report card, and he didn't. During one quarter, I got A's in spelling and language arts and English. Papa told me that spelling doesn't really count, and why do they even make that a goddamn subject when all you do is memorize 20 words a week to spell correctly, but he knows it's an important part of writing.

Makena says that Papa used to write more often. While he was in the Army, he sent letters to Mama while she was pregnant with Makena. His nickname for her was "Love," just like he calls me.

"Love, are you taking care of yourself, staying away from those sweets? Eres un ángel, mi *Angelina, so true to your given name. Say hello to our Martín, my firstborn son. I want our Martín to carry on the José name like no other José ever has. Everyone will be hitching their wagons to my shining star."*

Makena stops and stays quiet for a minute, and I wonder if she's done and why Papa thought she was going to be his firstborn son, and that's when I realize that she turned nosy with Mama's private brown metal box too.

"I was supposed to be Martín," she says, "named after Papa's father."

All of a sudden, Makena springs up like a jack-in-the-box in her bed.

"I was supposed to be Martín," she keeps screaming, and I call for Mama and Papa, but no one hears me. When I get up and run for the door, Makena jumps off the bed and grabs the edge of the hood on my sweatshirt.

"Ryan said I couldn't live my whole life pleasing Antonio José," she cries. "He yelled in my face in my dorm room on that fateful night, 'Nothing is worse than wanting respect that's based on fear. I thought you were braver than that.'"

I feel Makena letting go of my hood, and that's when she plops onto the floor next to the bedroom door, shrieking "How could he forsake me?" and not caring that there's saliva dripping from both corners of her mouth.

"Truth, like light, blinds," she says softly, and now she's preaching to herself. "Falsehood, on the contrary, is a beautiful twilight that enhances every object."

72. construction of a creation of a construction

Papa takes me to his job sites only when the construction is close to being done because he says it's dangerous for kids like me to be around when his subs are laying the foundation and pouring concrete or framing the floors, and also when there's plywood and dust all over the place. Papa's favorite part is when the drywall goes up because this is when his masterpiece finally starts to look like a house.

I ask Papa if I can be his sidekick today at his La Cañada job site because I overheard Mama telling Tita Gwen that the house is almost done. I don't tell him the real reason, which is that it's getting harder to be around Makena, especially when she cries all out of control in her room or tells me not to stare at her please. I also want to make sure Papa's really okay enough to work after his mini gallbladder surgery, but don't ever tell him I said that.

"I'd be happy to take you with me, Love," Papa says, and he tells me I picked the right day because he needs to go through his punch list, which is the final inspection of the house, and of course we know that Papa is an expert at inspecting because he's "anal-retentive," which he hates being called by Xavy because Xavy is the same exact way. He needs to make only one list, but he prepares two because sometimes his subs get lazy towards the end, just wanting to finish the house already and who cares because it's not their house anyway.

For both lists, Papa carries a roll of blue tape and walks around the whole house, opening every door and cabinet and checking every little corner. At each spot where he sees something that needs to be fixed, he tears off a piece of tape and slaps it right on the mistake. Xavy says, "When Papa be bustin' out dat blue tape, betta run fur cover from all dem repugnant Tagalog an' *español* words flyin' atcha, foo'."

I hope that the La Cañada house doesn't have too many mistakes, or else being at home dealing with Makena and all the drama might be a better deal than watching Papa go into a mad rage with blue tape.

Papa pulls up to the curb of the La Cañada job site. The house reminds me of the mansions with tall pillars that you see on the cover of the *Frontgate* catalog, all deluxe and look at us, our house is so lovely and majestic. Papa tells me that the husband and wife who asked him to build their house are both lawyers who are *mayabang* and don't have any kids. "Hell, if you have all that dough," Papa says, "you might as well show it off and live it up."

I remember Lolo Martín was a lawyer, and I wonder if he had a lot of money too, so I ask Papa if Lolo Martín was rich.

"We had a comfortable life growing up," Papa says. "But the American dollar goes a long way in the Philippines. You can't compete with the wealth here in the States."

Papa takes my hand and leads me through the front door. The new-house smell of paint and wood and carpet is sharp and strong, like it's punching me in the face.

Papa points to the fireplace and says, "See that mantel? All the way from Indonesia. Check out the detail on this beauty."

I once watched someone on the Do-It-Yourself channel carve a piece of wood, and boy whoever carved this mantel must have spent a long part of their life doing this. There are scrolls and flowers and even lion faces that look real and menacing. Papa says it's made of mahogany, which is one of the strongest kinds of wood out there.

I walk behind Papa all around the house while he knocks on walls, opens and closes doors, turns faucets and lights on and off, and slaps on blue tape here and there. It looks like there aren't too many mistakes, so Papa keeps the curse words to himself. You can tell he's in a good mood because he's humming "I Will Survive," which was playing on the radio in the car.

"I Will Survive" was another of Tito Gus' favorite songs. There are so many things that remind me of Tito Gus, like Sara

Lee pound cake, snacking on slices of it like they were crackers, and Duck Duck Goose, playing rowdy outside restaurants while we were waiting for a table. Then we'd get the gimlet eye from the host, and we all would crack up when Tito Gus winked at him and made him red hot in the face as we walked inside together.

I always imagine how things would be if Tito Gus were still around. I'll bet he would have helped take care of Makena, and I'll bet Xavy would have had someone to be silly with and make everyone laugh and almost pee in their pants, especially whenever Makena rants about her stinging canker sores or why fossil fuels have both helped and destroyed our world.

I ask Papa, "Do you miss Tito Gus?"

We don't talk about Tito Gus too much these days, so I sure hope that my question doesn't make him angry or blue.

But Papa turns to me and smiles. Everyone knows "I Will Survive" was the song that Tito Gus had a blast singing and dancing to the most.

"Of course," Papa answers, but that's all he says. He notices a scratch on the wood floor in the family room and slides a piece of steel wool from his pocket and places it over the scratch.

He tries to rub the mark away all super gentle, and I wonder if he had steel wool inside his pocket because he knew there would be scratches to buff or if he just carries it around with him all the time.

Even though Papa tried to act all cool and I don't give a hoot during the *kuwento* about Gusdagard Vergon, Mama always tells me that Tito Gus is a sore subject for him, try not to bring up his name too much, and if you have to, just talk about something funny he used to do, like imitate Xavy talking ghetto but with a high-pitched voice. "I'mma down wit dat," Tito Gus would squeak out, and then he'd high-five Xavy while sticking out his butt at us.

But Papa acts different when you're alone with him because there isn't anyone else around to show off to. I watch my papa so calm with his steel wool, and I feel like I could ask him anything at this very moment.

"Papa, tell me how Tito Gus became a *bakla*," I say, and I feel my insides settle down when he answers right away.

"Your Tito Gus was born gay, Isabel. He was never meant to be a man."

Papa's voice feels heavy, but I keep firing away.

"Then does that mean Tito Gus was born happy too? And aren't gays still men?"

"Love," he laughs, "Yes, they are, but…not in the true sense. I don't know why, but men seem to be the only creatures that don't want to be who they truly are."

He looks away from me and tilts his head at another scratch on the floor. I can feel my eyebrows crinkling because "true sense" doesn't make much sense.

"Were you embarrassed to have a brother who was *bakla*?"

Papa makes wide frog eyes and twists his face into an expression of wow look at you, little girl.

"That's a loaded question," he says.

"So were you?"

I can feel my face twisting into a look of surprise too. I don't think Xavy or Makena or Mama would ever ask Papa these kinds of questions, one after the other, so maybe I should pat myself on the head again or something.

But after each question I ask, my body stiffens like clay that's all dried up and about to crumble because Papa might just turn capricious and start acting like Mafioso.

Papa doesn't answer me right away and keeps buffing the scratch with the steel wool, even though I don't think you're supposed to do it for that long.

If he tells me he was embarrassed to have a gay brother, he might feel waves of shame. If he tells me he wasn't, he might wonder if I think he's lying, because all those years that Tito Gus was a part of our lives, Papa never stopped making fun of him and letting the whole world know how gay his baby brother was, calling him "Gusda" and "Maricon" and all those names for *baklas* that Makena says are belittling.

"Like I said, your Tito Gus was born *bakla*," says Papa. "Even if he weren't, I don't think he would have ever changed."

Right when Papa says this, my heart goes ba-boom and feels like it's jumping ahead a few beats. This is the moment I try to decide whether or not I should share my secret about Lolo Martín and Tito Gus.

No one ever asked me to keep this to myself because I was the only one who heard what Lolo Martín said to Tito Gus on that day at the nursing home, so I think I can tell Papa without having to go to church and confess to Father Jack that I didn't stay true to my word.

"Lolo Martín told Tito Gus to change his life," I blurt out to Papa.

My heart's still making thud sounds, so maybe I committed a sin, and that's when Papa stops rubbing the mark on the floor and walks over to me.

He gets on his knees so that his face is closer to mine.

"Where did you hear this?" Papa asks, and you can tell by his gimlet eyes that he's trying to figure out, "Did someone feed you this bullshet," which is what Mama says when we repeat gossip from the *titas* or *titos*.

"I heard it on the day we visited Lolo Martín before he died. It was when he asked me to come help Tito Gus push him around in his wheelchair," I say to Papa while my heart keeps skipping beats. My words feel like they're crashing into each other as they tumble out of my mouth, so I hope Papa understands them.

Papa and I are still face-to-face, and I'll bet his knees are starting to hurt. He looks deep into my eyes to make sure they're not lying.

"*Don* Martín couldn't do anything about it," Papa says to me. "He tried. But he had 10 other children to look after. One of them, your Tito Ronnie, got sick with meningitis and passed on, remember?"

Before I can ask what Lolo Martín couldn't do anything about and also start to feel blue about Tito Ronnie dying in Papa's arms, Papa goes on.

"Rolling around your Tito Gus in that barrel was devastating. But I don't judge him for making us do it. He did what any father would have done during his time. He was a first-rate dad, *tu abuelo*."

Papa's eyes start to shine from the tears collecting inside, but he holds them in and continues.

"Don't ever doubt his love for his family, Isabel, even for his gay son. He and your Lola Carmen were responsible for all of us. We were their creation."

Papa straightens his shirt, and I follow him around the house again. He runs his hands over a few dents in one of the walls in the living room and grumbles *mierda* under his breath. He turns to me and says, "Love, give me a minute."

I go to the family room, far enough away from Papa so that I don't bother him, but I can still hear him saying *"Que te jodan,* Arturo" which means F you, and he's calling him a *gilipollas* and an *hijo de las mil putas.*

I watch my papa bust out new Spanish curse words that he saves for when he's going ballistic, my papa who is in charge of the superintendent and subcontractors and electricians and plumbers, and of all the other workers who help build his houses.

When Papa orders all of them to go back to this house and fix all the things covered with blue tape, they will be done. Papa says this is a fantastic feeling, when he sees the end product, something he worked hard on and saw from start to finish and took care of to make sure it came out perfect.

It's like the time when I made a hand imprint in first grade, I got to make the dough and smash it and roll it and press my hand into it and even carve my name on it before it was sent off to be baked. When I was finished, boy was I proud, especially when Mrs. Winters said we'd get to keep it. Papa hung it in my bedroom, and even now it makes me smile because I can't believe how small my hand was when I was only six years old.

But then the *mayabang* husband and wife who are lawyers will come live here to show off, and Papa will have to move on to the next house to build.

I wonder if the lawyers will notice all the things with blue tape that were fixed because of Papa.

I wonder if they'll buy a different mantel because it looks like something from Ethan Allen with menacing lion faces.

I wonder if they'll throw big parties with butlers who serve you food on silver platters and if their guests will make scratches on the wood floor with their deluxe and pointy shoes.

I wonder if Papa's sad because even though he built the house from the ground up, it will never be his.

73. cah-moose is crystal clear

"You're incarcerated in your own body. It controls you, and it won't ever let you control it. It eats up every last ounce of your dignity."

This is the kind of stuff that Makena preaches all the time now.

They join the ghosts that keep haunting my brain.

Damn him to hell, you cunt, you fucking bitch, you're a choker, you're a pussycat, I don't raise timid children, and why can't you just hold it, for crying out loud?!

Makena says she was with Ryan the first time it ever happened. They were hiking on one of the trails at Redwood Park in Oakland Hills, which wasn't too far from campus. Someone had painted the sky such a distinct color that afternoon, she tells me, a yellowish blue, almost like it was a viridescent green. The color alone gave Makena feelings that she called contentment, like she was finally making the right choices.

Ryan enjoyed the outdoors. He loved animals, trees, even the mud puddles on the trails. He liked to hold Makena's hand. He liked being with her even if they were just sitting together in the "shit-green o'd-lady Honda CRV" that Makena says Xavy always teased Ryan about. Makena and Ryan would sit quiet, listening to other cars whooshing by in the background, letting the other person just be.

They walked together for 12 miles that day. Both Ryan and Makena played college sports, so the hike wasn't too hard for either one of them. The rain had come down only a couple of days before and left mud puddles all over the trail. When they arrived closer to the end, Makena says she didn't care about the mud on her new hiking shoes. She was still feeling the contentment.

As Makena and Ryan passed by more puddles, Makena felt a twinge inside her stomach. She stopped at a tree stump, leaned against it, and groaned. Ryan asked her what was wrong.

She knew the pangs and rumbling weren't from being hungry. She remembers both of her legs starting to lose all their strength. She remembers the pain that arrived shortly thereafter, perhaps similar to what it would be like to give birth to a baby, jamming her way through her insides. She started to take slow, deep breaths, hoping to God each breath would stall the inevitable.

You remember your weakness, you remember your pain.

Makena asked Ryan how far the nearest port-a-potty was, but she knew there weren't any along the trails. When she started to crouch down to try to prevent what was coming, Ryan put his arm around her.

"You can go behind the tree down there," he told her. "I'll watch out for people, Kenz, don't worry." Makena remembers the calm in his voice.

She says they dated not even a year, but Ryan got to know her so well that he memorized every mole on her face, every shape, every size. He particularly adored her Belt of Orion, the spot on her cheek with three moles in a row, which, he liked saying, formed a comma.

Although they grew close in such a short amount of time, the one thing Makena says she couldn't get over was having to lock the bathroom door shut around Ryan, even if he was in another room far enough away.

That's when I start to giggle because Makena locks the bathroom door at home, acting like her family is a bunch of hoodlums who will kick down the door and announce to the whole world that she's making a gigantic poo pile inside the toilet, but now it makes me wonder if Papa, Mama, Xavy, and I are the bizarro ones who should be locking the door too.

Makena says she always made sure to throw her Always feminine pads in the garbage outside Ryan's apartment. If she needed to *utot*, which she calls passing gas because she hates saying fart or *utot*, she'd go to the bathroom or hold it in. She didn't even like to sweat around Ryan.

Ryan always laughed at Makena's prudish ways. He liked to tease her about saying "fork" whenever she was angry, especially while watching the news. He knew she had grown up with a father who burped in your face and a brother who sat on you and made rotten *utots* and tried pulling down your pants when he wanted to make you red in the face. *Titos* who pinned their nephews to the ground and pretended to lick their faces, *titas* who showed you the hair on their underarms to let you know that puberty was just around the corner.

Makena says she felt her heart sink when she could no longer stall the inevitable. She wanted to let out a long shriek and collapse to the ground. "How can I go in the woods like an animal, a beast in the wild?" she thought to herself.

But she remembers there was no time. She started down the hill to the tree that Ryan had pointed to earlier and walked through tall, wet grass. She found a shrubby area to surround herself with, to make sure the world didn't know she was about to go like an animal in the wild.

Then she looked up the hill at Ryan and asked if anyone was walking by.

"Coast is crystal clear," Ryan said with a little chuckle. Makena didn't appreciate the timing of his alliteration and wondered if he could see her unbuttoning her shorts and pulling them down. As she squatted, her legs started to wobble.

"God," she thought to herself, "I'm a hideous sight, defecating behind a tree. I don't even have the decency to dig a hole and cover it up. I know Ryan can smell it. I'm a barbarian."

Makena remembers pulling up her shorts and making her way back to Ryan, not wanting to face him. He looked sorry for her, but she knew he wanted to just unleash his laughter about it. She couldn't even bring herself to look him in the eye for more than a few seconds.

She wanted to hide inside a well and stay there forever.

Makena says they walked without saying anything for a few minutes before Ryan whispered, "Kenz, don't be such a spoilsport. It's me."

But she didn't care if he was okay with it because *she* sure as hell wasn't, with any of it. What was her problem? Why couldn't she hold it? Even her kid sister could hold it.

Remember his calm, remember there was no time.

Ryan and Makena weren't holding hands anymore.

Makena starts to lie down on her bed as she finishes her *kuwento* to me. Her eyebrows are like twisty wire, evidence of her worry and her serious ways.

All of a sudden, she turns super crazy dramatic.

Why would Ryan want to touch me after this, and what was he really thinking?

That his girlfriend can't even hold her shit for five fucking minutes?! That she might as well wear diapers, like a helpless infant or one of the meek elderly wasting away at a nursing home?

I was luckier other times. At my apartment or at Moffett studying, the toilet just down the hall, well within reach.

How would I have known this was all an omen?

I wake up in the morning, I labor, I sleep. I push the boulder up, and it rolls back down. I go back to sleep, and I start over.

It's absurd, and it punishes you. It can turn happy and wow to self-pity, to dejection in a matter of seconds. It can break you.

After I listen to what sounds like a speech, I watch Makena fall asleep. When her eyes are finally shut, I try to make her comfortable by straightening her blanket and pulling out the book that's stuck under her right shoulder.

It's called T*he Myth of Sisyphus and Other Essays.* I notice the author is Albert Camus.

Hey Alberto Cah-moose! I think you have joined the ghosts that keep haunting my brain. You seem to be everywhere with your intellectual quotes that my Papa and áte *always preach, and you are just like that picture of Jesus, whose shadowy eyes won't stop following me, and oops sorry I called you "Alberto."*

I imagine being broken into pieces. A puzzle with pieces not fitting where you think they're supposed to go, and you sure can't force them in.

Puzzles are meant to be put together. But if there are pieces that don't fit, do you put them back inside the box? Or do you just throw them away?

74. tomás the tool

Sometimes Papa introduces us to his business associates, and one time, he brought home what Mama calls a bigwig in the Philippines. This guy was named "Tomás Ignacio Eduardo Moreno the third" when he was born, but Papa still calls him Iggie Boy, even though he's already a grown-up. Xavy always makes fun of Filipinos when they name their kids Boy or Baby or a dumb repeating name like Jun-Jun, saying they're cheesy and "Who da hellz in Flip history started all dis jive?"

Papa says Iggie Boy used to be a tool, which to him means nerdy with a shaggy haircut and teeth that looked like they weren't brushed too often. And of course the thickest pair of eyeglasses you'd ever seen, which would always fall off his face because his nose is flat.

"Goddamn, were those schoolboys at Ateneo relentless," Papa would tell us, then he'd shake his head and make tsk-tsk-tsk sounds when he started to remember all the contemptible things the boys at school made Iggie Boy do. One time they forced him to shove bubble gum into his mouth until it was so full that his jaw cramped, and when one of the boys yelled at him to swallow it, Iggie Boy started choking and turning green.

That's when Sister Agnes had to rush over and do that maneuver called the Heimlich, where you hug someone from behind, even though it looks like dogs humpin' according to Xavy, and then you start pressing your knuckles firm below their ribcage so that they can cough out whatever they're choking on.

Papa witnessed only the very end of the bubble gum scene, and the nasty thugs had already run away so he couldn't help Iggie Boy, but Papa promised he would protect him the next time anyone messed with him.

All the schoolboys at Ateneo were scared of Papa from the time he was in kindergarten. But they also looked up to Papa because he was the leader of the pack, always so *masayang kasama* and let's go do this and that and who cares if we get into trouble because all the nuns adore me.

The nuns did adore Papa, but not so much when he got all the schoolboys to steal BB guns and shoot lampposts and all the lights you could see at school and on the streets. Another time, Papa had everyone tie paper bags around the heads of all the stray cats, and boy they all thought that was the funniest thing ever, watching cats run into poles and trees and walk in circles everywhere. Even though I don't really like cats except for Hello Kitty, that sure was a cruel and unholy thing to do to them.

Iggie Boy told us that God gave Papa all the charisma and good looks and even brains, but at least there were leftover brains for Iggie Boy, who graduated from the University of the Philippines, which they call U.P., and was awarded Summa Cum Laude just like Papa.

Then he got into an MBA program here in America called Harvard University School of Business, and he made the highest honors there too. He went back to the Philippines after going to all those elite schools, and many years later, he worked hard to be in charge of all the Shangri-La Hotels in Asia.

Iggie Boy ran into Papa at the Starbucks on Colorado Avenue near Best Buy, and that's the night when Papa brought Iggie Boy home to our house.

When Papa introduced Iggie Boy, they both had watery kinds of eyes, but you could tell they weren't sad or mad kinds of watery because Iggie Boy kept looking at Papa as if he made a friend for a whole lifetime.

After Papa told him to make himself comfortable and asked if he wanted some of Mama's homemade *bibingka* with goat cheese, Iggie Boy started to make *kuwento* with his thick Tagalog accent, but real proper and maybe even using king's English, about how Papa protected him when he was a little tool at Ateneo.

Your father, Antonio, he was so well-liked, the type of person who could get away with anything because of his charm. Just like that Ferris

Bueller character from the movie, the one who plays truant from school for one day. The difference, however, was the administrators adored Antonio as well.

People like Antonio would never be caught dead mingling with eggheads like me. Ah, but Antonio was different. He rubbed elbows with high-ranking officials and the undignified alike, and he was always quick to defend those who could not defend themselves. I will never forget what he did for me, although it happened very long ago. Thirty-eight years, to be exact.

After classes had concluded one afternoon, Cesar Panlilio, the king of the hoodlums, walked up to me and jerked my eyeglasses off my face. My vision was already poor at the age of 12, thus the bifocals, so naturally, I scarcely could see a thing. Cesar's hoodlum friends proceeded to tear off my clothes, and before I knew it, buttons were flying and all that remained on my body was my underpants. Cesar and his friends were yelling, "Sissy, geek, para siyang *Einstein," and they started to kick my entire body: my thighs, my stomach, my back, sometimes even my head.*

Amidst my screams, all I could hear were the humiliating chants of "Sissy, geek, para siyang *Einstein."*

Cesar asked that I remove my underpants for the nuns, to "give them their kicks," he had said with a smirk. When I refused, he and his friends jumped on top of me. Suddenly, out of nowhere, I heard a shriek from one of the hoodlums. Then curse words in both Spanish and Tagalog, from a voice demanding everyone to lay off me or else.

The voice was Antonio's. Cesar challenged Antonio to a fight right on the spot. Antonio chuckled, raising his fists, but little did he know he would be sabotaged from behind by one of the other hoodlums. As Antonio was forced to the ground, Cesar gave him a swift kick to the ribs and pulled out a pocket knife. I shouted for a nun, but soon I felt a hoodlum's hand muffling my cries.

I watched Antonio retaliate, kicking kung-fu style and eventually defeating Cesar and his gang. He carried me all the way home to my parents, although he had been hurt badly too. My mother was a nurse, thank the Lord, and she cared for both me and Antonio that evening. Antonio was in much worse shape, his entire face and body covered with bloody gashes.

We listened to Iggie Boy finish the story of how Papa saved him from the bullies, and before Iggie Boy left, he thanked Papa again for being his protector and offered him a free hotel room at the Shangri-La in Manila for as long as he wanted. We all looked at Iggie Boy with our mouths wide open, and then my eyes stopped at Papa. Everyone could tell he was trying to keep his cool, but I saw something else.

It's the puzzle of connect the dots, and it's making a new and better picture, which Makena would call impressionistic, like the paintings of Claude Monet, one of her favorite artists, the one who creates those colorful and blurry scenes that force your eyes to figure out what they're really looking at.

When Papa told Iggie Boy that he might take him up on his offer the next time he was in town, we all knew it was just like Papa, so proud and don't let anyone know I like free hotel rooms too, but Papa was all talk because you could tell by the way he looked at Iggie Boy, with his gray eyes like polished glass, that he realized he made a friend for a whole lifetime too.

75. being body bionic

There's a lot of screaming and yelling going on these days. I don't understand why because my *áte* is sick, so shouldn't we all be pleasant to each other during a time like this?

Papa and Mama fight almost every day about something, whether it's about how late Papa's coming home or why Papa should tell Xavy off when he's not helping out. Or how did Mama's cooking go to the birds or why don't Mama and Papa do it anymore, which is the one thing I don't understand because what are they not doing?

They do so much every day and every moment, with Mama running all over the house putting everything back in its place and cleaning toilets and grocery shopping and making sure Makena's comfortable, and Papa working all day long at his job sites and coming home to a sick Makena and not having any time to rest, and when you add these things up, it can sure make your head feel like it needs to and even wants to pop.

It's June 16, 2003. This is what it said on Mama's kitchen dry-erase board because I still can't find my calendar book. Today, Mama and Papa fought about me.

I sat right outside their bedroom door and listened for a long time while Makena and Xavy were asleep. I could hear Mama and Papa even though they were whispering, which Xavy and Makena say is uncanny, and that's why Xavy calls me Bionic Ears.

Papa and Mama used to watch a '70s show called *The Bionic Woman*, and every time I ask Xavy how the woman's ears turned bionic, he says that the main character Jaime Sommers was in a skydiving accident and doctors put cybernetic implants inside the places where she got hurt, including her right ear, but he insists that I have cybernetics in both my ears.

Mama thinks her littlest girl is growing up too fast. Papa doesn't believe this because I have a lot of spirit, just like Makena. He tells Mama that I'll learn so much from this experience and it'll make me tougher, but Mama says she doesn't want a tough little girl.

She wants a girl who plays with her dog and her dolls and all her toys. She tells Papa that her baby used to have beauty contests with her stuffed toys and Barbies, and suddenly she had to be in charge of making Jell-O for her *áte* who couldn't chew her food because her mouth was filled with 17 canker sores when we found out about this cancer shet.

I decided to go back to my room after listening to all of this cancer shet, oops I mean cancer stuff, because I didn't want Ms. God to see that I was eavesdropping.

Ms. God, I was still being a little girl when I would make Jell-O for my *áte*. I had fun mixing the powdery stuff that turned jiggly after I stirred both hot water and cold water with it and stuck it inside the fridge. It made me feel like a scientist in a laboratory.

Maybe one of these days instead of becoming a doctor or a nurse, I can create potions that will help get rid of all the cancers in the world, always and for always.

Ms. God, I'm still a little girl because I'm not tired of my Groovy Girls yet. I don't really like Barbies that much anymore, but my Let's Go Camping set is cool to play with sometimes. I do have a grand old time holding beauty contests for all my stuffed toys and making my Snoopy beanbag win first prize every single time, even if he isn't fluffy anymore.

I keep reading *Harry Potter* in Spanish, even though there's too much hell breaking loose in the house to be able to focus on books, but I do like Hermione Granger because her hair is big and stringy like she doesn't care, and not just because she's smart but also clever like a fox, or even a foxy flawless fireball.

Ms. God, I am a tough and hard girl like Papa is raising me to be, even though he probably wishes Makena and I were boys like Xavy.

They say I have bionic ears, but I'll bet you can help me make my whole body bionic, and even my soul so that the Lord doesn't have to take it when it's time to take the ride.

I never get sick, not even a cold, and sometimes I forget to take my vitamins.

I can hold in my poo piles for a long time even if I eat too many Ligo sardines.

People make fun of my tree-stump legs, but don't ever mess with them man, because they can kick solid and bike to faraway places, a whole 18 miles from Playa del Rey to Redondo Beach and back.

Ms. God, when I'm not being bionic, do you think you can help me show the piece of my heart that's like a sponge?

You know what I'm talking about, right, Ms. God? Can you help me squeeze these feelings out, especially when everyone is looking?

76. a baby blanket *bakla*

I wonder what kind of life Tito Gus had, being a *bakla* and someone his papa didn't want him to be. Makena keeps telling me that to be attracted to someone who's the same gender as you is natural, but why would Ms. God create gay people if she knew that sadly xenophobic people would always make them feel small and tell them to become something different?

Xavy says he would bag on Tito Gus nonstop, but he loves that they vibed super well, doing disco dances together and going bowling once in a while. Makena didn't get along with Tito Gus the same way, but that's because she never makes time for anyone.

Tito Gus would even tell her, "Slow down, my sweets, life doesn't have to be such a whirlwind."

Of course Makena would answer back and tell Tito Gus that his life was just as much of an uproar. And we all knew she was right because Papa used to tell us that Tito Gus thrived in the fast life, frequenting the gay bars and even spending a few nights in jail here and there for the irresponsible things he did when he was high on drugs or just drunk.

Xavy made a movie about Tito Gus called a documentary short for his film class, and every time we watch it, our bellies hurt from all the wacky laughter. The first thing that makes me giggle is Tito Gus' nostrils flaring wide, like the suction cups on the legs of an octopus, and also his hands waving this way and that as if he were shooing away flies.

Papa always cracks up about the way Tito Gus used words wrong and awkward, like "My partner's fastidious ways furnished me with a coronary infarction" or "Thank you very many," but he says Tito Gus does it on purpose just to get the snickers. One time when Tito Gus and Makena practiced taking the SAT together, Makena couldn't believe it when Tito Gus got a 740 on the verbal section, because he sure doesn't act as smart as he looks and talks.

Ay Diyos, *where do I begin? Xavier, be a pal and please do not focus too closely on my nose. It is not my most pleasant-looking feature.*

All right, my sweets, take it away. Gusberto Ramón de la Viña Yen José, live from Arcadia, Californi-aaay.

My brothers, they are all assholes. The biggest one of them all is that macho little piece of shet, Vito. Puta siya! *He stands perhaps only five feet high and acts like he is God's gift, karate-chopping and aya-ing as if he could kick another man's ass.* Sino ba siya*? Who does he think he is?*

He fails to remember I possess a deadly weapon: my fifth-degree black belt in Kajukenbo. He has procured only a third degree, so I will punt that microscopic ass of his to that big moon in the sky when I can no longer tolerate his shet.

Tito Gus, it's shit, not shet, and quit with the procuring and all your show-off vocab. This is a film, dude, people need to understand it. An' couldya pleeez talk 'bout *you?*

What in hell? Ano ba iyan*? Fine, I will obey you, Master Xavier. And please, I cannot stand to be disconnected when I speak.*

I will bet you anything in this galaxy, even the fantabulous Gucci watch Jerome gave me, that Vito's wife Marion will punt his little ass to Jupiter before anyone else does.

You said punt his microscopic ass to the moon, not Jupiter. And you're still rippin' on everyone else.

Ay*, did I say moon before?* 'Susmarijosep! *Moon then, you smart aleck, you. Now can I please continue, my handsome nephew?* Ay naku, *where was I?*

You were talking *shet* about Tita Marion instead of telling me about your own shet.

Ay Lord Jesus Christ, that wife of his frightens me. At your Tito Sal's party last night, I was sitting in the dining room conversing with your mother and your titas *when out of the baby blue, I could sense Marion's largeness behind me.*

From the corner of my left eye, madre mia, *I spotted a hand on my shoulder, and I froze as if a tarantula were crawling up my leg.* Diyos ko po, *I am not being facetious, her hand felt like it was the paw of that bigfoot, and I have never been acquainted with any Sasquatches in my entire life.*

Ay, *but I adore that Marion.* Talagang mabait siya—*she is so warm, so* simpática. *Not one bad bone in that colossal body of hers. She makes the most delectable* bibingka *con queso de cabra.* Diyos ko, sarap na sarap ang *goat cheese! Makes my belly crave for more.*

Do you know who is also kind? That eldest of theirs, Magda. Oh Lord, please do not drop an anvil on my head, but she is the most objectionable-looking one of my nieces. She looks like a rat, you know, the kind with the pointy nose and beady eyes like little munggo *beans. Did you know your father nicknamed that family The Good, the Bad, and the Uglies while we were playing* mahjong *the other night? I giggled so profusely that I wet my new silk panty from Neiman Marcus. And it was not even on sale!*

[Loud snorting from Xavy]

Your father, he can be very fiendish. He calls me the Bakla, Maricon, *Gusda…* Ay, *there must be at least five more names. You know he is the Lord of nickname-giving,* 'di ba? *He calls your Tito Carding an overweight Benjamin Bratt, and he furnishes your Tito Vito with* loko *nicknames, like Mini-Me or R2-D2 because he is vertically challenged. And your Tito Sal they call* Pilay *because his left leg is shorter than his right. Poor* Pilay, kawawa naman, *that is the reason he inserts pads into his left shoe and never wears shorts when he plays tennis.*

Tito Gus, sorry to *disconnect* you again, but tell me, is there anything positive you can say about the Josés if that's all you're gonna talk about? Is this the only thing you guys do? Get all up in their Kool-Aid?

Ay anak, *let me tell you, this family is brutal. Are you not aware this is a Filipino trait? We are all* pintaseros. *We live for the* tsismis, *the* kalokohan. *We put each other down, gossip, and act like screwballs yet still possess fierce love for one another. Any one of my brothers and sisters, they would die for you. What you call taking a bullet or walking over hot coals for someone you so dearly love.*

So, tell me, Shaaa-vier, I am your favorite uncle, 'di ba*? Come now, I promise I will not tell the other* titos.

Aw man, Tito Gus. Don't put me on the spot!

Shaaa-veee, darling, you better make nice-nice to me. Or Santa Gus shall ignore your Christmas list and buy you a panty from Neiman Marcus!

Dude. Come on, man, we better finish this segment.

[Trying to hold back laughter]

Ya needs to stop talkin' smak 'bout us Josés an' start givin' me da 411 on *you.*

Ay, *but let's talk about the little Josés first. You are all much smarter than your* titos *and* titas, *but at times I wonder how all of you will turn out. Take that tenacious big sister of yours,* Doña *Makena. That girl will be a survivor. That is, if she survives your father—or even herself.*

[Silence, then suddenly looking up from his Camcorder, goggle-eyed]

She is simply a girl on the outside, but inside, ay naku, *she is a hoodlum. Do you recall that one evening I took her and Scrappy-Doo Isabel to see* Toy Story*? We were tootling back to the parking structure, and I noticed all the lights were out.*

Do you know what your áte *did?* Diyos ko po, *she grabbed the car keys out of my hand and inserted one key in between each of her fingers when she saw the lights in the parking garage were out. She wanted to rampage into there by her lonesome and fight anyone who tried to jump us!*

Papa showed her the thing with the keys. Papa's taught us sum hellzacoo' shit.

Your father taught me some cool shet too. All of us. He protected me. He was the leader of the family.

But wasn't Lolo Martín the leader?

[Silence]

Tito Gus?

[Long pause]

Yes, he was. But your father, he was easier to follow. He led you to believe that his heart was made of concrete, but in reality, it was like Cream of Wheat.

Ya kiddin' me?

I am not being facetious. However, do not get me wrong about your abuelo. *He taught us discipline, diligence, respect, all those things you need to grow up properly, even if his methods were tyrannical at times. He also taught me the most important lesson in life. It is about loving something and setting it free.*

Aw, everyone knows *that* one. If you love something, set it free. It if comes back, it's yours. If it doesn't, it was never meant to be. But that's supposed to be about lovers. Dude, Makena would scold you for being so cliché.

No, there is much more to it, my sweets. You will learn in due time. It might bonk you on the side of your thick ulo *one day, but you will learn. Just remember, darling, when you stare at something for too long, you fail to see it.*

That's deep, man. Deep. You're dope, Tito Gus.

Ay Xavy, please pardon me, but I need to visit the comfort room. I do hope you have something other than Charmin. That Charmin, putangina, *it is like wiping your asshole with a baby blanket.*

77. yan yans

Mama and I are shopping for fresh Dungeness crabs at 99 Ranch, which is where we go on Sunday after church sometimes. 99 Ranch always smells like a mix of burnt rubber and fish that's about to spoil, but Mama says that they have everything she needs to make Papa his favorite Filipino and Chinese food.

While Mama waits in the seafood line, she tells me I can go pick a special treat for myself and to come right back, so I go to my favorite section where they have Yan Yans, which are cookie sticks you can dip in chocolate.

I look for the aisle where the Yan Yans are and I see there aren't any left, only the sign that says "Yan Yans $.79." On the shelf above the Yan Yans are Pockys, which are chocolate-covered biscuit sticks, but those are no fun because the chocolate is already on the stick. I try to think of what else I can get, and I start to walk back down the aisle when all of a sudden, I feel someone tugging at my shirt and asking "Ahr you loookeeng por dees" in a cold and nasty voice.

It's Lola Zeny with a box of Yan Yans, and she sure looks fuming mad.

"Why deedn't you tell me your *áte* ees seeck?" asks Lola Zeny in her accent that's fat and choppy.

I look into Lola Zeny's gimlet eyes, just like Mama's right when she's about to shake her finger at me and yell all kinds of *Ay buhays* and *Ay nakus.* I don't say anything because shrugging my shoulders like I don't know won't do me any good. That's what I learned from doing it so many times and getting scolded even more.

"Ahn-sehr me now." Lola Zeny is speaking in Tagalog, which means she's trying not to make a scene, but of course that never works and just does the opposite. So now a bunch of short Asian ladies who look like Lola Zeny and are holding too many pink plastic bags and smell like fried noodles are whispering and pointing at us.

I want to say to Lola Zeny that I couldn't tell her that Makena is sick because of her high blood pressure and her stroke that I heard was mild so I didn't want her to worry, but I remember only one thing that Papa keeps reminding me, and that's what I blurt out to her.

"Because I'm not supposed to tell you anything about our family," I say like a machine running low on batteries, and it sure doesn't feel right.

When Lola Zeny starts to shake and cry *Jesusmarijosep*, I don't know what to do or say, and now the Asian ladies are surrounding her and asking her if she can breathe and do you need a doctor.

I run like a hurricane down the aisle and look for Mama who isn't in the seafood line, so I peek down all the other aisles, catching whiffs of whatever is on the shelves, and boy it all sure smells like feet. The sweat drops collecting on my forehead trickle down faster and wetter every time I don't see her.

I look for her dark brown head in the checkout lines, but all I see are other Asian-looking ladies. When I finally see Mama holding up a pink ticket to one of the guys behind the seafood counter, I let out a long sigh.

I wrap myself around her, and she asks me what's wrong. My tears push against the backs of my eyes and I tell her there were no more Yan Yans and I take a deep breath and hold her tighter.

Mama looks down at me and strokes my head and says, "Why don't you find something else, sweetheart," but I can't stop thinking about the Yan Yans that Lola Zeny was squeezing tight in her veiny hands, and now I'm not so sure I like Yan Yans anymore.

78. stale stench of suffering

It's 7:03 in the morning. In our backyard, I can see our green lawn, all perfect rectangles and triangles and different patches of it surrounding our tennis court, which means Arturo was here early with his grass trimmer and probably trying to make up for something that his workers stole from Papa's job sites.

I can also see orange, bright yellow, purple, hot pink, and electric blue. The colors can blind you if you've stayed inside the house for too long. June is almost over, and all the flowers have been blooming for some time now.

But my *áte* sure isn't.

Makena doesn't keep her eyes open for very long or say much to us these days. She moans a lot and whispers things to me like "Please, Isa, I don't want you to see me like this."

Today, hospice care workers from Arcadia Methodist Hospital are picking up Makena because it's becoming onerous, which was one of Xavy's favorite SAT words, taking care of her here at home. Dr. Witt's wife Karen comes over and helps us out a lot even though she works all the way in San Bernardino, but she has to go back to work full-time on Monday.

I wish Surfer Girl could help us, but her schedule is too full with all her other patients at Dr. Minor's office. Dr. Witt and Dr. Minor recommended many home health nurses to Papa and Mama, but they thought that taking Makena to the hospital was the right thing to do so that she gets the highest quality kind of care 24 hours a day.

I watch Karen give Makena sponge baths, which you would think is simple because all you do is wipe a wet and warm washcloth all over someone's body, but Karen has to turn Makena in all kinds of positions, and sometimes I help undress Makena when Karen's extra tired after a long day at the hospital where she works.

I didn't realize how hard it was to change someone else's clothes, even if that person is supposed to weigh 50 pounds more than she usually does. And it's even worse when the person you're helping change can't move her arms or legs for you. It's like trying to put clothes on a doll that's the size of a person, but the difference is the doll is filled with sand.

Karen gives Makena painkillers every three hours on the dot, and when Makena starts to sweat and her clothes get soaked, Karen asks me to tell Mama to fill up a basin of hot water for Makena's next sponge bath and to gather lots of clean towels, which Mama always piles high on Makena's dresser next to her many changes of clothes.

Makena's room smells stale now, and every time Papa walks in, he grumbles that we might as well be living in a goddamn hospital with this stench of sickness in the air. I wait for Mama to scold Papa for being insensitive, but she knows he's just mouthing off from all the stress and sadness that Makena brought to our lives.

Yesterday, we had to change Makena five times, so we're lucky it was Karen's day off from work because Mama always whimpers when she has to give Makena a sponge bath. Papa and Xavy tried to help one time, but Papa was all thumbs, afraid he would hurt Makena when he turned her on her side. And Xavy was too embarrassed to see his *áte* naked, even though they're brother and sister and we're all family.

Makena doesn't eat anymore, so her lips and the inside of her mouth are always dry. Karen told me that when this happens, I should get a wet Q-tip and run it over her gums and both sides of her mouth. I don't really like doing this because when I push my fingers between Makena's lips, the smell is worse than Lolo Carlo's Listerine breath was, like leftover food that's been sitting in the sink for too long after dinner.

Mama still says a novena every night before she goes to bed, and one time when I went to the bathroom at 4:14 a.m., she was still praying. Her light was on but on the lowest setting so that she wouldn't bother Papa, but his snoring is way worse than a bright light.

Frida plays and hangs out with us on the couch. She sleeps a lot, and she gnaws on beefy knuckle bones because they take longer to get through than the digestible bones that Mama buys at PetSmart.

Frida also knows something isn't right. I can tell by the way her face pleads with me, like she's asking why, why can't you do anything about everything, but she just keeps chewing.

Papa and Xavy have been spending more time in Papa's second office these days. Britney Spears is falling apart from all the dart holes, and Papa's coffee cup is filled to the top with cigarette butts and ashes.

Now I'm mad at Ms. God for making Makena sick, even though she did it when she was a man-boy God. I shared my feelings with Sister Iris at catechism last week, and she made me sit in the corner and think about my inappropriate words and why on earth am I calling God a "Ms."

Of course I don't hate Ms. God, that sure would be a wrong and unholy kind of feeling to have, so when I told her that hate is different from anger, Sister Iris slapped the top of my hand with a bendy plastic ruler and told me I'm supposed to know that God has a plan for all of us, we've been learning this all year.

I keep hearing about Ms. God's mysterious ways and all these plans she has, but I want to know why she gave sickness and suffering to Makena. When Sister Iris asked me to remember the story of Jesus, I told her I didn't feel like remembering.

"I don't want to learn about Ms. God's plans and Jesus' story anymore," I told her, and that's when she sent me to Father Jack's office to wait for Mama to pick me up.

Father Jack is cool. He's known our family for years, and Mama says he was so glad when she and Papa decided to take me to catechism at his church in Glendale, even though we live in Arcadia now.

Father Jack sure isn't like Sister Iris. He talked to me like I wasn't nine years old on that day in his office.

"Isabel, it's perfectly acceptable to be mad at God. I mean, 'Ms. God.'"

"But Sister Iris told me to think about my words that weren't appropriate and then she hit my hand with a ruler even though it didn't really hurt," I told Father Jack. I looked around his office, and there was that shady picture of Jesus again. I wondered for a second if Father Jack might have a quote in a frame by Albert Camus too.

"Sister Iris needs to find her way out of the old school," said Father Jack.

That's when I thought about Xavy and even Papa saying that all our grandparents were from the old school, but did they ever try to find their way out?

"Father Jack, does Ms. God have a plan of sickness and suffering for Sister Iris too?"

"No, Isabel." Father Jack started to laugh, but then he cleared his throat fast and sat up straight in his tall chair.

He arranged the papers on his desk into a neat stack and looked at me and said, "Isabel, I've known your sister since she was a 6-year-old climbing the monkey bars."

"She went on the monkey bars when she was six?" I asked, and I couldn't imagine Makena swinging across all those bars because everyone says that Makena was way smaller than I was when she was younger.

"She was the only one who could go across," said Father Jack. "On one cold day during recess, she came running to me and asked me to warm up her hands with mine. They were so cold, and I saw her blisters had popped, so I took her to the nurse's office. While we sat waiting for the nurse to bring over her supplies, I was still warming Makena's hands and noticed how tiny they were. She was so small and fragile, like a porcelain doll."

Father Jack kept talking, and after a while, he wasn't really speaking to me anymore. He just kept staring down at all the papers on his desk and went on and on about Makena, and boy I don't think he ever stopped shaking his head while cracking the widest smiles.

79. is money money

I'm telling Mr. Baluga all about running into Lola Zeny at 99 Ranch and how she cried *Jesusmarijosep* and started to shake and that it made my insides tie up into tight knots, and he just laughs his gorilla ha-ha's, but this time in a rude "That's what you get" kind of way.

"Oh, the hullaballoo of it all," he says, and he pats me on the head. "Sorry, Kid, I know she's your grandmother, but after everything she's done to your parents, it's impossible for me to give her even one ounce of respect." Then he makes his tsk-tsk-tsk sounds and mutters *sayang* to himself.

Lolo Carlo

Lolo Carlo, you sort of remind me of Mr. Baluga, and one reason is that Papa says you're set in your ways and stoic when you want to be, and that's so true because one time last year before you went to heaven, when you took me with you to your barber shop, you acted like a robot to the guy who wasn't your regular barber, whose name was Alistair, with hellos and thank yous that were super stale, and you didn't even have a double quarter pounder, which is usually what happens after you get whiffs of the aftershave that Alistair always rubs all over your neck and chin and cheeks, right after he's done cleaning up the gray stubble from your beard.

You and I used to watch The Price Is Right *together, and you'd laugh so hard and clap your hands together three times when I overbid by $10,000 during the Showcase Showdown, but sometimes I did well in that one game that asks you if the price of canned food or other stuff you can buy at the supermarket is higher or lower than the price they give you, and you* *would pat me on the head like Mr. Baluga does and say "Thatta boy" even though you knew I was a girl.*

You used to make the tastiest ice cream, which had frozen avocado chunks mixed with milk and sugar in those little ice cube trays, and you stuck toothpicks in them so that we could eat them like they were mini popsicles. You also used to make the creamiest vanilla ice cream with bits of corn in it. You'd buy the freshest stalks of corn and slice all the kernels off and pile them up into a bowl next to your ice cream maker, and when you were done churning, I would be super crazy excited to lick my first scoop of vanilla corn. One time, I told you to sell your vanilla corn to 31 Flavors, but you said that capitalism wasn't your cup of tea, which reminds me of what Makena told me about Ultra Charmin.

You once started to say in your deep and scratchy voice, "Ah, my sweet Eesabel, money doesn't make the world go 'round, contrary to what the rest of the miserly people on this earth think. Remember, don't ever let it come between you or anyone else, especially the people you love."

I wouldn't know what to do about this family feud if I were Mama because how are you supposed to choose between your own mama and your own husband? I'd pick my mama, but that's because I don't know what it's like to have a husband. Makena says that your partner for life becomes your family, sometimes even thicker than your own blood, so of course Mama made the right choice.

I overheard Papa telling Makena and Xavy one time that money is just money. It isn't a means to an end or an end to all means, it's just goddamn money. But when I think about Papa's words, I still don't understand, because you need money for everything. A house and a car and food and clothes, and if you don't have enough, you won't have a place to live and you can starve and even freeze to death, but that wouldn't happen because it doesn't get too cold here in Arcadia.

Sometimes Mama and Papa fight about money, like when Papa asks Mama if she thinks his salary grows on trees. One time, she went mad at Macy's and bought 17 pairs of shoes because she got an additional 50 percent off the lowest-marked price. Then

Mama answered back to Papa that he bets way more than 17 pairs of shoes whenever he plays baccarat or roulette in Las Vegas, but I keep hearing that it's so much fun to watch Papa play high-stakes because he loves punching the air and making hullabaloo, tipping the dealers and high-fiving the pit bosses and getting everyone pumped up with him.

Then of course there's Xavy, who spends too much on Volkswagen car parts that are just for show, like his special and shiny tire rims or his restored original steering wheel. Or Makena who asked Papa if she could buy La Mer, this really expensive cream that J. Lo uses all over her face and body so that she doesn't get wrinkles and will look younger than she really is when she's old. That's when I expected Papa to ask Makena if she thinks our money grows on trees, but instead he told her to become famous and trashy just like that Jennifer Lopez and you can buy all the goddamn La Mer you want.

I don't think J. Lo is trash, she is gorgeous and classy and talented just like Makena, and she's even engaged to Ben Affleck, who isn't too wretched-looking for an older boy, and now I'm not sure what to believe about money because it can be both good and evil.

It's not supposed to make the world go 'round and it's just money, but it's the reason why I don't have an *abuela* anymore.

80. *diyos no*, no, stupid nurse

It's June 23, 2003, and I am nine years and 14 days old.

Last night when Mama was about to dry my hair before bed, Xavy all of a sudden appeared before us with shaky hands that were trying to hold his cell phone steady. Then Mama dropped the hair dryer which banged on to the cabinet and almost hit my leg.

She ran down the hallway screaming, and I followed her with sopping wet hair asking, "What Mama, what Mama," and that's when Xavy told me to find my shoes that I grabbed two left ones of, and then he barked at me to hurry my big ass over to the garage so that's what I did.

In the car, Mama kept saying, "Oh Lord our God, why couldn't I have been there," and I sat squirmy in the backseat having a super hard time putting the other left shoe on my right foot and trying to stay quiet and keeping my questions to myself even though I think I already knew the answer to them, except for how did the Lord become God all of a sudden?

Xavy drove like those RTD bus drivers who think they're in charge of the streets in downtown and even sped right through a red light, but Mama didn't notice which she usually does and then sighs *Ay Diyos ko*, but this time she said *Diyos no* in a whisper that sounded like it already gave up.

I knew where we were going when Xavy turned right on Huntington Drive, but I kept my mouth shut while Mama said "Why couldn't I have been there" and *Diyos no* over and over again and again as if the words would change the way things were.

After Xavy turned into the hospital entrance and parked the car, Mama started to tug at my arm because I was walking like an *abuela*. She dragged me through two automatic glass doors that slid open too slowly to each of their sides and we rushed through one hallway and then another one with some of its ceiling lights flickering, and when we got to the hallway where we were supposed to be, Mama stopped.

Xavy's skater shoes made a skid noise like tires screeched, and when I looked over towards the row of medical carts to see why everyone was frozen, I saw Papa cradling Makena like he was holding a newborn baby, except the expression on his dark face was an oxymoron made of both proud and weak.

Now he lays you down
to sleep, his golden angel
with no soul to keep.

All kinds of doctors and nurses dressed in those scrubs that still look like green pajamas to me were trying to talk to Papa, but he kept roaring like a lion protecting his cub when someone came close. Tears were skidding down past his neck, and he walked noisy steps up and down the hallway like he wanted to show off the scene he was making, kissing Makena's head and holding it close to his wet face.

Makena was wearing a white hospital gown, the kind that looked like Lolo Martín's when the whole family visited him and gave him rides in his wheelchair, but this time the dots all over the gown looked like hearts, which all seemed darker purple surrounding her chest.

Her eyelashes weren't as curly but still looked like those spiders resting near the corners of walls and ceilings, and this time I think they knew where to crawl to next.

Mama's face turned pasty whitish gray as she fell heavy to the floor on both her knees even though she was wearing one of those shorter muumuus that didn't cover her kneecaps, so boy that must have hurt. Then Xavy wrapped his giant arms around her and hiccupped and started to gasp like something got trapped inside his sumo wrestler chest.

She died in your arms
But did she forsake? It is
hard to know if you

made a mistake that you can't
unmake, and boy does it ache.

When I walked down the hallway towards Papa and Makena, I spotted a man with thick black hair slicked back with gel that looked like it never dried. He was leaning against the wall and wore dark sunglasses and a long black coat with a belt tied super tight around his waist that all looked bizarro because summer just started.

He noticed I was looking at him, but he turned his head away fast which sounded like it made his neck crack, and then he scrambled his cloggy black shoes in the opposite direction.

I felt sweat drops racing down my forehead and my heart going thud. One of the nurses with pink pajama scrubs grabbed my hand in a firm squeeze but pulled it gently, and that's when all kinds of ambivalence, like pushpins poking but not too deep because the pin parts are short, all came alive inside both my brain and my body.

There will be no hullaballoo. Of any kind.

Papa yelled, "Go with the nurse, Love, go with the nurse," but I didn't want to go with the stupid nurse.

All of a sudden, there were tears near the corners of my mouth that tasted salty, and I couldn't stop licking each drop that passed by my lips, drops that weren't skidding or rolling but just kind of, just sort of, falling down.

I felt a strange rumble in my heart and not a thud this time, and this was the moment I realized I wasn't crying for Makena.

"Your *áte*'s spirit is gone now, Isabel," Papa sobbed. "Please. Go. Go with the goddamn nurse."

81. souls for always

On June 24, 2003, Ramona Quimby, the plant who we all thought would be living for always, lost her last dry leaf two days after Makena took the ride. I had watched her leaves turn yellow and brown during the past month, and then one day I noticed they dried up and got crunchy and started to fall off, one by one.

I kept watering Ramona Quimby, telling her that she was allowed to keep living without Makena, but her leaves didn't want to be green, even with little speckles of yellow.

When the last leaf fell behind the toilet and down to the floor, I placed it inside a Ziploc bag and brought it over to the oak tree in our backyard. I broke through the dirt with Mama's garden shovel, and I wondered where Makena's special place was, where she dug up a hole for her bloody towel.

I imagined the leaf and the towel finding each other underground someday, and when they did, their souls would finally get to play.

Bionic souls that just play, they are never meant to keep and never meant to take.

Then I prayed. I prayed for a towel and a goddamn weed.

82. sit on this

Seeing all the *titos* and *titas* and cousins again at Makena's funeral made me wish the Josés were still friends, everyone going back to their roles on the same old TV show. Eating and dancing and singing loud at parties almost every weekend, playing with the girl cousins even though we fought all the time, taking sides and pulling hair and scratching faces and biting arms, sometimes going home early when things got out of hand but always making up at the next party like nothing ever happened.

The party I remember most was when Makena taught me how to play "Heart and Soul" on Tito Dante and Tita Carlie's baby grand piano. Loud witch cackles echoed from the kitchen, where Papa and Tito Sal were playing gin rummy. Everyone knows that Tito Sal is the biggest cheater in the world, and Papa is the only one who can still beat him when he's cheating, so Makena took me to the kitchen to watch them in action.

"Come on, Lek-Lek, I really have something to show you," Tito Sal called over to our cousin Alex. Tito Sal whispered into Papa's ear and gave him a high-five so loud that it echoed and boomed in the kitchen.

"No," Alex said. He stood far enough away from Tito Sal and Papa and chewed on the collar of his shirt, keeping an eye on the kitchen door. All the cousins know that whispering and high-fives mean that the José brothers are up to no good.

"*Halika dito,* Lex," Papa said, trying to act cool, waving him over like he wasn't up to no good.

Alex took super small steps to Tito Sal and Papa, and then he folded his arms in front of them like a genie, like he was all tough nails.

All of a sudden, Tito Sal grabbed both sides of Alex's green gym shorts and pulled them down to his ankles. Even his Spider-Man underwear made it to the floor too.

"*Ay*, Lar, that is harsh," said Tita Lourdes, shaking her head along with the other *titas* in the kitchen. I looked at Makena with her sour face, and I already knew what she was thinking, that "harsh" wasn't the word she had for Tito Sal.

I didn't think it was *that* mean because sometimes the cousins do rotten things to the *titos*, like when Benji put maple syrup in Tito Vito's bottle of gel or when Jeannie and Marie ordered fake lottery scratchers on the Internet and stuck one in Tita Malou's wallet, and boy you never heard so many screams of "You little shets, I thought I was rich!"

I couldn't help giggling a little at poor Alex, even though I'd want to hide out in a cave for a long time if someone pulled my pants down, but I didn't want to show Makena too much laughing, so I bit down on my lip and checked Papa to see if he was going to join in on the fun.

Poor Alex looked like he was stuck in quicksand, and not because he was frozen but because he wanted to be sucked up by it. He was so embarrassed that he forgot to cover his private parts, which of course I was trying hard not to stare at.

All of a sudden, he went from embarrassed to red hot pissed off, the kind of angry that decided to make a fist and point it at Tito Sal.

"*Uy!* Lek-Lek wants to fight!" Tito Sal yelled. Then he got up from his seat and started to karate-chop and dance at the same time. He looked kind of dumb in his tight Levi's with a high waist and a light blue stretchy shirt that was clinging to his bony body. Makena was noticing his outfit too, and her face turned even more sour while she checked him out from head to toe.

As Alex backed away to give Tito Sal room to show off his fake moves, Tito Dante pulled up Alex's underwear and shorts and lifted him onto his lap, trying to look like the good papa in front of his brothers. He poked at Alex's sides and kept telling him that his *titos* were just fooling around, giving him a hard time.

Alex was still pointing his fist at Tito Sal. Then all of a sudden, his middle finger appeared, like a waffle stick popping out of a toaster.

"Sit on *this*," he announced, trying to sound like a gangster, but you could tell he was trying to keep his voice hush-hush so that his mama Tita Carlie wouldn't hear.

I couldn't believe what Alex was doing, and I sure was proud of him, even though Mama keeps nagging me about respecting my elders. I yelled, "Go Alex," and right when Makena heard this, she tried to pull me away.

Tito Dante screamed all kinds of Tagalog curse words while he grabbed Alex's hand with the middle finger still sticking straight up and held up a dainty kind of sorry hand to Tito Sal. Tita Carlie's face turned white, and all sorts of *'Susmarijoseps* and gasps of *Ay naku* came from the *titas.*

Tito Sal stood there for a moment, wrinkling his eyebrows and looking up at the ceiling. We were all wondering what he was up to while he started to scratch the sides of his body like an animal with fleas. He stretched and yawned all innocent, and then all of a sudden, his smile turned evil.

Alex's eyes were shrinking so fast that you could have blindfolded him with a shoelace. When he raised his other middle finger at Tito Sal and glared at him with his gimlet eyes, more *'Susmarijoseps* flew out of the *titas'* mouths.

Then Papa, who was sitting real quiet on the side the whole time, stood up and said, "All right, Lex, I'll sit on this."

That's when he sat right on top of Alex's left middle finger, and you could tell it was being bent the wrong way.

More curses and gasps and giggles and howling kinds of laughter exploded from everyone and made the house shake. I howled too and then yanked myself out of Makena's hold and ran over to Papa, who gave me a fist bump and said to come sit on his lap.

Makena looked at me like she was done with me forever, absolutely not for always, and stormed out of the kitchen. I watched Alex follow Makena while he cradled his middle finger and kept blowing at it, his face crazy pink like a watermelon radish.

"Dante, that son of yours must be *bakla*," Papa burst out, and he gave me a noogie that kind of hurt, but of course I didn't let him know that.

Tito Dante laughed hard with Papa about his remark, but I could tell it was forced by the way he was trying to keep his face from drooping when the word *bakla* came out of Papa's mouth.

I felt Papa's body crumple underneath me. I knew that he realized he had hurt Tito Dante's feelings, so he pushed me off his lap and told me to go play with the cousins. I went looking for Makena, and while I walked up the stairs, I heard her voice.

"Everyone here has grown up watching this sort of thing, and you start to believe it's justifiable. 'Just take it like a man, goddamit,' the *titos* keep saying. Or 'Cold-cock that bastard.' It's nothing more than fraternity hazing. Initiation into what they think is manhood."

"Kena, joke *lang*," I heard Tita Gwen tell her. "Your father and the *titos*, they just like playing. *Mahal nila ang kalokohan*."

"I know they're just joking around, and I know they all love the craziness. But when I tell Isa that the *kalokohan* isn't always okay, she scowls at me like I'm a spoilsport. So I stop. And every time I do, I wonder what will become of her."

I made sure they didn't hear me, and then I tiptoed back down the stairs and looked for Papa. He and Tito Dante were high-fiving and making their witch cackles with all the other *titos* in the kitchen, making *kuwento* about what they did to Alex and how *loko* he looked when he stuck his fist out at Tito Sal.

I sat on the carpet in the small hallway between the stairs and the kitchen. I listened to the high-fives and the cackles downstairs, and I could still hear the low and serious voices upstairs. I looked both ways, up and then down, and I didn't really know which way to go.

Makena

Your full name was Makena Alexandra Santos José, and you were born on October 29, 1983, at 3:14 p.m., at Huntington Memorial Hospital in Pasadena. You died all super crazy dramatic in Papa's arms at Arcadia Methodist Hospital at 6:32 p.m., on June 22, 2003.

You played number one or sometimes number two singles for Cal's tennis team, depending on who the coach liked better on match day, and you were supposed to graduate last month in the month of May, and don't forget that it doesn't rhyme with José.

Papa and Mama told us that the biology and psychology departments honored you during the graduation ceremonies with "On Eagle's Wings," which I'm sure you remember complaining is one of the most syrupy and sappiest but sweetest songs ever. You know, the one that Mama asked you to sing and play piano to at Lolo Carlo's funeral, the one that you made tampo *about because you had to sing it in a different key to match it with your alto voice, but it got everyone at the funeral to sway and hum and even made people who didn't know or like each other hug and weep, all to the music you performed with your voice so full-toned, with your long royal-like fingers that pranced light and airy on ivory keys.*

Tracy and Ally told me that all your tennis teammates brought a wide banner with the words, "We'll always remember your wicked forehand, Makenzer Wowzers," which they all shouted together so loko *and loud. When their chants started echoing throughout the auditorium, they held up the banner higher and mightier and yelled even louder in the section they were sitting in.*

You got sick with colon cancer when you were almost 20 years old, which was a random freak occurrence according to Dr. Minor, who never stopped saying "Hi hi hi," even though you said he might. Dr. Witt, who found your tumor that was the size of a big yellow peach, thinks there are genes that still need to be researched and that your cancer might be hereditary, which Mama and Xavy say will make Papa go ballistic because he's afraid of getting screened, and then he'll think he's a weakling if he becomes sickly or turns into something he wasn't supposed to be.

You went to chemotherapy every week for 10 months, and you're the reason why our family stopped making pasyal, *but that's fine because all it means anyway is to get out of the house.*

Some people didn't like the way you lived your life, all proper and high and mighty, and "Don't you dare roll your eyes at me because you think I'm a princesa," *but you trained and cared for scuzzy SPCA dogs, and whenever you shampooed their fur that was coated with fleas and mud, you told me that you would watch their bath water turn powdery brown and sometimes even black, and then you would watch your tears fall like raindrops into the tub, just like Tito Gus' did into that basin where Papa removed the stinky fish from all over his little body and his cloggy feet.*

When you were a golden girl, life kept giving you royal flushes, but I noticed whenever we played pusoy dos, *you were never dealt the two of diamonds, which I don't think really takes charge of the whole game anyway if you ask me.*

Because of you, I learned many new and long words that weren't on the vocabulary lists that Ms. Langevin gave us every week, like gastroenterologist and misogynist and oncologist. And guess what, some of these words I can make into an alliteration, which I know you would have been so proud of, even though they sound like tongue twisters, such as "Chemotherapy and colonoscopies can carry on capricious" and "Believably that ballistic barium brought big bilirubin beneath your belittled but beautiful body and brain."

On the day we talked about our dreams, I can still picture your doll face, watching it turn into what looked like real porcelain, so hard but crystal-like, with an expression that kept trying to figure out the things you never finished.

Oh Ms. God, my heart hurts, it hurts like it's hissing and huffing, because whenever I think about Makena's dream, the one that was derogatory and demeaning and maybe even dubious, I realize that you didn't let her finish her life.

83. the color of herself

The last time Makena went rambling, her eyes, the light brown that everyone used to brag about, were more golden than usual. Golden like the leaves of fall, almost like amber which is Mama's favorite, the color of hope.

Makena's amber eyes shimmered while she made *kuwento* about the first time she shot Papa's Walther PPK. She said shooting a gun was one of the most exhilarating experiences of her life.

I always thought that Makena would be against having guns in the house, because she hated violence and would try to cover my eyes when the bloody and gory parts on TV came on, but she said she felt safe knowing we had something to protect us from intruders. Right after her eighteenth birthday, she asked Papa to show her how to use a gun.

Papa usually takes his business associates to the shooting range, where Papa tests out his Sig Sauer, Glock, and Walther PPK. Mama never stops grumbling, "Shet, I can't believe we have weapons in our house," but Xavy keeps reminding her they're hidden in the gun safe and that I would never crack the code and she's not interested in guns, so just relax man.

Makena was right, what if a burglar decided to rob us or hurt us, so I'm secretly glad too that we have guns. But I'd never try to open the safe because I'm just a kid, and Papa and Xavy are here to guard us anyway. Mama still hates it and tells Papa and Xavy to never tell a soul that there are guns in our house, or else boy would she hear it from church and the PTA and the mothers' club she likes to bake goodies for.

Makena told me that Papa took her to Lock, Stock and Barrel in Azusa. Papa flung open the first door to the lanes, where Makena read a sign that said, "Ear and Eye Protection Must Be Worn at All Times."

Tito Gus opened the second door. He liked shooting with Papa. When Papa wasn't busy making fun of Tito Gus, he would tell everyone that he's the toughest *bakla* you'll ever meet, with his fifth-degree black belt in Kajukenbo and stellar shooting skills.

It smelled like the Fourth of July inside the range, Makena remembered. Bullet shells lay scattered over the carpet, and the shooting lanes reminded her of that carnival game where you squirt water into a clown's mouth with a toy gun. But these lanes weren't a part of any kind of game.

Makena felt her body jerk every two seconds from the sounds of other people shooting in their lanes as she, Papa, and Tito Gus walked over to the lane assigned to them. Another sign that said "No Loading on Counters" hung on the window behind their lane. Papa kept reminding Makena you're allowed to load your gun only inside the lanes. Makena was afraid to sit down or lean against the wall, wondering if there was some sort of shooting range etiquette.

Makena couldn't hear what Papa started to tell her, so she lifted her ear protection and removed her plugs.

"Watch and learn," Papa said, pointing to Tito Gus. Makena remembered Tito Gus acting self-important and masculine, making his voice all husky and posing like he was a man of the world. His body wasn't stiff, the kind that was trying to show it had perfect posture, and there were no smiles or flaring nostrils. Tito Gus was all manly business that day.

Makena watched him clip his target on to the conveyor and hold the button down until it reached 30 feet. He placed his right foot behind him, held out the gun in front of him, and *bang*. Five shots in a row. Makena said it made her shoulders tense up in an instant.

Tito Gus pressed the button again. The target shook and swayed on the conveyor, the outline of bullets growing bigger and wider as it came closer. Makena could see that the bullets formed a small star.

"Macho man," Papa said, and he gave Tito Gus a high-five.

Makena was still shocked about Tito Gus knowing how to use a gun and shoot it that well, and she couldn't believe her ears when Papa called Tito Gus "macho." After Tito Gus was done, Makena observed Papa in action, and it turns out he was a sharpshooter too. He shot his Sig Sauer, bang bang bang so lickety-split that Makena felt a huge thump inside of her, like she just swallowed a firecracker.

She glanced over at Tito Gus, who was inserting another cartridge for his second round.

When Papa handed Makena the Walther PPK, she felt her insides go thump again.

"Let's start with this one first, Kena, since it's easier to handle," Papa said. "Don't forget to put your thumb here. Line up the sights with the target. Then relax and shoot."

Makena took the gun from Papa and went over to the lane, like she was walking the plank. He set the target for her at 25 feet. It was Tito Gus', the one with a burglar wearing a ski mask. Makena imagined a real burglar and squinted her eyes.

Papa told her, "You're a lefty, so keep your left foot behind you for leverage." Then he took Makena by her shoulders and adjusted her stance. For a moment, Makena recalled the way Papa had positioned her next to our front door and demanded she stand still for two hours.

"Take the motherfucker out," Papa egged her on. "Come on, Kena Beach." Makena remembered Papa shaking his fist at her.

Makena rested her left index finger on the trigger. She waited. "Will the kick be so strong that I'll drop the gun?" she thought to herself.

She squinted at the target again and imagined someone she wouldn't mind opening fire at. Then she shut her eyes for a split second.

She saw a figure. No, it couldn't be.

She was expecting to see Eli, Papa, or even Bill Van Gelder.

Instead, what she saw was herself.

She tried to shake off the image and held the gun as tightly as she could, even though she was supposed to relax.

She went ahead and pulled the trigger. It wasn't as loose as she thought it would be. The gun shook.

BANG.

An orange spark, a shell flying past her. She inhaled gun smoke and let out a cough.

"YES!" Papa raised his hand to Makena for a high-five. Tito Gus clapped and saluted Makena like she was a general in the military.

Makena shot a gun, a real live gun. She remembered the rush, her body overcome by a flood of chills. "A rush that you could cling on to for the rest of your life," she had said.

Papa pressed the button to the conveyor. When the target met him face-to-face, he flinched.

"What's wrong?" Makena asked.

"You hit the bastard square in the heart," Papa said, his eyes widening from all the surprise. He grinned at her and shook his head.

"*Ay naku*, Doña Makena," Tito Gus said. "Now you're prepared to take out that ogre father of yours. Anytime, anyplace, with just one badass shot to the *puso*, my darling." Makena laughed when she remembered the "*bakla* Tito Gus" bursting out of him, his nostrils flaring and arms waving this way and that. But right when she said that she was describing the gay coming out of Tito Gus, to me it meant he was just being happy for her.

Makena had said that her thoughts were clouded by the image she saw and shot, then she felt her eyes following Papa carefully. What he thought about Tito Gus' remarks was more important at that moment.

She waited for his reaction.

Remember his fist, remember the rush.

But he was too busy admiring Makena's target.

As Makena finished her story, I remember waiting for her reaction. She didn't look scared. Her eyes, the color of fall, were still shimmering.

84. hard to know

It's two days after the funeral. I'm hoping Makena won't visit me, but Mama keeps reminding me not to be afraid of her spirit. Frida's standing at my bedroom door, looking at me like she has to go pee, so I walk downstairs with her to the dog door in the kitchen, which is great timing because I was thinking of sneaking some Swedish Fish out of the pantry.

What flavor are you, Swedish Fish? You aren't strawberry or raspberry or cherry, what you are is just right and just red. You are an enigma of soft and gooey goodness, not like some gummy bears that are too hard to chew, probably because they're made from pork gelatin, which is what Makena used to complain about, and if you ask me, that is the best oxymoron ever.

At the bottom of the stairs, I hear loud sniffling, and just when I think it's Makena's ghost, I notice some more stuffy-sounding noises coming from Papa's office. I got in trouble with Mama yesterday for eavesdropping and was asked to turn off my bionic ears please, so I better stay away from the door.

I decide to go back to my room while Frida finishes her business when all of a sudden, Tito Carding appears from Papa's office with puffy eyes.

"Isaboo," he says. "You're so big now."

Tito Carding used to call me "Isaboo," even though he knows I hate it.

"I think you're so big now too," I say, and I feel my face twisting into an expression that says oops sorry I didn't mean that.

He laughs, and his belly that's trying to hide behind his clingy shirt bounces up and down. "Isaboo Scrappy-Doo, *mahirap pa ring malaman ka*," he says, which means "It's still hard to know you," but not in a rude way.

Papa comes out of the office next. He and Tito Carding both just stand there, staring at me.

I can't figure out what kind of staring it is. Papa's eyes are swollen too, but not as much as Tito Carding's. I notice my *tito* is looking more like Papa now with his high cheekbones, but his hair is even thicker and darker, sort of like Dr. Minor's tumbleweed look but flatter because you can tell he uses gel.

Tito Carding nods to Papa. Then he does the same to me, but it's a half-nod, the kind that men make to each other when they're greeting you or saying goodbye. They tilt their heads up, raising their chins, but they never bring them back down for a full nod. They think they're so cool, but they just look like gangsters acknowledging each other, Makena would say.

Tito Carding reaches out his hand and messes up my hair. He walks down the hallway, making a wrong turn into the kitchen. That's when I realize he hasn't been to our house in a long time.

I wonder what he thinks of it, if he likes it better than our retro ranch-style house in Eagle Rock that was a few houses away from his, where Papa and Mama used to throw the most epic dance parties, according to Xavy.

I wonder if he and Papa talked about Makena, and is he sorry and sad at all for making our family fight for so many years?

Tito Carding almost trips over one of Frida's squeak toys in the living room, then he accidentally kicks Xavy's Magic 8 Ball. He grumbles *putangina* under his breath, and my eyes follow him as he lets himself out the front door, closing it all delicate like it's made of cardboard.

I ask Papa, "Was he saying goodbye?"

Papa's gray eyes look purple, like the sky he screamed at as a young college boy. When I look deep into them, the blues and the reds that become this purple seem to make his spirit turn blurry and dark.

"It never waits for you. It's the sum of all your choices," he mumbles, but he's not answering my question probably because he's quoting Albert Camus again.

"Go to bed now, Love," he says. He bends down to kiss me on my head, and it feels kind and gentle.

I find Frida. We walk back up the stairs to my bedroom. When I lift my covers, Sarita is lying on her side with her gangly legs curled up to her belly, and her hair looks like it got wedged under something heavy, maybe Frida's big beagle butt.

Bouncy and peppy hair makes for a bouncier and peppier lifetime.

Frida plops right next to Sarita and nuzzles her head against the softness of my blue and yellow Snoopy pajama pants.

I smile at my *áte*'s little dog, whose name Makena liked reminding me is "peace" in German. She also made sure I would never forget that Frida was the only full-bred beagle ever to turn up at the Pasadena SPCA.

I smile again because Frida is really *my* little dog. She always has been, from the day Makena brought her home from the shelter.

I was waiting for her, and she was waiting for me. We'll both keep waiting, *siempre y para siempre.*

It's hard to sleep. I close my eyes, and I see different scenes that are rewinding and fast-forwarding and never pausing, like when people say your life's flashing before your eyes, but what's queer is that I'm not sure whose life it is.

All of a sudden, I remember I didn't have any Swedish Fish, so I flip my covers over and start skulking like a panther back down the stairs.

As I move closer to the bottom step, I spy the Magic 8 Ball that Tito Carding cursed at. I pick it up.

It says, "Cannot predict now."

I try to picture Tito Carding's half-nod. I can't help laughing out loud at the way he messed up my hair and called me Isaboo and adding Scrappy-Doo, even though I hate it.

But I never really hated it.

wakas

colorín, colorado
este cuento
se ha acabado

ALL THE BONES
THAT ARE
GOOD
LIVE INSIDE OF
YOU,
YOUR SOFT HEART
IN A WORLD
WITH TENDENCIES
TO BE VILE.
YOU
ARE STRENGTH'S
BEAU IDÉAL.

YO. WASSUP,
CHI. "YOCKS!"
DA BRUDDA
WHO
ALWAYS
SHOCKS.
LIFE WILL
BE DANDY
AS LONG
"YOU AH"
IN IT,
YA
GANGSTA-
TURNED-
GRAJITUT.

MAN OF MY WORLD, YOU
ARE JUST YOU. THE SUM OF NOT
ALL YOUR CHOICES, YOU
DIDN'T BECOME THEM. I AM
BECOMING, STILL. YO SOY YO.

REFERENCES AND WORKS CITED

Amstein, Jürg; Burkhard, Paul; Parsons, Geoffrey; Turner, John. "Oh My Papa," 1939.

Anka, Paul; François, Claude; Revaux, Jacques. "My Way," 1967, 1969.

Armstrong, Billie Joe. "Church on Sunday," 2000.

Camus, Albert. *The Myth of Sisyphus and Other Essays*, New York: Knopf, 1955; *The Stranger* (translated by Matthew Ward), New York: Vintage, 1989; *The Rebel,* New York: Vintage Books, 1956.

Cates, George; Elliott, Jack. "Adiós, Au Revoir, Auf Weidersehen," first release by Lawrence Welk, 1971.

Deutsche Weile, "Rudi Dutschke and the Struggle of the 1968 Movement," 2012.

Henry, Patrick. "Give Me Liberty or Give Me Death," 1775.

New England Primer, "Now I Lay Me Down," 1784 edition.

Sheed, F.J. *Society and Sanity,* New York: Sheed & Ward, 1953.

Thompson, Linda; Morricone, Ennio. "You're Still You," 2001.

Thoreau, Henry David. *Walden (Life in the Woods),* Boston: Ticknor & Fields, 1854.

White, Barry; Sepe, Tony; Radcliffe, Peter. "You're the First, My Last, My Everything," 1974.

ABOUT THE AUTHOR

i.b. casey cui was born in a badass beach town in Southern California, and her ancestors hail from Madrid, Bilbao, Xiamen, and the western coast of the island of Luzon in the Philippines.

She earned her BA at UC Berkeley, where she studied human society and its social problems while taking cool courses like Tagalog and Pedagogy of Movement. At Mills College, she engaged in fiction and nonfiction writing workshops and was teased about kinda-sorta minoring in journalism with the undergrads, as well as serving as the tennis team's practice partner. She graduated with an MFA in English Literature and Creative Writing.

She is considering pursuing another graduate degree, but if she becomes a prolific author, she may forgo this plan.

She co-heads a private foundation whose mission advocates arts and language enrichment, literacy development, and the education of underrepresented children, along with the physical health and well-being of dogs.

She is a well-nigh 26-year colon cancer survivor. She's an enthusiast of stream of consciousness, sushi, Swedish Fish, sonatinas, and Snoopy.

She hopes to transition effortlessly from tennis to pickleball in the near future. She rediscovered piano 25 years after she stopped taking lessons.

She has enjoyed and continues to reread the works of Cleary, Camus, and Capote, just to name a few. She also has become a recent fan of alliteration and unabashedly overuses it, overzealously. She writes haikus and tankas in her spare time, but only for select friends and family.

ms. i.b. casey cui owns residences and is a part of two cohesive communities in California and Utah, where she—together with her hairless yet handsome, hardworking hubster—is a co-parent to two yare and yappy boys. And: a gorgeously gleeful, godlike goldendoodle.